Acclaim for Paula

The Snow

"Love and loss, and courage and compassion collide in this brilliantly told story of survival against the odds. Based on the true story of her grandmother, Paula Lichtarowicz's exquisite novel takes readers on a family journey full of passion, longing, regret, and eventual acceptance of choices made a lifetime ago. In these riveting, heartfelt, and brutally honest pages, Lena keeps a lifetime of secrets and dreams from her loved ones but never allows them to stop her from loving in return."

—Heather Morris, *New York Times* bestselling author of *The Tattooist of Auschwitz*

"Lichtarowicz delivers a dramatic story of a Polish woman's coming-of-age during WWII...The gripping narrative of Lena's wartime experiences contrasts bleak deprivation and suffering with sumptuous scenes of familial affection and the ache of true love. This will transport readers."   —*Publishers Weekly* (starred review)

"Lichtarowicz is a writer of great talent, with the ability to portray hardship and grief shot through with humor and hope. The gorgeous prose, compelling story line, and emotional depth ensure that *The Snow Hare* remains in the reader's mind long after the last page. I can't wait to read her other books."

—Frances Liardet, *New York Times* bestselling author of *We Must Be Brave*

"*The Snow Hare* is an extraordinary novel of fate, hope, love, and determination. Lichtarowicz's beautifully drawn story, set against a backdrop of real historical events, is every bit as heart-wrenching as it is inspiring. *The Snow Hare* brings the past to life in a vivid, evocative way—reminding us that history echoes through time, and hope can sustain us even through the most difficult of circumstances. This is one of the finest historical novels I've read in years."

—Kelly Rimmer, *New York Times* bestselling author of *The Warsaw Orphan*

"This is historical fiction at its absolute best — epic in scope and intimate in detail. Paula Lichtarowicz reminds us that even in the most brutal of circumstances, hope, love, and forgiveness sustain us." — Lauren Fox, *New York Times* bestselling author of *Send for Me*

"*The Snow Hare* is a profound and moving novel of the first order. Lichtarowicz brings a lost world to life with vivid and electric prose, attentive to the richness of her characters and acutely aware of the coming tragedy looming over their shoulders. At the center of all this is Lena — as unforgettable a protagonist as one could imagine in contemporary fiction: driven, brilliant, and haunted. Her story turns in unexpected directions that are so masterfully crafted as to feel like the inevitability of history." — Brian Castleberry, author of *Nine Shiny Objects*

"There is much to admire in *The Snow Hare:* the crisp and vivid prose, the lively portrayal of family dynamics, the taut pacing and tension, the skillful conveying of historical context. From the very beginning, I knew I was in the hands of an expert storyteller. I especially loved the character of Lena. Spirited and stubborn, fierce and flawed, she carried the story from the villages and mountains of Poland, to the brutal labor camp on the Siberian steppe, to her final days in England. *The Snow Hare* is an excellent novel, and I relished every page." — Melissa Fu, author of *Peach Blossom Spring*

"I loved this book, though it left a huge crack in my heart. A beautifully written, enthralling story of an unforgettable family caught up in a conflict that takes them all the way to a Siberian work camp. The main character, Lena, is determined and compelling, and the novel a brilliant study of what it means to survive both the best and worst of times." — Joanna Quinn, *New York Times* bestselling author of *The Whalebone Theatre*

The Snow Hare

Paula Lichtarowicz

BACK BAY BOOKS

Little, Brown and Company

New York Boston London

In memory of my grandparents Krstyna and Piotr Lichtarowicz,
and their daughter, Marta

Also by Paula Lichtarowicz

The First Book of Calamity Leek
Creative Truths in Provincial Policing

Copyright © 2023 by Paula Lichtarowicz

Hachette Book Group supports the right to free expression and the value of copyright.
The purpose of copyright is to encourage writers and artists to produce the creative
works that enrich our culture.

The scanning, uploading, and distribution of this book without permission is a theft
of the author's intellectual property. If you would like permission to use material from
the book (other than for review purposes), please contact permissions@hbgusa.com.
Thank you for your support of the author's rights.

Back Bay Books / Little, Brown and Company
Hachette Book Group
1290 Avenue of the Americas, New York, NY 10104
littlebrown.com

First United States hardcover edition published by
Little, Brown and Company, January 2023
First Back Bay trade paperback edition, December 2023

Back Bay Books is an imprint of Little, Brown and Company, a division of
Hachette Book Group, Inc. The Back Bay Books name and logo are trademarks
of Hachette Book Group, Inc.

The publisher is not responsible for websites (or their content)
that are not owned by the publisher.

The Hachette Speakers Bureau provides a wide range of authors for
speaking events. To find out more, go to hachettespeakersbureau.com
or email HachetteSpeakers@hbgusa.com.

Little, Brown and Company books may be purchased in bulk for business, educational,
or promotional use. For information, please contact your local bookseller or the
Hachette Book Group Special Markets Department at special.markets@hbgusa.com.

ISBN 9780316461351 (hc) / 9780316461375 (pb)
LCCN 2022943460

Printing 1, 2023

LSC-C

Printed in the United States of America

Lena sees the girl far off on the steppe, running towards the horizon where a red sun is sinking. Her elbows jab the air as if to break it. Dust flies up from her heels as she runs.

Lena can't take her eyes from this girl. She's tiny, the child, she shouldn't be out there alone.

'Wait!' Lena shouts to her. 'Please wait, I've something to say to you.'

But the girl keeps on, running towards the departing sun.

England

A figure is moving in the shadows of Lena's bedroom.

There's a rustling sound, a ripping of plastic. A woman is speaking, the voice telling her something is here now to ease the pain, to help her sleep.

Her right arm is turned, her inner elbow padded with soft fingertips. 'Just a sharp scratch, Magdalena, then a good rest.'

A door closes softly. Lena opens her eyes and sees the familiar pale walls of her bedroom, the pine wardrobe standing where it's been since the day she and her husband and JoJo moved in. She sees the stretch of her legs beneath the bedcovers, a tented hillock of toes.

What is it she has to say to the girl?

Lena turns her face towards the window where rain is smacking the glass. The sky outside has that sullen air, the sort of weather that knows itself unloved. Which is perhaps why a wind is bullying the cherry tree in the centre of the lawn, howling and hurling branches onto the grass. Never mind, that tree was always a puny, ridiculous thing. Her husband's idea. She scans the back fence, the yew, the patch of concrete they learned in time to call a patio. The blackbird won't be out, not in this weather.

Lena turns from the window and reaches for the piece of amber she keeps on the bedside table. How snugly it fits in the scoop of her palm these days. She presses it to her throat, rubbing the place where the malignancy grows. Her head slides back against the pillow and the bedroom recedes. There is something she needs to say to the girl. Her eyelids close. Her thoughts swirl with the howl of the unloved wind.

Przemysl, South East Poland

'But you need wind.'

Who's saying this? The girl?

No, it's Ala. Ala is speaking to her. Her sister is saying, 'Ulka told me. But it can't be any old June breeze. It's got to be a south-westerly, and a strong one, otherwise they'll end up elsewhere. And they have to come here, they simply have to.'

Where is Ala saying all this?

The geranium pots.

Really?

Yes, Ala is teetering between Papa's rows of red and pink geraniums in a slit of sunlight at the sitting-room window. She's sucking on her plait ends and pressing her nose against the glass to stare down the deserted lane.

And she, Lena, where's she?

There's a godawful smell – a reek of hot fat and bone – she must be at the hearth, boiling up a rabbit's head in a pot over the coals in the interests of science.

'Who won't come here?' she says, taking her tongs to prod an ear back under the churning water.

'The gypsies, stupid. Ulka says they only travel on south-westerlies. And if they don't come I'll never get them.'

'Get what?'

'Are you a complete and utter idiot, twig? My life's fortunes.'

It's entirely unintended, the hoot that comes out of Lena.

Ala glares.

'Sorry.'

Because both Papa and Ulka have said she's not to laugh at Ala. This has been mentioned on separate occasions, and repeated, so undoubtedly there's strong feeling in the household about it. Lena focuses on pinching an ear with the tongs, professional autopsy instruments that she's unwrapped even though it's not yet her birthday, and that are proving most satisfactory; steel-sprung with a pleasing snapping action. It only takes the slightest tug for the skin to peel away from the skull. From under the settee, a damp nose appears, followed by orange eyes, gleaming with anticipation, then the rest of Ivan Pavlov scrabbles out.

'Sit, Pav. Be a good boy. Look at the skin, Pav, good boy. Concentrate on the lovely smell of boiled rabbit.'

The dog's tail beats on the rug. If Lena's hypothesis is correct, saliva should begin to leak from his mouth. These emissions should be more plentiful for the familiar-smelling rabbit than for the mole she boiled yesterday. She may send the results to Moscow for the behaviourists to add to their research. Scientific progress depends on collaborative principles.

'You stink of rotting flesh, twig.' Ala's plaits go flying as she turns, tutting, back to her vigil. She bangs on the window and waves at Ulrich, leading his cows down the lane for milking.

Sunday brings the first confirmed sightings of the south-westerly wind in Lena's town. Three hundred people witness a breeze licking Father Gorski's skirts on the steps of St Lukasz's after Mass.

Two days later Ulrich rolls the week's milk churn to their doorstep, shaking his fist at the sky as he goes. This is all born of a storm in the Carpathians, he mutters. It is making his heifers cry. Only storms from the Ukraine do that.

By Thursday forked lightning strikes the old quarter. The air cracks to an unseen whip. In the convent schoolyard Lena's friends lift the flaps of their blazers and grow wings.

'Rumour has it they're directly overhead.' This is what Widow Manowska tells Ala and Lena when they are blown into the baker's on an errand for Ulka.

'You mean they're *here*?' Ala clutches Lena's arm. 'Above us right *now*?'

Widow Manowska takes Ulka's list. Casting an eye to the rattling windows and the black clouds scudding over the roofs, she crosses herself. 'I didn't think they'd return so soon. I was heavy with child when they last came to town.'

'You've seen them before?' Ala whispers. 'And did they give you your fortunes?'

Mrs Manowska leans close. 'Every one of them.'

'Go fuck yourselves!' Adam Manowska shouts, so Lena jumps. He's crouched like a baboon on a heap of sacks in the shop corner. Mama says when Lena and Adam were toddlers they would sit inside these sacks for hours playing bakers. They would emerge giggling, covered in dust. 'Fuck you all.'

'Hi, Adam,' Lena says. 'Nice to see you.'

Mrs Manowska sighs. She loads the girls' basket with rye loaves and caraway rolls. She reaches into a drawer under the counter and throws in a handful of wrapped cream fudge. 'Make sure one or two survive for your father.'

Lena opens the bakery door and steps out onto the street with the basket, lowering her head, her eyes scrunched against the whip of the wind. 'Will you goddamn come on!' she shouts to Ala, hanging back in the entrance, watching Mrs Manowska unwrap a fudge for her son.

'Mrs Manowska,' Ala says, 'did they tell you when you were pregnant that—'

'They told me everything, child.'

'And do you really truly think they're here?'

Mrs Manowska shrugs. 'They have the south-westerly behind them, they'll land by morning if their course is set straight.'

Tired of waiting, Lena tucks her chin into her jacket and sets off up the cobbles, leaning into a grey wall of air.

All Friday morning, Ulka scowls at the sky. After lunch she curses and knots her apron and climbs the ladder to the roof to secure the guttering.

'It may be I saw a hint of cape,' Ulka tells Ala on returning to earth and regaining her breath. She takes up apron corners to pat her cheeks dry.

'A cape?'

'It may be.'

'Oh, Ulka, do you think that—'

'Beneath their flying capes the gypsies keep their tents and caravans and their dancing bears? It may be so.'

Lena snorts and Ulka turns to shrink her with a stare.

'They have dancing bears?' Ala spins round and round and claps her hands.

'It may be so. Although I was told it's the blackest clouds you want to keep an eye on. Behind these clouds lie the gypsies' sacks. It's said these sacks contain the world's sorrowful histories. That's why it takes such a wind to drag them along.'

Lena swipes the head off a white rose. 'Ridiculous.'

Ala stops spinning, hovering on one foot. 'But, Ulka, what happens if the gypsies' sacks get spilled?'

Ulka narrows her eyes. 'I think you can work that out as well as I.'

Lena is on her bed. It's now Saturday, the 16th of June to be precise, and the wind has vanished from town. She's unwrapped her medical encyclopaedia and has all afternoon to read it. But Ala's here, dancing about in the doorway, saying she must come with her and come now, and somehow she always ends up doing what Ala wants. It's ridiculous, she has her own brain in her head, and functioning vocal cords to form the words 'go away', but here she is, tagging along downstairs and into the conservatory where their mother's resting, her face gabled by song sheets.

Ala is standing in front of the daybed, blocking the light from the garden doors and is stamping her foot, saying, 'Mama, we simply must go right now. Francesca went this morning. All my friends are going. It's already two o'clock. And it is Lena's birthday.' Ala elbows her.

'It is my birthday, Mama.'

At last she is sixteen. Admittedly not much can be done with this fact itself, but one more step has been taken. Now it's only nine years until she'll be a qualified doctor. Which is only three thousand two hundred and eighty-seven days, taking leap years into account. The medical encyclopaedia has five hundred and thirty pages with an average of three ailments to a page. If she's to be ready to practise by the time she's twenty-five there's really no time to lose.

A sheet of cantatas lifts and Mama peeps out. 'Mother of God, it's hot today.'

'Please, Mama, everyone's going, simply everyone.'

Behind the girls, by the open doors to the lawn, the potted palms begin to rustle and snigger. Ala glares at them then returns to business.

'Mama, please.'

'We are not everyone, Ala, my darling.'

Lena considers her mother on the daybed in her white smock, her hair – Ala's hair really – splayed all bushy and gold. 'You look like you're laid out at the morgue.'

'The things this child says!'

'Mama,' Ala says, 'no one in their right mind would miss it.'

The palms whisper, 'I'll give you odds of a hundred to one against that.'

'And I'll kill you, Romek, if you don't shut up. With these hands I will.'

Mama's cantatas slip to the floor. 'Blessed Mother, this family! Romuś, my darling boy, you really are too close to the draught over there, you know what Doctor Janucek says. I tell you it's too bad of your father to be away so much when I have my recital season upon me. What about the standards of his own children's education? Listen to your mama, girls, under no circumstances are you to marry school inspectors, they are no better suited to marriage than travelling peddlers, if I'd have only known when he limped into the convent that . . .'

The conservatory door swings wide. It's Ulka with honeyed tea for Mama's throat after all those encores in the town hall last night. Ivan Pavlov is lurking in her skirts where he believes he can't be seen. Ulka says the dog thinks himself far cleverer than he actually is, so Lena will test his intelligence this summer using Ulrich's sheepdog for a comparative study.

Mama raises herself to take her tea and Ala moves to deploy the hair, flinging her plaits about, so Mama can't help but smile at all this flying gold.

'Please, Mama, even Pavlov wants to go.'

'Mother of God, what a name for a dog.' Mama's hand flaps at the nose snorting along the daybed for crumbs. 'Ulka, what to do with these girls?'

Ulka folds her arms on her belly and dispenses one of her looks towards Ala and Lena, before turning it to silence Romek in the palms. She bends to Mama's ear.

'Thank you, Ulka darling. Not your best shoes, girls, stay together in the forest and be back by six for Lena's birthday celebrations.'

Mama's eyes close and she begins to hum. Ala and Lena kiss her on each cheek and race from the room.

She is running. Running after the girl but the steppe never ends.

Brown dust coats her eyeballs and sticks to her teeth. It rides on her breath into the depths of her lungs. Lena runs until her legs turn to lead and she stumbles, scouring the empty land to the horizon.

Heat vibrates the air around her. And on the heat a scent is rising; a scent too pungent for this parched land. It is a smell of cut pine and bleeding resin, it is forest soil after rain.

Blood beats in her ears. It roars through her skull.

A whisper slides up against her: 'I've a question for you, Magdalena.'

She spins round, barely daring to breathe, blood rushing from her head. Perhaps this time. This will be the time—

'Do you think it would have made a difference to your own fortune if you hadn't gone with Ala to see the gypsies that day?'

She spins and spins again but she can't see the form of him anywhere.

'Well, Magdalena, what do you think?'

How to name this desire to bring to life each scrap and flake of him? To conjure a thumb's split nail, resurrect the thinnest of hairs on an arm? The need is here in her stretched and seeking fingers; a yearning to recreate the curve of a shoulder so she may scrape her knuckles against a clavicle ridge, so her thumbs might take their rest in the hollow at the base of a stubbled throat. It is an ache that has never left her.

'Grigori?' Blood floods to her heart as if it might drown her. 'Where are you?'

Silence.
'Why can I never see you?'
There is only silence.
Again she begins to run.

Przemysl, South East Poland

She runs with Ivan Pavlov bouncing beside her, deviating now and then to crash through bulrushes after a whiff of vole. She runs with Ala's hot hand yanking her along the path on the banks of the glistening San.

'I want a count, or an officer at the very least. He'll have a chateau in the mountains and an apartment in Warsaw,' Ala pants. She is very pink-cheeked. 'What about you?'

Lena is far too sweaty to care. 'Can we slow down?'

'Come on. What do you want?'

'I don't know.'

'You must know. Think.'

She is. She's thinking about breath. The white branches of the birch trees sound as if they're wheezing above them. Asthma is the term for wheezing in the branches of the lungs. You would prescribe adrenaline injections for acute attacks, otherwise treat with oral ephedrine.

Ala lets go of Lena to unfasten her plaits and shake her hair into a crimped yellow sheet. 'Maybe my count will have a younger brother. I mean the brother will be poorer, obviously, but he might be a teacher or something. You'd take that for a fortune, wouldn't you?'

Bronchus, bronchi. Latin, originally from the Greek. And before the Greek?

'Come on, twig. What would you choose, really, and don't say an emperor or a pope or something ridiculous.'

Lena stops dead, so Ala turns back, her eyes dancing with apartment-owning counts and officers. 'What now, twig? What-ever is it?'

It is, truth be told, quite a disappointment to see Ala like this. Because what's the point of an elder sister if she is not in solidarity with you against the world? She looks at Ala with her bouncing hair and count-crammed eyeballs and once again she can't understand how, from the same biological starting point, they've ended up such ill-matched beings.

'Suit yourself.' Ala shrugs and she's off so fast that Lena almost loses her.

But opening out from a narrow path between the oldest birches is the clearing. And Ala's waiting, waving, and behind her, dominating the centre, is an enormous tent, pale as a mushroom, its peak taller than the crowns of the trees, guy ropes like jungle roots across the grass. By the tent's entrance a bear in a sequinned waistcoat jiggles its hips on a planked stage. In the spaces between the guy ropes, stalls are selling *barszcz*, or spiced apple punch, or slivers of suckling pig rotating on spits. There are games too; hoops to throw, hammers to lift, and right on the clearing's edge, a line of men wait to hurl knives at a spinning wheel.

A bearded man, dressed in Cossack style, leaps up on the stage beside the dancing bear. Lowering his horn he begins to shout, offering midgets and strong men and sword-swallowing ladies – in fact every known wonder of the world, and several unknown ones too – and all this inside the tent this very afternoon for five zlotys only. Five zlotys is all the lucky ladies and gentlemen will need to watch the most unforgettable show this side of heaven.

'No,' Ala says. 'No way.'

'Yes.'

'Goddamn no, twig.'

'Goddamn yes. It's my birthday.'

'We're here to get our fortunes.'

'And it's my birthday, Ala.' Lena stares at her without blinking. If she keeps it up long enough Ala will give in. She just has to wait it out.

*

It's gloomy inside the tent, smoky from the paraffin lamps staked between the rows of benches and around the sawdust-strewn ring. Lena has to put a lead on Pavlov to stop him scuttling back out after a taste of roasting pig. Ala complains that it reeks of sweat and ale.

Luckily Lena spots Julia, Ala's best friend, sitting on a bench halfway back from the ring, and even better Danushka's with her, Julia's younger sister who's in Lena's class. Except, what's this? – when they go up, Julia is sobbing into her handkerchief.

Danushka rolls her eyes at Lena. 'My sister had her fortunes given to her.'

'Were they good ones or bad ones?'

'No one knows. There's too much snot for any understanding.'

Lena sits down beside her. 'And yours, Dan, what were you given?'

'*Quod plerumque*. What you would expect.'

Lena laughs out loud. Danushka is not one to be easily impressed. Dan is the best in school for Latin, and Lena for General Science.

'But Ala's fortunes are looking good.' Danushka nods towards the opposite side of the tent where three men in dark uniforms are taking their seats.

Lena snorts. 'Goodness what polished belts, and look, their mamas have done a lovely job of pressing their cap corners.' She gives Ala a nudge: 'Officers, straight ahead.' At once Ala begins flicking her hair about like a fly-ridden horse, so Lena can't help but lean to Dan's ear. 'It's not just acrobats performing today.'

The horn is blown, the tent flaps close, and a juggler runs into the ring with flaming torches, throwing them into a fiery wheel. Lena cups her hands around her mouth and shouts, 'Keep them up!' And Ala closes her eyes.

'He's looking this way,' Dan whispers, 'my life on it he is. The officer in the middle; the one with glasses.'

'He's spotted you,' Lena tells Ala, 'the officer in the middle. The one with the glasses is staring.'

'Go to hell, twig.'

'On Romek's lung, he is. His spectacles imply that he opens a book now and then. Should I go over and warn him what you think of education? He's not so bad when viewed from a distance. I can confirm two eyes, a full complement of legs, and arms of functional length. Goodness, what shiny boots he's got. Mama's going to adore those.'

From a platform high above them, a flashing parcel comes tumbling down a rope, unravelling into a silver-cloaked woman with a rapier clenched between her teeth. Lena jumps up. 'This I've got to see!'

Ala grabs her skirt and yanks. 'Sit goddamned down!'

The sword-swallower, a slight young woman, strides along the front benches flexing the glinting blade. She steps up on a box in the centre of the ring, wide-legged, opening her mouth and leaning back, holding the rapier directly above her like Damocles's sword. Slowly the metal descends towards her stretched lips, then the blade begins to disappear down her throat until only the rapier's handle protrudes.

Lena leaps up to roar her approval. Ala puts her face in her hands and inches away along the bench.

'Thank the blessed Virgin that's over,' Ala says when the world's strongest man has been and gone, and the flaps are raised to daylight. She's standing and heading for the exit.

'You can thank me when you marry your officer,' Lena replies, trailing behind.

But Ala ignores her. She's off, running down to old man Bosko, who's turning his chestnuts on the griddle, wiping his face because of the heat of the coals. Old man Bosko knows everything worth knowing. Lena watches him raise his spatula and point south. Ala turns back and waves at her, 'The marshes, come on.'

Once they're out of the forest, Ala stops and shields her eyes to scour the land alongside the river. The brown-crusted ground is an acre wide and thicketed with reeds and bulrushes, dry enough to walk on in summer, but a bog, alive with trout and carp as soon as the October rains fall and the San bursts its banks.

'There! Over there!' Ala cries. 'I see them!'

A dozen or so hoop-framed caravans stand in a row near the thin silver river, shaggy ponies hobbled in the vehicles' shade. It seems very still in this open space after the noise and action in the tent. Little knots of townspeople wait behind the caravans, fanning faces or smoking pipes, or simply gazing at distant herons' nests or the squabbling geese.

'Which one, twig? Which caravan?'

'Does it matter?'

'Of course it matters. There could be any number of fortunes out there.'

Lena looks over the caravans, unpainted and tatty. She shrugs. 'They all look alike to me.'

'They can't be.'

'All right, go for the most popular one, where the most people are waiting.'

'But they might shut up business for the day before I get to go in.'

'The least busy then?'

Ala looks at her. 'You think?'

Ala is off, running to the farthest caravan, one with a dirty red sheet hanging at the back. A man comes out, squinting in the sunlight at the top of the wooden steps, then he hurries down and away. No one else is waiting so Ala lifts her skirts and jumps up. She pulls back the curtain and disappears inside.

Lena looks around for something to do. She considers heading back to the birches and breaking off a switch to continue her investigation into a left shin–right shin pain disparity. Understanding pain will no doubt constitute an essential part of her medical training. Or she could go down to where the marshes get really boggy and see how far she can hop on the log path before she sinks. But in the end she just sits down watching a damselfly zipping through the reeds. Pavlov leans against her and she pulls his ears for him. 'Pray that Ala gets her officer predicted, Pav, otherwise there'll be foul weather at home for days.'

But then Lena remembers she doesn't need to worry about Ala.

This is what her father always says.

Ala is like a seed from a dandelion clock, Papa says. She'll be happy whichever way the wind blows her.

As Papa always tells it, Lena had shaken her head furiously when he first explained this.

'But me, Papa?' she'd apparently said. 'What am I?'

'You? Magdalena Luiza?' He'd had a good titter. 'You? Let me see . . .' And he'd laid down his trowel – they were in the bean rows at the time – and scooped her up, upending her and lurching along the canes so furry pods brushed her bouncing face, going up and down laughing as she screamed at him to stop. When he planted her back on the ground and got his breath back he'd leaned over his cane so their blue eyes were level. 'Well, little miss, it seems obvious to me that what you most resemble is a short brown stick—'

'Papa! I'm not a stick!'

'– one that seems to have grown for the sole purpose of poking and prodding at whatever has the misfortune to lie beneath.'

She'd shook her head at him, several times, fish-mouthed with protest. At least this is how Papa always tells it, mimicking her outraged expression when he does.

How old was she then? Four? Five? She'd lowered her face and charged to butt him in the stomach. 'I'm not a stick, I'm not a stick!'

'I'm afraid so, Magdalena Luiza. There you have it.'

'But, Papa, can sticks be happy like dandelions?'

'I fear you won't be entirely content until you've turfed an army of ants over your toes. Please do not pummel me, Magdalena Luiza. We may struggle to contain our essential natures, but your mother assures me it is a mark of a civilised society to make a show of concealing one's mood.'

'Twig? Twig! Wherever are you?'

Standing on the top step at the back of the caravan, Ala is waving with both arms like a person summoning assistance. Except she's grinning – thank the devil himself for that. Words start spilling out of her before Lena even gets close. 'A man in uniform! Someone here will be in my future – right to the end of everything – but before that we'll make a great journey together! A man in uniform, twig, and children – two if I'm lucky, she said. She said I'd be luckier than others in life.'

'Everyone is luckier than others in one way or another, Ala.'

'Not everyone.'

Lena opens her mouth and closes it. Then she can't resist. 'Oh, Ala, think about it for one second, if you can manage that. "Luckier than others" – it's an entirely meaningless statement. What is luck anyway? It's not even something that exists.'

Ala is gaping at her. Lena looks away. Ulka has promised cherry cake for her birthday. 'Come on then.'

'Where do you think you're going?' Ala hasn't moved.

'Home?'

'You can't.'

'Observe how legs work: nerve, muscle, sinew, bone in perfect synchronicity.'

'Not yet, I mean.' Ala is suddenly at her side, keeping pace. About to seize her elbow. 'The thing is, twig, she wants to see you.'

'Excuse me?'

'Send in the child who's sulking by the river, that's what she said.'

'Well it can't be me because I don't sulk.'

'Twig, listen. You have to go in there.'

Lena kicks at the reeds. 'I don't have to do anything.'

'She said send in that child, I have a gift to make her, that's all she said.'

'You told her it was my birthday? Oh, Ala, you goddamn told her!'

'Would it matter if I had?' Ala smiles all sugar and cream.

'Goddamn you, Ala. I mean goddamn. Really. Fine, I'll god-damn go. But only for the purpose of investigating the irrational. Though quite why I should be forced to do these things on my birthday is quite beyond me.'

She stomps off towards the caravan and thuds up the steps with little grace.

England

'Ma, are you awake?'

JoJo. Here, sitting stiff-shouldered by her bed. She raises a hand as if to touch his cheek. How big he's grown. She should tell him this. Tell him what a man he has become.

He takes her hand, pulls it to his lips. 'You need something, Ma? A drink?'

She moves her head slightly from side to side. His eyes are sad. Poor boy. She would like to tell him not to worry about having to speak when he makes these visits. She'd like to say, 'It is enough for me to see you moving through the air; to hear your breath in the room. It is enough and it is everything.'

'Is there something else I can get you, Ma? A cloth for your face?'

Again she shakes her head, smiling till dampness comes to her eyes. If she could loosen her throat and talk freely she would like to tell him how he used to stand stiff as a pikestaff – four years old – holding up the feed bucket as the Clydesdale thundered down from the hill. She would say how Blackie came only to him; this soot-haired, fierce little boy, who never stepped back, who always held his ground. She'd recall for him the time Blackie was sold and he refused to eat for five days. She'd tell him how much she has always adored this fire he keeps burning in his heart. She'd like to lie and tell him he was never second best.

She digs her thumb into her throat. 'Darling, are you eating?'

And he looks at her and snorts. He slaps his thigh and starts to laugh. The image of his father, of course. 'Ma, honestly!'

But she doesn't laugh with him. She should try for more words because who knows if this chance will return. Tell him to fill himself with fat, spoon it in, say, 'Listen, child, you can never eat enough in this life. Lay flesh on your bones and the fat on top. Keep your body strong and whatever you do stay standing. Do this and you might just avoid the grasp of the god beneath the soil.' This is what she needs to say.

He wipes his eyes with his thumbs, looking to the window. 'Papa's blackbird's back,' he says. 'Look, Ma.'

She turns to see the bird hop along the sill, blinking and peering in. 'Sure,' she whispers. 'He's wanting his breakfast.'

Przemysl, South East Poland

Lena is out on the path waiting for the cart to arrive, waiting too for Ala and Mama to finish their fussing. It's a warm evening, a week after the gypsies came to town. In the pink dusk, bees are working over Papa's jasmine above the lintel. Lucky bees who aren't forced to wear white satin confirmation dresses with peach bows stitched on 'for interest', who never have to go to pointless parties. She walks down the path to wait at the gate, slipping her fingers into the pocket she asked Ulka to stitch down the seam of the dress. She's decided to bring it, the gift the gypsy gave her. As soon as the mothers are occupied she can take Danushka aside and consult. With any luck Dan will have an idea what to do.

'Did your sister intend to dress as if she was in one of the cheaper Black Sea resorts?'

Lena sniggers and looks down the hall where newly arrived guests are batting bursts of chit-chat back and forth, tapping heels on marble, waiting, no doubt, for a measure of champagne to warm their tongues. Ala and Julia are loitering under the chandelier right by the front door, practically boring holes in the wood with their eyes. Danushka has a point, if a sharp one. Ala's wearing one of Mama's recital gowns and has somehow defied gravity by stacking every strand of her hair high as a sand tower on her head. A turquoise feather perches on the top like a flag in peril. She shrugs. 'It's practically certain,' she says.

It's practically certain Ala will marry the officer from the gypsy tent. Everyone's agreed on this. When they got back from the forest, Ala had gone straight to the kitchen and, with

Lena as witness, informed Ulka of the events in the tent and the fortune readings the gypsy woman had given her. Ulka agreed there might be promise in them, and told Mama over breakfast on Sunday morning. Mama couldn't help it all coming out to Julia's mama after Mass, and Julia's mama clapped her hands and said an invite to Julia's name day celebrations must be sent to the barracks at once; that would be the thing to do. She'd despatch her maid, Elena, who was fiercer than a terrier when it came to digging out persons of interest, no matter how deep their burrow. On Tuesday Ulka bumped into Elena at the butcher's and received confirmation that an invite had been issued to three men of officer rank in the Engineering Corps who'd been in the gypsy tent on Saturday, one of whom was a spectacles wearer. There followed a forty-eight-hour period of silence, during which Ala chewed down her nails and stacked up her hair twenty different ways, before word came in a note from Julia, rolled along the floor to Ala during their graduation exam on Thursday afternoon. The officers had accepted the invitation.

'Which can only mean one thing,' Ala said to Lena in the bathroom that Thursday evening, a flush on her cheeks.

'You've messed up the exam?'

'No, you know, it's—' Ala's lip began to wobble.

'Practically certain?' Lena offered with more enthusiasm than she felt.

After all, it was only what everyone else was saying.

'They'll be engaged by autumn, I suppose.' Danushka licks cream off her thumb. It was a good decision to position themselves by the kitchen door where a finger might slide onto a tray of warm canapés. 'Will you be bridesmaid?'

Lena puts her hand in her pocket and turns over the gypsy's gift, wondering when to move the conversation to weightier matters. She shrugs and says she hasn't really thought about weddings. 'I'll probably be settled in Kraków by then.'

'Very wise.' Danushka is tapping her riding crop against the toe of her boot. Lena admires her friend's fortitude in choosing breeches even though her mother fell to her knees and pleaded for lace. 'I don't think I could bear it myself. Why anyone wants to marry is beyond me. I've already warned Julia she'll have to use our cousin to hold her train when the time comes.'

'Dan, listen, you know when Ala dragged me off to get her fortunes—'

'But speak of the devil.' Danushka raises her crop and points down the hall. 'We have company at last. I mean the only sort of company anyone's interested in. Shall we? For the sport of it?'

Linking arms they waltz to the front door. The three officers from the gypsy tent have actually materialised and, in an even greater miracle, seem to be propelling themselves willingly over the threshold. This done, the door is being shut behind them, and possibly also bolted. The men click their heels and fold themselves in bows to Ala and Julia and the mothers, taking slender white-gloved fingers and pressing them to their lips.

Lena sniggers. 'Lambs to the slaughter.'

'Hapless toy soldiers, popped out of their tin by accident and can't find a way back in.'

'Danushka, at last! We were about to send out a search party!' Dan's mother's arm extends with a swift and unerring grabbing motion. 'My dear girls, we're just being introduced to Lieutenants Bem, Machek and Dabrowicz of the Engineering Corps. Gentlemen, you will please forgive my younger daughter's attire. We've every hope she'll grow out of it.'

Lena tries to catch Ala's eye, but her sister has turned terribly grey in the face. She runs through the correct procedure for treating fainting fits. 'Everyone stand back, give her air,' she'll have to shout. 'Get me a stool. You there, soldier, kneel down and raise her legs!' Alternatively she might just need a bucket.

Mama makes a flapping grasp at Lena's peach bow. 'Gentlemen, my younger daughter, Magdalena.'

The officers swivel their boots in Lena's direction. They bow simultaneously and so gravely that she has to suck in her cheeks to keep from giggling. When Ala's officer – Bem – resumes the vertical, resettling his spectacles against his nose, the irises of his eyes appear so pale as to be almost colourless. There might be a medical condition involved, possibly a hereditary one. Ala will need warning.

'But we've encountered each other before,' he says to Lena.

'I don't think so.'

'In the gypsy tent last week. As I recall you were very taken with the show.'

'It was an extraordinary display of anatomical capability.'

He glances back at his friends with a thin smile. 'Is that so?'

'What else could you call it? Do you know how many pairs of oesophageal muscles need to be relaxed to enable a blade to slide down the throat?'

Still with that smile: 'I have no idea.'

'Have a guess.'

'No idea.'

'You can guess, can't you?'

'Lena darling.'

'Yes, Mama?'

'It's quite all right, madam. Would it be ten pairs?'

'More. Come on.'

'Lena darling—'

'Fifteen?'

'Fifty.'

'That I did not know.'

'I mean there's no way someone like you would be able to do it. And I wouldn't recommend you even try. Even the smallest injury can lead to a perforation of the heart, lungs, stomach or small intestines. The outcome would certainly be deadly.'

'Lena darling, please. I'm sorry, gentlemen, my daughter has these enthusiasms.'

'Not an enthusiasm, Mama. Medicine is neither a hobby nor the pursuit of amateurs. I'm not sure why I have to keep telling you this.'

The officer casts his small smile towards Mama.

'Well, Doctor Magdalena,' he says turning back her way, 'if I stay away from gypsies' swords, will you tell me if your fortunes were good?'

'I am a rationalist, sir. I hold no store in five zloty fables.'

'Lena, please!'

'I don't, Mama.' She doesn't have to look at Ala twitching beside her to know she's no longer pale and delicate. 'But my sister's fortune reading was excellent, sir. It said that Ala is to marry a man in uniform.'

'Mother of God, Lena!'

'Indeed? Well, miss, I confess to a certain curiosity as to whom you think you might marry if it's not the person the fortunes decree.'

'But that's really none of your business. You will excuse me but it is not.'

'It's no one's business yet. You might say it's not even mine. I've years of studying ahead of me before I begin to think of marriage. That's if I do. I'm not convinced there's a tremendous amount to recommend it.'

For a moment nothing is said among the little group by the door. The officers to each side of Lieutenant Bem are occupied in coughing into their fists. Ala can be heard emitting a sort of monotone, something in the way of unhappy pipework.

'Time for that powder room.' Mama's grip tightens and she starts to steer Lena away. 'Gentlemen, I apologise most sincerely for any impropriety in my daughter's speech.' She hisses in Lena's ear, 'I've no idea what devilment has taken you, but tonight, darling, you offend us all.'

'Please, madam, wait.' Bem steps after them. 'I confess I'm not offended.'

'You're not?'

'One might hazard it a notion to be celebrated; the fresh air of youthful ideas.'

'In these modern times,' his colleague smirks behind his hand.

'Quite so, Machek.' He turns to Lena and makes a brief bow. 'If I'm not mistaken, a mazurka may be starting up in the ball-room. If you don't find music counter to your rationalist principles, I wonder if you'd do me the honour?'

Lena stares at him. 'Excuse me?'

'Will you dance?'

'Mother of God save us,' Mama whispers to the ceiling.

'No. No, I don't think I will.'

'No?'

'No?' Mama whimpers.

'It's a kind offer, sir, but I don't dance.'

'Everyone dances.'

'With respect that's completely untrue.'

'Lena!'

'What now, Mama? Take Papa, for example, it's a straightforward fact that when your left foot has been blown off by a Prussian sniper you can't perform a polka, much as you might believe otherwise. I like to run with my dog and I'm not the worst skater if you must know, but dancing at parties is dull beyond words. There's never enough room to be entirely free, which is the only way to go about it. Besides which there are far too many people watching. So, thank you, but no, it's not for me.'

Danushka is bent double, her shoulders shaking violently. The coughing officers have exploded into great wails of mirth, and this grave-faced watery-eyed officer is staring at her like she's a book he doesn't know where to shelve.

'My sister dances very well. Better than anyone I know. You should give Ala a try.' She flops down in a ridiculous sort of curtsey and bolts for the front door.

Goodness it's a relief to be out in the night with nothing but cold air in her face. She runs down the stone steps and round the side of the house to the back lawn. It takes a lot of running to leave the lights and music behind. It's far too grand, Danushka's house, and the lawn is too vast, and all that noise of partying people who haven't just messed up their sister's future is much too loud. She wishes Ivan Pavlov were at her side, bumping her fingers with his nose. How much easier it is to talk to dogs. Dogs do not ask people to dance. Dogs know when to leave someone alone.

As she runs it knocks against her leg, the gypsy's gift in her pocket. Stupid to have brought it. Stupider not to have thrown it in the San straight away. Whatever is happening to her rational thinking?

'So you made it in the end.' That's what the gypsy woman had said, squinting from her samovar as Lena pulled back the curtain and stepped into the dark. The air inside the caravan was stifling; rough with smoke yet sweet as the killing stall where Ulrich's diseased cattle await their bullet. A square of peat burned beneath the samovar's stand. Above it, a gash in the fabric roof was only open enough for the fumes to escape and for a trickle of dusty daylight to fall in. Lena backed up against the curtain, her hand to her mouth, her eyes watering.

The woman took up a tallow lantern from the floor, her thin body crooked like an old nail. A scarf was pulled tight across her skull and knotted under her jaw. Cataracts clouded her pupils.

'Turn around, daughter, I would see the whole of you.'

Nodding to herself, she returned to her samovar. 'Not what I expected, but as good as any other.'

'I don't have any zlotys on me, you should know that.'

'It's not your money I need. Sit down, take some tea.' She turned the tap and poured steaming brown liquid into a glass.

'No, thank you.'

The woman dropped a brown sugar crystal into her glass, and stirred the liquid, squinting up at Lena as if deciding something.

'I only came here to spare Ala's feelings,' Lena said in the silence. 'She believes in fortunes. But I'm a rationalist not a fool. You should know that.'

'So you think you'll have the future you choose?'

'Papa says such things are entirely possible for women in the twentieth century. I haven't decided on marriage, but I will be a doctor.'

'Is that so?'

'Ours is an age of progress. Women are piloting aircraft now.'

The woman said nothing. Lena watched her blow on the tea. For a moment Lena thought herself forgotten, then the woman looked up and grinned.

'How easy it is to plot a journey through life when you're looking down from the sunny heights of youth. Nice view when you see the world laid out in every direction below.'

She returned to her tea and Lena waited. When the woman spoke again her voice came at a crawl. It seemed to drag something heavy in its wake. 'My daughter, at this moment your future seems no more perilous than a stream you might follow down from your mountain, isn't that so? But what happens when other people jump in this clear stream of yours and muddy it with their boots?' She held Lena's gaze. 'What happens when love creeps up and puts its hand on your shoulder, what then?'

Lena looked away quickly. 'You're mocking me, I can tell, and that isn't a kind thing to do. I don't believe in any of this, so actually it doesn't matter what you say. But still I would like you to stop talking this way or I'll leave. You can't keep me here, you know.'

The woman laughed, the sound gurgling in her throat. 'Don't lose this temper, child, it may help you get through the worst of things. Anger has its uses.' She drained her glass and threw the dregs onto the smouldering peat. 'But the particular course of your life is neither here nor there to me. I've no interest in weighing your portion of sorrow. It's hardly going to be unique.' Drawing back her lips she smiled black-gummed at Lena. 'I wish only to make you a gift.'

'Why would you do that?'

'It's your birthday, I'm told.'

Goddamn goddamn Ala.

'Mama says I shouldn't accept gifts I can't repay.'

'You haven't seen it. You'd reject a gift without seeing it? Do I scare you that much?'

'You don't scare me at all.'

The woman laughed again. She dug into her skirts.

'I don't want it, I told you,' Lena said, her voice far too loud. She stepped back against the curtain. 'I don't want your gift.'

'But you want to be a doctor and help people. Do you think doctors can choose who they aid?' Her ancient hand was clasped over an object. There was a giddiness in her dim eyes, a flickering feral exhilaration. 'Help me now.'

Lena shook her head. 'I can't.'

'You can and you will take it because you're a good girl, we both know that.'

It was her legs that moved her forward, Lena remembers this much. Her head was refusing, but Lena's feet shuffled towards the woman.

'Happy birthday,' the woman grinned, holding out her hand.

Lena took the gift. She opened her fingers and saw a smooth lump about the size of a duck's egg, warm and slightly waxy. 'What is it?'

The woman had moved back to the samovar. She filled a glass and threw its liquid on the peat. Smoke rose up in hissing tongues.

'Baltic resin.'

'But what am I to do with it?'

Without seeming to hear the question, and without giving any warning, the woman bent her face to the tallow lantern and blew out the flame. But for the small pool of daylight above the dying fire, darkness was everywhere. It was all Lena could do not to cry out. Fumbling behind her she found the curtain and pulled it so sunlight sliced in, a hard yellow blade of it, illuminating the woman now settling herself in a nest of tattered blankets in the far corner, her slipped scarf revealing a mottled skull, bald but for a few colourless strands of hair.

Lena backed beyond the curtain into light and warmth. 'I said what do I do with it?'

'You say you're a rationalist. So do nothing.' The woman closed her eyes. Her hands were clasped over her chest. 'Do nothing, child. But know this amber for what it is; a thing of solidity. It will not decay like flesh. It won't warp like love nor rot like dreams of the future, and you, my daughter, will need something solid to hold on to in life.' The woman lay narrow and unmoving, her blackened soles poking out beyond the blankets. 'And now, it's time to go.'

Lena can't stop shivering, but it's a July night and she's running, so really she should be warm. The lawn is long and sloping, it curves away past a summer house and a row of marble statues, down to the willows and brook. It's quiet here, there's only a plash of water over pebbles and the odd stoat or vole scrabbling along the bank. Lena can just make out a thin black ribbon, and suddenly she's taken with a wild idea that she might jump in this stream and follow it all the way home.

Someone's behind her.

There's silence, but it's the careful sort. Lena knows she's being watched.

She turns. Him – Ala's officer.

'I was taught it's rude to creep up on people.'

He tips his head, not enough for it to be a sign of agreement. 'You didn't care for the party?'

'Should I?'

'Young people generally seem to like them.'

'Not all of us.'

She kicks at the grass, already wet with dew.

There is a sudden dry hissing sound from the trees across the stream.

'That was a female barn owl,' he says.

Lena says nothing.

'The pitch of their call is always a little higher than the males.'

'Look, I don't want to be impolite, but I was just in the middle of thinking about some things I really have to think about right now. So could you please go and listen to your owls somewhere else? The lawn's plenty big enough.'

He pinches his nose and smiles, although she really wasn't joking. 'My apologies if I disturbed you. I was concerned.'

'Me?' Lena can't help laughing. 'You've decided you're concerned about me?'

'Actually your mother was wondering. Coffee and sweets have been served in the dining room. She sang a delightful aria followed by two encores and now carriages are beginning to arrive.'

'Do you usually perform errands for anxious mothers?'

He says nothing. The night's noises do nothing to fill the space between them.

She digs her toe into the moss in the grass, scuffing it up. Her shoes are soaked and now also muddy. 'Thank you for coming to find me, but as you can see I'm quite well. Please return word to my mother that there's no need for concern. I simply wanted some air.'

He clicks his heels. Ridiculous. His boots squeak in the grass.

She keeps her eyes on the brook until she's sure he's set off, then she turns to watch him head back up the lawn, his strides of even length, as if every step has been measured to a precise specification before being handed out to him. His arms are swinging metronomes. Tick tock tick tock tick tock.

'Goddamn it!' she shouts to no one in particular. 'Goddamn you all!'

She pulls the amber from her pocket and turns it in her hands, walking along beside the brook looking for the darkest corner. There's no need at all for Danushka's advice, or anyone else's for that matter, as to what to do. She lifts the amber above her head and hurls it into the black water.

England

Bright light. Behind it someone is speaking.

A straw is being pushed at her lips.

Someone is asking her to drink. It keeps on at her, the woman's voice. 'Drink, sweetheart. You must drink. Just try a little for me.'

She allows the straw between her lips and is praised for it. The liquid is a sludge tasting of berry. Oramorph in there, she supposes. Ten milligrammes or perhaps twenty. Someone is wiping her lips and saying how about a little more, just a little? A kind person, doing the asking. Just like she was kind when she looked after people. Wasn't that what a doctor once told her? You'll be a great doctor one day.

This person is speaking in a strange language. She must tell them she doesn't know this language yet. She's only a child, isn't she? At least a moment ago she was only a child at Julia's party. She shakes her head.

'You did well, Magdalena,' the woman's voice says. 'Lie back now and rest.'

Przemysl, South East Poland

But there's no time to rest.

It's the summer break before Lena's final school year and there's too much to do. There's a medical encyclopaedia to memorise, canine intelligence tests to repeat, and besides all this apologies need to be offered as many times as Lena can bear and then double that number. At least this is what Ulka recommends when she sees Ala's damp face at the breakfast table the morning after Julia's party.

'Expect heavy weather,' she tells Lena, tailing her into the kitchen with the empty porridge tureen. 'There's no telling how Ala will grieve this.'

'But how can she grieve, nothing happened to her.'

'Precisely, twig.'

'Excuse me?'

'The loss of a future is as great a loss as any other.'

'But that's absurd.'

'You think so?' Ulka gives her a look and dumps the tureen in the sink. 'Apologise. And while you're at it, keep your head down.'

Lena keeps her head down. Fortunately there's no word from the officers, and just three days after Julia's party, the barracks are deserted; the entire Army Corps has left town. This is no wild rumour but fact, delivered as fast as unpreserved meat from Elena to Ulka in the market square. Mama is overheard whispering to Papa that this must be considered something of a relief given the circumstances.

On the fourth day after the party Ala drifts into the kitchen where Lena has been commandeered to stuff pierogi. Ala has a hairbrush in her hand.

She pulls out a chair. 'I can sit on my hair now.' She sits on her hair.

Lena and Ulka lift sticky fingers from the bowl and observe in silence.

Ala stands. 'I think I'll borrow your silver brooch tonight, twig.'

She drifts away and Ulka grunts, declaring communication restored.

'But what if I'd actually liked the officer?'

Ulka slams a doughy slab on the board. 'Shall we be grateful for small mercies?'

It turns out Ala is indeed happy this summer, and not just because she can finally sit on her hair. Ala has employment at the town hospital as a secretary in admissions.

'However can you stand the thought of it,' she says coming into the bathroom one evening where Lena is at the sink examining two of Pavlov's fleas under a magnifying glass. 'All those years of study ahead of you without so much as a zloty of your own to spend. Are you going to be long in here?'

Ala dumps a load of stockings in the bath and opens the taps. 'I'm going to the new picture house with some friends from work,' she says even though Lena didn't ask. 'I can't tell you how liberating it is, being in employment. For one thing you're in adult company at last. And now with this salary I can see all the Warsaw pictures and eat in any cafe I like, and buy the fabric I choose. Why I might even take an apartment of my own. Just you wait until there's no one to tell you what to do. I'm not going to let anyone tell me another thing ever. Shove over, I need the light.'

Lena folds the fleas in a napkin and watches Ala dot rouge on her cheeks. There's a whiff of cigarette to her sister these days. Ala applies the stick to her lips.

'How do I look?'

'Like your mouth's bleeding. Excuse me.'

She finds Ulka grating beetroot at the kitchen sink, crimson juice streaming down to her elbows. But when informed of Ala's plans, Ulka surprises Lena. Ulka merely laughs.

'Don't you worry, twig, your sister's going nowhere while there's hot water in the bathroom pipes, supper on the table, and shoes that turn up polished outside her door in the morning.'

'But she always said she'd be married by autumn. That's all Ala ever wanted.'

Ulka scoops up dripping handfuls from the sink, dumping them in a cut-glass bowl. 'Perhaps you're learning your sister is not as simple-minded as you'd imagined. People change. They grow up and want different things.'

'Not me.'

Lena returns to school in September for her final year, determined to keep an eye on Ala's metamorphosis. She might even begin a study on female psychological health. But two weeks into term, she's distracted from all thought of Ala by an unnerving encounter on a Thursday afternoon after school.

When Lena returns home she resolves to see out the evening quietly, before retreating to her bedroom to turn things over alone. And for a while the evening progresses harmlessly enough; Papa grumbles through a newspaper in the armchair by the hearth, airing his stump on a footstool, and Mama occupies herself at the piano with a tricky Brahms sonata. Romek's nowhere to be seen which means he's probably somewhere beneath the piano drawing up odds for his classmates' Latin exams or attempting card tricks or some form of levitation. But then the front door slams and Ala bursts into the sitting room in a fit of excitement so great she can't get her arm out of the sleeve of her coat.

At the table Lena closes her maths book. 'I think I'll finish off upstairs.'

'Don't you want to hear what Julia's family are planning for next spring?' Ala says, whirling and shaking at the coat on her arm. 'It's quite extraordinary. Did Dan say anything to you, twig?'

Lena stares at Ala. Just about every day now she returns like this, with rumours still warm from the admissions desk, lobbing them into the sitting room like she thinks they're buns for the starving.

'What are they planning?' Mama abandons Brahms and swivels on her stool. When it comes to gossip, Mama is one of the starving.

'They're packing up and leaving the country.'

'Nonsense!'

'It's true, Mama. Ania was on a break and she overheard Mr Meyer telling Doctor Janucek he's booking the family on a boat to Britain. From there they're planning to head to the New World, probably Argentina. They're leaving in April.'

'Nonsense, darling, that beautiful home—'

'Is going up for auction next month. Mr Meyer said he thought it the safest course of action, what with the world heading the way it is. I can't believe Julia's said nothing. Twig, Dan must have spoken to you about this.'

'But Krystyna Meyer is Polish,' Mama says. 'She does all the flowers on Holy Days, that must count for something. And the two girls are being confirmed at Christmas. I must say this all sounds very extreme. What do you think, Jozef?'

Papa's eyes are closed and a news-sheet is slipping from his lap to the floor.

'Jozef! The Meyers are leaving the country.'

'Possibly overheard to be saying they're leaving the country, my dear. Information acquired by someone we don't know in the slightest.'

'Ania is a very good friend of mine actually, Papa. She swears it's true.'

'She probably swears a lot then.'

'Romuś, darling boy, please. But this is awful. Say it's awful, Jozef.'

'Jan Meyer is known for his sense.'

'But this is awful.' Mama jumps up. 'I must tell Ulka.'

'I'll come,' Ala says. 'Wait. What's that you've got?' She crouches down to peer under the piano. 'What on earth are you fiddling with down there, worm? Come on, out with you, strange creature.'

She drags Romek out by his ankles. He stands up gangly as an urchin, his fingers grimy and closed over a clutch of objects that look like black duck eggs.

Lena gathers her books and heads for the door.

'Brother, you truly are a filthy piece of worm skin,' Ala sighs.

'I can juggle five lumps of coal with my eyes shut. I'm working up to six, then I'll move on to carrots, then butter knives, then daggers or cut-throat razors.'

'That's not all coal.' Ala pokes at his cupped hands. 'What else have you got in there? I knew it! I knew I saw something odd. My God, Lena, you'd better come and see what I've found in the worm's disgusting paws.'

Lena waves a departing hand as if above such minor concerns.

But this is to underestimate Ala's zeal for meddling. 'Give it here, thief. It's a low business to steal from your own family.'

Mama sighs, 'Very low indeed, darling.'

'If you must know, Mama, I borrowed it today.'

'Impossible,' Ala says.

'Want to lay odds on it?'

'Romuś darling, you remember Father Gorski's final warning, we are not to have gambling in the home.'

'Goodnight then,' Lena says and heads for the hall.

'Lena,' Ala calls, 'come back a moment. Is the worm telling the truth?'

'Excuse me?'

'Did you give him the amber?' Ala is staring at her now, and it's like every cog in her brain is straining to connect with its neighbour. 'Because you told me you threw it in the brook at Julia's party and that was the last you saw of it.'

'Until it found its way home today,' Romek says. He starts to throw four pieces of coal in the air and then the amber. 'Five is easy for a professional. And the amber is perfect. Watch it go round, I'll send it a little higher next time if you like. Do you want to see me try six? It takes an exceptional amount of concentration and skill for any number over five. Do you want to see six?'

'No, we don't,' Ala says. 'Wait, twig. How?'

'Excuse me?'

'How did you get it back? The amber went in the brook and now it's made a miraculous reappearance.'

'No miracles were involved, I assure you.'

'In which case—'

'Does it really matter?'

Ala's staring hard at her, cogs overheating, a suspicion slowly clicking into place like a tiny hammer coming to strike a chime. 'I'm starting to think it does.'

'Fine. If it's so vital for you to know, it was returned.'

'By whom?'

'Someone who found it, obviously.'

'And that someone was?'

'You're a funny colour, sis. Red as cherry compote.'

'Worm, you goddamn shut up right now or I'll shove every one of these coals down your throat into your withered lung.'

'Mother of God, Lena, how you speak to your brother!'

Ala begins to smile. It's a thin-cut sort of smile, nevertheless she is buttering it all over the air. It is a smile that somehow seems to imply both a question she has in mind, and the conviction that she knows the answer.

'Which someone, twig?'

'Ala, please,' Lena hisses. 'I can't believe this.'

'It's a simple question.'

'It is actually, darling.'

'Papa?' Lena begs, turning to the armchair.

But he doesn't take her side for once. He bends to gather up his fallen news-sheets. 'I'm a little confused. Are we talking about a man, Magdalena Luiza?'

Romek sniggers.

'Are we talking about an officer?' Ala says. 'A lieutenant, perhaps?' Back in town?

'Mother of God!' Mama's hand leaps for the pearls at her throat, 'Are we?'

'I knew it,' Ala crows. 'I just knew.'

'Oh, darling! This is so—'

'Unbelievable.' Lena hisses. 'You're all quite unbelievable.'

Papa unwraps a boiled mint humbug. For a moment they listen to the sound of sucking.

'Magdalena Luiza, do you have something to say, only people appear to be waiting?'

And there really is no escape now.

'Well, I'm sorry to disappoint you all, but there's not much to tell. He was at the gates after school. It turns out he'd found the amber in the brook at Julia's party. He said he'd seen me throw something in the water – although he really shouldn't have been spying – and he decided he felt responsible for me doing that – though I can't see why he should. Then he said he didn't want me to regret anything from that night, so he went back the next morning and fished the amber out. There was no time to bring it round because they were sent off to a summer training camp. And now they're back in town for a while before they head to their base in the mountains, which, you'll be sorry to hear, is a very long way away. There. A great mystery solved. Now if you'll excuse me, I'm going to finish my equations in my bedroom.'

'But this is wonderful news!' Mama cries. 'Did you hear, Jozef?'

'Dear heart, I did. Magdalena has regained possession of a missing lump.'

Later that evening, Lena creeps downstairs to listen to her parents in the sitting room. You can hear a lot when you position yourself with a dog and a tick hook outside the crack of a draughty door.

Mama is doing most of the talking.

'A mother thinks ahead, Jozef,' Mama's saying. 'She can't help herself.'

'Magdalena Luiza is sixteen years old.'

'I was barely eighteen when you swept me off my feet.'

'Dear heart, I could hardly stand on my rotten foot, so how you think I swept anyone anywhere I really don't know. Would it be wise to remember we know nothing about this man? Not even his age. He's hardly a schoolboy.'

'Something to be grateful for.'

'I'm not so sure.'

'Very well, I'll make enquiries. That should be easy enough to arrange.'

'Zosia, please, you're leaping ahead of yourself.'

'Nonsense. It's a mother's duty to see her daughter safely bestowed. I'm a little disappointed, frankly, that I need to point this out.'

There's a moment of quiet. Possibly Papa is refilling his glass.

Mama sighs, sounding wistful. 'To think Lena is the first with a suitor! We shall have to think about doing something about her teeth. I'd hoped they might straighten, but that's your mother living on, husband.'

'Who has a suitor, my dear?'

'Good heavens, Jozef, have you been listening to anything tonight? Lena of course.'

'But Magdalena Luiza has only just turned sixteen.'

'So you keep saying. We seem to be going round in circles. I'll write a list of questions. Mrs Meyer will have the connections to find out.'

'What sort of questions?'

'Questions, husband, about the lieutenant. Are you overtired, Jozef? They work you far too hard. Really you need to be thinking about slowing down, because the day won't be far off, darling, when our babies . . .'

Lena can bear it no longer. She shoves back the door, Ivan Pavlov on her heels, snorting in excitement. Mama looks up, needle in hand, an ostrich-feathered headband on her lap.

Papa raises his vodka glass, beaming. 'What a surprise. We were just chatting about – whatever was it, Zosia, that we were talking about?'

Lena runs to his armchair and takes his hands.

'Papa, promise me right now that I'll go to medical school and you won't let Mama interfere. You know how she does it – starting all slowly, like a dog licking a sore, so you think it's only a bit of fur the dog's bothering and you forget to keep an eye on things. Then suddenly there it is one day – a gaping hole in the skin – and the dog's worried right through the fat and muscle to a lung or kidney or something vital.'

Mama's needle stops mid-stitch. 'Lena, my darling child, are you calling me some sort of—'

'I'm sorry, Mama, but it happens to be true. Papa, listen, you know Mama's like this – she gets what she wants every time. But you have to promise me tonight, here and now—'

'My darling,' Mama interrupts, 'you misunderstand my intentions.'

'Do I?'

'These are worrying times. Your father and I agree on this. Mother of God, your parents are old enough to remember such suffering that no human should ever endure. It's my fervent hope my children never encounter anything like it.'

'I'm not a child any more, Mama.'

Mama gazes at Lena for a moment. She lays aside the headband and comes to her, running her fingers through her hair. 'This fluff! Darling, you're right, of course you're not a child.'

'Thank you, Mama. I have things to do in life and I will do them.'

'You're a butterfly just opening your wings to dry in the breeze.'

'A butterfly?'

'Yes, darling.'

Papa snorts into his glass.

'And while your wings are gaining strength, your parents, who have lived in the world for some time, want to help their little butterfly take to the air in the safest possible way.'

Lena shrugs her hair out of Mama's grip. 'See, Papa, she's started. You're a witness, this is exactly how she does it.'

'That's all any parent wants, Lena darling. You'll come to see it with your own children one day. My mother, of course, wanted only the convent for me.'

'And you chose against it, Mama. You made the decision.'

'I went against my own dear mama and it was not easy. Love for your father compelled me. You might ask me one day if I have regrets.'

Lena waits while Mama wanders to the mantelpiece and lifts the photograph of her mother and father, caressing the silver frame with her thumb.

'I know my interests, Mama, at any time of life, and this lieutenant isn't one of them. I'm going to be a doctor, is that clear? And, Papa, if you let her meddle and mess things up, I'm telling you now I'll never forgive you either.'

She marches out of the room with Pavlov hightailed at her heels. Behind her she can hear Papa tittering like a child into his glass.

Lena lies on the bed with the shutters and the casement windows open, listening to Ulrich's heifers shuffling in the field below. Pav is snoring at her feet. Holding the amber towards the light from her bedside lamp, Lena studies the twisted filament in its core. She tosses the amber from hand to hand wondering how it must be to end up trapped for all eternity. Really there couldn't be anything worse.

'But I threw it away.' This is what she'd said to him when he unwrapped his white handkerchief and held the amber out, ovoid and glassy in the sun. 'Don't you see,' she'd stepped back, shaking her head, 'I don't want it.'

He'd been standing under the lime trees and the spots of light between the dark September leaves threw blotches on his pale face. 'I can't keep what isn't mine,' he said, his hand outstretched.

'But I don't want it. You really might have thought about that before you went fishing and got your boots all soggy.'

He'd inclined his head but said nothing. She studied him then, trying to understand why he was back; there was really no sense to it. Danushka was right, of course, they were exactly like toy soldiers, these military types, taken out of their tin every morning and wound up with a key in the back. He looked no different from how he'd been at the party except for his khaki clothing and the addition of a moustache, one so thin it looked drawn on, and what would be the point of doing that?

Her school friends were filing out of the gates, goggling and nudging each other. She turned her back and waited for him to speak again. When he didn't she said, 'I have a lot of homework to get on with. I have to go home.'

'I thought you might come to regret throwing it away.' Behind his lenses his pale eyes were on her, narrowing as if that key at the back was cranking them closed. Still the amber sat in the white handkerchief in his palm. 'When we come into possession of something precious it can take a while to understand its value.'

She didn't know what to say to that.

'I had it examined for you, I hope you don't mind. It's an exquisite piece. Baltic, as the best are, uncommon due to its size and clarity, and then there's this insect – some sort of ancient fly – you can see the trace of a wing in the core. Rare to see a wing so well-preserved, I was told.'

'Sell it then. You found it, you can sell it. Give the money away if you like.'

But he didn't lower his hand. 'It wouldn't be proper.'

'Do you always do what's proper?'

He frowned, his lips tightening.

'I'm sorry,' she heard herself say. 'I didn't mean to offend. I'm always getting told I speak without thinking. I need to learn not to for when I'm a doctor, you see.'

'Yes.'

'I will be a doctor, you know.'

He didn't say anything to that and it made her feel suddenly unsure why she'd said it. 'It was good of you to come to return it.'

'In which case you'll do me the honour.'

So she took the amber from his handkerchief.

She watched him fold the handkerchief into quarters and tuck it into his trouser pocket.

'Good,' she said in a manner meant to indicate a conclusion to their business, and she turned to cross the street.

'If I may?' he said, and there he was, at her side, matching his strides to hers. 'Rather warm,' he said, 'for this time of year.'

He pointed out two jackdaws on a wall, and three sparrows sitting in guttering, and left her at the gate to her house saying he wouldn't intrude. She'd had to laugh then, saying her mother would be most disappointed when she discovered Lena hadn't invited an officer home.

'In which case?'

'Disappointments are good for mothers.'

He mentioned he'd be in town the following Thursday. She found nothing to say to that. He bowed, clicking his heels and strode away down the lane.

Ulrich's cattle are ripping the grass in the field below, the sound is rhythmic and comforting. There have been cows grazing for as long as she's been in this room. Sixteen years. This is comforting too. She should shut the window and turn off the lamp before any more moths fly in. Perhaps she dozes off for a moment, but suddenly she's wide awake, her heart pounding, thinking of boots in streams, thinking of ancient gypsy women gurgling tea. The amber is still in her hand. She leans over her mattress and throws it under the bed without watching to see where it goes. Pulling the casement shut she takes the medical encyclopaedia from her desk. C: *Carcinomas*. She finds her place and begins to read.

Carcinoma: a cancer that starts in the cells of the skin or tissue lining the organs. Like other types of cancer, carcinomas are abnormal cells that divide without control.

'But I never asked him to do it,' Lena complains in a hiss to Danushka one Thursday afternoon in November as they pull on their winter coats. In the school cloakroom dozens of eyes flicker her way. She may as well be stuck in a nest of snakes. Lena slumps on the bench. 'It's his choice how he spends his free time. If he wants to use up Thursday afternoons walking along Linden Street beside the tramline, that's his business. I myself will be going straight home to spend my evenings with my studies. In advance of Kraków.'

She's not even sure if Dan's listening. Danushka is fully buttoned and booted for the weather, but she has her journal out of her satchel and she's pushing back her grey coat sleeve, two fingertips pressed to the inside of her left wrist. They've just come from Latin where Dan has a crush on the mistress – evidenced empirically. Every time the teacher enters the classroom Dan's pulse increases thirty per cent.

'I can't bear everyone goddamn staring at me.'

Dan stops counting and takes a pencil to add figures to a column on the back page. 'In the fifteen minutes since class ended my pulse has fallen to sixty-two. They're jealous, that's all.'

'Why should they be jealous?'

'Are you that much of a simpleton?'

'But why?'

Dan slaps her journal shut and slides it into her satchel. 'So you are a simpleton. Very well. Give me your hands.'

She turns Lena's palms and sniffs at the left one. 'Interesting, yes, very. First I will speak of the fortune I see in your right . . .'

'Really, Dan, you sound like Ala.'

'Please don't interrupt, miss, a moment of sustained attention is all that's required. Quite fascinating . . . now I see
it's very clear. In this hand you hold a marriage of status, a
comfortable home with champagne, fine linen and orderlies.
The lines on your left palm are fainter, but let's see what we
have. Yes, I believe I can just discern a cold university lodging
room, a student studying late into the night, fretful, recalling
a dissection that day when she fainted and a co-student jeered
and offered to escort her back home to her parents.'

'Nonsense. I would never faint like that.'

Danushka looks up, intent behind her black-rimmed glasses.
'So which hand would you choose?'

'Do you even have to ask?'

'Left or right?'

'Why the left of course.'

Danushka swings her satchel over her head and starts for the
door. 'We will see, Miss Sadowska, we will see.'

'Wait, Dan. Whatever do you mean?'

At the door Dan hesitates. 'Nothing.'

'You do mean something.'

'Very well. You really don't care for this man?'

'I care for my future studies. You know that.'

'So take care of your future studies.'

'What do you mean? I'm working as hard as I can.'

Dan sighs. 'Take care things don't get in the way of your
future, that's all.'

'What's going to get in the way?'

'I really have to point it out?'

'Muddy boots,' Lena mutters. 'Or very clean ones.'

'What did you say?'

Lena shakes her head, dragging on her coat. 'Listen, Dan,
come back with me for supper, why don't you?'

Danushka shakes her head, groping under her coat sleeve for
her wrist again.

'Ulka will do *naleśniki* with blueberry compote if you come.'

Dan smiles pityingly. 'My poor little doctor girl.'

'Please, Dan. Just tonight.'

'I can't tonight. I've an errand to run for Sister Kaminska. It's remarkable. Even when I'm nowhere near, I only have to think of her and my pulse jumps to seventy-five.'

Lena collapses onto the bench, wondering how long she might stay undetected once the lights are off and the school is entirely empty.

'They'll lock the gates and you'll freeze to death in here.'

Lena glares at Dan.

Dan shrugs and goes out the door. 'Just tell him no. Don't let things slide. No is easily said.'

Outside the winter sky is heavy and quiet, the grey-trunked lime trees naked in their row like old men with nothing to hide. For a minute she thinks he isn't there; he's given up on her now all the other girls have come out and gone. Just to be sure she could always turn left rather than right and head past the tram depot, then double back through the medieval quarter. She could even run the first stretch of it, just in case.

But just then something shifts by the closest trunk across the road. Him, stepping forward, a pair of binoculars in his left hand. He lifts them slightly, not enough to wave, sufficient only to get her attention. She crosses the tramway to him.

'A couple of blue jays up there,' he says, pointing with the binoculars. 'Rare to spot them in town without the cover of foliage. They're rather shy of humans.'

Lena glances up and sees nothing as usual, and remembers again how little appeal there is to be found in constantly crooking your neck.

'Beautiful creatures. Intelligent and loyal in their pair bonding.' He offers her the binoculars but she declines. 'Shall we then?' and they set off along the pavement.

Lena walks with her head down trying to resist the urge to scuff her toecaps against the cobbles. Trying not to look at his shining boots matching her shoes stride for stride. She'd like to break into a run, or hop in a circle; anything to disrupt this metronome rhythm. *No is easily said.*

'You have something on your mind, Miss Sadowska?'

She shakes her head but she can't clear it out. Very well.

'You don't have to wait, you know, for me, every Thursday. You must have other things to do.'

'Not at all, as it happens. It's my free afternoon.'

'So why spend it like this?'

'Why not?'

'Well, I might have things to do soon, on a Thursday.'

'Preparation for your university years?'

'Yes, exactly.' She stops and looks at him, beaming. 'Yes, that's *exactly* right.'

He nods to himself and runs a finger along his moustache, from side to side and back, like a zip he doesn't know whether to open or close. They walk on.

'Forgive me, Miss Sadowska,' he turns suddenly, 'but I feel I must ask, it's not uncomfortable for you, is it, me accompanying you home in this way?'

Lena stares down at their four unmatched feet as he speaks.

'After all, it's but a few short months and then, as you say, you'll be off to Kraków, and I shall be returning to the mountains. So you see, I myself can think of no harm in passing the time with a little afternoon companionship, that's all. A break from your studies and an escape from my barracks. Unless . . .'.

She glances at him pushing his spectacles up the bridge of his nose. 'Unless?'

'Unless perhaps you think a walk might lead us elsewhere?'

'Oh goodness no! No, I don't think that for a moment.'

'Indeed,' he says. 'Indeed.'

'Not even for a second!' Lena begins to laugh. 'So you do understand, thank the devil for that!' It comes from her like a great honking, this laughter, like she is a goose flying away beating her wings. She almost sees herself climbing slowly but resolutely into the clouds. She slaps his arm. 'What a relief! Although Mama will be terribly disappointed. She wants us all married off, you see, she's quite determined.'

'Is that so?' He smiles very slightly, squashing it to nothing between his lips.

'Obviously I love her, but she gets these silly ideas at times. Papa says it comes of too much romantic music and too little time in the real world. Really she's to be pitied and loved not condemned, that's what Papa says.'

'Indeed.'

She shrugs out her shoulders and they walk, and it is he who has to keep up with her now. She throws in a skip or two and a spin on her heel. She begins to talk – events of the school day come pouring out of her – and suddenly it occurs to her to think of him like a young uncle, or a much older brother, this man, not at all like the useless worm, but a mature, wise brother who might be able to offer advice. He might even provide information on male ailments – without mocking her like Papa does – surely the only one-footed man who believes himself in perfect health. She laughs and talks and Captain Bem listens, only putting his arm out to stop her at the street corner where the columns of the provincial bank building block the view of the tramway. The tram bell sounds.

'It's at least thirty seconds away,' she says. 'We'd be fine to cross.'

'Indeed. Are you always so impatient, Miss Sadowska?'

She grins. 'Are you always this cautious, captain?'

They wait. The tram rattles round the corner and passes them by. He pats her arm and they step out into the street.

'Lena, darling, is that you?' Mama appears in the hallway, panting and touching her hair. She has a bright pink smile on her lips. 'I didn't hear the door. Where's Captain Bem?' Her smile slips. 'You didn't invite him in? Mother of God, I suppose you're going to tell me you forgot again?'

'You have lipstick on your teeth, Mama.'

Mama turns to the mirror. 'I think I must write him a little note directly. That will be the thing to do. He will be thinking us all so terribly rude.'

'Don't worry yourself, Mama,' Lena says bouncing past, beaming.

'Really?' Mama's eyes are drilling into her.

'Really.' She runs to intercept Ivan Pavlov who's clattering down the stairs to greet her, and gives him a kiss on the head. 'Everything's completely fine.'

The days shorten. Winter creeps into the town like a thief bagging up the colours of autumn, leaving only black and grey. Ice coats the bones of the trees and the ground snaps with frost. One morning in early December, a letter arrives for Papa, typed and bearing a Kraków postmark. The cream paper is too heavy for the contents to be guessed in the light, the gum too thick to steam off. It waits two days in the tray on the hall sideboard while snow delays his return from an education symposium. On the third day, when Lena arrives back from school, the letter is gone.

'Is Papa back?' she asks Ulka, checking behind and beneath the sideboard. The letter is definitely missing.

Ulka puts a finger to her lips. She's standing by the sitting-room door and beckons Lena to join her at the crack in the hinge. 'They've been at it a while.'

'At what?'

'. . . And behind my back, Jozef!' Mama's voice – raised.

'I could very well say the same.'

'Not at all. We both agreed I would make investigations. It was a joint decision. Unlike yours.'

'I don't happen to remember that.'

'How convenient, husband.'

'I doubt I would have agreed if I'd been asked.'

'It was one call to Mrs Meyer. Don't make that face, you know the connections the woman has. She told me on good authority that Captain Bem's elder brother is a man of increasing influence in Warsaw.'

'And your point, Zosia?'

'He's been earmarked for a senior position within the state department. At the highest level.'

There's silence now. Drifting like a gas cloud. Lena looks at Ulka. Ulka presses in her chins and picks at a crust on her apron.

'The highest level of government. You have no opinion about that, husband?'

'Ulka has excelled herself with the poppy seed cake.'

'About Captain Bem's brother.'

'Does Mrs Meyer know who's filling the other state department roles and who might lead the next cabinet, not to mention what the outcome of all this posturing in Berlin and Moscow might be? And, wait, could she let me know whether it's going to rain next Tuesday, I'd rather not take an umbrella on my inspections?'

'You're making fun of me and it's beneath you, darling. May I remind you of your own words: in this nation we live as hens between the fox and the wolf.'

'You'd have us all jump on a boat to England now?'

'Of course not. But nevertheless—'

'Nevertheless what, my dear?'

'Foxes and wolves, Jozef. Don't you pull that face. Every blessed morning when you pick up the newspaper it's the only thing I hear from you. The world worsens. You say so yourself, every day. Or have you forgotten this too?' Mama's voice drops so it's hard to hear. 'The Bems hold influence in places that matter, that's all I'm saying. We might be fools to throw valuable contacts away.'

'Is this really about Magdalena? Or is it more about fishing for connections using our daughter as bait?'

'That is beneath you, Jozef.'

Silence again.

Papa suddenly appears at the sitting-room door, pulling his cane from the stand. 'Get your coat, Magdalena Luiza. You and

I are taking tea by the skaters. We have matters of importance to discuss.'

'Look, here comes another one! Now observe closely the chap in the red sweater – see him, Magdalena? – wobbling all over the place. And here comes the fence. Look up, man, look up! Wham! Did you see it? I don't think he did! That's got to hurt.'

'Papa, please try not to sound so thrilled, the poor man might be injured.'

'Nonsense, it's all part of the fun out there. Watch this fancy lad now, going at it backwards, backwards I ask you! It won't impress the ladies when you crash that backside into the Christmas tree, young fellow—'

'You're incorrigible, Papa.'

He wriggles in his seat and giggles. The moment they passed the pastry display his mood began to lighten, and now that the waitress has put them at a window table where they can tally up skating collisions on the lake, he can barely contain his glee. Lena looks out of the tea room's steamy glass at the dark sky sagging over the castle turrets. Braziers have been lit on the ramparts. The ice shines like a pane of blue glass, the tall pine in the centre shimmers with candlelight. And to be sitting inside the cafe in the warmth – she wrinkles her nose happily – well, just about every particle of air must be coated in sugar cream.

'Do you remember coming down to the lake with your sister and brother some years ago?' Papa's little blue eyes are gleaming. 'You and Ala took a spin on the ice. Romek wasn't much more than a howling bundle, as I recall, bumped along between you without mercy.'

'Wasn't that the time you insisted on having a turn even though they refused to give you skates?' Lena grins. 'Mama always says you threatened to sue if they wouldn't let you on.'

'Nothing would fit my foot, that's what they said. I'd be a danger to myself and others. What claptrap. If I can walk on a wooden foot I can certainly shuffle on one, and what is skating but a form of shuffle?'

'Mama was begging them to keep you off. I don't think that helped.'

'I had taken a small helping of schnapps, I admit it.'

'A small helping! Mama says you had half the barrel.'

'Your dear mama is blessed with many gifts. One of which is a talent for exaggeration. Did you see the shine on that ganache?'

'I did, Papa.'

He scratches his beard, eyeing up a dark slab of cherry gateau heading to the neighbouring table, and leans forward conspiratorially. 'May I suggest we take the full tea menu this afternoon. Although I'd hazard it's unnecessary to mention back home. Too much reflection on my cream consumption would only cause anxiety before her recital.'

'What a considerate husband you are.'

Papa giggles. 'Our secret then?'

Lena smiles and wonders whether to tell him how it feels when she's sitting with him all to herself in this way. How sometimes it's like a blaze ignites inside her; a rushing inferno; how the feeling comes quite out of nowhere. She laughs, suddenly reminded of Mama's bedside statuette of the Virgin with a flaming heart. Ridiculous. She's becoming sentimental. Like Mama. She shudders. She must desist at once.

Suddenly Papa reaches and takes her wrist, a look of mock mourning on his face. 'How did this bone get so long? When did it grow? Did I keep an eye on you over my papers? Was I taking enough notice day by day? The look on your face gives me hope, but I don't know. It can be no more than a moment since I lifted you from a cot, and the only thing I know is that I can't go back to that time.'

'But it's all right, Papa, because we're here and there's lots of time ahead of us.'

He shakes his head. His eyes are glassed with tears. 'What a speeding business this life is, Magdalena Luiza. When I think of the time I've wasted staring at reports or newspapers, or even with my eyes shut up in sleep; all the hours I've spent not looking at my children. From now on I shall do nothing but watch you all. Every day and late into the night. How does that sound?'

'Dreadful. Just imagine, you'd have to sit through Romuś's conjuring shows.'

'Hell and damnation, I hadn't thought of that.'

She throws back her head and laughs.

He blows his nose on the napkin. 'You know what I wish for right now?'

'Cherry gateau? With extra cream?'

'For time to stop right where it is. No more forward motion. We stay right here, you and me.'

'For ever?'

He leans forward, 'Where's the magic button to do it? It must be about here somewhere. Under the table? There's always a button under tables.'

Lena shakes her head, snorting as he fumbles under the table-cloth. 'But Papa, there's a flaw.'

'Always you with the flaws.'

'You could press the button—'

'I shall, I shall, just let me find it.'

'Only if you do it means I don't get to take possession of my life. I don't get to live my future and do the things I need to do. And really, Papa, there are so many things I need to do.'

Papa rubs his beard. 'Yes, on consideration that would certainly be a tragedy.' Then, bending sideways to look under the table, 'But this button must be somewhere. Goddamn it, where is it?'

The waitress arrives with the cake stand and bad news about the gateau. Papa requests extra cream for the scones and enquires of her brother, now a barrister in Lublin, no less.

'Do you hear this, Magdalena? A great career ahead of him and at thirteen this boy had a stammer you wouldn't believe. A mind as quick as a rapier but barely a word made it past his lips. Isn't it something, what this young man has achieved?'

Papa shouts after the waitress for three glasses of champagne to toast her brother. They confer and settle to the sandwiches first. Out of nowhere a slice of cherry gateau which had been sold out materialises, but no one is really surprised to see it because people perform this sort of magic for Papa all over town.

Lena waits for him to produce the letter from Kraków, which is after all why they are both there. But he's busy with his gateau and she loves watching him eat; his eyes squeezed tight in appreciation, his head shaking in wonder as he lifts his napkin to dab the corners of his beard.

'It's only kirsch sponge, Papa!'

'Only nothing, Magdalena Luiza! This here is joy in its purest form; rich and moist and served simply on a plate.'

'You'd better not tell Mama she's so easily supplanted.'

'But now you talk of love for which no recipe in the world exists.'

'Aren't we actually here to talk about something else?'

Papa looks unsure for a moment. He lifts the teapot lid and calls for more hot water. 'We are?'

'You know we are. The letter.'

'Ah yes. I thought you'd never ask.'

'I thought you'd never tell.'

'Well, well.'

'In your jacket pocket, Papa. The top left.'

He grins like a crafty magician, opening his jacket and pulling out a narrow cream envelope with a flourish.

And in that instant Lena's throat constricts.

The entire cafe – tables, customers, walls – untethers and drifts away. This pale envelope in Papa's hands is the only thing of substance in the world. Her teacup motionless halfway to her lips, blood crashing in her ears, she watches Papa extract a fold of paper from the envelope.

'Well now, twig, I'll plunge straight in.'

'If you would, Papa,' she hears herself whisper.

'I want to tell you I received this letter earlier in the week from Professor Szafran at Kraków University. We studied together in what you'd consider to be Neolithic times.'

'Professor Szafran is the dean of the medical school.'

'Indeed he is. I wanted to enquire of him, to put it bluntly, whether your dreams have any prospect in the world as it is, or whether it would be wise to open our minds to alternative options.'

'I don't want to be a nurse, Papa. You know that.'

'I enclosed the results from your summer examinations along with glowing letters of commendation from your science mistress and the principal. I won't heat your ears by repeating how highly they regard you at school. But I will tell you I mentioned to Szafran that you'd already skipped a year grade, and after all this appalling bragging I asked for a realistic assessment, friend to friend, of your hopes of getting on the medical foundation course, the world being as masculine as it is.'

Lena lowers her cup slowly back onto its saucer.

Papa blows out his cheeks. 'But this I did not expect.'

'What?'

'No, I did not expect this at all.'

Papa fumbles for a handkerchief, his hands shaking, and Lena can't help herself. She reaches over and takes the letter from him.

'He writes that they're opening the medical school to women. Four will be permitted as a trial scheme. My exceptional results and commitment to my studies suggest I'm an ideal candidate.'

Papa is nodding and sobbing and blowing his nose so loudly into his napkin that the waitress hurries to the table and asks if there's anything she can do.

'Bring more champagne,' Papa sobs. 'A bottle. Put a second on ice.'

Lena reads down the letter a second time, sipping quietly at her tea.

'My daughter the trainee doctor,' Papa sobs. 'Incredible.' He blots his face with a second napkin and looks at her. 'You're very quiet. Tell me your papa was not wrong to make this enquiry? This is what you wanted?'

'Of course it is. It's just I never doubted it as you seem to have done.'

He roars then. Papa roars and drums his fists on the table, and he shoves back his chair so firmly that something cracks, but never mind, he is up and dancing, leaning on his cane, waggling his booted stump in the air, and shouting for more champagne – a glass for everyone in the room, because this is his very own twig, right here! See how she's grown! Has he told her how long her bones have grown?

Lena has always loved to ride with Papa in the traps returning from town, watching him tip his hat to the butcher or toss handfuls of fudge to the children racing by the side. If Mama's come along she'll always shake her head in mock censure but with laughing eyes. 'This school inspector is better loved than the king of Poland!' To which Papa will reply with mock solemnity, 'Dear heart, this pony is better loved than the king because Poland no longer has a king.' But now, as they sit on the padded leather seat in the back, the sheepskin over their knees, waiting for the driver to slap the pony's rump with the reins, Papa is staring at his boots. It may be the effects of the champagne or the frost in the air causing this sudden melancholy, but when Papa looks up, tugging at his beard, Lena is immediately nervous.

'Of course there's an impediment to all this that we haven't yet discussed.'

'There is?'

'That lieutenant or captain or whatever he is now. Bom.'

'Bem. Oh him.'

'Your mama tells me his intentions are obvious.'

'Mama romanticises.'

'He's of good standing, that does seem to be true unfortunately.'

'Unfortunately?'

'These things have more power than you think, more than they should have in a modern society. Societal power is not always easy to resist.'

Lena laughs. 'You make it sound sinister.'

Papa shakes his head. 'This sort of power works in insidious ways, Magdalena. It worms inside a person's insecurities about their place in the world and feeds on what it finds. Consequently I fear it is a most pernicious force.'

'Has Mama been up to something?'

'A little research I believe.' He stares out at the streets unravelling behind them, narrowing from elegant stuccoed arcades to close-built timber buildings on cobbled lanes. 'She's thinking of you in her way.'

'It's OK, Papa, really.'

Papa turns to gaze at her for a long while. 'Do you have any thoughts as to why I do the work I do?'

'Because you believe in education.'

'Be more specific. Why do I believe in it?'

'It's a door to opportunity for anyone who wants it.'

Papa tips his hat to Widow Manowska and Adam taking in a flour delivery at the bakery.

'Go fuck yourselves.'

'Good day to you, Adam. But what does opportunity really mean, Magdalena Luiza?'

'Choice.'

'Of course, choice. But to put it more pertinently, education is the key to freedom. What a world it would be if each of us were free to live as the best of our natures and dreams intended. I don't mean for our individual selves, although the psychological benefits would be immense. No, I believe the greater point to be made here is that if every person is given the freedom to achieve their unique potential, so humanity itself takes a step forward. We all progress together.'

The trap is twisting through the medieval quarter, the pony's hooves slipping on the cobblestones. Here the low-timbered houses lean so close that people are said to be able to reach from the upstairs windows and hold hands with their neighbours across the street. Mama says at least one couple will find love this way every year. Lodgers have been known to rent the top-floor rooms just to try their luck.

'You believe in progress, Mama in romance. What a strange alliance you are.'

'Education is never to be squandered, Zosia, not even when it seems a foolish course. Not even when other paths look safer.'

'It's Lena, Papa.'

He looks at her. 'What?'

'I said it's Lena.'

He nods several times before he smiles. 'Of course it is. My little twig.'

Lena watches him rubbing his beard, which is a sign there's something more to come. But the Jewish cobbler is waving a pair of boots to get his attention and calling out a greeting and Papa is shouting down, asking how his boy is faring at the Grammar. 'A marvel for the algebra,' he tells Lena, 'a genius, this man's son.' Then Ulka is spotted with a full basket of potatoes and the trap is halted to give her a lift, and talk on the back seat turns to the likelihood of snow. So it happens they never go on to discuss exactly whose education might come to be squandered, or indeed why.

The sudden roar of a train rages without receding.

Lena hears a long drawn-out squeal of wheels on rusting rails.

Not yet.

Please not the train yet.

Let her be somewhere else.

Somewhere there's quiet. A place where nobody cries.

Snow. Is Ulka about somewhere, talking of the likelihood of snow?

No, this snow is smothering, silent. There are deep drifts on the hills.

She and a black-haired boy, who will not hold her hand, are trudging uphill, calling out in search of buried sheep.

No, it is not this place either. It's somewhere where there's still no boy: some other sort of snow.

A touch on her arm.

Him.

Of course. Him in the snow. Yes, he must be standing with her in the clearing, she can see the bay mare's breath steaming behind them. His hand will be reaching for her coat. A smell of resin fills the air; always this scent, the forest he brings. Her heart pounds.

'Kiss me,' he whispers.

A hurricane rages in her head. She turns but there is only this voice.

'You have to do it because that's how it starts.'

'What starts?'

'Our story, Magdalena. We have to get to us.'

England

Lena opens her eyes and knows at once where she is.

Say it then. She's alone in the house where she's too slow about her dying.

Old fool woman. There's no other place she can be. She could almost laugh. No one tells you this about the end. No one talks about the goddamn dreams.

A glass with an inch of liquid and a straw has been left on the bedside table. There's a note from Margaret saying she popped in and she'll be back later in the day; a prescription list is on the side too. Margaret knows how she likes to see it.

Something's tapping on the window.

Lena turns carefully to look. Cheeky one.

The blackbird steps along the ledge, tipping his tail feathers, looking for the margarine tub where her husband kept bread-crumbs and bacon rinds, and the scrapings from rissole pans.

What to do about this cheeky bird? Something will have to be done.

Once when she was out in this garden hoping to bury some memories, he came to her. He waited beneath the cherry tree, his wings tucked but close, so she might touch them if she'd needed. He didn't leave her to cry alone.

So many things she's planted out there: that miserable tree, the shrubs and what have you, along the borders. Things she thought might grow and fill up empty space and time. But the soil was poor. She never dug deep enough for roots to take hold, or bothered to learn the names of the plants, and after a while she stopped replacing the dead ones.

'These are boxes for hiding in.' This is what she had said to her husband the afternoon they sat in the car waiting for the estate agent to show them round the crescent of squat silent houses with identical facades and front doors.

He said nothing. She told her husband she was reminded of animal hutches with bolts to keep living things inside.

Her husband continued to say nothing, staring through the windscreen at the show home ahead of them. He never complained when she was like this. He cleared his throat. 'If you don't care for this place we can look at others. We should try to be happy.'

She touched his arm. 'We should,' she said, not knowing whether she believed it or not. 'And we have things we wish to lock away. Perhaps they will come to lose themselves here, and then we can be happy.'

Anyway they took the house. They put down a deposit that day. Here as well as anywhere. This is what she had thought.

Although as it turned out nothing had allowed itself to be lost, no matter how she re-dug the borders and made herself busy moving bulbs east to west and back. Because they had brought grief with them, and it could not be locked away or even hidden from view. Because their grief did not have substance, it was not like treasure, say; it could not be nailed down in a crate and buried in a single spot. No, it turned out grief was more like the ghost of a corpse that crawled out of its plot every night. Grief lay sprawled on its back on the lawn waiting to be discovered in the morning when she drew back the curtains. It shifted its place every night, but always showed up by dawn.

The subject wasn't ever discussed but they wouldn't move again. A house was simply a house, after all. There were many reasons, they agreed, to be grateful. The weather in this country was mild, their workplace warm, and food plentiful. And Jozef – a blessing not a burden, her husband had been right about that – grew up a cheerful child. He played rugby for the local team and they watched from the sidelines. Every Saturday they visited the local nature reserve. In the evening there might be canasta with the couple three doors down, and in the morning her husband went to church. Time passed them by in this regulated way, and the world let them be. JoJo left home, but did not go far. When her husband was no longer able to walk, she hung feeders in the yew and he made tallies from the chair by the bedroom window. Yes, they had made a life of sorts. They had done what they could.

In the yew now, the blackbird is singing. He always sings after breakfast.

Przemysl, South East Poland

'It's better if I tell him myself, don't you think? I thought about asking Mama to do it, but we'd probably end up goddamn engaged.'

Danushka blows a smoke ring at a wasp creeping along the frame of the settee. 'I've no idea why you let all this companionship drag on so long. What is it now, eight months? You'll have to be far more decisive when you begin at Kraków.'

Lena puts out her finger and nudges the dopey wasp onto it. 'It's actually been very useful, like having a brother – a functional, sensible one. He told me all about his childhood measles. And he's a demon with geometry.'

'So now you cut him loose, before the exams? Not better to wait until after?'

'I have to be ready for Kraków, I won't have time to schedule walks in the summer. Anyway I told you, it's not like there's anything to cut.'

'Just the odd strudel together in the tea room.'

'It was good place for geometry revision.'

'And the occasional walk by the San.'

'Once only; an expedition to study his hay fever.'

Danushka exhales through her nostrils. 'You're sure?'

'No question.'

'Your poor Mama.'

They're sitting on the floor in the summer house at the end of Danushka's vast lawn, surrounded by packed tea crates. It's hot, but this is the only safe place for smoking cheroots and Danushka needs to practise. As soon as the summer exams are done Dan intends to convince Sister Kaminska to elope with her to Warsaw before ships can be boarded. She must demonstrate to her teacher that she's no longer a child and cheroots are the way to do it. 'When are you going to tell him?'

'This afternoon after school. It'll be simplest that way.' Lena turns her finger, observing the wasp. 'Ala's walking out with a Prussian officer now, you know. We're keeping it from Mama given what happened to Papa's foot. But do you know what she said to me?'

Danushka crawls along the crates and pulls a silver flask from beneath a stack of linen.

'Ala claims she isn't serious about anyone. Not even this officer. She says she likes to imagine herself standing in a cafe in front of a display cabinet. On the shelves are a dozen varieties of cake. Should she take the plum tart, the cherry gateau, or perhaps just a simple babka?'

Danushka takes a deep swig from the flask and begins to cough. 'What does she choose?'

'She says babka because she fancies something uncomplicated at that moment with her coffee.'

'Makes sense.'

'But here's the thing. When it comes to her table she's glad to see it but—'

'There's always a but with Ala.'

'– but if she has to eat it every day for breakfast, lunch and dinner for the rest of her life, is a boring old babka really the best choice to make?'

Danushka whistles slowly and drinks again. 'Look at that. The girl has grown sense from somewhere.'

For a moment they sit in grudging admiration of Ala's unexpected wisdom. Dan passes Lena the flask. 'Poor Papa's been hunting for this all week.'

Lena takes a gulp, shaking her head as fire roars down her throat.

Dan laughs. 'Go again, it gets easier. So? What about your officer? Bom?'

'Bem. Captain Bem. Not my officer,' Lena says and drinks, trying to summon his face with his thin wire spectacles and narrowing eyes, but whenever she tries to think of him he's moving away, heading out of the door into fog.

'Babka, I'm betting, slightly stale at the crust?'

'Toast,' Lena whispers, coughing. 'Toast with the burned bits scraped off.'

He bows to her under falling lime flowers, commenting on the fine June weather and the blossom's scent, also the acid brightness of the leaves. Shaped like hearts, he adds, pressing his lips as is his manner of smiling. 'Shall we?'

They begin to walk.

She wishes for a glass of water. Her stomach's queasy and all that brandy seems to have thickened her tongue just when she needs it to be lively. 'I have some bad news.' That's all she has to say.

'If I may venture something, Miss Sadowska.'

She looks up, startled by the gravity in his voice.

'It's a matter of some significance actually.'

'Me too,' she says quickly. 'I've got something I really need to tell you.'

'Indeed.' He runs a finger along his moustache. 'Well, perhaps if you'd permit me to speak first, my words might impact on the nature of yours.'

'Or mine on yours.'

'Quite so.'

'Quite.' Her stomach is churning terribly. A glass of milk would sort it.

He smiles at her. 'Of late, Miss Sadowska, I confess to having been engaged in a period of reflection.'

'Me too.'

'Indeed?' He glances at her. 'During this time, I began thinking it has existed a while now, this association of ours—'

'It's not been so long really,' she interrupts. For some reason she can feel her heart starting to quicken. 'I mean it's only a matter of months, and just once a week. And each of those occasions hasn't been for very long, certainly no more than half an hour at a time, although the geometry help is going to prove exceedingly useful in the exams. I'm very grateful.'

'It's been nearly a year since we noticed each other in the gypsy tent.'

'Wait,' she says, 'what do you mean by that?'

But he can't have heard her because he's going on, 'Long enough for things to become clear to me. Long enough to realise things have begun to develop.'

'Things?'

'Feelings. Honourable ones, I assure you. Strong ones, if I may be permitted to put it like that. I must tell you from the first moment I saw you, so full of energy and—'

'Stop!' Every inch of her skin is suddenly crawling. 'Please don't say another word. I'm sorry but you can't have feelings, that's just not possible.'

'My dear Miss Sadowska, we did agree I would speak first.'

'No, I'm sorry, this isn't possible, it's just not actually possible. You've seen me once a week for eight months – at most – so what's that, thirty times? If you add it up that doesn't even make a single day.'

He smiles tightly. 'That's an odd way of accounting, wouldn't you say?'

She stares at him. 'We said we'd be friends.'

'We did.'

'All we ever talk about is school and birds and more birds and ailments. So you see it's impossible – absolutely impossible – for anyone to have feelings from that.' Now she's started, words are crashing over each other in their haste to be out. 'The fact is you don't know me at all and I have no idea about you. I mean there are biological and social details we're both aware of, but beyond that – nothing. That's the cold hard truth of it, I'm afraid. Not to mention Ala's babka.'

'Babka?' He looks confused.

'Never mind the babka.' She's waving her arms and shouting. She knows she shouldn't raise her voice on a busy summer street or flap her hands in a man's face, but this must come out of her. He must hear all the reasons why a future between them is impossible and then it will be over. Harm will not have been done.

He's pinching his nose, nodding to himself, rubbing at those two pink marks he always has where the pads of his spectacles press too tight.

Lena spins away from him. 'You see, that's just your look. That's how you look at me, like I'm a book and you need to work out where to shelve me. Well, I'm not a book. I'm not a book. I'm not—'

'My dear Miss Sadowska, this manner of agitation is—'

'And at Julia's party you were supposed to come for Ala. Goddamn it, I don't know why you had to be so, well, so questioning of me and demanding of dances, because that was all a big surprise I have to say. We agreed it was a few months of friendship. That's what we both agreed. So now you can't possibly tell me it's not. That isn't fair. And besides all this I don't have the time for any more friendship because my place is waiting for me, you know that, this autumn in the medical school, there's a place waiting for me—'

'Miss Sadowska, I must ask you to take care, you're stepping very close to—'

'– I mean I know you really like birds, but I like dogs and dogs like chasing birds and I could never live without a dog, so you must see even after Kraków it would all be quite impossible. I mean we never really laugh together, do we? I don't mean to say you don't smile because that wouldn't be fair because you do, but I like to laugh until my stomach hurts and I feel sick and—'

'Miss Sadowska, please watch your step . . .'

She moves back away from his hand, '. . . and sometimes . . .'

He grabs for her. 'Miss Sadowska, please—'

'Sometimes—'

'Lena!'

'Sometimes I forget your . . .'

Here it comes; the roaring. It comes with a tremendous whoosh and a glinting and a ringing in her ears.

Lena sees a blur of red metal and she's flying. She's a spinning top hurled in the air. How strange it is to be shooting up and up, limbs whirling everywhere . . .

When she lands on the cobbles every sense goes from her.

All that's left is pain.

Tatra Mountains, Southern Poland

In an apartment for married officers within the mountain garrison of the Second Army (Engineering Corps), Major Anton Bem's wife goes to bed with a Kraków-stamped letter beneath her pillow. It's not that she believes this is the only means to safeguard an agreement, it's simply easier to get to sleep this way.

'Undoubtedly there will be a period of adjustment,' her husband says on the first morning of their life together at the base. He's spooning boiled egg into his mouth at the far end of the dining table in precise, quick movements. From Lena's position, it's hard to see his eyes as he has his back to the bright window. 'Army life has its own peculiarities. You'll find the wives a tight group, but welcoming. I'm sure they'll have the guidance you require regarding etiquette, appropriate dress and so forth.' He dabs his moustache with a napkin. It hangs a little lower these days. 'It goes without saying I've every confidence in you.' She watches his fingers pinch the handle of the tiny china coffee cup and raise it to his mouth. By the side of his plate is an open notebook. 'But tell me, did you hear the nightjars just before dawn? I rather hope this year we may be lucky enough to discover a nest in the vicinity.'

'I didn't hear them.'

'A pity.'

If Lena looks past her husband to the world beyond the window she can see the track that links the soldiers' barracks and officers' apartments with the Mess Hall and from there various administrative huts, training rooms and stores. The base is larger than she expected – almost like a small town – the track busy with jeeps or soldiers striding. A security fence lines the far side of the track where bushy columns of spruce and mountain pine push their tips through the loops in the wire. What is beyond all these trees she doesn't know.

'Lena, my dear?'

She looks across blankly.

'I asked you if you had any thoughts? About what you'll do with your time. I could ask some of the wives to pop round.'

'It's eight months to September,' she says quietly.

'I'm aware of that.'

'Then you'll understand you don't need to worry about me adjusting to life here for long. During the day I shall be occupied with my studies for Kraków and my strengthening exercises as we agreed.'

'Nevertheless, with your permission I shall ask Mrs Machek to call on you. A day without company is a long time alone.'

'I have Ivan Pavlov.'

Anton pushes back his chair. 'Nevertheless . . .'

Lena feels under the table for the head resting on her knee. Her husband stands, turning towards the window. The words pound in her skull. *Her husband. Her husband. Her husband.*

'I believe I'm right in thinking this was discussed on the afternoon we reached our understanding? As I recall your father himself acknowledged the importance of integration into this life I lead.'

Lena takes a triangle of toast from the rack. She lays it on her plate.

'Your father himself said—'

'Please,' she says quietly, keeping her eyes on the thin white toast, 'don't.'

She hears coffee being poured. When she looks up he's at the window again. She takes in the narrow shape of him, the tucked shirt, and straight cut of his blond hair an inch above his collar. He stands motionless but for his elbow levering the cup to his mouth. She slides her toast under the table to Ivan Pavlov.

An orderly waits by the sideboard in this dining room keeping a second pot of coffee on a silver salver. He looks no older than Romek, but he must be. She needs to get used to this – people planted about the place with blank expressions and eyes that stare into nothing. Ulka would bang the coffee on the table and shout, 'Get it while it's hot.' Right now, in fact, she'll be doing just that and Romuś will be lunging from his seat for the jug, while tipping honey onto his porridge with his other hand. Mama will be praying to the ceiling that the Virgin excuse her son's farmyard manners, but all the while she'll be smiling to see him eat so well. At some point the door will crash back and Ala will come flying in for a slice of babka to take on the tram. When she flies out everyone will start coughing from an excess of violet fumes.

And as for Papa?

Well, what of him.

'You must do as you see fit,' Anton says.

'Excuse me?'

'With the apartment. Furnishings and the like. I'll make enquiries of my colleagues as to an allowance sufficient for your feminine necessities.'

He turns from the window, laying his china cup carefully in its saucer and he comes down the room to her, his boots slicing through blue diamonds cast from the window light on the parquet. It occurs to her she has never seen him in anything but boots. *Her husband. Her husband.* Under the table Pav begins to grumble. Lena drops her hand to rub his ears.

'And the leg this morning?' Anton glances at the crutches she's leaned against the door. She can smell camphor on his skin. He pulls out the chair beside her and sits, rubbing at a watermark on the table close to her plate. 'Any pain today?'

'Very little.'

'That's good.'

Silence. He is waiting, it seems, for her to look up at him.

'My dear' – because this is how he addresses her now – 'it would be entirely expected if you were to feel a little homesick at first. Whatever I might do to alleviate that . . .' He pauses and rubs again at the stain on the table.

'Thank you, Anton.'

'Gratitude isn't required. I'd simply have you understand your happiness is paramount to me. As I said in the hospital, I'd do anything for you, Lena.'

She runs a finger through the crumbs on her plate. 'I know you're a good person, and I'm to think myself lucky for that. But we don't need to talk about it all the time. I know I'm to be grateful to you and your brother. I understand that. But let's not think about it, could we, Anton? That might help a little. With the homesickness, I mean.' She takes a sip of her coffee, lowering her cup onto the table.

'Better here, I think,' he says, lifting the cup into its saucer on the linen place mat. 'Never mind my brother, all I wish is for you to consider whether we might try to be happy together. Things can grow in surprising places.'

'Things?'

He stands and looks at the clock. 'I need to go to work.'

Lena sits at the small desk in her bedroom trying very much not to think about breakfast.

Nor can she think about home, only twenty-four hours ago: Mama wrapping her in a stole, tutting and brushing hair from her forehead, Romek sloping into the hall to astound her with a final five-card trick. Most of all she's trying not to think about the shape of Papa at the upstairs window, as she banged her crutches down the path to the waiting staff car; Papa who might have been watching as she glanced back. In the light it was hard to tell.

Her bedroom overlooks the infirmary roof, the only building painted white. As they were driven into the base, at the end of that long, awkward journey from the chapel, Anton had pointed it out, suggesting she might find occupation in her spare hours. His white glove had capped her knee. 'I want you to know it's important you're happy here,' he'd said. She would have liked to ask him, 'Important to whom?' or, 'Happy how?' but just in time she remembered Mama's parting words: 'try to be kind', and anyway happiness was something best not gone into right then, so she had simply nodded.

From her desk she can see an even split of sky and roof. This simple division of metal corrugations and empty air is pleasing. She tells herself it is the sort of view that restrains a mind from wandering from its purpose. She unpacks a trunk, ordering her books on the shelf above the desk. There are other cases to see to and clothing to sort – all Mama's clothes really – but she opens the cover of an infectious disease manual and turns to the index. With a sigh Pav tucks himself into a lump on her feet.

Everything is black outside the window when Anton knocks on her bedroom door, a peaked cap under his elbow. He's wearing a dark uniform, a multicoloured strip of medals pinned to the chest of his tunic.

'You've forgotten.'

'What?'

'We're to dine in the Mess tonight.'

'Goddamn it, I'm sorry, you're right, I did forget.'

He looks at the floor with a slight frown.

'You don't care for how I speak?'

He glances at the pile of dresses flung on the bed – Mama's spare recital gowns that Lena hasn't yet put away. 'Would you need me to assist in some way?'

She looks over the gowns – soft pinks and sage greens – Mama's favourite colours, and wonders what a good wife would do now. She'd probably enquire as to which dress her husband prefers. 'I think I can still dress myself.'

He colours. 'Of course. I'll be in the hall.'

After he leaves she selects a rose-coloured gown with chiffon sleeves. She holds it to her face and Mama's ghost drifts through the lilac scent. She closes her eyes, letting the ghost kiss her cheeks and smooth her hair from her brow.

White gloves in the evening, darling, do make sure you brush out this fluff, and do try to be kind, sweetheart – a seed well planted often grows.

When she comes out into the hall, leaning on one of Papa's canes, Anton's fingers freeze on the buttons of his coat. There's a flush to his cheeks. It's how he looked when he watched her come up the aisle of the mountain chapel – as if, just for a moment, everything that was rigorous and rigid inside him had turned molten.

'It's only Mama's dress for Tchaikovsky and other romantics,' she says, flicking at the hem with the cane. 'It's been around for ever.'

He clears his throat and glances away. 'It suits you.'

'You should smile like this more often. It suits you too.'

Anton helps her into her long sable. By the door is a gilt-framed reproduction of the Black Madonna of Częstochowa carrying the infant Jesus in her arms.

'From my mother,' he says, seeing her looking at the picture. 'We all got one. She believes it keeps us safe.'

'Do you?'

He pinches his nose. 'I'm not sure I'm Our Lady's greatest priority.' He opens the door still smiling. 'You'll let me know if you tire?'

'Why should I tire?' she says. 'Which way do we go?'

He walks on the side of her good leg and they head up the track towards the long timber Mess building, its windows fogged and flickering yellow light. There's a din coming from the interior; voices laughing or disputing, and a clattering of plates. A soldier salutes and swings back the door.

'You mustn't worry about all the shouting,' Anton says in her ear. 'They get a little raucous, but the men need their means to relax.' They step into the noise and heat. The air is thick with smells of sweat and tobacco, wine and meat.

Two banqueting tables run the length of the hall, furrowed either side by men in identical dark uniforms. Dozens of heads lift and turn. Spoons hover over glassy consommés while white eyes make silent assessment. Pulling her fur tighter Lena wishes she had not worn so insubstantial a dress and that her foot might stop dragging like a dead thing has been tied to her leg. She straightens her back.

A shout comes from somewhere: 'Love and long life!'

The shout is repeated, accompanied by a beating of fists on wood.

'Are there no wives here?' she whispers to Anton.

'Not tonight.'

'Is that usual?'

'As it's your first time, it's traditional.'

'I'm to be paraded?'

'The men simply want to celebrate.'

'What?'

He looks at her. 'Our marriage. Shall I take your elbow?'

'I can manage.'

'As you wish.'

She's been placed at the head of the senior officers' table. Anton is on her left. On her right is Machek, the officer she last saw at Julia's party, grown rounder and balder; quite turnip-faced now with a bulbous nose. He seems to have control of the bottle of claret, and much of it is going his way.

Gurning sweatily, he rises as they approach and kisses her hand. 'Enchanted, my dear child. Although it's tricky to know who to congratulate most.'

'I'm not sure what you mean,' she says, glancing at Anton.

'Come now,' he tips his glass in a toast, 'it's quite some match your family achieved. Then again, you didn't fare so badly, did you, Bem? The teeth aren't dreadful. In fact I'd have to say the whole package is more than adequate, once you straighten out that gammy leg.'

Anton leans over, cupping an ear from the general din. 'What's that?'

'Buy as fresh as you can afford. Isn't that what they advise in the provinces?'

Anton jerks away, his face white and tight. 'You go too far.'

'Relax, man, I'm only pulling your pizzle.' Machek waggles the claret bottle. 'Shall I fill up your bride or will you be doing that later yourself?'

For a moment Lena doesn't get his meaning. She watches his palm slam on the table, as he roars, his teeth and tongue black with tannin.

Anton leans forward, his face tight, his finger an inch from Machek's nose. 'You need to control yourself, friend, I warn you. Any more and we'll face difficulties, you and I.'

Lena looks down at the consommé in front of her, Anton's voice in her ear, telling her to try it. What does she think of it?

'Yes,' she whispers, 'yes.' There's nothing else to say. Everything in her head has simply been whipped away like one of Romek's flapping magic sheets.

They'll have finished supper at home by now. Will they be thinking of her at all? Discussing how it is for her here? Ulka, for one, will never believe that Lena seems to have lost the use of her tongue so quickly. She must write in the morning – tell them everything – of a hundred staring eyeballs and pounding fists, and this overwhelming feeling of being reduced, as if sprinkled in shrinking powder, to the size of a mite with the brain of a mite and no voice at all.

'You're not eating?' Anton says. 'My dear, you should eat.'

She picks up her spoon. Anton turns to his left to discuss a military matter with the man beside him and voices blur into a humming swarm around her head.

Over dessert Captain Machek elbows her.

'Well done, sweetie.'

'Excuse me?'

He raises his eyebrow and adopts a stage whisper. 'I take my hat off to you.'

'I'm sorry I don't understand what you mean.'

'Of course you don't.' He winks and says, 'Got my own beloved very excited when she heard about your doctoring dreams. Most inspiring, she said. Can't wait to meet you.' He raises his voice loud enough for the men down the far end of the table to prick up their ears. 'Have you heard about Mrs Bem's plans? We'll have to take care to perform our marital duties adequately, gentlemen, otherwise every wife will start demanding their own careers. It's the beginning of the end for us, I tell you!'

The officers tip back their throats and laugh like walruses.

Lena pushes back her chair. Reaching deep inside herself for her voice she turns to Anton. 'I'd like to go now please.'

They start the walk back to the apartment in silence. Once or twice he's cleared his throat and she's cut him off. 'Don't apologise,' she says, 'I needed to understand how it would be here, and now I know.'

He's gripping her elbow but even so she's bent over her cane like an old woman.

'You're tired, Lena. This was too much for you, I think.'

'I should have brought the crutches, that's all.'

'With your permission,' his arm moves round her waist, 'let me take some weight.'

'I'm fine, really.' But she leans her head against him and they hobble on, their breath forming brief clouds in the dark. Here in the mountains it's colder than any winter she's known. Her left thigh bone is beginning to throb. The sole of her boot scrapes the ground, and she thinks of the eyes watching her stump up the hall. 'You never talk about my limp,' she says suddenly. 'Not once since the accident. Why is that?'

'Perhaps because I don't notice it.'

She scoffs. 'It's hardly attractive.'

'Really, Lena.'

'Well, the men in the hall certainly noticed.'

'Do you think?'

'I think they looked at me and pitied you.'

'I happen to disagree.'

'So it doesn't bother you?'

'Not at all.'

She laughs. The sound is too loud in her ears. 'Mama said most men would have turned and run after the accident. Why didn't you?'

He says nothing, his face closed. She's reminded of a Baltic crab she saw once, brought into the school by a teacher after the holidays, how it had tucked its legs beneath its shell to escape the girls' prodding. She's also reminded of how she had elbowed her way to the front and asked to turn it over to see the hidden limbs, to see if they could be pulled out and scrutinised one by one.

'It wasn't your fault, you know, Anton. My accident.'

He says nothing.

'You didn't cause the tram to mangle my leg.'

He turns his head to look at her and squashes a smile, that's all he does.

'Don't you have anything to say to that?'

'Lena, with respect, may I ask what's the point of all this? You're very tired, we just need to get you home.'

But she isn't anywhere near home and anyway she can't stop her thoughts now. 'I'm just telling you I know it wasn't your fault. I wonder if perhaps sometimes you think it was?'

'Is that what you'd like to hear from me?'

She stops dead. 'I really don't know.'

'Are you starting to remember any of it yet?' he says quietly.

'I can see you waiting under the lime trees and then there's an awful screeching noise. And between those two things, I'm not sure. Were we talking?'

He's staring at the ground. 'One day I'm sure it will come back to you.'

'Except it's too late now, isn't it?'

'I don't know what you mean.'

She isn't being kind, she knows it. She's never been kind and he'll have to learn that, and he might as well start now because she mutters, 'It's too late because I'm here, aren't I? Mrs Bem.'

For several moments he doesn't speak. Then he looks at her and frowns, 'You need to wear warmer clothes, Lena my dear.

You're shivering. Even a chill can be dangerous in the mountains. Hypothermia kills.'

She wants to tell him not to speak to her like a child, say she knows all about hypothermia and much more besides. Rage rises in her quickly these days; it is a serpent in her throat. But her thigh is burning too much for her to speak. Pain radiates from the break and her good leg is spasming from compensating. Even though it's well below freezing, she's starting to sweat.

He's glancing about the track. 'We should find a jeep.'

Go slow and regular, inhale and exhale in beats of five, the nurse said in the hospital. Use your breath as a tunnel to crawl through the pain.

'Did you hear me?'

She looks up at his face which seems to have grown waxy in the night. Some distance behind him there's the yellow fuzz of the Mess windows, a vague burble of singing.

'I said I'll carry you the rest of the way.'

She shakes her head. 'I'm fine.'

'I must insist.' At once he bends and scoops her up, carrying her as you would a child. 'Put your arms round my neck.'

His overcoat smells of wool and camphor, his breath is thick with beef and claret. Her forehead bumps on his buttoned epaulette. She doesn't know where to look. She closes her eyes and swallows down her pain and rage.

Once inside the apartment he carries her into her bedroom, turning on the light by the door. He lowers her onto the chair by the desk. 'Do you need further assistance?'

'I can manage perfectly well on my own now, thank you.'

He nods, looking at the jumble of gowns on the bed, the open trunk on the floor. 'Lena, forgive me, but you're sure you won't reconsider our arrangements? My room is much more spacious.'

She pushes her fist into her thigh where it burns. She waits for him to leave.

'If you were to require help in the night—'

'I won't.'

'But my dear, if—'

'We agreed it would be best for my recovery to get an undisturbed night.'

'Of course.'

But he doesn't move. She straightens her leg and begins to flex her toes. 'I need to get on with my exercises, you'll have to excuse me.'

'Perhaps then we should consider swapping rooms for the duration of your recovery. After all this bed is—'

'Perfectly adequate.' It's true, there's plenty of room for her, and also for Ivan Pavlov, who's tucked himself up on the counterpane, pretending to be asleep and unmoveable. She rotates her ankle to the left counting to twenty, then to the right. She can feel his gaze on her.

'I'm sorry, but it goes much better if I do this alone.'

'Of course.' She hears him step towards the door.

She waits to hear the door close.

'I wondered if perhaps you might wish to pray together, Lena?'

She looks up. 'Did you say pray?'

'Is that such an unusual idea?'

'I thought you knew Mama's the devout one in my family.'

'I often find it beneficial in settling the thoughts for sleep.'

'And does it work, do you think, asking for things like that?'

'There's more to it than asking. There's being grateful, and remembering all you've been blessed with.'

'And you believe these blessings came from God?'

'As a matter of fact I do. Like the vast majority of people.'

She is suddenly weary beyond measure. 'Thank you, but I don't have any trouble getting off. Goodnight, Anton.'

'As you wish. Goodnight then, my dear Lena, sleep well.'

At some point in the dead of night she's woken by a tapping sound, a shy sort of half sound, as if unsure whether it wants to be known. Lena lurches up, staring in the dark, trying to locate its direction. Under the covers, Ivan Pavlov lifts his head and snarls.

'Lena?' a voice says beyond the door. Anton's voice.

She stares at the handle; a vague ivory globe in the dark.

'My dear, are you awake?'

The handle doesn't move.

'I'm just turning in and checking you're not in any discomfort.'

She reaches for Pav and pulls him to her, watching the door.

There's a moment of absolute silence then the slight skidding sound of leather soles in the hall, followed by the click of a closing door.

A long exhalation comes from her.

Calm down. Nothing happened.

She listens to the quiet seeping through the apartment, smooth as spreading oil. She lies down and pulls the blankets high. Her breathing is fast, too loud.

Nothing happened.

And in this darkness it begins to seem to her as if she's no longer high in the mountains, but sinking to a place underground – somewhere deep and close-walled like a cave, or the bottom of a mineshaft, somewhere the air is frigid and thin. From nowhere she can see, a weight now seems to descend on her chest, suffocating as a pressing stone.

There are twenty-six bones in the human thorax. The bones form a protective cage. The ribs, the costal cartilage, the sternum. There are two types of ribs. Typical and atypical. The typical rib consists of a head, a neck and a body. She lies very still in the dark with only her lips moving, describing each bone, one at a time.

At breakfast Lena watches Anton take his knife and tap three times on the side of a boiled egg. He unhinges the shell and asks after her sleep, spooning clots of yellow and white into his mouth. Now and then he turns a page in the leather notebook by his place on the table, taking up his pencil and writing. The forecast is for snow, he says. That is something to be seen in these mountains. He drinks his coffee and pockets his notebook, and he comes down the room to her. Twelve strides it takes him today.

'You're not hungry?'

Lena reaches for a slice of toast.

He pushes the butter dish towards her. 'You need to keep up your strength.'

She waits, because for a moment she thinks he's going to bend and kiss her hair, but he turns to the mirror. She slides the toast under the table to Pav.

Anton runs a finger over his moustache, his eyes on his reflection. 'Good to remember that in the military we try not to waste food.' His hand touches her shoulder. 'Enjoy your day, my dear.'

She listens to the tread of his boots down the hall. The front door closes and the clock on the mantel ticks towards the chime at eight-thirty. Lena sits at the table and watches the second hand quivering as if uncertain what to do next.

She looks at the rack of cold toast. Mama once swore she saw baby Jesus's handprint in a slice of griddled rye, but the evidence had been swiped by Pavlov before it could be taken to St Lucasz's for confirmation. How long ago had this happened? A year? Two? Despite Papa's teasing and Romus offering odds on a third coming, Mama had made Ulka griddle the rest of the loaf in case the holy infant's spirit was still hovering in the kitchen waiting to assume carbonised form.

The clock marks the half-hour. Lena blinks back water from her eyes. She empties the rack onto her plate and feeds buttered slices to Pavlov. When she leaves the table, she asks the orderly for a ream of paper and envelopes for mailing. It would be a shame if they've forgotten about baby Jesus's handprint at home.

'Would you care for Patience?' Anton says to her after dinner. They're in the sitting room, he with the day's newspaper and she with her encyclopaedia of infectious diseases, making notes on smallpox. Ivan Pavlov is stretched close to the grate, embers pinging into his fur.

'Excuse me?' She turns a page and scribbles a note on her pad.

'Patience. Would you like to learn? My mother enjoys the game very much.'

He folds his newspaper and gets up from his armchair, bringing a card table in front of her armchair. Pav raises his head and shows his teeth.

'That dog of yours.'

'He's just a little unsettled.'

Anton pulls his armchair to sit opposite her, brushing the baize. 'How's the leg? Did you do your exercises today?'

He looks down at her open encyclopaedia. 'Interesting reading?'

'They called it the speckled monster,' she says. 'A very nasty business as you can see from the illustrations.'

'Indeed.'

'Did you know the Chinese began inoculating people a thousand years ago?'

'I did not.' He opens an ivory case and removes a pack of playing cards. 'Shall we make a start?'

'Once infected a person has a thirty to fifty per cent chance of death.'

'Is that so?'

'If you're lucky enough to survive you could be left blind.'

On the edge of her vision Anton is laying out cards. When she glances up, the cards are face down on the baize in columns of increasing numbers.

'The snow didn't arrive today after all,' he says. 'But when it does, it comes down like nowhere else.'

She hears him clear his throat. She looks up.

'I was talking of the snow. When it comes we must train hard. It's imperative the communications equipment withstands winter conditions.'

She watches him straightening the deck, setting it parallel to the edge of the baize. 'Would you like a war to come?'

'What sort of question is that?'

'You missed Papa's one. You're a soldier so I'd think it's what you want, because if there isn't a war you're spending your whole life pretending. I'd want the real thing if I were you.'

'There's more to my work than pretending, I assure you. Come, let me show you this game. Maybe one day you'll play my mother. She's very exacting so we must make you a match for her. We set out seven columns, our aim is to build four suited foundations using all the cards.' His pale hands move across the baize turning cards at the edge of each column. 'We can only build foundations from an ace. Patience is about drawing out the aces.'

She closes her books. 'Do you love your mother?'

'What manner of question is that?'

'Some people don't.'

He stares across at her, his pale eyes blinking. 'This is the thing I cherish in you, dearest Lena. From one moment to the next it's impossible to predict what you might say.'

'But you didn't answer my question.'

He turns the top card on the deck. 'Which in particular have I not attended to?'

'Well firstly, is there going to be a war?'

'We must hope not.'

'Hope?' she hears herself spit the word back at him. 'That's all you can say for it? Your brother certainly predicted one.'

Anton looks down at the baize. Lena opens her mouth but has nothing – or far too much – to say. She thinks of the expression on Mama's face the afternoon the Warsaw brother appeared on the doorstep in his dark city suit. They had sat around the dining table and the man had slid a sheaf of documents from his briefcase and started to speak about the potential of a continental conflict. She thinks of the shine in Mama's eyes as she turned to

Papa on one side, then to her on the other. *You see,* Mama's eyes said, *no more arguments now.*

'It was a geopolitical assessment, Lena, not a certainty,' Anton says quietly. 'One puts one's trust in our leaders' diplomacy. Pacts are being signed that would suggest all may yet be well.'

She stares at him.

He unhooks his spectacles and cleans the lenses on a handkerchief. She watches his thumb on the fabric moving in circles. How quietly he had sat at her side two months ago as Mama read the Warsaw brother's documents, crossing herself now and then. Mama had met the gaze of the brother, grave-faced at the head of the table, his eyes darting to his pocket watch and no doubt thoughts of his return train. *And my daughter,* Mama had said, *with this disablement of hers, she will be taken care of?*

I give you my family's word.

Anton had reached for Lena's hand. He pressed it between his own.

Lena looks at him now, this man she has been sworn to for life, and the serpent hisses in her throat. 'Your spectacles are too tight. You'll get sinus headaches from the pressure. What sort of soldier needs lenses anyway?'

'One working in communications behind the lines.' He replaces his spectacles and tucks the handkerchief in his pocket. 'Patience is most generally a game for one. In some countries it's known as solitaire.'

'You know you don't look like a soldier. You probably don't even have a gun. You look like you'd be happier studying birds or maybe just trapping them.'

'It's what my family does.'

'Trap birds?'

'Protects our nation.'

'Have you always done what your family tells you? I can't imagine a mother would really want her son to fight. Not if she really loved him.'

For a moment he is silent, then abruptly he pushes back his chair and goes to the decanter on the other side of the room.

'Have I offended you?' she asks. 'Only it's hard to tell sometimes.'

'Some people prefer not to paint their emotions on their skin.'

'Which can make it hard for people to see they have them.'

'That's one opinion.' He returns with the decanter and a vodka glass, settling in front of her, a smile held tight between his lips. 'Now with your permission,' leaning forward he takes her hand, moving it to the first column, 'we turn the card. You're lucky. Our first ace. Clubs. We build our foundation from here.'

Lena isn't asleep that night when the handle on the bedroom door begins to rotate.

Nor is she asleep when the door turns on its hinges.

She doesn't shift her position as slippers slide into the room and something is thrown to Pavlov on the end of the bed.

A figure comes to stand over her. She's not asleep but she must seem to be.

She can feel a gaze narrowing, driving down like a screw.

His irises will be pale but his pupils dilating in the dark.

She hears air drawn in between teeth, a quick swallowing sound.

But she herself must not swallow, not once. No, she must freeze her reflexes, pour wax in her muscles and nerves. There are forty-three muscles in the human face. They are controlled by the seventh cranial nerve. She must relax them all.

Heavy snow falls that night. For hours after he left the bedroom, Lena had lain awake not thinking herself able to sleep. Now all of a sudden she's aware of pale light under the curtains' edges.

Pav is stretched on the floor. The rug is undisturbed. She gets up and looks outside. Thick white crusts overhang the infirmary roof and weigh on the forest branches.

When she goes in to breakfast Anton has already finished his egg and is flicking through his notebook. He looks up, watching her lean her canes against the table and sit down.

'I've been meaning to ask if there's some other breakfast you'd prefer? I find egg and toast perfectly adequate but perhaps you'd care for an omelette, or porridge instead?'

She thinks about Ulka's porridge, soaked overnight in cinnamon water and served with honey, grated apple, raisins and cream.

'Porridge, I suppose.'

'I'll inform the orderly. In the meantime perhaps we shouldn't waste this toast. Did you see the snow? It must be a metre deep in places. Fascinating how it pacifies the natural world. Yet I always seem to wake.' He shakes his head, smiling. 'Isn't it strange that it's the silence that wakes you?'

She takes a triangle of toast from the rack without meeting his gaze, scraping butter into the corners, making the sound go on and on. 'I'm a deep sleeper.'

He clears his throat. 'Another downfall is forecast this morning. I'd advise staying indoors.'

'Pav needs walking.'

'I'll instruct the orderly. You don't want to open the break in your thigh when it's mending so well. Besides, I'm sure you have plenty of studying to occupy you.' He closes his notebook and smiles. 'I'm going to ask Mrs Machek to stop by if she can make it through. No arguments please, my dear. It's time you had company.'

Pushing back his chair Anton turns to the window, taking a pair of binoculars from the sill. 'We should string some bacon on the fence and throw down oats. I should imagine the ground feeders are starting to suffer in this weather. Actually, Lena, I've been wondering whether it might be an interesting hobby to begin a daily tally – a survey of ornithological habits and the like. I've never found the time before which is a pity.' He pauses, glancing back. 'Perhaps that might be something we could embark on together?'

Lena cuts her toast into pieces.

'What do you think?'

'If you wish.'

'You look a little pale under the eyes, my dear. I hope you're not overdoing your books while I'm out.'

'I'm quite well enough to study, thank you.'

'But this toast goes uneaten and you never touch an egg. You must keep up your strength.'

'I'm not so hungry in the mornings.'

'This is not the girl who could eat three slices of strudel and take a hot chocolate to follow.'

She raises her coffee cup and sips slowly. 'Perhaps I'm no longer that girl.'

The telephone starts to ring in the hall and he leaves to answer it. The call goes on and she takes her cane and stands at the window looking out.

It was Ulka who advised to do this.

'Remember the sky, twig. We all share the same sun up there. If you feel homesick look out at the sky and you'll find a sense of us.'

What rubbish.

She should write and tell Ulka this.

She should say, you'll want me believing in gypsies next.

Suddenly she wants to talk to Ulka. It comes like a thump in the gut. If she could only go into the hall to this telephone and hear Ulka on the other end snorting like a horse. Ulka will know what to do about doorknobs turning in the dead of night and slippers inching onto bedside rugs.

Anton is coming back up the hall. She doesn't move from the window.

His palms touch her shoulders. His fingers rest on the ridge of her collarbones.

'Is there something upsetting you this morning, Lena?'

She smells the soap on his skin.

'You're missing home, I suppose, that will be it. When I was first posted after college I remember feeling as if I'd been sent to the moon.'

'I was wondering,' she says quietly, 'has any mail arrived for me yet?'

'There's something you're expecting?'

'Just a letter or something from home perhaps.'

'I'm afraid it takes a while for correspondence to make its way up here. It could be a week or so. The snow won't be helping, but I'm sure you're not forgotten.'

Dan. She would like to speak to Dan, far away in England, right now. Dan will know what to do about fingers sitting on bones where they don't belong. Dan always knows what to do.

The clock chimes the half-hour. His hands lift.

She watches him in the window's reflection as he drops his face and kisses the crown of her head. 'Just a small gesture of endearment,' he murmurs, turning away.

Lena forgets to count his steps down the hall to the front door. Not that it matters. There will have been eighteen of them and a pause to make his prayer at the Madonna. She listens to the clock hand jerking towards the chime at eight forty-five. Outside the snow is coming down again, falling as if hurled in a fury. Nine o'clock chimes and she's still leaning on her cane at the window, watching flakes creep up the corners of the frames, suffocating the light.

Under the table Pav begins to bark. She follows him to the front door.

'Hello, my dear. Mrs Bem, I'm presuming?'

The woman beaming on the doorstep is large and well dusted with snow. 'I'm afraid I come to you looking rather like a mountain. Please resist all urges to ski down me.' A mole trembles on her chin. 'With this weather I thought I'd better get you out of the way early. Maria Machek – Misha to my friends. Goodness this damp is ruinous for a wave.'

Lena steps to the side as the woman enters, shaking out her headscarf.

'Piotr was right, you're but a slip of a thing, aren't you? Well it takes all sorts. She must be quite something, I said to him, to steal our Anton's heart at a dance where I hear you did not dance. Of course when tragedy struck, well goodness, we all told Anton he mustn't blame himself, but he had to announce he was taking you, ruined leg or no!' The woman shakes snow from her coat. 'The romance of it all! But the truth is, my child, when our menfolk fall, they go down heavily. And your major has tumbled harder than most. This dog, my dear, is he always so fond of strangers?'

Lena takes Pav's collar. 'It's your coat, he has a liking for mink.'

The woman – Mrs Machek – hangs her coat and headscarf, eyes the Madonna and goes bustling down the hall. 'You don't mind me making myself at home? I'll ring for the orderly. Successful hosting must be thought of not as a talent but a skill that can be picked up by anyone who only wishes to apply themselves. Let's take coffee by the fire and whatever there is in the way of cake.'

Seated in armchairs, Mrs Machek opens the conversation with talk of her embroidery group which welcomes all wives, regardless of ability or rank. A tip here, she says. In conversation it is advised to commence with a general topic before moving on to specific news. This avoids the appearance of being interested only in gossip. Is that understood? Mrs Machek moves on to describe several 'Useful Persons' at the base – women of decency, interest and influence as she calls them, before draining her coffee and lowering her voice to list those ladies currently best avoided. She concludes with an outline of her four children's achievements to date. Discussion of family must always bring up the rear of any social occasion, she says, to avoid the appearance of bragging. Anton, she mentions in an aside, has been a wonder with her boy. Anyone can see he has a way with children. This comment is left in the air to settle where it will while Mrs Machek's thumb attends to the crumbs of her apple cake. Lena takes the opportunity to ask if Maria knows anything about telephones and how to connect with someone overseas?

'Goodness, that would be a challenge. This person must be very important.'

'Just a friend.'

'We all need those. But the telephone, you say. There's no telling these days which towns have them and which do not. Wouldn't a telegram work?'

'I'd really like to speak to her. She's studying in England.'

'A modern country, but still. How about a letter?'

'That would take weeks.' Lena hears a sudden tremor in her voice. 'Please excuse me,' and she turns away for a handkerchief.

Mrs Machek lays aside her plate. 'Oh, my dear, I see it now. You're homesick, of course you are, and you need to unburden yourself to a reliable listener.' Her hand reaches for a consoling grip on Lena's knee. 'Perhaps the opening marital moves are not what you anticipated? Am I right?' She watches Lena blow her nose. 'Disappointment is a land to which women journey, my dear. I've been there myself, believe me, all women have. Perhaps I was not quite so fresh as you my first time, but the good Lord knows I've been in your place. Should you wish for a listening ear, Misha is here for you.'

'Just the telephone, Mrs Machek.' Lena blots her eyes. 'Even a call to my family.'

Mrs Machek takes up her fork and sucks the prongs thoughtfully. She waves it in the air. 'Home is home of course. There's simply no replacement for it. Let Misha see what she can do.' She reaches for a second slice of cake.

That evening Anton sends word he'll be late. Lena takes supper by the fire and goes early to bed. She must have fallen asleep in her clothes, because she's lying on top of the counterpane when the door handle turns. She lurches up, startled by Pav's barks.

'I don't mean to disturb you, Lena. I'm just checking you're well.'

'I was asleep.'

He stands in the doorway in his long grey overcoat, a damp cap under his elbow. 'I hear Misha came by today. Did she mention that she runs a group who sew clothes for the village children? The ladies meet on a Thursday morning, I believe.'

Lena nods, hugging Pavlov to her.

'Very good. As I say it wasn't my intention to disturb you. I'll leave you be.'

The bedroom door closes. Lena buries her face in the dog's neck. When she catches sight of her hands they are trembling. They don't even look like her own.

Halfway through breakfast Anton mentions he's been informed that she wishes to make use of a telephone.

'I must be honest, I'd rather you'd come to me about this. However it does sound an excellent idea to have you speak with your parents. If you like I can make enquiries as to how to reach them.'

'I'd be grateful.'

'Whatever I can do.' He smiles, scraping out the shell of his egg. 'Did you manage to hear the nightjar last night? There's definitely a female out there. I noted her at 5.45, still a good way off dawn.' He lays his palm on a larger notebook to the side of his plate. 'I was thinking perhaps we could start our observations by noting that female. I've ruled a few columns. Date, time, location, species description and observed behaviour. What do you think?'

Lena holds his gaze without speaking.

'It wouldn't have to be anything more than that,' he says.

'There is something else actually, Anton.'

'Yes?'

'Last night, you came into my bedroom.'

He lays down his spoon, pushing his plate to the side of the mat. 'Maria Machek mentioned you were perhaps feeling a little out of sorts. I was concerned.'

She forces herself to take a sip of coffee. 'And the other nights when you've come in?'

'Excuse me?'

'The other nights. There have been a few.'

He nods several times. 'An old habit. In the academy we were taught to make a check of the cadets before turning in. Think nothing of it.'

'I'm not a cadet, Anton.' She grips her cup, holding his gaze. All the way to his end of the table she holds on until he looks away.

'Indeed, no, you're not.'

Her coffee cup clatters as she places it on the saucer. 'Thank you, Anton.'

When he's gone Lena walks in the hall raising her bad leg in front of her. It will have to be strong for all the bicycling to be done in Kraków.

She says this out loud in the silent hall. 'I am going to Kraków soon.'

She tells Pavlov scratching at his collar on the floor.

She turns and speaks to the mirror. 'Kraków.'

She has to believe it is still possible.

'Anton believes it possible,' she says to the mirror.

At least that's what he always told her after the accident.

Every Thursday afternoon he would turn up at the hospital, bringing a wrap of flowers, two slices of strudel and a frown of concern. Arriving at four precisely, so the nurses joked that they set the ward clock by him. 'You'll get to Kraków eventually,' he'd say, never seeming to notice her leg strung high in its cast. 'You of all people.'

And she was grateful to hear it. Very grateful. But still she would look away and mutter that she didn't know what he meant.

Because after the accident nothing was clear to her any more. During those long motionless weeks she'd had to remind Papa time and again to write to Professor Szafran for a deferral of her university place – Papa who claimed no recollection of writing the first letter, and seemed to have aged in the time since that June day. The deferral couldn't be brought up with Mama who'd sat with the doctors and heard the initial prognosis and now seemed to believe Lena's future lay within nunnery walls – if walking was even possible with such a serious break. Ulka and Ala, delivering daily pierogi and gossip, were also strangely silent on Lena's prospects. Even Romek was low on jokes at first. In that sense Captain Bem's Thursday visits brought solace. He alone seemed convinced her leg might mend, and her dreams remain unbroken. He'd even brought in her beloved encyclopaedia from home.

So she didn't see the bombshell coming, the Thursday after she finally got home from the ward, swinging on crutches, but upright – more upright than anyone dared hope.

Anton had been sat by the hearth with Mama and Papa, taking tea and discussing something to do with Moscow, when she came into the room with a journal she'd requested months ago from the national psychological library. She burst in saying something like, 'Look, it's here at last!' except Anton was speaking and Mama was listening, leaning close, and they looked up and all smiled at once, so Lena said 'What?' and Mama shook her head and said to Anton, 'Please go on.'

Lena sat at the dining-room table and engrossed herself in an article on the Viennese method for curing hysteria. It was raining heavily outside. As a consequence she barely heard Anton lay down his teacup and clear his throat and wonder aloud about her hand in marriage.

The first she really knew was Mama's pearls bouncing over the floor, rattling like hail. Because Mama had pulled so hard on the necklace at her throat that it broke. It seemed like they were all looking at the pearls for ages.

Anton had turned to her then, a flush on his cheeks. 'A married student will be better protected.'

'You'd do that? You'll take her as she is?' Mama said. She was up and running to kiss his nose and forehead, his chin and cheeks. 'My son, my son!' she'd sobbed, 'This mother thanks you from the depths of her heart,' and Mama was coming at Lena, flapping her handkerchief and crushing her in a lilac embrace, and all this before Lena had had a chance to knock the shock from her throat and say a single word.

It was Papa whom she'd looked to. Papa who was silent, sucking on a humbug by the fire. She waited to hear him say something, come out with words that would reorder things, put crazy ideas back in boxes. 'Hold it, everyone,' he'd say, 'Magdalena Luiza and I need to discuss what she wants from her life. Only then can we make decisions about what needs to be done.' After all, it was only what he'd said to her sitting in a winter cafe a year before.

'Papa?' she said. But Papa was no longer that man.

'Anton's taking Lena,' Mama cried, rushing to him.

'He is?' Papa said, unwrapping a second sweet.

Ulka had been summoned at once with vodka and glasses, and a toast was being made to Lena and Anton's happiness. He'd looked at her with a blush and that pressed smile of his that suddenly seemed to be more about keeping things in than letting joy out, and right then she'd felt it inside her, it was like a bone cracking all over again, except this time it happened deep in her core. Whether this was a result of panic and confusion or plain disbelief, she didn't know. But there was no time to think further because Ala was charging into the room, and everyone was embracing as though this were the most natural turn of events in the world. Mama sat down at the piano and got stuck into a polonaise, even Papa seemed to be smiling at his empty glass. And through it all not a word had found its way out of Lena's throat to say, 'No, I don't want this, I don't want this at all.'

It had felt like being thrown in front of a second tram, that's what she told Ulka afterwards in the kitchen.

'But you drank up your vodka to the union.'

'I was in shock.'

Ulka refilled their glasses. 'Perhaps it's not so bad an idea all things considered,' she said.

'What?' Lena screeched. 'I thought you were on my side.'

'There are no sides, twig.'

'That's what you think.'

The following morning Mama, Ala and Lena had been halfway through breakfast when Papa thundered in, waving his cane in the air.

'What's this Romek tells me? Lena's to marry that Bom fellow?'

Everyone looked at him. He was wild-haired and in pyjamas.

'That's right, darling,' Mama said. 'Captain Bem. Come and sit down.'

'This is some sort of joke presumably? How old are you these days, Magdalena Luiza, sixteen?'

'She's seventeen and a half. Have some tea, darling.' Mama went for the pot. 'Shall I fetch your gown?'

'I don't want a gown or any goddamn tea. I want to know what you've been conniving behind my back.'

Ala looked at Lena and shook her head faintly.

'Am I talking to my family or a goddamn heap of stones?'

'Jozef, please, there's no need to shout so.'

'Crap is what this is, a stinking heap of it. Lena's going to Kraków to train to be a doctor. I've a letter from Szafran saying as much.'

'She's going as a married woman.'

'Over my dead body.'

Mama nodded and quietly laid a bowl of porridge his way. 'You agreed to it, my dear.'

'Rubbish,' he said.

No one spoke.

'Sit down, darling,' Mama said. She pulled out a chair for him.

Romek came in juggling butter knives. 'Somebody die in here?'

Ala sprinkled a shower of sugar into her coffee. 'You know I can't actually see what all the fuss is about. Captain Bem is about to be made a Major.'

'Thank you, darling, that's right, there are lots of benefits to the match.'

'Lena?' Papa said, his blue eyes on her. 'What do you think about this?'

She stared at him and felt her hands start to tremble.

'It's all settled, Jozef. There are many benefits to the match. Not only with her leg, but with the world as it is.'

'May I enquire what's so wrong with the world?'

Mama had looked at him and then at Ala and Lena and she shook her head. 'Anton's brother in Warsaw is in a position of some importance, Jozef. He hears things.'

'Well I'd like to hear them too, if you don't mind, Zosia, before we start despatching our children to any suitor who comes calling.'

Mama sat down slowly and bowed her head over her clasped hands.

Papa banged his palm on the tabletop. 'I will hear these matters before I agree to anything. You understand? I will hear them.'

'We'll ask the brother to come then,' Mama said softly, 'and afterwards that will be the end of it.'

'They say one man's the same as another in the dark of the night.' Ala whispered this to her in the conservatory that evening, where Lena had been sleeping since she came home from the hospital. They lay top to tail on the daybed, Lena, at the bottom, tossing the gypsy's amber from hand to hand, Ala fiddling with the gas lamp, turning it up as bright as she could. 'You shouldn't worry too much, twig.'

'But I won't see him in the dark of the night.' Lena threw the amber high in the air towards the ceiling lampshade, half hopeful of lodging it somewhere beyond Ulka's reach. Ulka had been insisting on keeping the amber near Lena's leg in accordance with some irrational healing notion she'd picked up in the market.

Ala held the ends of her plaits to the lamp and began to separate out split ends.

'I said I won't see him in the dark. We'll have separate rooms.'

Ala didn't reply. She was nibbling off hairs.

'Goddamn you, Ala. Will you just spit it out, whatever you're chewing over?'

Ala shrugged. 'You'll be married. I expect he'll expect you to share a bed.'

Lena thought about this. 'I won't let him.'

'You think you'll have a choice?'

'Of course I will. I'll say my leg's bad.' Lena turned the amber in her hand trying to spot the wisp of wing in its core. 'It's not like we'll be married properly. It's just a piece of paper to make Mama happy because her daughter's a cripple. You really think he'll expect it?'

Ala sighed. 'It's time to grow up, little sister. You might come to love him, do you ever think that?'

'Unlikely.'

'It happens to lots of people. It's probably what he's hoping and Mama's hoping, and he's really not that dreadful, you know. I should imagine the spectacles come off at night. And all these promotions he's getting, they're very good signs.'

'Of what?'

Ala said she wasn't sure but that most of her friends thought Lena was very lucky in the circumstances.

'I don't intend to be crippled for ever, if that's what you mean.'

'I didn't say that.' Ala swapped plaits. 'Do you think they favour floral scents?'

'Who?'

'The officers' wives. Whatever are you throwing about down there?'

Lena held up the amber. 'You and your blasted gypsy woman. It's brought nothing but bad luck.'

'You don't believe in luck.'

'Maybe I'm changing my mind.'

Ala laughed. How was it she always sounded happy when she laughed? Her laughter was never mixed up with other stuff. It never had another intent. 'You can't see your good fortune, that's your trouble.'

'So you always say.'

They lay silently for a moment. Lena stared at the ceiling.

'Mama's very worried about Papa you know,' Ala said. 'Yesterday he forgot how to get home from the market. He spent five minutes completely frozen to the spot, and when she asked what he was doing, it seemed he couldn't choose a direction. Then he got angry at her pointing out the way. He took her wrist and shook it. And after this he asked why she was crying and then of course he started crying too. The grocer came over to check they were all right.'

Lena leaned her head on an elbow. 'And what am I supposed to do about it?'

Ala shrugged. 'Nothing. I don't know. Make it easy on Mama, I suppose. Be nice?'

Lena hurled the piece of amber as hard as she could at the wall.

Ala looked up from her plaits at the crack in the plaster. She got off the bed and went to the dresser under which the amber had rolled. She got down on her knees and pulled it out, returning to Lena. 'It'll be all right, you'll see.'

Lena couldn't trust herself to answer. She swiped her eyes and blew out hard. Then she sat up and threw the amber again at the wall.

But look how far away Ala and her plaits are now. It's hardly likely they'll have this snow falling over them at home. It never snows much in February so it was quite stupid for Ulka to go on about everyone sharing the sky. Not that much of the sky can be seen from the kitchen anyway. Right now Ulka won't even be in there, she'll be cursing the laundry in the cellar, and Ala will be leaning over the admissions desk, like she's being passed state secrets not pointless tittle-tattle. Romuś will probably be in detention juggling pencils, and Mama hammering the piano. And as for Papa? But she can't think of him. She mustn't. Her stomach turns to stone when she does. Really there's no point at all in thinking about home at all.

The following day she's late to breakfast.

Anton looks up from a newspaper. 'You seem to be walking better.'

'I'm sorry I'm late, I slept in. I was studying last night.'

'Interesting work, I trust?'

'The arterial system.'

'Well, you'll find breakfast waiting. I hope it's not cold.'

There's a tureen of porridge on the table, and by her place, a small silver jug of cream. She takes a ladle of porridge while he smiles at her like a parent watching a present being unwrapped. 'Is it good?'

'Thank you, yes.'

'So you see?'

'What?'

'We can make you feel at home here.' He watches her reach for the sugar bowl. 'Nevertheless, I do want to suggest you reconsider your study hours.'

'I haven't been late to breakfast before.'

'It's simply that I fear we shall become complete strangers to each other if our routines don't align at least slightly.'

She meets his gaze as levelly as she can.

'Reading in daylight puts less strain on the eyes,' he says, folding his paper and coming down the room. 'I speak from experience in this.'

Lena looks down as he approaches. She pours cream into the porridge. 'I'll do my best.'

'So you slept well.'

'I did. And you?'

'Indeed, yes.'

Neither of them mentions the chair that was jammed against her bedroom door, or the handle that tried to turn in the night.

She asks him about his progress in arranging contact with her family on the telephone.

'About that,' he says, 'I must take full responsibility. The truth is we don't have a contact number. Neither your family nor the neighbouring farmer are on the exchange.'

'We could send a telegram and ask for an appointment to be made in town. As I understand from Mrs Machek it's quite straightforward. We tell them to go to the bank or the postal office at a certain time on a specified date. You could send a telegram this morning. I could do it myself if you're too busy.'

Anton pulls out a chair next to her and sits down. He removes his spectacles and breathes on the lenses. She watches his thumb turn circles on a handkerchief pressed to the glass. Five rotations on each. 'I've been turning this over carefully. Please believe me when I say this, Lena. In this regard I think we must tread with caution.'

'In sending a telegram so I can speak to my parents?'

'Indeed so.'

'I don't understand, Anton.' She lays aside her spoon quietly. 'Please explain.'

'When I first started at cadet school I was twelve years of age. I didn't have contact with my mother for six months.'

'And you think that was a good thing?'

'It was necessary, Mother said, and I've since come to believe it was. When humans are subjected to a change in circumstances the physical body adapts far quicker than the psychological system. Time must be allowed for the mind to catch up.'

'I still don't understand. What's a telephone call to my family got to do with your schooling?'

He replaces his glasses. His hand is now beside hers on the table. She stares at the nail on his thumb which is very clean.

'Lena, my dear, I'm simply proposing that we wait until you're more settled, a few weeks, that's all, perhaps when you've achieved something you'll enjoy passing on, and that your parents will take pleasure in hearing about. After you've joined the embroidery group or hosted a party. My mother keeps my first letter home from cadets. Apparently it's full of delight at exploring the woodland around the school and the prospect of winter theatricals.'

Lena finds herself suddenly standing, looking down at his hand that is now flat on the table. 'You've changed your mind.'

'I've reflected overnight and reached a decision.'

'You haven't reached a decision, you've changed one, and now you're preventing me from using the telephone to contact my family.'

'I wouldn't put it quite like that.'

'How would you put it?'

He looks at her. 'My dear, I believe a little calmness is called for. Let me send a telegram on your behalf if you've something urgent to relay.'

'That's not speaking to them.' She hears the rise in her voice. 'That's not listening to Papa laugh.'

'And I'll find a way to make that contact happen, I promise you. But a little patience is called for.'

'I want to speak to Papa.'

He is silent, nodding. A teacher, she thinks, with a difficult pupil.

'Anton, I want to speak to Papa today.'

'Indeed you do, Lena. When you're young it's only natural that you expect everything at once. With maturity comes an understanding that sometimes it's more fruitful to take things slowly in the beginning. To act on reflection, not impulse.'

She stares at him.

'To think of the future,' he adds.

'And do you yourself adhere to these principles in your maturity?'

'I'm afraid I don't understand your meaning.'

She snorts. 'Of course you don't.'

The clock chimes the half-hour. He pushes back his chair. 'We can continue this discussion later if you wish. I'm afraid it looks like another day indoors. More snow is forecast and the track may be impassable by noon.' He touches her shoulder. 'Perhaps you might reflect on what I said.'

Lena stands in her small bedroom, leaning on her cane, looking out of the window at the snow piling on the infirmary roof. There are no vehicles to be seen. The track itself is gone. Even the trees beyond the fence have been consumed by the blizzard. The only noise comes from inside her body, an incessant whine in her ears.

Papa, as he once was, would not have asked her to stay here. Not in this place against her wishes. She shouldn't be here. This was not meant for her future. She has plans. Papa would say as much now, if she could only hear his voice.

Lena opens her wardrobe before she can change her mind. She pulls scarves from the rack, strapping them round her weakened thigh. She dresses in her thickest skirt and sweater. For a moment she glances at her desk and the opened encyclopaedia, then she goes out of the room. In the hall she puts on her fur, a deerstalker hat and sheepskin gloves, glowering at the painting of the Madonna with her gold halo and slashed cheek. Taking a deep breath she opens the front door.

'Let's go, Pav.'

They step out into the blizzard, the bitter air making her cough. Ivan Pavlov slinks between her legs as she lurches, canes slipping, across the deep white track to the fence. She'll be able to grip the links and walk in the shelter of the trees. One truck, defying the storm, that's all there needs to be out there, making its way down the mountain to the village and the train station. She just needs to will one truck into existence to take her home.

Laughter.

All of a sudden there's laughter, the sound rolling like a purr in her ear.

It stops the blizzard in mid fall. Flakes vibrate around her, a mesh of white. The trees and fence vanish away.

Her heart thumps at her ribs.

'Please,' she whispers. 'Bone man, please, I want to see you.'

'I'm here, Magdalena, you only have to look for me.'

'If I do will our story begin? Will it be different when it does?'

She hears him laugh, and she turns after the sound.

'You're here.' She says it in case she cannot trust her eyes. 'You're real.'

Because in this white world, whatever world it is, it may be one to come or one long gone — and Lena no longer knows which — she sees him. He is standing by her side.

His flesh is as real as her own. He wears his long sheepskin coat, epaulettes of snow on his shoulders. His arms are wide open, waiting; a scarecrow or a man to be crucified. Dark-red hair, thick as a pelt, falls in a clump over his eyes. She stares at the curve of his brow, his cheek's hollow, the wisps of breath leaving his grinning lips. If she stares at him without blinking perhaps he cannot go.

'What's troubling you?' he says. Always that fox's grin.

She shakes her head. 'How can you smile so easily' — her words splinter, coming apart from each other as they fall — 'when you know how our story ends.'

'Oh, Magdalena, we're getting a little ahead of ourselves, don't you think?'

He throws back his head and laughs. It echoes like the falling of forests around the world. He laughs and she blinks, and suddenly she sees nothing but a blizzard on a mountain track.

'Bone man?' she screams. 'Don't you dare leave me. Don't you dare go!'

Tatra Mountains, Southern Poland

Anton pulls on the handbrake and turns off the ignition. The headlights die, leaving the jeep in darkness. 'In the name of God whatever were you thinking?' He doesn't turn to look at her as he speaks. All the way back to the base, he's kept silent, his eyes on the track, his expression fixed. So this is the shape his anger takes; it is high and impenetrable; a cold cliff set against her.

'I'm sorry if I embarrassed you.' Even to her the words sound insubstantial; puffs of ice dissolving in the dark. 'I didn't mean to cause trouble with your colleagues.'

'I don't care for such ideas, Lena, I care for you.' His palm strikes the steering wheel. 'Am I never to understand you?'

Through the fogged windscreen she can see lights in the apartment windows. The door opens and an orderly comes onto the step with blankets and a lantern. Further up the track a generator thrums and a string of bulbs, hung from tall posts, flicker into balls of orange light.

'You could have died out there, Lena. And to leave no note as to where you thought you were heading . . .'

'I planned to telegram from the station.'

'Saying what exactly?'

She shoves her fists under her thighs, trying not to shiver. 'I was going home.'

'Home?' His eyes are tiny vials of frustration. He stares ahead unblinking. 'This is your home.'

Lena says nothing.

Anton passes a gloved hand over his face.

Where were the trucks? There should have been at least one in all that time she was on the track. How is she to get home without a single goddamn truck driving down the mountain?

'Thank God the infantrymen were on exercise. I suspect that's all that's saved you from hypothermia.'

The orderly comes to his side. Anton gets out taking the blanket and tells the man to prepare a hot-water bottle and to call the doctor.

'I don't need the doctor.'

He comes round to her side of the car.

'There's nothing wrong with me,' she says, but he lifts her out anyway, laying her over his shoulder like she's a loaded sack. In the rear of the jeep, Pav starts to whine.

The air in the apartment feels dense with heat. Anton carries her through the hall and into her bedroom, kicking back the door and lowering her onto the bed. He looks round the room at the clothes tumbled everywhere.

She watches him gather scarves from the rug and return them to the wardrobe. 'I'm sorry for your trouble today. It wasn't my intention to inconvenience you.'

He pulls the chair from her desk and sits, dropping his head into his hands. 'I doubt you even thought of me.'

'That's not true.'

'Isn't it?'

'I promise you, Anton, I didn't mean to cause trouble.'

'So will you also promise me not to try this again?'

She doesn't know what there is to say to that.

'Don't forget Pav. He hates being alone. Will you send the orderly for him?'

'What?'

'Pav'll be very hungry and cold, he needs bringing in.'

The orderly knocks on the door and Anton goes to speak to him in the hall. When he comes back into the bedroom he tucks the chair under the desk and hands her a hot-water bottle.

'Did you tell him about Pav?'

'With your permission,' he says.

'My permission for what?'

He sits down on the bed beside her and he lifts her boot onto his knee. He begins to undo her laces. 'This foot is like ice.'

'You don't have to do this. I can manage.'

'The physician will be here shortly.'

She sits up. 'Anton, please, there's no need. I know it was a stupid thing to do, but I'm fine, really. I don't want a doctor. Please, Anton, send him away.'

He turns to look at her.

'Very well, as you wish.'

He gets up to go to the phone and she lies back on the bed, clutching the hot-water bottle against her chest. Now she's in the warm her body is starting to throb. She will sleep where she is, with one boot still on for that matter. Her eyes close.

And then Anton is in front of her, looking down.

'I'm fine,' she says, half-opening her eyes, her voice a slur of tiredness. 'You've been kind. You're always kind but I can manage. Where's Pav, is he in yet?'

Anton doesn't answer. He turns and closes the bedroom door, then sits on the mattress beside her and continues to unlace her boots. She lies like a stuffed doll, leaned forwards and back as he removes her coat and her hat and her gloves. Her feet are lifted onto his lap.

'This is how frostbite starts, Lena.' He caps his hands over her toes, squeezing the joints, working warmth from his skin into hers. 'Tell me,' he says quietly, 'is it really so miserable here with me?'

She shakes her head slightly. It is so heavy. Her eyelids ache.

'What can I do, Lena? There must be something.'

'I don't know, Anton,' she mumbles. 'Honestly I don't.'

He looks at her. 'Because I love you, Lena. You must see that.'

She can barely keep her eyes open.

'You're tired, forgive me, now is not the time for this.' He pulls back the bed covers. 'You were out for hours in sub-zero temperatures. Let's get you under the blankets, it's essential we get your core warm.'

He pulls the blankets over her shoulders and tucks the hot-water bottle beside her. He lays an extra woollen blanket over the counterpane, and she closes her eyes and waits to hear him leave.

But there are other sounds in the room, movement and rustling. She forces her lips to move. 'What are you doing, Anton?'

'It's essential we get you warm.'

'I am warm.'

But he doesn't seem to hear her speak. When she forces her eyes open she sees a blur of him sitting on the chair by the desk with his coat off. He is pulling at his boots. He's unfastening his jacket, working down the buttons one at a time.

Of course she needs to speak now. She needs to say something like, 'Shouldn't you do that in your own room?' Or, 'Please leave, I'm tired', or anything; she should say anything at all that will stop him from removing his tunic in her room. But all that ice seems to have frozen her throat.

'Anton . . .' she says. 'Anton, please.'

He's unbuckling his belt and stepping out of his trousers. He's folding them over the back of the chair and unhooking his spectacles from his ears. His skin is pale. Blond hairs curl from his vest, hairs lie flat like thin threads on his narrow blue shins. 'With your permission, Lena, we'll make you warm.'

'Anton, please.'

'It's all right, Lena, it's all going to be all right.' And he comes in his socks and underwear to her bed.

She can go anywhere she likes when her eyes are closed, this is the thing. There's no need to stay in this room where the mattress is sagging and Anton's body is pressing down next to hers. There's no need to feel his breath on her cheek as he tells her she'll be warm soon enough, that this is what must be done in cases of hypothermia, it's standard procedure, the only way.

She can take herself to a library full of the books she needs to read for the first term. Better still, she can fly home to her own bedroom to read them with the view of Ulrich's cows grazing in the field below, a cup of honey tea on the desk.

If she turns her face to the wall, she can go anywhere she likes, and she won't hear Anton speaking in her ear, 'Oh, little Lena, whatever were you doing out there? You can't go running off in this climate, my dear, impulsive girl.' She won't feel his hand moving on her hair. 'You gave me such a fright. Are you sleeping now? Because you need to rest, you need to recover your strength.'

As he talks, she feels the weight of him shift, and the top button at the neck of her blouse begins to move in the fabric, popping from its hole. One after the other, from her throat to her belly, buttons are pressed through. The flaps of her blouse are pulled from the waistband of her skirt, each side folding back, as though she is a cabinet opening on its hinges. 'Let's just make you comfortable,' Anton is saying in her ear. 'You'll sleep better this way. Are you warm?'

Anton is talking and talking. He's speaking of the mountains in summer. There are many beautiful hikes they can make when her leg is strong. The waterfall is perfect for summer bathing. All the families go to the pastures for picnics in August. Children love to play in the streams and climb trees. A wonderful summer lies ahead. Lena's skirt is being rolled above her waist. 'Are you asleep? Are you warm?'

Go somewhere warm.

She could run with Pav along the river in August sun or roll with Danushka down the slope of her grand lawn.

Why then does she find herself looking into the face of a gypsy laughing in the dark of a caravan? Why is that where her mind takes her?

Lena would even stay with this old woman, but the caravan is flying up into the sky, and the woman is pointing at the curtain, telling Lena to leave as she came, to get out because she can't fly, not the way gypsies can fly.

Two people can become very proud of each other, Anton is whispering, a good life can built between them, but it requires both of them to believe it's possible. And it is possible if you keep trying. Lena knows that, doesn't she? Just like him, she believes anything is achievable if you try your hardest. There is this ambition in both of them. This is something they share.

Suddenly her eyes are wide open and they won't close, not even to blink. It's like the lids have been peeled from her eyeballs.

His face is over hers. His eyelids pouched, the tips of his moustache dangling. His eyes meet hers and look away. He's fumbling between his legs, his breath quickening, holding a thing in his hand that is not her. 'Don't be afraid. There's said to be pleasure for you in it.'

'No,' she says – at least she thinks she says this, but it may be that her tongue is stitched to the floor of her mouth. Her heart is not her own, that is certain, it must be the heart of a shrew she once dissected, hammering a thousand beats in a minute.

'I'd never hurt you, Lena, you know I'd never hurt you.'

She feels a motion at her pants, a hard tug and a ripping, and they are pulled aside. Now she knows what's different – he's no longer wearing undershorts. His body moves above her own like a slab tilting over a grave. She can feel his dry thighs and the shaft of his penis knocking against her, the bristles of hair at its base. A cry forms in her, a bubble in her throat.

He's parting her legs, lifting and bending them at the knee. 'You mustn't be afraid. It's right we do this. It's time to do this, Lena.' His pale eyes narrow in their pouches above her. 'It's what we have to do.'

Lena tries to fly up from her body. She makes it as far as the ceiling, but can go no further. She cannot fly. From there she looks down and watches everything that happens to her on the bed.

Flickers of silver dance in front of her vision. They crouch and leap so at first Lena thinks them fish moving in the reeds in the San, where she's running with Pav. It takes time to see the silver for what it really is: sunlight catching the rim of a tray on her desk. Her encyclopaedia has been closed and returned to the bookshelf to make room for this tray. Sunlight hits a boiled egg's brown dome and a rack of toast. There's a gleaming coffee pot and white china cup, a folded napkin, and a sprig of spruce in a slim glass vase.

Her body is limp. It is an abstract entity, unfamiliar to her. But her head, this she feels weighted against the pillow like a boulder. She can't stop staring at the tray, cloudy thoughts drifting in her mind, evading her grasp. For a while she was dreaming of running with Pav by the river. The dream had been as real as this room. A moment ago it was the only place she existed. If she touches her cheek it might still be cold from the breeze rolling across the marshes. She closes her eyes willing a return. But the vision is thin and tearing like dawn mist.

There's a glass of water on the tray. Minute bubbles cling to its inner sides. She'd like to drink this water. But when she sits up she's transfixed by the sight of her arms. The nightdress she's wearing is unfamiliar; a short-sleeved cambric smock in cornflowerblue. Surely she's in another dream. Then she remembers. It must be her mother's. Ulka packed it for the summer months. But there's all that snow on the roof outside. It isn't summer yet.

She moves to reach for the glass of water on the tray and a stabbing pain between her legs makes her gasp. Sliding her hand under the sheets she pulls up the nightdress and puts a finger inside herself, wincing. When she takes it out, it's stained bright red. It smells of blood and carbolic soap. And there's something else – an unfamiliar odour her school friends have sniggered about during biology lessons.

Lena wipes her finger on the front of her cornflower-blue smock. She creeps her body down under the bedcovers until all sunlight is gone. Here in the dark a sound trickles from her mouth, an animal whimpering she can't stop. Outside the bedcovers the sunlight moves off the tray and onto the floor. It moves along the far wall and leaves the room.

'My dear child, are you ill? Or are we playing hidey games? You cannot still be sleeping, that much is clear.' A woman's voice is speaking in the bedroom, close to Lena's face. 'I've been on the step knocking for quite some time. Thank goodness the orderly let me in. You must know it's past noon, half the day is gone.'

The counterpane is peeled away from Lena's head.

'But I didn't ask you to come,' she says without opening her eyes.

'It was your dear husband who requested I stop by, and I'm very glad I did. Are you unwell in some way? It wouldn't surprise me if you were. I heard about your little adventure in the snow. A blessed miracle you were spotted at all. Anton is having a Mass said in the chapel, I believe. Whatever were you thinking, my dear? And with this leg?'

'Go.'

There is a moment of complete silence in the room. Perhaps also the world.

'I beg your pardon?'

'Please could you just go.'

'Go?'

Lena whispers as loud as she can. 'I'm very tired, Mrs Machek.'

'Misha please.'

'I'm sure you'd like to hear that I'm grateful to you for coming, but I'd prefer it if you could leave me alone.'

'Well I . . .'

Lena hears a tut, followed by several more, rather as if an abacus was totting up an unnecessarily costly purchase. A sigh comes with the reckoning.

'My child, I fear it is incumbent on me to now speak plainly. I believe your mother would want this from me, as I would wish it for my own daughters should the circumstances necessitate. I must tell you the truth without a drop of varnish and I'm afraid you will have to listen.' Mrs Machek clears her throat. 'Firstly I must say you are lucky to have a husband who wishes to find a wife foolish enough to take herself off in the snow. There are men here who would gladly leave their helpmates to the frost, if not the wolves, yes, I am afraid that is so. But Major Bem was a man out of his wits yesterday. Therefore I must ask you to consider whether it was fair to behave in such a selfish fashion? Is this what the man deserves after his many kindnesses? After all those months spent nursing you back to health?'

'He had his reasons, Mrs Machek.'

'I beg your pardon?'

'He had his reasons for staying around.'

'That, my dear, is a very low thing to say.'

There's a period of silence, presumably to allow Lena to contemplate on her lowness, then a further string of tuts culminating in a second sigh. 'Woman to woman, I fear I must continue to speak frankly, Mrs Bem. Your husband is nothing if not a good man. However, he's been embarrassed by your actions, there can be no question about that. People talk and they are saying the major cannot keep his wife – even a young lame one, taken not from society but the provinces. I am sorry, my dear, but this is only what people are saying. If it happens again, well, let me simply say no husband likes to be humiliated in front of his colleagues, especially not a military man. Spousal nudges in

the quiet of the home are all well and good, but public performances, my dear, these are not the thing at all.'

'It might need removing.'

Lena has opened her eyes.

'What, dear?'

'The mole on your chin. Have you had it assessed for malignancy?'

Mrs Machek laughs, touching herself lightly. 'What a strange
creature you seem at times, Mrs Bem.'

'People surprise you, Misha.'

Mrs Machek opens her mouth to speak then decides against
it. Lena watches her turn to take a good look around the small
room.

'All these clever books you have here. Can you understand
them?'

'I try.'

'Well, you mustn't stop.'

'Excuse me?'

'Don't ever stop all this reading, promise me that.'

Lena looks up curiously. 'I don't intend to.'

'Your ambition is to be a doctor?'

'Why, was it yours?'

Mrs Machek laughs. But the sound lacks its customary peal.
'It was the bar I dreamed of. I was the best debater in my school.'

'What happened?'

'What always happens to our sex, my dear.'

Suddenly Lena is gulping and Mrs Machek is at the bed, taking Lena's shoulders.

'Cry it out, child. They say it's imaginary but I know of one
girl who never made it through her homesickness, a terrible tragedy that one. But this won't be the way for you, my dear. You're
a tough little nut, I can see.' Mrs Machek reaches into her handbag and brings out a folded handkerchief and a flask. 'My very
own medical equipment. Blow your nose and then you take a
nice big sip for me. There we go. Can you taste the plums? What

did I tell you, it's a miracle worker, I can already see some colour back in your cheeks. What a lovely complexion you have, pretty as a swallow's blush, it's no wonder your husband's smitten.' Mrs Machek takes a gulp for herself. 'Day by day things will begin to feel better. Don't look so doubtful. I promise you, it happens the world over. Every nest is flown and each fledgling finds strength in their wings. It is only nature's way.'

'Some don't. Some fledglings fall and break their wings or they starve.'

Mrs Machek avails herself of a second drink. 'That is also nature's way. But spring is ahead of us, and the alpine flowers are something to be seen. Now let's get you up and into a bath. It's also in the way of human nature for a man to like his wife presentable.'

She doesn't know where to go after the bathroom so she sits at her desk watching words slide on pages. Pav lies with his chin on her feet. At five o'clock she hears Anton return, talking in the hall with the orderly. From the gramophone in the sitting room comes the trickling sound of a Chopin prelude. She gets up from the desk and wedges the chair under the door handle.

Some minutes later Anton's slippers are moving across the parquet in the hall. Lena steps back in her room, her folded arms tight across her chest, her heart beating against her ribs. Eventually she hears a tap on her door and before she finds her voice to stop it, the handle turns, but the door is held shut by the chair.

'Lena, my dear, are you well?' His voice is low on the other side of the wood. 'I was wondering because Misha Machek—'

'Stay away from me,' she hears herself say, her voice high and thin.

Silence. Only Chopin from the sitting room.

'Lena, my dear, I wondered if I might come in and speak to you—'

'I said stay away.' She steps back shaking her head. 'Please stay away.'

Anton might be taking off his glasses now, or else shifting his feet. 'I don't mind saying I find this a little troubling, my dear. Is there's anything I can get you?'

'I'm studying,' she whispers.

The prelude comes to an end. The apartment is very quiet. She doesn't even know if he's still behind the door. Then she hears a cough.

'I'll ask the orderly to bring in a plate of stew. Misha said the breakfast tray was untouched. If you're disposed to it, perhaps you might join me by the fire for a hand of rummy later. Have a think. I wanted to tell you I spotted a female white-tailed eagle today. We were out in the mountains setting up a telegraph system and she circled overhead. I fancy she was curious to discover what we were up to. A wingspan of more than two metres, grey plumage and great fingered wings. Large but extremely graceful.' He pauses. 'I thought you'd like to know.'

A few moments later Anton's slippers recede down the hall. Lena folds her arms and stands until she is no longer shaking, and goes to bed.

A letter lies beside her plate when she goes to breakfast the next day. Anton glances up as she sits. He is dark under the eyes. He has not started on his egg.

Lena pours coffee and takes toast, buttering the slice thickly because she finds she is very hungry and somehow it matters that he see this.

The letter is an airmail sheet, almost transparent with a British stamp. She gobbles her toast, licking her finger and running it over the turquoise handwriting on the folded paper and all of a sudden she's grinning, ripping the seams.

Dan. Who else would write with such freakish timing, asking if Lena's still alive after marriage and whether the leg is bearing up and when's she going to Kraków? That done the rest of the sheet is crammed with the details of a deep attachment to her Ovid lecturer who happens to be married – currently. Her family, she says in parentheses, have sailed for Argentina. Dan is staying in Cambridge. But the college food is dreadful and the British seem to think drabness a style imperative. In a postscript, she asks for news from the mountain to distract from her *amor peribat*.

Lena folds the sheet and butters a second slice of toast.

'Good news?' Anton asks. He has still not taken his spoon to his egg.

'All news from friends is good.'

He's about to say something more, then he simply stands and turns to the window. 'You know, Lena, in a couple of days all this snow will start to melt . . .' He stops, like a man who has stepped on one stone across rapids and is unsure whether to venture further. 'It's extraordinary how green the world becomes in these parts. Everything unclenches and comes to life. You haven't seen it yet but spring is wonderful here for anyone who loves nature as much as you or I.' He turns from the window. 'I was also thinking about what you said and you're right, we should make arrangements for contacting your parents on the telephone. I'm sure Mrs Machek will be able to help with that.'

'You want me to call home?' She stares across at him. 'You're not concerned about what I might tell them?'

He comes down the room and sends the orderly to the kitchen.

'I'm not sure what you mean,' he says quietly, taking the chair beside her. The smell of camphor is strong on his skin. She sees soap like a rind in the rim of his nails.

'My dear. If you're referring to the matter I tried to raise with you last night—'

'*If* I am?'

'Then perhaps you'd allow me to effect an explanation.'

'I would have thought you don't believe you need one.'

'Lena, please understand . . .' His voice is a whisper addressed to the table. 'I must tell you I regret what happened deeply . . .'

She clenches her hands in her lap to stop them trembling.

'Will you believe me if I say I lost myself for a moment? That the better part of me fell prey to a moment of desire. If I was driven by anything in this matter it was an excess of love.'

Suddenly the chair is on the floor behind Lena. She's standing over him, looking down at him. 'An explanation won't be necessary.'

'Please, Lena, I feel so much for you I must explain how—'.

'Stop.' Her hand is flying up, without a conscious decision to raise it. It might not even be a limb, but a barrier held against a storm tide. 'Please just stop.'

She stands with her palm in the air between them holding back his words. Her hand falls to her side and she takes Dan's letter from the table and heads for the door. 'I've changed my mind about contacting home. They have worries enough. Would I add to them with my truths? Or were you thinking I should distract them with some lies?'

Then she walks out of the room.

In her bedroom Lena tears a page from her notepad and writes down a list of necessities. She sends the orderly to the depot.

That afternoon she hammers a latch on her bedroom door and a hook on the door jamb. The hammer she puts on the floor under the bed. She checks it for reach. After this she sits at her desk and writes to Danushka.

> *News from the mountain:*
> *I have become a woman. Or, to put it another way, I'm no longer what I was. The event did not occur in a manner of my choosing but I'm trying not to think about that. I read it's good mental hygiene to do so after instances of trauma. With my husband I am trying to forbear until Kraków. Recent events make me certain of my course. How long ago it seems, that afternoon in your summer house with the goddamn brandy (and that goddamn tram), I shouldn't look back but I do, and I almost believe it was a different person's life. Goddamn it, I miss it. I miss us.*

That evening she puts Liszt on the gramophone in the sitting room and sits to play Patience while her husband files papers at the bureau desk in the corner. When he has finished they play rummy in silence by the hearth.

In early March alpine plants force bright tips through the snow. The pines shrug off the last crusts of ice, sending them crashing. It's as Anton said, all around the barracks and army buildings, the mountain is casting out winter. Grass and earth and bushes emerge sodden but triumphant.

Each morning after breakfast Lena goes walking through the forest, Pav zigzagging in pursuit of squirrels. Some days she doesn't even use a cane. There's a path she's found that emerges to a panoramic view of the summit range. Some days she takes Anton's binoculars and leans against a warm limestone crag, tracking the white-tailed eagle to her nest in a copse beneath the snowline. In the meadow, primroses and saxifrage start to show their heads, then heart's-ease and crocuses emerge, dotting the green slopes with yellow and purple far into the distance. Lena gathers posies as she walks and arranges them in tea glasses around the apartment. The sight of the mountain flowers makes her smile.

There are other discoveries Lena makes this spring. She learns it's possible to cultivate a version of a self just as scientists are now cultivating cells on Petri dishes. It's easy enough for this self to smile at herring-soaked colonels and gossiping wives and even, on a good day, enjoy some aspects of embroidery. She shares this finding with Danushka. *Don't scoff but it's true,* she writes, *stitching needlepoint patterns can be imagined as a journey along the route of the arteries. Suturing can be practised if you choose to see closing a cushion that way.*

And in the evening, while her husband reads newspapers, or communication reports, or writes up sightings of white-tailed eagles, she sits across the hearth in a neat dress quietly turning cards. Twice now she has handed him a slip of paper with her own sightings jotted down.

Is this what comes to form our identity as much as any inner notion we might hold of ourselves? Lena writes, responding to Dan's five sheets detailing the consummation of her passion for the Ovid lecturer. *Is the brutal truth that we let the course of our lives – indeed our very character – take shape according to what others expect of us?*

Speak for yourself! Danushka replies in a short note. *But stop dressing everything in riddles! and tell me WHAT'S ACTUALLY GOING ON!*

But of course that would suppose Lena knows what's happening. And she isn't sure. Only that life is not so bad and that she must simply keep on. There are barely six months until she starts at Kraków, and perhaps time will pass quickly enough when ignored.

As if in proof of this, April arrives like a surprise, with Easter to be thought about and gifts to be sent home. Lena realises it would not be unreasonable to visit. She might even do it without warning and turn up for the Sunday feast, bringing crocheted doilies and dried flower arrangements to amaze them all. For a few days this plan cheers her and she makes a special expedition to gather flowers. But one morning she wakes with barely enough energy to get out of bed.

'Not hungry?' Anton's voice, at breakfast, seems to come from a long way off.

Lena looks at the unbroken boiled egg on her plate. The thought of the odour inside is appalling to her. She presses a napkin to her mouth.

'Embroidery is it today?'

'Excuse me?'

Anton's at the window, his binoculars trained on the tree-tops. 'Your sewing group. What marvels are you stitching at the moment?'

She can't think.

He puts away his binoculars and comes down the room to her. 'Lace doilies? Easter bonnets?'

She can smell the coffee on his breath.

'We're making rag dolls for the village children. I'm not sure what to stuff in my doll's head.'

'No doubt Misha will advise.' His hands press lightly on her shoulders and then he is out of the room and down the hall to his Madonna. He tends to pause a little longer with her these days. The front door closes and Lena drops her head listening to the clock's second hand making its rounds.

Most of all she'd like to go back to bed, but she drags herself to the embroidery group to save herself the knock on the door that an absence would provoke. She takes a seat by the open window where the air is inoffensive. But it seems she's barely selected her thread when Mrs Machek comes up and asks her into the hall, advising, in a whisper, a visit to the garrison nurse.

'Because I yawn over my stitching? Thank you for your concern, but I didn't sleep so well, that's all.'

'Because you can't bear to share the room with a coffee pot, and your head droops at ten in the morning. Because you say you can smell my cucumbers when the kitchen's three doors away. Any mother knows the meaning of these things. Mrs Bem – Lena, forgive me asking, child, but how long is it since your last bleed?'

It can't be true.

The thought beats inside Lena's head like a thing alive. She's running from the Macheks' apartment, pulling on her coat, a rag doll falling on the path. Misha is behind her, blathering about understandable shocks and unexpected joys, and how a mother recognises these feelings, a mother isn't wrong.

Never mind the ladies staring out of the sitting-room window, Lena is shouting as she runs. 'Actually you are wrong about this, Mrs Machek, completely wrong, do you understand?'

'Mrs Bem, please wait, the paving is slippy and your condition vulnerable.'

'I have no manner of condition, do you hear? I'm tired, that's all. What you presume isn't possible. Even if it were, it's none of your goddamn business. You'll mention this to no one. No one, you hear?'

Why won't the goddamn woman shut the door?

A truck passes on the track. The stench of diesel is overwhelming, causing her to stop and retch. When she straightens, wiping her mouth, Mrs Machek is picking up the doll and heading inside. The faces at the window retreat into shadows.

It can't be true.

She returns to the apartment in a daze.

Inside the hall reeks of beeswax. She runs to the bathroom. There's a fresh block of soap on the sink. She gags, vomiting into the basin, rubbing her forehead against the cold ceramic, avoiding her face in the mirror.

There was a smell of this soap between her legs the morning after he'd lain with her. It was there with the blood and the soreness when she stepped into the bath to wash him away. It's here now; its smell embedded in the pores of her skin. Shaking, she elbows the soap into the bin. She wets a towel and presses it to her throat and neck.

The apartment is silent, but for the sound of clocks marking time.

It would have been quiet like this when he got up from her bed and gathered his clothing and did – what was it he did next? Undress her? Clean her? Hunt for a gown? What order was it all done in? Why can't she remember? She was there. She should be able to remember what he did. He would have had to remove her stockings and torn pants, and turn her or reach behind to unclip her brassiere at the back. Everything would have come off – she'd have had to be stripped to her skin like a corpse before he put the nightdress on. Did he look at her then – like a mortician? Did he touch her? Where did he touch? And the smell of soap, the soap which meant he must have—

A figure's standing in the hall.

The towel drops from her hands.

'Anton.'

He walks up and hands it back to her. 'I heard retching. Are you well?'

She is holding the towel to her mouth. She turns away. She doesn't want his eyes on her. She doesn't want to think about how they must have looked her over when he returned to her room with a basin to wash between her legs. She doesn't want his body's scent near her. That soap. A new block it had been.

'You look very green, Lena.'

'Something I ate, that's all.'

'Are you sure I can't get you anything?'

She shakes her head, her gaze on the bathroom floor, the square black and white tiles between her stockinged feet. She keeps a foot on each colour. 'I didn't think you were here.'

'I mislaid some paperwork.'

She stares at her feet on the tiles. A thin ladder runs from a hole in the stocking at her left toe.

'Well, if you're sure there's nothing I can do . . .'

He walks down the hall and opens the front door. 'There's a screening of a new Warsaw comedy in the Mess tonight. I think it features that actress you like. I'll stop by the Macheks and see if they're going. Might you be interested if you're feeling improved?'

She doesn't look up. A great dizziness is rising in her. There's a crack along the white tile beneath her foot. If she doesn't keep a hold of the sink, a thing of solid substance, she might fall through this crack. She might never stop.

'We can decide later,' he says, a world away from her. 'Get some rest.' The front door closes.

In her room she sits on the edge of the bed.

She can't remember the basin he used, its colour or shape. Was it enamel or porcelain? A bowl from the kitchen presumably. It must have been while she slept that he'd brought it in and opened her legs to soap her down. Were the sheets soiled? Had he noticed this and rolled her aside, taking the linen to the incinerator late at night like a murderer with evidence to burn? Or did he leave it as a job for the orderlies? Did he think if everything was clean when she woke she wouldn't recall what had happened? But she was there. It happened.

She gets up and pulls the sheet off the bed. There, it's there on the mattress, a rust-coloured stain. It's been there waiting to be brought into the light. If she spreads her palm, she can almost cover the stain. She lies down and closes her eyes, trying to shut off images unspooling in her mind: the bending and parting of her legs, the head of his penis jabbing then pushing then shunting inside her; the burning splitting friction as her body gave way. His spittled teeth, and the hiss between them, as he shuddered and fell down against her at the end of it. And through it all, her silence as this was done to her. A silence she kept between them like a shield.

But look, it had been no shield.

A curious dream comes to her as she lies on the mattress.

It's a dream of an easy death; of falling down the slope of a snowy mountain, tumbling through softness, so in fact it doesn't really feel to her like a death at all. At the bottom of the mountain she finds herself rolling into a warm lake where she floats at first, rocking in the shallows. It's comfortable here, but buffeted by waves and pulled by the tide, her body begins to drift towards deeper water. Liquid slips inside her, seeping into her stomach and lungs. Slowly now she sinks beneath the surface, through darkening blues, to a place far from the world in which she was born. She comes to rest on a silt floor and she watches the last bubbles of air slip from her mouth. They rise up like a ladder that has served its purpose and is being lifted away.

Lena wakes from this dream feeling refreshed. She remakes the bed, then pulls undergarments from her drawer and packs them in a satchel. 'Please summon a jeep as a matter of urgency', this is what she tells the orderly. 'Pavlov is showing signs of distress and requires a vet.' Finally she goes into the sitting room and takes the money box from the bureau.

'So you're feeling improved?'

She turns, her purse open, banknotes in her hand. Anton is standing in the doorway looking flushed and out of breath.

She pushes the banknotes into her purse. 'Anton. I didn't hear you come in.'

'The orderly mentioned you require a jeep?'

'Pav's not well. One of the wives recommended a vet down the mountain who has an understanding of canine conditions.'

'You wouldn't think of consulting me?'

She closes her purse and moves towards the door. 'It's quite urgent. You'll have to excuse me.'

But he doesn't step aside. He comes into the sitting room, shutting the door behind him. Nothing is said for a moment. Anton has his back against the door.

'The dog seems fine.'

'He isn't.'

'Forgive me, Lena, but I must ask you to tell me the truth about why you need the jeep.'

'I told you.'

'You did. But garrison policy prohibits the requisitioning of vehicles for domestic animals.' He removes his spectacles, taking a handkerchief from a pocket inside his overcoat to clean the lenses. 'But that isn't the reason you want the transport.'

For a moment no response comes to her. He hooks his spectacles back on and tucks away the cloth. 'I think we both know that.'

Lena stares at him and suddenly she laughs once, hard. 'God be damned, Anton. She told you. That woman told you, didn't she?'

'If you mean Misha, she shared some thoughts with me out of concern for your welfare.'

'Lucky me to have such a good friend.'

'Indeed.'

He's not moving, not a step from the door.

'Anton, please,' she says quietly, 'I need to borrow that jeep. We can talk about whatever you like when I'm back.'

'Come and sit down with me, Lena. Just for a moment.'

'No, thank you. No, I don't think I will.'

'I see. Well then, you must listen to me carefully' – and he begins to speak in a slow, soft voice; it's as if she's a wild creature that mustn't be startled, at least not before a net can be fetched – 'I understand you may be feeling anxious, that's only natural, but I must ask you to confirm if it's true what Maria told me about your condition.'

'Did you wash me?'

'I beg your pardon?'

She steps towards him. 'After you'd done your business with me?'

He recoils as if slapped.

'Only it's the thing I can't recall. Obviously I remember the pain and your spit and grunting – but afterwards . . .' she shakes her head. 'I don't know. Isn't that strange? I'd like to remember, Anton, that's the thing. I'd like to know what you did to me.'

The clock alone moves in the silence between them. She holds his gaze. 'Well?'

'You should know I didn't ever intend to act in a way that would distress you.'

'Should I know that?'

'Lena, please. I understand you're upset, but please believe me when I say what occurred between us arose from an excess of love. I was tempted in the moment, I was weak, it had been several days since our wedding and—'

'Just the facts, Anton, just tell me the facts concerning that night. Did you wash me?'

Outside, orders are being shouted on the track. A lorry passes and the window vibrates. Anton looks away, clearing his throat. 'You were exhausted. I didn't want you to wake up in the morning and be afraid when you saw the blood.'

'How considerate of you.'

'I'm sorry, Lena. You must understand me when I say I'm more sorry than you'll know.' His hand is lifting towards her, wanting to touch her arm or shoulder. She backs away.

'No need to apologise. After all, as you say you were only helping yourself to what's legally yours.'

For a moment he stares, stunned. His mouth opens and closes.

'Would you believe me, Lena, if I said it isn't that some people can't feel but that they feel too much, and it's this that drives them to actions they'll regret for the rest of their lives? Would it help you to know they'll never forgive themselves even if others come to see what happened as a moment of aberration, not the definition of their character. Please, Lena. Please know it isn't who I am. It's not who I want to be.'

But as he stands in front of her, his red-rimmed eyes avoiding hers, she understands there may as well be a chasm opening in the floor between them. When she watches him talk it's like she's looking at a far-off actor speaking his lines in a language she doesn't know – a man from a different country, a place she'll never travel to because it will always be too far away. She is suddenly weary.

'It's not right, is it, Anton? You know that as well as I do. We shouldn't have this life, that's the truth; it's the wrong one for both of us. It's like a sea creature and a land animal trying to exist in the same place. One or the other will always be struggling to breathe. You must see that, don't you?'

'I know you didn't want me. You think I was blind to that?'

'Yet you decided to have me anyway.'

The clock on the mantelpiece chimes the quarter hour and the sound fades.

'How can you want us to do this for even a second longer?' she whispers. 'Even if you had certain hopes before, you know I'll never be able to find love for you now. Perhaps it's best if I make arrangements to return home.'

'Home?'

'We can wait out the terms of the contract without any more unhappiness between us. It'll be easier for us both to get on with our lives that way.'

He stares at her.

She hears the sound of an engine idling outside the apartment.

'I have to go,' she says.

'Go?' He moves towards her. 'But we haven't discussed the present situation.' And she realises that in the other country, where he belongs but not her, her condition is not an impediment to be removed, but a thing of wonder. And with a lurch she sees it is also a padlock that might fasten two people from different worlds together.

'I have to go now, Anton. Could you step aside.'

'Is it true? Lena, I have to know.'

She opens her purse and rifles the notes, a tremor in her hands. 'I'm not sure if I've enough. Do you have any spare money?'

'Forgive me, I don't understand what you mean.'

'I was wondering if you had any idea of price? Perhaps one of your friends knows the going rate in the valley villages? It would be best to take more than enough to cover the cost, don't you think? It's not the sort of thing I'd want to haggle over.'

His expression stiffens. There's a knock at the sitting-room door.

'I'll just be a moment,' she calls. 'Would you like to come with me, Anton?'

'With you?'

'For the procedure?'

He looks at her, colour gone from his face.

'You don't think I could keep it in me,' she says, 'knowing how it started?'

'For the love of God, do you have any idea what you're saying? You're talking about—'

'Excising a malignancy – an unwanted growth.' She finds she's smiling at him, smiling with relief, because it's been said now, the way forward can be seen by them both. Papa always told her this when she was small and in a fury with Ala for some reason or other: *There's a reasonable solution that works for the two of you. Go and find it.* 'This is it,' she tells Anton. 'A reasonable solution for us both.'

'Lena,' he whispers, 'you're not thinking straight.'

'I disagree.'

'You can't possibly believe I'd let you do this.'

'But it's the only answer. There isn't another. Surely you can see that.'

The jeep's horn sounds outside. Anton looks up after the noise. His expression hardens. He steps towards her. 'Listen to me. This is insanity.'

'How so?'

'There's the danger to you for one thing. I could never allow my wife to subject herself to an insanitary procedure that might threaten her life.'

'Your wife?'

'Yes, Lena. My wife.'

Behind Anton the walls of the room seem to vibrate and bend. Rage rises in her. She tastes its heat on her tongue. 'But every action comes with a risk. I'm surprised they didn't teach you that at military school. Besides it's hardly a novel operation. It must go on everywhere women are made pregnant by men.'

She makes a move to pass him for the door. He grabs her coat sleeve, his hand gripping her elbow, pinching to her bone.

She tries to pull away but he holds her.

For a moment she's too shocked to speak. She looks into his face. That cold high cliff.

'Let me go.'

'I'm sorry, Lena. You're young, you hear things without understanding the full implications. Rash decisions are easily taken when you lack experience. This is an impulse of youth. The only thing it sows is regret.'

She looks at his thumbnail pressed bloodless above her elbow. 'Let go of me.'

'Lena, listen. What you're talking about is illegal. It goes against the laws of man and God.'

'No one has to find out. If they do, you can blame me, say you didn't know.'

'People already know, Lena. Everyone hears everything in this place. They know I know.'

'Do you care that much for their opinions?'

'My family would be shamed and yours. The consequences would be unimaginable. I'd lose my commission. They could lock you up. Is that what you want?'

'Take your hand from my arm. You're hurting me.'

There's a louder knock on the door.

Anton lets go of Lena. 'Enter.'

The orderly salutes and announces that the jeep is waiting outside.

Anton doesn't take his eyes off Lena. 'Send it away.' After a moment he follows the soldier into the hall, shutting the sitting-room door behind him.

Lena stands very still listening to the faint mumble of voices. The room is cold and she shivers, clutching her purse.

When Anton returns a few moments later he's without his overcoat. He walks without looking at her to the fireplace. Outside the window the jeep is driven away.

'Let's sit down for a moment.'

'No, thank you.'

'We should take some tea perhaps. Collect ourselves.'

'No, thank you.'

'I'm sorry I held your arm as I did.'

She looks at the door. It can't be more than seven or eight steps away.

Anton runs his finger up and down the mantelpiece tapping the wood.

'This isn't a terrible event, Lena,' he says quietly, his back to her.

She makes no answer.

'Most people would think it quite the opposite in fact. With time perhaps you'll come to see this news for the blessing it is.'

'A blessing?'

'Presumably there's now a heartbeat?'

'There'll be other heartbeats in the world.'

Anton is staring into the grate. 'It's a sacred thing. A life is forming, one with as much right to existence as you or I. It's the life of our child, a being with a beating heart that will have a smile one day, and a future all its own. Perhaps it'll be a girl with her mother's blue eyes and joyous laughter.' He turns around to face her. 'We've no right to take that life away. Whatever we did to be in this position it's clear God wanted this child to exist. He chose us for parents, Lena. It's a sacred undertaking.'

'Whatever *we* did?'

'I've no doubt you'll come to love the baby with all the breath you have. You'll be a wonderful mother, I know it.'

Lena laughs darkly. 'You think?'

'To talk as you do, is nothing less than to suggest murder.'

'What about my life, Anton?' Lena hears the rise in her voice, the struggle for thoughts to find air. 'What do you think God supposes will happen to that?'

'I understand you're frightened. But there isn't a woman alive who doesn't love her children.'

'I have a letter from Kraków university. I have plans.'

'And I know you'll come to adjust, Lena. I know you will. I'll do everything I can to help you.'

'I'll say it was my decision alone. I took a jeep without your knowledge. Please, Anton,' she whispers, 'After Kraków I'll do whatever you want. Only I can't have a child, not now. Not like this.'

He comes to her and he takes the purse from her hands. 'I'm sorry, Lena. What you're talking about is a mortal sin and I must forbid you. There's no more discussion to be had.'

'You can't forbid me,' she screams suddenly, running to the door. 'This is not what I want.'

He follows her out of the room, standing in the doorway, watching her run to the front door.

'This is not what I want, this is not what I want,' she screams, pulling on the handle. There is no key in the lock. 'You can't forbid me, this is not what I want.'

The door doesn't open.

He watches her slide to the floor.

'I can, Lena, and I'm afraid I must.'

Crying.

Somewhere now where there's crying.

The train. Yes, there's always this crying in the container.

From one moment to the next it never sounds the same. Right now someone's taken to whimpering. Earlier the noise resembled a series of barks, as if grief is a bestial business. On occasion several voices might come together in chorus; a cloud of weeping, floating above the stench on the floor, or a single throat will hiccup out sorrow. Tears might fall down onto the planks hard as lead pellets, or patter like summer rain. Inside this container she learns more sounds for sadness than human language will ever know how to say.

Is that why she's been put inside the train? Is this what she needs to learn?

He laughs in her ear. 'You think life's for learning?'

'You again.'

'Me again.'

'Touch me, bone man. I need to feel your hand on my skin. It's so dark in here, I can't see you. I need to feel you.'

'I'm here, Magdalena.'

'But I can't feel you.'

'I'm here.'

'Tell me, when will this journey end?'

'Every journey ends.'

'But when?'

'Only you have the answer to that, Magdalena.'

'But I need to know what it is I have to say when it does.'

'To me?'

'To the girl on the steppe.'

'The time for that will come.'

'But what if it doesn't? What if I'm stuck here for ever with the crying on this train?'

Silence. Nothing moves.

And suddenly she's not on the train. She's nowhere at all. Adrift in blackness.

She hears her voice start again. It is hesitant, faint as a distant echo. 'Will I see her again when my journey ends?'

He laughs, a long time he laughs to hear this.

'Oh, Magdalena, my heart's breath, why ever are you asking me?'

Tatra Mountains, Southern Poland

Sometimes, during the summer of her pregnancy, Leńa thinks she can put all the words she and her husband exchange in a week into sixty jerks of the hand on the clock. Sometimes she presses her forehead against her bedroom wall and whispers into the paint:

Tuberculosis, vascular degeneration, arteriosclerosis
Encephalitis, fistula, pneumothorax
Angina, typhus, pox

The trick is never to let words connect and never to say the same word twice. She'll put her lips against the wall and take a breath, and on the exhalation she'll incant medical conditions for as long as she can. Afterwards she'll stand back and look at the lozenge her breath has left behind. Some days she doesn't allow herself to blink until the breath vanishes and the wall has taken her words into itself to keep them safe.

For a month she doesn't leave her bedroom. She writes to no one and keeps her hands from her thickening belly. On occasion she gets up and takes the amber from her desk and lies down with it on the floor by the half-inch gap at the bottom of the door. She rolls the amber along this gap, scrutinising the turning fly within. She might do this for a minute or an hour before she returns to the bed. Anton and Maria Machek are in frequent conversation in the hall. Occasionally she creeps her ear against the woodwork to listen. Antenatal psychological norms are their preferred topics of discussion. Rarely do they try the handle.

I have become a creature of superstitions, she whispers to Danushka, whom she sometimes conjures up smoking a cheroot cross-legged beside her on the bed. *I'm seeing ghosts crawling in the paint.*

Rot and nonsense, Dan retorts, exhaling through her nostrils. *Your brain's understimulated and overindulged. Get up and find something to fill your time.*

I'm invaded, Dan. I want it gone.

And self-pity will help? Dan inhales and puffs out a chain of smoke rings. *You have to think clearly. There are still plenty of ways out. Many childless families are desperate for newborns. Once it comes there'll be alternative actions, other homes for it; families, orphanages, baskets on rivers. This isn't the end of choice.*

Easy for you to say. No one's ever trapped you. I was given no choice.

She traces the word on the wall. *Choice.*

Danushka is silent on the matter.

Do you know, Dan, sometimes, when Anton and I are facing each other in silence at different ends of the dining table, I wonder what would happen should an incision be made down the length of my stomach with the knife that has been used for slicing the pork belly. I imagine taking the tip of this knife and unpeeling myself, dropping the outermost layer of me like grape skin on the floor. I wouldn't mind the blood. I think I'd quite like to see it congealing there. That would be a choice, at least. But I look at the knife lying by the meat and I do nothing. Why?

Danushka stubs out her cheroot and starts to fade into the wall.

Because you're too busy feeling sorry for yourself, she replies as she goes.

When five months of her pregnancy have passed, Lena finds apartment keys beside her plate at the breakfast table. Anton is at the window scribbling in his notebook.

'You're taking a risk,' she says quietly touching the keys.

'My dear?'

'You presume I'm too far progressed to go down the mountain to the village women? If you do you underestimate me.'

He closes his notebook and returns to the table. 'Five barred warblers enjoyed the pumpkin seeds this morning. I was attempting a rather poor sketch of them.'

'Show me,' she hears herself say.

He looks at her.

'I'd like to see it.'

He hesitates, then brings the notebook to her. There's a slight blush on his face. 'No Matejko, you'll agree.'

'The proportions are fair enough.'

Anton glances at the notebook and shuts it. He pours himself a second coffee.

The light at the window is hard and white. Hard as a door, Lena thinks.

Anton clears his throat. 'Lena, I need to tell you I've shared our news with your family. I'd like to suggest you go home for a while, perhaps even for the birth. Understandably they're thrilled and most keen to see you.'

Her hand moves to her belly. 'You told them?'

'I'm afraid I couldn't see an alternative. Think how your mother would feel if she missed out on this important time. There's a letter for you on the sideboard.'

Lena turns and sees the envelope on the tray bearing her mother's handwriting. Torrents of lilac-scented joy will gush out when she opens it. She presses her napkin to her eyes.

Anton comes down the room and sits beside her. He puts his hand to her shoulders.

'My dear Lena, I can't tell you how it troubles me to see you like this. I had hoped you would be cheered by hearing from home.'

Her voice is barely a whisper, 'Don't let it worry you.'

'But I am worried. I would dearly like us to be friends. After all, no one can stay enemies for ever.'

She sniffs and turns to look at him. 'You think?'

'Perhaps we could try to start trusting each other.'

Lena says nothing. She blows her nose watching Anton go to the sideboard.

Lena takes the letter from him and the keys by her plate. She pushes back her chair to return to her room.

'Think about it,' he calls after her. 'Your family would love to see you. I could arrange a car by the end of the week.'

Home. She speaks the word slowly so the pain will not be a sharp one, standing in her bedroom sniffing the envelope for a trace of lilac.

Why not go home? Dan whispers at her shoulder. *What are you afraid of?*

Who says I'm afraid?

It'll be easy there. Mama and Ulka will fuss over your every need. Ala will dote. None of them will be able to keep their hands off you.

Lena puts a hand on the mound of her belly, thinking of Mama delighted by the coming of this child, no doubt also pleased by the falling away of other ideas about Lena's future. It occurs to her that Mama couldn't have planned it better.

You see how impossible it is, Dan.

And yet it twists her guts, the desire for home.

Leaving Mama's letter unopened, Lena goes walking in the forest for hours. Her leg is strong now, as strong, she thinks, as it has ever been. When she returns she tucks the letter inside her medical encyclopaedia and writes back to Mama that she feels settled for the birth where she is. It is a short note. She concocts a few lines about cravings and dreams. In a postscript she promises to visit once the infant is born. That evening she gives the letter in its envelope unsealed to Anton.

'Have a look if you want.'

He glances at her, unfolding the note. 'Are you sure about this?'

'About staying here?' She shrugs.

'You can always change your mind. Any time you want to go, tell me.'

She turns away, biting hard on her lip.

'The Macheks are planning a picnic in the meadow this weekend. It's a beautiful spot. We could join them perhaps? Have a think, don't answer me now. See how you feel.'

'No, it's all right,' she says quietly. 'We'll go.'

'Really?'

'Yes,' she says, stepping back from the sudden light in his eyes.

The leaves of the mountain ash turn orange, its berries red. The nights thicken and the first frost spikes the apartment windows. One Saturday morning Lena's standing at the stove making porridge as she now likes to do, when Anton comes into the kitchen.

'I'm not disturbing you?'

She stirs the pan waiting for what's to come.

He asks if he might touch her belly.

She turns a little towards him. She says nothing to object.

The next morning he repeats the request.

This time she lays down her spoon and unties her apron. She takes his hand and guides it to the left, beneath her ribs. 'She's kicking, can you feel it?'

'She?'

'Yes, of course, it's going to be a girl.'

A smile spreads across his face. 'I can feel it.'

'That's her heel, or an elbow.'

'Yes, I can feel it.' His eyes blink with wonder. 'Her elbow. Or her heel.'

And this then, is how it goes. Each morning he walks down the dining room and pauses by Lena's chair. 'Here,' she will say, 'a heel' or 'a fist, I think, over here' until the baby is too big to move inside her. But even after this, he comes to place his palm on the hard high dome of her stomach. Some days the clock will strike eight-thirty and he won't have moved away.

At the beginning of November, Anton is required to lead a training exercise at altitude. In his absence Mrs Machek assigns herself the duty of appearing at the door each morning to assess the descent of Lena's belly and dispense words of anticipation, as if she fears it might be lacking within the apartment. 'You wait,' she tells Lena, 'when this child comes love will reshape you. You won't be the same person after this child. Everything changes my dear. It's a wonderful thing. You just wait and see.'

Lena makes no response to this kind of talk. Once she may have laughed at such platitudes; a few months ago it would have alarmed her. Now Misha Machek's words merely wash up against her. She's grown large, an ocean liner, as she glides through the apartment from window to window watching autumn rain bend pine branches and turn gravel to mud. Books no longer strew her room, but folded stacks of muslins rise in towers from the desk, along with gowns and knitted booties provided by the embroidery wives, and packages of blankets sent from home.

One morning there's some excitement beyond the dining room: a jeep is stuck on the track in driving rain. Soldiers drop their shoulders to push against the back, and cadets pull on a rope tied to the front. They skid and slip in the mud. Lena is watching this drama so intently that she fails to notice a giving way inside her. It's only when a sensation of warmth rushes down her legs that she looks and sees fluid drenching her shoes, splashing on the floor.

The doorbell rings. She curses and shouts to the orderly to please tell Mrs Machek she's gone out. Leaning for a moment against the windowpane, she considers her soaked stockings. Ivan Pavlov is standing watching her closely.

'Come, boy,' she says and grabs his collar, dragging him into the hall. 'Don't give me that look, I've no choice either.' She calls out again to the orderly to take Pav for a walk, in fact, she calls, the dog is not to be brought back until the next morning. Her husband wishes her to have complete rest and an undisturbed night.

The first contraction comes as she bolts the front door. It doubles her over, pulling breath from her body. She grips the door frame until the pain passes, then she takes her sable from the coat-stand and goes to the bathroom where she undresses. When her body convulses a second time she's ready, dropping against the side of the bath, hissing through her teeth, pushing her forehead against cold enamel. The pain is a giant closing its fist over her. When the convulsion fades she breathes quietly, squatting, counting, waiting for the giant's return.

Her. It is a girl who slides out behind Lena onto the tiles, coming quickly in a slurry of watery blood.

Scrawny as a frog, Lena thinks, gripping the bath and staring down at the being that is shaking its fists on its back on the floor. Between them hangs the gristle tether of the umbilical cord. Beyond the bathroom door there's no sound.

Sweat falls from Lena's chin and elbows. Fluid drops from every point of her. She hangs her head, staring at the infant's heels, white with grease. A second thought rolls through her head: it is done.

The baby bellows on the tiles crimson-mouthed with rage. Elsewhere in the apartment there's silence. The front door is bolted in two places. There's no one here but her and this furious child. The child that a moment ago was not.

Lena stares at the infant's heels, and she waits for her brain to turn to joy.

But there is no joy rising in her, only a cold, congealing sensation of loss. A life has begun and one is being lost, that is what she thinks, looking down at the child. This is the exchange that has been made. That is the truth of it.

And it is like ice water in her brain, the realisation that comes to her.

Startling in its simplicity.

Because she has a choice now, in this silent, locked apartment. She can't ever say again she doesn't have a choice.

What needs to be done can happen quickly. A few seconds – no more than a minute – that's all it need take. The baby has not even opened its eyes. There will be no suffering, and after it has been done Lena's life can resume a proper course. It won't be wasted. Because this was never meant to be her life. Not here. Not this.

Lena looks down at the tiny body. A little courage is all she needs.

The baby gulps. It stops bellowing. Lena watches puffy eyelids part to reveal a murky amphibian gaze. Courage, she thinks, a minute, that's all it need take.

Lena looks away.

When she looks back, the baby is starting to shiver, its lips puckering into an O. A tip of red tongue protrudes and retreats so Lena isn't sure she's seen it.

Lena rubs her face against the bath, tears dropping in a chain from her eyes. Beneath her the baby is shivering, blinking its eyes.

Human newborns can't see, Lena tells herself, even with their eyes open.

The baby blinks again.

Crying silently Lena reaches between her legs and takes up the child. She lifts it to her breast and throws her sable over them both. She is wearier than death.

The bathroom is dark and cold when Lena wakes. She lifts the coat and looks at the shadow hunch of the infant body against her belly. She puts her face to the scalp and sniffs its mossy dampness. She uncurls a wrinkled fist then lifts each bowed leg, stretching it to see the knee straighten, pressing her thumb to the pliant bone. 'Still here, little frog?' Her voice sounds too loud in the tiled room. 'I didn't want you to come. If I'm to be honest with you, little frog, you should know this. But you're here now so I suppose we'll have to make the best of it.' And gripping the baby and its afterbirth, she pulls herself up against the bathtub and goes to the sink. She leans her face beneath a stream of water, letting it splash the back of her neck, then she drinks, unlocks the door and takes her child to bed.

*

Agata, it might be as well to name the child after Anton's dead sister. His telegram arrives the next morning, a few hours after the bolts are broken and Lena and the baby are discovered in bed with no harm having come to anyone.

When Misha has ceased giving thanks and directing orderlies to the bathroom with pails of bleach, she draws a chair beside Lena's bed and reads out the telegram. Would Lena not prefer to lie in the marital bedroom where there's more space? A cot could be placed by the side of the mattress. This is what Misha, in her experience, would suggest.

Lena would not.

Perhaps she'd like to hand over the infant and take some time in a hot bath?

Lena is silent.

And Misha can't help noticing an urgent need for the application of nappy cloths, unless Lena wishes the counterpane, sheets and indeed the mattress itself ruined beyond repair?

Lena smiles.

Mrs Machek sits back and reflects. She goes to the window. She tells Lena she's hopeful the sable can be saved. Lena unfurls her daughter's fist and looks at the palm, creased and pink. When she next glances up Mrs Machek is back with panic fluttering her breath. 'The doctor is imminent. Heavens, Mrs Bem, never mind the linen, what are we to do about your own lack of clothing? One might hazard, as a matter of some urgency?'

'But I don't need a doctor. Who sent for him?'

'Gracious, child, every new mother needs the doctor. There's the afterbirth for one thing.'

'Our pulses are regular, as are our functions. There's nothing to be gained from his visit. Best not to have him waste his time because I won't see him, I assure you.' Lena shifts the baby to her side and curls herself around her. 'Whatever are you doing over there?'

Mrs Machek is at the window opening the latch. 'How can I put this delicately, my dear child? There's a certain pungency in the room.'

Lena listens to the rain beating in the world outside. The cold air is not unpleasant on her face. Under the covers their bodies are warm. Piss squirts from the baby, and Lena realises she is grinning. The baby shits a coil of meconium which Lena scoops out and throws on the floor, wiping her fingers on the counter-pane before sliding them back into the warmth. Halfway to the door, Mrs Machek comes creeping back. Under her eyelids Lena watches the woman bend and scoop the black excrement into a white handkerchief and tiptoe out, shutting the door. The baby snores, sprawled against Lena's chest, and Lena grins.

'I came as soon as I could.' Anton stands in the bedroom door-way. 'We were caught in a storm, forgive me.'

Lena looks up and smiles. He is all steaming overcoat and peaked cap and boots; his very being held together by uniform. But when he glances towards the bed, she sees a hesitancy enter his expression – something that could be called shyness even – and suddenly the man in the doorway doesn't look to her like a lieutenant colonel in the Engineering Corps, but an uncertain boy waiting to be told what to do.

'I suppose you'd like to see what I'm hiding,' she says, finding she can't help the grin that curls with her words. 'Come closer, she doesn't bite. In fact she's a very lazy thing, she sleeps most of the time.'

Anton takes the chair by the bed. He is hesitant, like a man sliding onto the pew of an unfamiliar church.

'Here she is.' Lena lowers the sheet to expose the baby's dark blonde head turned against her breast, her eyes closed, lips pressed into a beak. 'Your daughter.'

She watches his face closely for his reaction; to see light ignite in his gaze.

'Anton?' she says. Because he isn't looking at Agata. He's star-ing down at his hands, clasping and unclasping them on his lap.

Lena touches his knee. 'Take a look at her.'

He nods and his shoulders shake. He looks up quickly and then pulls off his spectacles and wipes his eyes with the heel of his hand. His chest shudders, and he gives way to sudden sobs.

'It's all right,' Lena says, watching him. 'It's all right.'

'But there's nothing wrong with her.'

'Of course not.'

'She's perfect.'

'She is.'

'I'm sorry, Lena. I'm sorry.'

'It's all right.' She smiles at him, waiting while he wipes his eyes on his handkerchief. 'Get my stole from the wardrobe.'

Lena rolls the fur around the baby, kissing her nose because she looks pink as a sausage in pastry. She holds her out to him. 'You can't break her. She's going to be a tough one, I can tell.'

Lena watches Anton settle his daughter against his forearm. He's breathing easier now. His fingers flutter over Agata's head and Lena smiles. It's as though he thinks her conjured from spider silk or moon dust; as if by breathing too much or shifting the wrong way he might cause her to vanish for ever. 'She has a swirl.'

'At the crown, yes.'

'And very fair eyelashes.'

'She does, yes.'

'These fingernails—'

'Are sharp I can tell you.'

His thumb hovers at the curve of Agata's downy red ear.

Lena pushes back the counterpane and gets out of bed. 'I'm going to take a bath. Talk to her. She should hear you. Agata is a good name for her. I call her my little frog.'

She touches his shoulder as she leaves.

Over the next few weeks the atmosphere in the apartment undergoes a transformation. Small and sleepy Agata single-handedly expels the sterile military air. In its place come infant smells, animal mewls, and soft, marvelling voices. To Lena it's nothing less than a revolution. She no longer counts the taps made by a knife on an eggshell. She doesn't attend to the direction boots take in the hall. Because life doesn't run in straight lines any more. Some days when she's been out with Pav, she'll open the door and the air of reverence in the apartment reminds her of entering a church. She'll find Anton by the fire, dozing with Agata against his chest. Winter settles over the mountain but in the apartment the world turns round a different sun. In this world Lena notices little as the days drift by but the changes in her daughter. Agata's amphibian legs straighten. She takes on fat at the chin and wrists. And one day she bestows her first gurning grin on Pavlov as he chases a rabbit in his dreams.

There is a morning when Lena's changing Agata's nappy at the desk in her bedroom and Anton taps the wood of the open door and comes in.

He stands beside her watching Lena fold cloth at Agata's belly and pin the fabric. 'How well you do that.'

'Misha advises me on modifications to my technique every day.'

'Indeed she would.'

She glances back at him and they share a smile. Lena lifts Agata from the desk and kisses her nose. 'Do you want to hold her?'

'I'd like that very much but there's a staff meeting I'm required to attend.'

She leans Agata towards him so he can kiss her forehead as has become his habit when he leaves in the morning. As it has become hers to say 'Enjoy your day.'

At the door he turns. 'Forgive me, Lena, I had a question.'

Lena has Agata against her shoulder, rubbing her back.

'It's very small in here. I've been wanting to ask whether you might consider moving into the main bedroom. Not immediately, but perhaps sometime soon.'

'To sleep there?'

'Yes.'

'With you also present?'

'That was my thought. Families should be together, Lena.'

Lena puts her face to Agata's hair, breathing in the milky scent.

'I give you my word I'd never allow myself to overstep in any way. Indeed I could take a cot bed on the floor while you slept with Agata on the mattress if that would give you assurance.' His voice grows hesitant. 'If my word is sufficient. Please don't answer me now, take a few days to reflect. But please reflect.'

When she lifts her head he's gone.

She goes quickly to the bedroom door. 'Wait,' she calls to him in the hall. He's taking down his overcoat and cap from the stand. 'I don't need a few days.'

He pauses. 'Are you sure?'

She nods. 'We've been happy of late.'

'We have, haven't we? I knew it was possible.'

'So I think it better if we don't make any changes.'

He seems to freeze, his arm halfway into his sleeve. 'But this situation—'

'There's space enough for Agata and myself in my room. This is the situation we have at present and it's working, so I think we must keep on with it.'

'At present?'

She presses her lips against the crown of the baby's head. 'I can promise nothing, Anton, please understand me.'

'But Agata seems to change so much.' He looks at her, his eyes blinking. 'I've not been wrong about that?'

'She does, she changes everything. And yet I wonder whether it's possible for everything to change and also nothing at all.'

He turns away. When he shrugs on his overcoat it seems to Lena to press heavily on his shoulders. He doesn't look back as he opens the door.

There's a photograph taken of them around this time. The regimental photographer is visiting the base and Anton makes a request for a personal record.

Lena sits by the unlit fireplace, the mantel wreathed in advent holly. She wears a high-necked cream blouse, her hair pinned back from her face, holding Agata in a crocheted white shawl. Anton stands behind in dress uniform, all braiding and buttons, his white-gloved fingers a picket row on Lena's shoulder. The image is set in a gilt-edged card and sent home in time for Christmas, with an apology scrawled on the side. The winter conditions are too treacherous to attempt the journey with a newborn. In the spring, Lena promises, I'll bring your granddaughter home.

A new year begins and more days float by. The atmosphere in the apartment sustains its somnolent calm. Some mornings Lena finds the air so dense she feels as if she is living beneath salt water. She sees little point in dressing, let alone opening the front door to go outside.

It's on a February day like this, while napping with Agata on the bed, that she's jolted awake by snow crashing from the infirmary roof. She gets up and goes to the window, staring out at corrugated metal, exposed after weeks of white. Cadets are sprinting to clear the debris. The scene is disconcerting; for a moment it's as if she's lost her place in time. Then she realises the activity is simply a repeat of how the snow fell down a year ago when she was sitting at the desk with her medical books.

For the first time it occurs to her that another woman must be now studying in her place in Kraków. At this very instant this woman might be frowning over notes in a library, or jotting down a diagram in a lecture hall, having taken her seat there without a thought. From nowhere Lena feels a swell of grief and jealousy, it comes like a drowning wave. She sits at the desk and waits for its passing, because what else can she do? And of course this woman can't be blamed for taking a university place. To her no student called Lena has ever existed; the place she takes is entirely her own. What was once Lena's future – before the accident of pregnancy – has become this woman's destiny; it's not for her to wonder about what has been lost by a person she doesn't know.

Lena doesn't know what to do with these thoughts, so she takes paper and starts a letter to Danushka, who sees neither accident nor destiny in life, only actions driven by will.

Behind her Agata starts to grumble and kick her heels. Lena abandons the letter and takes Agata into the sitting room to feed her by the hearth. Listening to her daughter suckle, she recalls

Ulrich's cows plodding to the stall twice a day to be milked. Do they also experience it as a sensation of placid relief, of the brain itself draining? Does it calm an animal's thoughts or dull them? For a moment she feels herself an onlooker – watching a young woman by a fire with a child at her breast. Accident, destiny or will, she says aloud. I must be here by accident or destiny – because this was not my will. She watches the coals in the grate pulsing from orange to pink and disintegrating into a crumble of white.

On the occasion of Lena's nineteenth birthday in June, Anton presents her with diamond earrings. She holds them to the chandelier in the sitting room and watches the teardrops spark with rainbows in the light.

'They're exquisite.'

'My grandmother left them for my future wife, so rightfully they're yours. May I help you with them?'

They stand at the mirror in the hall, his breath on her neck as he fastens the clasps. She tilts her head from side to side then stops. 'I am becoming Mama.'

'Your mother's a charming woman, talented and very kind. I've always respected her.'

Lena turns from her reflection and moves away. 'Shall we go in to dinner?'

The candelabra has been lit in the dining room and places set next to each other at the head of the table. Anton pulls back her chair and the orderly opens a bottle of champagne.

She watches him turn his glass on the table, then lift it to hers. 'It's three years to the day since I noticed you in the circus tent, cheering on that sword-swallower and her fifty pairs of oesophageal muscles.'

'You remember me telling you that?'

'Naturally,' he says quietly, 'it's rather hard to forget.'

She smiles, thinking how it is between them now; a thing exists, and if it cannot exactly be called love, then it is at least a sort of affection – a mosaic put together in bits and pieces, bound by a shared devotion.

Anton reaches for a bowl of caviar, putting a spoonful on her plate. 'You need to try this, it came from my mother.'

'You've been very thoughtful to make all these arrangements.'

He pushes a teaspoon heap of caviar onto a blini. 'How was Agata today?'

Lena pulls a face, shaking her head. 'You really want to know?'

He fingers his glass. He looks tired tonight, she thinks. 'Of course.'

'In which case it pains me to report it hasn't been her finest day.' Lena sips her champagne and starts to recount how their daughter spat out every mouthful of marrow at lunch and shoved the bowl so it fell off the table onto the dog. She speaks slowly, in detail, and Anton listens without interrupting, nodding now and then. It is easily enough done, this manner of suppertime conversation, keeping the air between them busy. She's found that an hour, even two, can pass in a volley of little nothings reported from the day. Were someone to stop by the table and observe, Lena has no doubt she and Anton would appear to be a well-matched union. As to what she feels about this, she prefers not to think. Many other things do not need thought at present, such as the encyclopaedias she no longer reads, and the letters she doesn't send to family and old school friends, and the conviction she now carries that another woman exists inside her skin, a doppelganger who looks just like Lena but who crams her day with nursery songs and lullabies and knitting, and when Lena wakes at night in a cold sweat, is there by the bed raising a finger, whispering hush.

There's lamb to follow and dill creamed potatoes. Anton takes the champagne from the ice bucket and stands it by his plate. She watches him refill his glass, which is the moment to enquire about his day.

'What you would expect,' he says.

'You seem tired.'

'Everyone's tired of late.'

'But still . . .' she says and then she leaves it there. She doesn't point out there's an increasing tension in his expression when he comes home these days, like a tautening of strings behind his eyes. Nor that he seems to spend every evening with a bottle to hand. His notebook hasn't been out of the bureau for a while. She asks him if the military situation is worsening.

'Who can tell.'

'We should take a trip somewhere as a family.' She knows this suggestion will please him. 'Go away one weekend, take a resort chalet perhaps.'

He smiles briefly and drains his glass. 'I'm afraid this isn't quite the time.'

The plates are cleared, and with the absence of anything obvious to talk about, silence falls down between them; it is like a weighted cloth trapping them in their separate places.

'Did I tell you she tried to crawl again today.'

'Is that so?'

'It won't be long now.'

He reaches for the bottle. 'I don't suppose it will.'

'She's very determined.'

'I'm sure.'

The silence is lifted by the orderly bringing in a pavlova piled high with cherries and redcurrants. Lena claps her hands in delight. 'How thoughtful, Anton. Wherever did you find redcurrants?'

He looks up from his glass.

'The pavlova,' she says. 'It's wonderful.'

'It's your favourite dessert.'

'You knew that?'

'Yes, I knew that, Lena.'

She lays her fingers on his wrist. 'You need to take care of yourself, Anton.'

He looks down at her hand and he says quietly, 'What's mine?'

'I beg your pardon?'

'What's my favourite dessert?'

'Cheesecake? Possibly strudel with cinnamon?' She smiles, shaking her head. 'Am I close? Or a tart – plum and almond?'

He pushes back his chair.

'Well?' she says, 'am I?'

'Yes, you're close.'

She looks at him standing, draining his glass. 'But we haven't finished eating.'

'You'll have to excuse me. I find I'm not so hungry tonight.'

In the sitting room they sit either side of the unlit hearth. The windows are open, letting in a wash of midsummer light, and the sound of soldiers laughing as they make their way back from the Mess. She has an unfinished hand of Patience on the baize, and he a newspaper on his lap. He uncorks a bottle of vodka and pours a glass. 'Do you think Agata is happy?'

Lena looks over at him and laughs.

'What do you find amusing?'

'She's a baby, of course she's happy.'

'Character develops young. Not all babies are happy ones.'

'Well, then our daughter has been born with a cheerful nature.'

'You believe it?'

Lena lays down the cards in her hand. 'Whatever is it this evening, Anton? Are you thinking you weren't happy as a child?'

He sips from his vodka. 'I was, but I had siblings round me.'

'So that's where this is heading.'

'It's heading nowhere like all our conversations.'

'You're drinking too much, Anton. It's not like you.'

'What do you know?'

'Excuse me?'

He is staring at her. 'What do you know is like me or not like me?'

'I know it's not this.'

She gathers up cards to start over but watches him from the corner of her eye, tipping back his glass, pouring another. Outside, voices are singing rambling ballads about German whores, trying to outdo each other in volume. Anton's expression tightens and he moves to get up.

'It's high spirits,' she says. 'Let them be. It's nice to hear some laughter.'

'It's filth. There are women and children around.' He goes to the window and leans out and the singing dies away.

She watches him return, sitting down heavily in his chair. 'Anton, I'd like to understand whatever it is tonight that is making you this way.'

'Forgive me, it's just the occasion.' He does not meet her eye.

'The occasion?'

'Reflecting on the last three years.'

'What about them?'

His hand is unsteady on the bottle, vodka spilling over the rim of the glass as he pours. 'Being here with you, I suppose.'

'Being with me is the problem?'

'Night after night, it's always the same.'

Lena puts down the cards. 'How is it the same?'

'Sitting together but so very distant from each other.' He shakes his head.

'I would like to understand, Anton.'

He drinks and refills his glass. 'Very well. Allow me to explain in the simplest terms. Night after night it's as if there's a sore where my heart should be.'

'Anton please—'

'No, let me speak. You see, Lena, the truth is I'm a fool. I never listened to those who warned me. You yourself warned me. But I couldn't help myself. I still can't. My heart aches because I can't stop hoping in some way. That's the ridiculous thing. Hope is a ridiculous thing.'

She lifts her head, turning to the door.

'What is it?'

'I thought I heard Agata. She hasn't been settling lately. Hope isn't a ridiculous thing, Anton.'

'No?'

'Of course not.'

He pours another glass and drains it. 'Perhaps you're right. I mean we've been closer of late, haven't we? There's a warmth between us – a flicker now and then?' He is staring at her, she feels the intensity of his gaze. 'You can't say I'm wrong about this?'

'You're not wrong.' She looks down at the undealt deck. 'You and I have a shared love. That's bound to reflect warmth between us.'

'Reflect warmth?'

'Yes.'

'It's not there of its own accord?'

'Please, Anton. You're working too much. You're tired. This isn't the time.'

He laughs, stuttering. The sound is almost like choking.

Lena stands. She puts away the cards and folds the table.

'You're going?'

'Agata needs me.'

'She's asleep.'

'Yes, but—'

'But what, Lena?'

She shakes her head. She doesn't say how it is for her. She won't make it worse and tell him how impatience starts to rise in her from the moment she lays Agata on the bed, that every evening she's simply filling time until she can tiptoe into the room and wrap herself round her child for the night. How can she explain this contradiction that she craves to be more in life than mother to a child she hadn't wanted, and yet nothing matters more than lying with her palm on Agata's chest as she sleeps, marvelling at the diaphragm pumping life.

'One day, Anton, there'll be someone who loves you as you deserve.'

He laughs bitterly and throws back his vodka. 'You really don't understand, do you? Perhaps you don't want to understand. I don't want someone else's affection.'

'Perhaps one day someone will—'

He corks the vodka bottle and stands unsteadily, rocking on his heels. 'No, Lena, you don't want to see it. There was only ever you. There will only ever be you in my life. That's just how it is. I can do nothing to help it. Nothing. And it eats me alive. You wanted to know my punishment for what I did that night? This is it. Every day and every night of my life, this is it.'

He nods at her. 'Sleep well,' and he goes from the room.

It's a hot Saturday two months later and Lena is preparing for a picnic with the officer wives when Anton walks into the kitchen, a file tucked under his elbow.

'This is for you.'

She glances up from the tomatoes she's slicing and the knife slips in her hand.

'Are you ill?'

'Open it first, then I'll explain.'

She looks at him and wipes her hands slowly. Shifting aside the heap of tomatoes she spreads the contents of the file on the kitchen table: travel cheques, a pouch crammed with banknotes, a train ticket for Warsaw and her passport with Agata's details added.

'You'll need the letter too.'

There's an envelope with an unfamiliar name and address in the capital.

Lena grips the table and forces herself to breathe. She stares at the tomatoes and their spill of pink glistening seeds. When she turns to Anton she sees it isn't just exhaustion on his face, he looks like a man in receipt of a terrible diagnosis. 'What's going on, Anton? You must tell me.'

He takes off his glasses and pinches the sides of his nose.

'Whatever it is, tell me everything.'

He nods and then very quietly he begins to speak. 'I can't say for certain that what we most fear is going to happen, but it's time to prepare for that eventuality. I need you to go and pack as much of the silverware as you can, also all your jewellery.

I've written a list of other valuable pieces. Take your warmest clothes and medicines.'

She hears herself say, 'Take them where, Anton?'

'When it's quieter outside, you go down to the sentry. I've arranged a jeep to take you to the station. Don't leave it too late.'

She stares at him. Outside the window she can hear families gathering in the sunshine with their hampers and rugs for the day's picnic. Children are running and screaming, no doubt dangling worms or kites, women are cackling, bartering gossip. 'But what about all the other families?' she whispers. 'We're supposed to be in the meadows this afternoon.'

'I'll send word you're unwell.'

'But you can't know anything for sure. I mean you said yourself you can't say for certain.'

'I can't. However I've received information.'

'From where?'

He rubs the bridge of his nose. 'The exact source isn't important and I really can't say.'

'Your brother? It's him again?'

'Lena, please. It's vital you get to Warsaw as soon as possible, that's all that matters right now. If we're in luck there'll be time enough.'

'Time enough for what?'

'The name on the letter is my brother's alias. Memorise the contact details on the letter. Memorise everything in the file. Get to him and he'll arrange your onward movements. I'm sorry, Lena, this is not how I'd wish it.'

She needs to keep gripping the edge of the table because the room is tilting. She is staring at her passport and the envelope of money surrounded by the tomatoes that need salting if they are not to be wasted. 'Just like that? You want us to leave just like that?'

The dog is pushing his nose at her skirt. 'Ivan Pavlov, what about him?'

Anton rubs his eyes. 'I'm sorry, Lena. The orderlies will keep an eye on him.'

'He'll hate that. He'd be no trouble in Warsaw.' But even as she speaks she hears her voice weakening.

'With God's blessing you won't be staying in Warsaw. There's a limited number of seats on flights out of the country. If you hesitate, even for a day, your seat will be taken by someone else. There's very little time. Please assure me you understand?'

'And my family?' she whispers. 'What happens to them in all this?'

'Get to Warsaw, Lena.' Anton turns and walks out of the kitchen.

She runs after him into her bedroom where he's lifting Agata from her cot, raising her above his head. He begins to spin her, whooshing her like a boat riding waves. Agata flies on the unseen waves, chuckling. Round and round they go, surfing in and out of the sunlight from the window. Lena watches them spin, the light like a shutter closing, printing the image in her mind.

'And you?' she says.

'Me?'

'Yes, you, Anton. I'll need to contact you. There'll be all sorts of news. I'll have lots to tell you. I mean for one thing she'll be walking soon.'

She watches his frame stiffen as if absorbing a blow.

'From now on it would be better if you acted without thought of me.'

He lowers Agata and cradles her in his arms. Then he kisses her brow. 'Go to Mama now, my little one.'

Lena settles Agata on her hip and turns away. It benefits no one to see the water rushing to her eyes.

'You need to get your spectacles resized.'

'What?'

'I've been meaning to tell you for ages. You always get pressure marks by the side of your nose.'

He says nothing, his mouth opening and closing. He nods and clears his throat. 'I must return to work.'

'Wait,' she says, stepping towards him. 'There's something else.' She lays her hand against his cheek. 'You're a good man, Anton, I do know that.'

He looks at her. His lips are pressed and trembling.

'A good man,' she says.

'I must go back to work.'

She follows him into the hall. Sunlight streams from the glass panel above the front door, dust particles trapped in its beam. The light is so strong it seems to Lena to have solidified; to go into the hall is to enter a white-walled tunnel.

Anton walks away from her towards the door. He turns the handle and steps outside. Lena watches him melt into the sun.

She stands in her bedroom, a case open on the bed. Agata is rolling in Lena's sable coat on the floor. Pav watches her from the door, his tail tucked between his hind legs.

She has packed exactly as Anton told her; jewellery rolled in scarves, their warmest clothing, Agata's rag rabbit. She has added the amber, remembering Anton said it had some worth. From the dining room she has taken the silverware and all the money from the bureau, from the kitchen she has wrapped the loaf and cheese she was planning for the picnic. The track outside is quiet, the families will be splashing in the water meadows now. She returns to her room. It is surprising to her how methodical she's been, how quickly and mechanically she moved to take what was needed, avoiding an excess of thought. She closes the case and feels its weight. If she wears both her coats there's still space inside.

She stands looking round the small room a final time and steps to the shelf by her desk. Dust lies on the spines of books she once opened every day. When she pulls down her medical

encyclopaedia, the pages bulge. An envelope slips to the floor.
Lena picks it up. A letter from Mama. There are other envelopes,
six of them, unopened, pressed inside the book. She takes them
out and lays them in a row on the desk beside Anton's file.

She sits down in front of them. What scent they might have
once held is gone. Before she can change her mind she rips open
each envelope pulling out sheets covered in loose curling blue
script, staring at the long chains of words.

Mama's voice enters her head just as if she had stepped into
the room.

> *Anton writes that you're expecting a child! I can't tell you the
> joy in my heart at this news. It's all a mother could wish. Come
> home for the birth, darling. Please consider it. And write with
> details of your health, we want to know everything!*

In the next letter Mama mentions that Papa's health is declining.

> *Your poor Papa's memory grows poor, a tremor now
> affects his right hand.*
> *I pray this letter finds you, my darling, and finds you well.*

In another note he is wandering at night. He has fallen in town,
grazing his forehead.

> *Can you believe it, Lena my darling, he wonders most even-
> ings when you are home from school. I don't tell him you
> yourself have a child now. We try not to add to his con-
> fusion. I pray you are happy, my darling girl, that no news
> means only good things . . .*

Mama writes in purple ink in January thanking Lena for the
wonderful Christmas postcard.

> *How elegant you all look. Little Agata is the double of you!
> The postcard is on the mantel and already quite tatty from
> receiving its daily kiss. Ulka says I ruin it with my lipstick, but*

I shall carry on until I get to hold my granddaughter in the flesh. On a sad note, we seem to have the doctor here every week. I think of you and how it is hard caring for a baby, but you're strong, darling, I know that. I imagine Agata must be smiling by now, is she taking well to your milk? . . .

Ala starts one letter, writing a page with hospital gossip. Mama continues overleaf.

I wanted to add a word, darling, to say not to worry if little Agata cries in the night. I remember thinking my exhaustion would never end, but this time will pass. Rest in the day when you can. I wonder on her eye colour, it will be settling by now. Impossible to tell from the postcard, of course. Ulka tells me she will be blue like her mother. But will that blue be the colour of cornflowers or sapphire or clouded skies . . .?

The last letter arrives five days after Lena's birthday.

We celebrated your day with a cherry cake. Nineteen, Lena, my darling child. Ala thinks me mad to go to the window after every motor car, but I will trust in my prayers. But let me think, Agata is approaching eight months now. I've added your infant photograph to the mantel to compare. You were ten months at the time, propped in Ala's lap. Quite a scowl you wore! Do you recall which photograph I mean? Your ever loving—

There's a knock at the front door. Lena wipes her eyes.

A soldier, saluting. 'Madam, I have orders from Lieutenant Colonel Bem. The jeep is prepared and the driver waiting. I am asked to escort you to the vehicle without delay.'

For a moment Lena stares at the boy.

'Madam, I have orders from Lieutenant Colonel Bem. The jeep—'

'Of course,' she says. 'The jeep, yes. Please give me a minute, I'll fetch my daughter and the dog. We have two cases, that's all.'

The soldier reddens. 'A dog, madam?'

'Is there a problem?'

'I was made to understand the dog is remaining here.'

'You were,' Lena says quietly, 'but there's since been a change to our planned destination, and the dog is coming with us. A moment please.'

England

Lena wakes to the sound of screaming.

Who? Who's yelling like this?

The girl? Where is the little girl?

'Hush, Ma, hush, you're awake, you're safe.'

A touch on her cheek, stroking.

'It's me, JoJo. I'm here. What is it? What do you want to tell me?'

The screaming goes on. It must be inside her somewhere. Because the images unspooling in front of her are silent, like scenes from an old film.

She sees the girl slip over the horizon out of sight.

'Wait!' Lena cries to her, 'there's something I need to say to you.'

'Ma, look at me. It's JoJo. Ma, look at me.'

Her wrist is lifted, fingers push against her artery, pressing against her bone.

'Ma, I'm going to call Margaret. Hold on, Ma, I'll be back.'

'Please wait.'

But the girl is gone from the scene.

There's only jolting blackness and a grinding of rusted wheels.

It doesn't stop. Make it stop . . .

The container again. Stinking of piss and sweat and shit.
It's only to be expected: after all these are the natural smells of

animals kept limb to limb in a place with too little air and too much heat. The only space inside is the gap that separates those bodies that breathe from the growing pile, hidden by a blanket against the wall. She mustn't glance at the pile. If she does she might see a stump protruding from under the blanket, tapping on the planks in time to the jolting wheels.

Nobody's saying anything in this container. Someone's keening backwards and forwards; Mama, taking a turn at making the noise for the rest of them. Lena puts her arm around her mother's shoulder and avoids Ala's blank stare. On her lap her little frog dozes, sucking her thumb, a finger rubbing the bridge of her nose. Lena closes her eyes but she can't shut out the sound of tapping on planks. She bites down on her thumb knuckle until blood leaks out, and she is grateful for the pain.

The train rolls on.

When the journey was just beginning there'd been a surge of energy in the container; a clamour for information about the sights they were passing; a need to locate the changing flora and pin down the position of the sun. Assessments were made as to their direction of travel, speculations thrown into the air about their probable destination. The train stopped every couple of days and a bucket of gruel would be thrown in. At this time there would be jostling for a view of the landscape. Once or twice there was a deserted platform to stand on with a flat brown world to gaze at for an hour or a day or through the night into the dawn. But all desire for knowledge of the outside world began to fade as days grew to weeks and supplies of food ran down. When the white mountains rose in crooked steeples beyond the container's slats, human voices fell silent. The air turned thin and the oldest travellers weakened.

Lena cradled Agata and Mama cradled Papa, singing lullabies to them both. She whispered to him in the night, unravelling the story of their life together. For a week or more perhaps, Papa's eyes watched Mama's face as she remembered. He took no gruel and then no water. His eyelids dropped and Mama sprayed her

*scent on her chest and held him against her, so he would know
her and be comforted. 'Say goodbye now,' she instructed her
children. Inside Mama's cradle Papa's breath broke apart and
stopped for good.*

*It was after the mountains that a rumour came to life in the
container. There was to be no destination for this train; it was to
run on rusting rails looping the earth, throwing out corpses until
no bodies were left on board. Then this rumour shrivelled away.
Only the crying didn't stop.*

*No one's said it, but something has to be done about the
pile against the wall. Flies are everywhere, this is one thing. It's
summer and warm, and the natural stinks of functioning animals must simply be borne. But this stench of things that have
stopped functioning? The putrefaction of an old man's body; a
father whose love could set a furnace raging in his daughter's
heart. How can this ever be borne?*

It is taking for ever, this journey in the dark.

For ever and ever.

*But it has to end, because nothing is for ever, is it? Bone man,
tell me, nothing's for ever . . .*

A sudden slice of white in the black. The air is quiet but for
a blur of movement. A figure pulling back the dark, stretching
light like dough in her hands – Margaret, opening the curtains.

Lena watches her quietly clearing smeared glasses from the
bedside table. Margaret is good at her job, a thing they like to
say in this country. It's a term of high praise. Better than good is
what they mean if they weren't being so mealy-mouthed about
it: wonderful. Margaret, you are wonderful.

She reaches out, indicating she wants to take Margaret's hand in
hers. It's strong, this woman's grip: fleshy and tough; a hand such
as she once had, good for pulling up vegetables, scrubbing milking stalls, or cross-sawing lengths of pine. There are all sorts of
uses hands get put to in their lifetime, without acknowledgement,
thousands of times in a single day. Margaret's hands are freckled

and always clean. The fingernails have been known to gleam with coral polish. Her own hands turned brown as tea from the forest peat. They bloated from frostbite. Her nails split up and down from malnutrition and fell off. Even when she and her husband took employment in a factory the nails never grew straight, her finger joints refused to flex. The skin held on to its tinge of earth. Her hands never trusted the factory's warmth. They never forgot.

She takes the amber from the bedside table and rolls it against her throat. She has become like one of her dogs during these last days. Which was the one? The Welsh sheepdog with the wolf's stare. That animal could tell a hundred-page story with those eyes, a neighbour once said, and make you understand every word.

Margaret comes over. 'Don't try to speak if it hurts.'

'Thank you, Margaret.'

'For doing my job? Give it a rest. Would you like me to run a bath?'

She looks pointedly at the clock on the wall.

'For you, Magdalena, I have all the time in the world.'

Lena makes a face: 'Goddamn liar,' she mouths.

Margaret laughs and lumps her rucksack onto the bed. 'I came across a grand-sounding bath oil. Bergamot and lemongrass, whatever bergamot may be.' She rummages through the bag's compartments. 'I thought you could do with a treat.'

It's stupid to cry. She commands her tears to stop. Stupider when her eyes are filling for a body that should have been dragged into the ground long ago.

Margaret sits beside her on the bed and pulls a folded tissue from a packet. Lena shakes her head. Don't be kind to me. I do not deserve your kindness, this is what she needs to say.

There's a tapping at the window. Lena looks out at the black-bird fluffing his feathers on the sill.

Margaret squeezes her hand and gets up. 'Let me get that bath going. I'll feed your friend while I'm at it. Persistent fellow, isn't he?'

*

She closes her eyes and he's with her. It happens in an instant. On the slide of a breath he's here.

All around them, the moan of trees under the saw.

She stares at him. So clear, the image she sees now; she can follow each wisp of steam rising like ghost serpents from his sheepskin coat. Ice crystals spark on his red beard. She could reach and touch every one if she chose. She could take the shiver of cold from his skin, keep it as her own.

He tightens the bay mare's traces. Behind the horse is the wide wooden sleigh.

'Come,' he says to her. 'I'll lend you the coat.'

'No.'

'You want me to order you?'

'Nobody orders me.'

'Is that so?' He laughs in her face. Easy as a lunatic, this is how he laughs.

'They say you're a murderer.'

'Is that so?'

'Are you?'

He slaps the horse's rump and stretches out his hand. 'Come.'

She knows the eyes of the working party are on her. She can hear the hiss and cluck of the apothecary's wife. She doesn't know why she follows him, but she does, drawn by the look he throws over his shoulder.

Her mother's face is white. A pellet of spit flies from This Molek's lips as he shakes his head. At the edge of her vision she sees the apothecary's wife leaning towards the count, a hand to her mouth, words spilling through the bone gate of her fingers. Still she walks behind him, stepping into the prints he's making in the snow.

Knotting the scarf under her chin, she tries not to stumble. The soles of her boots flap where the string's snapped and she's not had time to tie a fresh rag to keep them in place. Her mother is running, as best she can, through the drifts after her, calling out that there's the rest of the log to dismember, her voice climbing higher, calling to Lena to remember her quota, remember her child.

She lifts her boots high, careless of the energy it takes. She'll soon be out of hearing. And all the while she follows him.

'Magdalena?' a voice is summoning her through the snow. 'The bath's ready. Can you smell the lemongrass?'

His breath is warm on her face. She could reach out with her fingers and touch that face, do it now, lean forward from this bed and press through the icicles on his frozen beard. Lay her palm to the bone curve of his cheek, feel each pore on his skin. Tears stream down her face.

'*You are sad, Magdalena.*'

'*I should not have gone with you that day in the clearing.*'

'*Is that what you think?*'

Why is his hand not on her skin? His knuckles should be moving against her tears, taking them as his own.

'*But I couldn't help myself, don't you see?*'

'*Oh, Magdalena, do you really believe life's tapestry can be unpicked into a single thread?*'

'*I couldn't help myself. It wasn't chance or bad luck what happened. I need to tell Agata it's all my fault. I decided to follow you that day. I must find her and tell her. That's what I have to do. You have to help me find her.*'

A woman's voice.

'Come, Magdalena, the temperature's perfect. Can you put your hands around my shoulders? We'll take it nice and slow.'

Przemysl, South East Poland

Shifting Agata on her hip, Lena wriggles out of her coat and lets it drop to the path beside her suitcase. She peers through the window. The late summer honeysuckle is coiled in ringlets round the frame, bees humming in the blossom. She calls Ivan Pavlov from scratching at the door and shades her eyes to better see in. The sitting room looks just as it should; under the window pots brim with pink and red geraniums, the piano's lid is open, a pile of scores on the stool, Romek's school books are stacked on the dining table. Even Papa is where he should be, dozing by the hearth, looking just as he should. Relief surges in her. Lena taps gently on the glass.

Papa starts forward clutching the arms of the chair.

She lifts Agata's hand in a little wave. 'Papa, it's me. Look, I've brought someone to meet you, Papa. It's Magdalena Luiza outside at the window.'

But he doesn't turn her way. His eyes search the room, as if waiting for instruction. Now she looks more carefully she sees how stooped he is, and far thinner than she would have thought possible. His once round face is a narrow plane, his beard straggling and white. It's as if he's travelled twenty years into the future not two. Lena is staring when the sitting-room door opens and Mama enters carrying a glass of tea. Mama is thinner too, her summer dress hangs looser on her frame. Lena watches her saying something like, 'Here's your tea now, you must be careful, it's straight from the kettle.' Mama sets the glass on a side table and lays a hand on Papa's shoulder. Lena's eyes fill. She takes a deep breath and taps again on the window.

Mama looks across after the sound. Her mouth opens. Her hand moves to her lips. Lena watches Mama lean forward, gripping the back of the armchair, her head raised and stiff as she stares towards the window.

She feels a sliding wetness on her face. 'It's me, Mama, I'm home.'

Mama turns, walking slowly from the room.

The front door opens to Ulka throwing herself over Lena and Agata like a bodyguard in fear for their lives. Romek materialises from nowhere – which might be some new trick of his – grumbling that there's no chance of rehearsing his mentalist act with the racket Ulka's making. Agata is starting to cry from the noise and the crush and Ulka is snatching her up and dancing, kissing her, throwing her in the air, singing. But then Mama appears on the doorstep, standing without motion, maybe even without breath, the sun a halo around her yellow hair, and Ulka's commotion and Agata's wailing falls away.

Mama looks at Lena, she has her arms braced against her chest.

From inside the house comes a man's voice – Papa – shouting about a strange dog in the room.

Mama looks at Lena, a tremor pulsing her jaw.

Ulka and Romek go around them into the house and the door is closed.

'You must excuse my current manner,' Mama says when all the world is silent, 'only I had started to give up hope of seeing little Agata or you, my darling child, for some time.'

Lena opens her mouth, shaking her head to dislodge words that will not come.

'I fear I must have done something very wrong for you to have needed to hurt me in this way,' Mama says, each word weighted with formality. 'For whatever I did, I ask that you forgive me.'

Lena cannot stop shaking her head. *It's you who must forgive me*, this is what she wants to say, but all that rises from her throat is a great sawing moan.

And Mama's arms unfold. 'Come.'

Her arms open wide. 'You're here, my darling child. You're home now, that's what matters.'

Lena goes to her mother's embrace.

They stand on the step, pressed cheek against cheek. Lena can feel Mama's heart pounding beneath her dress. A shudder seems to pass between them.

Mama holds Lena at arm's length. Her fingertips move through Lena's hair as they have a thousand times. 'Look at this monkey fluff, darling, has it been brushed even once in these two years?'

Lena lays her head on Mama's shoulder, she is somehow the taller now, and she closes her eyes, breathing in lilac, filling her lungs with perfume.

It's like flour sacks thudding in a neighbour's cellar, the noises that begin that night. Only they have no close neighbours on the lane but Ulrich and he doesn't have a cellar. Lena lies in the dark, her eyes open, counting the thumps. She isn't sure when the sounds started, but they seem to be getting louder.

The bedroom door creaks on its hinges, a wobbling yellow light in her face.

'Get that torch out of my goddamn eyes, worm.'

'Come to the attic.'

Lena looks at the thrill in Romek's eyes. A child when she left, he's now a youth nearing manhood. 'Sorry to disappoint, but it's not close, whatever it is.'

'Don't be boring, sis. You never used to be boring.'

'I can't leave Agata.'

'When are you going to see something like this again?'

'Hopefully never.'

'Suit yourself.'

She hears him on the landing, dragging the ladder from the closet. The thudding sounds continue, coming in rapid clusters now, four or five at a time. Lena looks at Agata, flat out on her back. Didn't she once believe that everything that could be observed must be observed? Cursing Romek she creeps out onto the landing and up the ladder into the attic.

Her brother is crouched like a goblin at the window under the eaves, his white eyes popping. 'It's the most incredible fire show you've ever seen. Lublin's burning.'

'It can't be.'

'Take a look.'

The night sky to the west, normally a canvas of black, is punctured by orange specks. White smoke streams straight up from these holes, pouring out as if the earth itself is leaking. While Lena looks she sees three tiny bursts landing one on top the other. 'It's like a giant's throwing down firecrackers on the world.'

'Do you think people are dying out there?'

'I don't know, Romuś. I suppose they must be.'

'Do you think we're next?'

'Who are we to bother about,' she says trying to sound confident. She can't take her eyes from the view. There are too many explosions now, coming too rapidly to count.

'Who's doing it, do you think?'

'I don't know.'

'Where're our planes? Why aren't we fighting them?'

'I don't know.'

'Well, now I can go off and die because now I've really seen everything.' This is Ulka, her head at the hatch. 'Are you total simpletons? Come down immediately. And you with a child, twig. It's supposed to put sense in your head, not knock it out.'

Mama, Papa and Ala are out on the landing, soft and dishevelled in their pyjamas and robes. Papa hasn't got his foot strapped on, and is leaning on Mama. Rosary beads rattle in her hand. Ala is cradling Agata in a woollen blanket, Ivan Pavlov cowering behind her legs.

'Let's go,' Ulka says, cuffing Romek and taking his torch from him.

'Where?'

'Downstairs. No discussion.'

They process mute and obedient down the stairs into the dining room.

By the time Mama has persuaded Papa under the table, and started on her Hail Marys, the night is quiet again.

'Listen,' Lena whispers, smoothing Agata's hair, 'it's all over.'

'Really? It can't be.'

She laughs at the disappointment on Romek's face.

He crawls out from under the table to listen. 'But it was barely anything.'

Ulka grabs his leg and drags him back under. She glares at him. 'You wait ten more minutes. Tomorrow we clear the cellar.'

Mama glances at Lena and opens her mouth to speak, then she looks away.

A tower of *naleśniki* rises perilously from a platter on the breakfast table. The pancakes bounce with extra eggs. Bowls of cherry compote, sour cream and honey sit in glistening attendance round the platter's edge. 'Eat.' Ulka slams down the coffee pot and turns for the kitchen. 'There's more on the way.'

Grace is said and the pancake tower dismantled. Word comes with Ulrich and the milk delivery that ten bombs have fallen on the cathedral of St John the Baptist in Lublin. A human chain, a thousand metres long, is passing buckets from the Bystrzyca to the ruined nave at this very moment.

'What are the casualty figures?' Romek asks, delighting Agata by hanging a spoon from his nose. 'Higher or lower than ten per cent? Would anyone like to lay a bet they're higher?'

'Ignore him,' Lena says to Ulrich, taking his coat. 'We're trying to.'

Mama bows her head and prays that this is the end to the world's madness. Ulrich twiddles a little finger in his ear and mutters that most likely it is only the beginning. He has been up with his heifers all night.

'We are hens between the fox and the wolf,' Papa says suddenly. 'You are right, my old friend, you are right.'

The pancake tower is rebuilt, and Ulrich persuaded to take off his coat and help with a second demolition. He takes three onto his plate and Agata on his knee for a bounce.

The rumour, Ulrich adds, not quite meeting Lena's eye, is that the war will come at them from both directions. 'Only heaven knows how our soldiers will defend themselves in such an eventuality.'

Romek goes over to the radio set in the corner of the room and finds Warsaw on it. 'They're coming from the west in tanks.'

Mama looks at Lena. Lena looks away.

'They're not following the roads. They're driving across fields and through hedges and rivers.'

'Who's coming?' Papa says.

'Turn it off, Romuś, darling, right now please.'

'Come on, Mama, this is history happening right now.'

'Romuś, please.'

Papa's chair crashes back. He's standing, wielding his fork like a pikestaff. 'I asked who's coming. I have every right to know who's going to be in my house.'

Mama runs round the table to take his shoulders. 'Nobody's coming, darling. Romek was talking about friends from the city, that's all.'

'Then why didn't he say so?'

Lena goes over and turns off the radio.

'Unbelievable,' Romek says glaring at her. 'So we're just supposed to sit in ignorance and wait for whatever's going to happen to us?'

Nobody answers. Ulrich asks Ala to pass the cherry compote.

'Utterly unbelievable.' Romek stomps to the door. 'We should be preparing to fight them.'

'Wipe such nonsense from your head.' Ulka reels him back on the strings of her stare. 'You'll sit down and finish these pancakes, that's what you'll do. There's to be no more waste in this house. And then you're going to school.'

Ulrich wipes his mouth with the back of his hand and gets up, folding a pancake into each pocket. He's heading for a meeting at the town hall. He gives Romek's shoulder a slap as he goes, promising to report back with any news.

Ulka pushes the stack towards Lena with a shaking hand. 'I won't lose a second family to starvation. I will not.'

They lower their faces and eat in obedient silence. Mama tries to catch Lena's eye but she keeps her gaze out of the window where the sky is pale and calm and deceitful.

Mama follows her into the garden after breakfast.

Lena senses her coming up behind. 'Ulka said to check on the apples. To see if there were any early windfalls, but I can't spot any.'

'Darling,' Mama says, touching her arm so Lena has to look up. Mama's face is pale, dark under the eyes, 'Can I ask, does Anton know you've come back home?'

'Anton?'

'Did he suggest you come? Only as I understood it, his brother was going to help get you to a safe place should anything happen. That was clearly understood, I think, when we made the plans for marriage.'

Lena scuffs her shoes through the dew on the grass.

'Darling—'

'A marriage I didn't want, Mama. You knew that, yet you still packed me off to the mountains.'

Mama turns her head, as if Lena's words have slapped her. 'Anything I did, my darling, was to keep you safe.'

'Safe but unhappy.'

Silence, but for the rustle of leaves. 'I'm sorry, Lena, if you've felt that's been the case.'

'Do you know where I should actually be now, Mama?'

Mama says nothing.

'In Kraków. Papa would have understood.'

'You father is a romantic, Lena. He's always been one.'

She laughs scornfully. 'Really? Well, he says it's you.'

'No, darling, a mother can't afford to dream.' Mama's voice is quiet, her hand reaching out. 'She does what she has to do.'

'Oh please stop.' Lena turns from her grasp. 'It's almost funny when you think about it. You're saying you don't want me here. All my time away and all your pleading letters, and I come home to see you, and you actually don't want me.'

Mama comes after her. She catches Lena's hand and presses it between her own. 'A wound in my heart was mended yesterday when I saw you at the window. But this – to come back like this . . .' Mama shakes her head. 'I want you safe, Lena. I want you and Agata to be wherever's safest. You must see that. If there's a chance somewhere, somehow, you need to take it.'

'If it's going abroad?' Lena whispers. 'Leaving everything?'

Mama presses Lena's hand to her heart. 'You're a mother now, I know you know how these things feel.'

Lena looks across the garden where Ala is introducing Agata to the hens in the coop. Pavlov is wriggling on his back in the dirt under the roses, grinning at the sun. She looks where Ulka is red-faced in the kitchen window, scrubbing the frying pan at the sink. Everything in her had felt alive last night; supper at the table, even Papa had smiled at Romek's cup tricks. Ala had spent an hour reeling off unsuitable suitors in the bathroom. Her bedroom entirely unchanged. Everything had been perfect until the bombs began to fall. She shakes her head. 'And you, Mama? And poor Papa and Ala and Ulka and Romek with his goddamn lung, what happens to all of you?'

'It tears my heart open to ask this, but I'm begging you, my darling. If there's a chance for you and Agata to get out, Lena, you need to take it.'

The streets are quiet, so quiet it seems as if someone has sprinkled a sedative over the town. It's opening hour for offices and shops but nothing moves except the trams rattling along their tracks, the carriages empty, carrying only ghosts. Those people who are about are purposeful. They move quickly, their eyes on the distance. Hands lift in the briefest of greetings. No one crosses the road for conversation.

Ulka and Romek head to the market quarter to bang on shop doors and buy what food they can. Lena joins a queue outside the exchange to use a telephone line.

When her turn comes she goes to the booth and recites the number of Anton's brother in Warsaw. The operator listens to the connection. She looks up shaking her head. Lena asks her to try again. The operator shakes her head a second time. 'Madam, regrettably the line is down.'

Lena stands, the world a blur of movement around her. It is like the view from a carousel, only she's not moving. Behind her someone is asking her to step aside.

'Wait,' Lena says, 'wait. You're sure about the line? What does that mean?'

The operator shrugs.

'But what does that mean?' Lena feels the panic in her voice. 'When's it coming back? I need to talk to Warsaw.'

An exchange employee runs into the hall shouting that all the lines are down. People are to return home, or if they wish they may wait in another queue to send telegrams in the event that electrical communication is restored to the region. This cannot be guaranteed.

Agata is starting to grizzle. Lena shifts the weight of her on her back. Sweat is running down her spine and her face; how hot she is. She looks at the line of people stretching down the steps and along the street to the corner. The operator has shut the doors of the booth.

In the end she goes out onto the street to meet up with Ulka in the market square.

'How was it with Anton's brother?' Ulka asks. She and Romek are jubilant. Romek is dangling monkey-armed from a lamppost, Ulka sitting on one of the two sacks of barley they've acquired, along with a bottle of rape oil and six kilos of dried beans. More people are on the streets now the word is out that shops are open and the sky so blue that nothing murderous can possibly fall from it today. A woman runs past with an armful of furs. It was good they came when they did, Romek says, crashing to the ground. Prices are starting to double. Cocoa and sugar are gone from the shelves.

Ulka repeats her question. 'The brother, twig, what did he say?'

Lena shakes her head. 'There's no way of knowing. There are no connections to Warsaw.'

Lena tries to imagine Anton's brother flipping open a silver pocket watch in an elegant apartment, and Anton, who is heaven knows where, standing in some field watching tanks advancing over a hill. Three days ago she was preparing a picnic. She looks into the calm summer sky. Does Anton know she's not in Warsaw and may never get there, or does he believe she and Agata are in a foreign country by now? Her stomach turns. Does he think them safe? Are they safe?

They're eating supper when Ulrich stops by, bringing a gallon of cream and information from the town hall. All postal and news deliveries have been halted. The telephone and telegraph lines are restricted to official communications, but a public service is to resume soon. Ulrich says no one knows when soon is.

Ulka suggests they sleep in the cellar but is outvoted.

In any case, no bombing wakes them in the night. The sun rises red and throbbing, the sky softens, and Mama says grace at breakfast, wondering whether it hasn't all been a false alarm. As if to prove this Ala goes off to work in her usual flurry, and Romek is sent, protesting, to school. Lena doesn't know what to do.

'Come,' Mama says, taking her teacup to the piano. She begins with Liszt, while Agata crawls about, pulling herself up on the piano legs and collapsing down.

'It won't be long,' Mama says. 'She'll be up and running before you know it.'

Lena smiles. She tells Mama how nice the music sounds.

'I did hope one of my children would inherit the inclination. Maybe Agata will prove to be our concert pianist. Tell me, darling, do you have plans for the day? I was wondering whether you might try to reach the brother again this morning?'

Lena looks out of the window at the poplar leaves glittering like medallions in a breeze or a dream of money.

It's your decision, darling, but I'd suspect time is of the essence.'

'How, Mama? I don't know how to do it.'

'A letter perhaps. If the telegraph lines are still out of action.'

Plump blackberries gleam like baubles on the hedgerow on the lane. 'Here feels safe, Mama,' she says quietly.

'I know, darling. I'm glad it does. But sometimes what we feel and what would actually be for the best—'

'Can't we just go berry-picking, Mama, and not think about all this, just for an hour, can we not, like we used to? Ulka wants to preserve as much as possible. I said I'd help, and it's such a lovely morning.'

'And afterwards? We could go together to the exchange.'

'Sure.'

They walk down the lane, Ivan Pavlov leading the way. The brambles are heavy with fruit. How many times in her childhood have they walked like this, buckets rattling against their legs? Only the slightest twist, that's what Papa always said. Never tug the stalks. The berry has to be willing. 'A secret for you girls' – always said with a wink – 'everything has to be willing.'

Lena turns from the hedge, a handful of berries on her palm, to where Mama is sitting on the lane, Agata on her lap. 'They're absolutely perfect. Try one.'

Mama takes a berry and feeds it to Agata. 'He wrote to me you know.'

'Who?'

'Your husband.'

'Anton sent you a letter? You mean when he told you I was pregnant?'

'I mean three months ago, around the time of your birthday.'

Lena stares at Mama for a moment. She turns back to the hedge to think.

'It was a slightly strange note, I must say.'

'He was under a lot of pressure, Mama. We can see why now. Do you remember how Papa swore blind that the berries must want to fall into your hand? He said that every time.'

'Actually he wrote that he wanted to apologise. That he'd not behaved to you as he should and he wanted that on record for the future.'

Lena watches a fruit fly crawl along the underside of a berry.

'Something was clearly troubling him but he didn't say what.'

'I don't know why he felt he should make his apologies to you.'

Mama hesitates. 'I'm not sure I was his intended audience, not really.'

'Why didn't he just write to me then, if he was so keen on forgiveness.'

'You can be very absolute, darling.'

Lena empties her bowl in the bucket and slams it on the ground. 'Right. So it's my fault, what he did?'

'Heavens, no, darling. It's just the letter was something of a shock to receive, especially as you hadn't been in touch. I couldn't imagine him ever wanting to behave in a way that would hurt you. He seemed to have such deep and constant feelings. When I think of how he sat with you those first nights after the accident.'

'Perhaps the feelings were the problem.'

Mama looks up at her. 'What do you mean when you say "what he did"?'

'It doesn't matter now.'

'Oh, Lena, my darling child, tell me. Tell me whatever it is.'

Lena sees the fear in Mama's eyes. 'It's all right, it wasn't very awful with him. Not in the end. It just happened once. Your granddaughter came from it.'

Mama lowers her face and presses her lips to Agata's hair. 'So it was his desire he was writing about. Well, that makes some sense now.'

'You think so?'

'But of course, sweetheart. Men are creatures of passion. It's not unknown for them to become overwhelmed by it.'

'He's written an apology, so now I write back and forgive him?'

'That would be the Christian response. Imagine the trials he's currently enduring. And to bear this additional burden in his heart.' Mama shakes her head.

Lena steps back. 'You're taking his side.'

'There are no sides, darling.'

'Actually it feels like there've been sides for quite a while, Mama. And there's not many people on mine.'

'Come on, darling.' But Lena moves off quickly further along the brambles.

'I never get it right with you,' Mama murmurs behind her. 'I try, but it's never the right thing I say, and I'm sorry for that.'

Every day for a week, Lena picks blackberries, and every evening Ulka tips buckets into two vast pans. 'Compote here, conserve there,' she mutters, mashing fruit with sloshing satisfaction. On a Saturday evening Ulka puts on her lipstick and steps up her stepping out with the butcher. By Sunday lunchtime another pig's cheek or trotter has found its way into the cellar salt barrel.

Lena checks the plum tree in the morning and climbs the ladder for the first of the apples at night. Some days she leaves Agata at home and takes a basket into the birch forest for the early mushrooms, or joins the crowds bobbing up and down in the castle gardens bagging fallen chestnuts. After school Romek is sent complaining to try to net trout, and Ulka sets Mama to work digging up beetroot and onions from the garden. Agata sits in the soil at her feet, examining worms. One afternoon Agata tips forward, her bottom in the air. Gripping two onions by their green stems she wobbles upright and takes three steps after a butterfly, four for a honey bee, and she is off, as Mama exclaims it, running to bang on the kitchen window, 'Come see, come see, Agata is flying!'

Four weeks, maybe even five, pass in this fashion. Lena has made three more attempts to call the brother. The connection is still broken. She isn't sure what she thinks of this. If she's honest she tries not to think about it. Nor is there any word from Anton. He doesn't know his daughter hasn't boarded a plane but is flying in the garden, nor that his wife has taken her mother's advice and written a letter of forgiveness that she doesn't know how or where to send.

Then one morning all voices are gone from the radio; there's nothing but an endless polonaise. The next day Romek turns the dial and there's only static.

England

She will not drink the milkshake Margaret is offering. She shakes her head once, twice, she will shake it for ever if necessary. She's done with all that.

Margaret leaves the drink on the bedside table saying she knows better than to try to persuade her. 'Can I get you anything else before I go?'

She offers Lena a black pen and holds a white board.

Very carefully Lena writes I AM DONE.

Margaret sits on the bed to take Lena's wrist. In her lap, an ampoule of morphine sulphate. 'It won't take long, Magdalena. This pulse is not so strong.'

Once Lena would have asked with interest, how many beats? How regular? She would have asked about readings: systolic, diastolic, resting rates. But these are questions from another, abandoned life.

HOW LONG?

'A few days at most. Probably less.'

Lena stares at the ampoule. One hundred milligrammes would do it. Make it simple. No more delay.

HELP ME.

Margaret is silent a moment. She takes Lena's hand. 'Sweetheart, I can't do that, I'm sorry. But I promise there'll be no pain when the time comes. I'll make sure of that. Will you trust me? Let me give you a top-up now before I go.'

Lena closes her eyes and Margaret sets about finding a serviceable vein.

'When I come back we'll set up a drip and a catheter. You won't have to drink any more, but you need fluids to keep you comfortable.'

Lena hears the needle puncture the ampoule. She feels the sharp slide into her skin, the liquid's cold leak. How much feeling a body does for you, she thinks, how much pain and pleasure it takes into itself. Margaret is stroking hair from her face with light fingertips, just like Mama used to do. Did she ever do this herself, for her daughter or little Jozef? Did she do it enough?

As the opiate begins to seep through her, Lena hears her dogged breath. There's no terminal respiration yet. What is the name for it? There is a name, but Lena cannot think what it is. This body has always been too strong for the life it was given. It has wanted to carry on feeling far too much. Her eyes close, and she begins to float, counting her wheezing breath. One two three four . . .

Przemysl, South East Poland

One two three four. Romek has decided to teach Agata to count even though she's only a year old and yet to say a meaningful word. He's leaning her out of the upstairs window, pointing down the lane. The quiet farm road is alive with boots and red flags. One two three four. One two three four. The family crowd at the window watching an army march past heading for town.

'Look at all those empty stomachs,' Ulka says, shaking her head. She hands Lena a basket and they go racing through the fields.

But everywhere they try in the merchants' quarter, shutters are drawn, the interiors dark. A light is on inside the bakery. Lena runs to bang on the door.

'Who's there?' Mrs Manowska's eye is white at the crack.

'We have leeks to trade. It's Lena Bem.'

Mrs Manowska takes a moment for thinking, and the chain is loosened. 'Be quick, I think I hear them.'

One two three four. One two three four turning in at the top of the street.

Adam's dangling his legs in the pan of the sack scales. 'Go fuck yourselves!'

Mrs Manowska's hands fly to her hair. She ducks behind the counter and brings out two wheat loaves. 'These people, what will they do with my boy?'

Lena touches her shoulder. She hands over the leeks.

One two three four. A hammering at the door.

A voice, heavily accented. 'Open this up for the procurement division of the People's Army.'

Adam clamps his hands over his ears and begins to hoot. The women grab him under the arms and drag him into the storeroom. Mrs Manowska pulls open the hatch that leads out to the street. 'Take the back alleys. Stay safe.'

Lena hurries home through the old town's crooked passageways. There's not so much as a rat to be seen in the gutters. Whatever lives in the town has retreated into the spaces behind its walls. Nothing moves in the streets but a tide of marching.

When she gets back she finds Romek and Agata relocated to the gate to get a closer look at the horses and vehicles now moving down the lane. So many men have passed that the ground is rutted, the verge worn to mud. Romek is making a tally in a notebook, holding Agata on the fence, open-mouthed at the passing circus. The animals are fleabitten, their heads too large for their scrawny necks. Many lack saddles and bits in their bridles. The men on their backs are filthy and too young really to be called men. Ulka is coming and going from the house with buckets of water for those permitted to pause to drink.

The soldiers hear her accent. They thank her and call her sister.

'What manner of conquering is this?' she says; she is shaking her head.

A man with more uniform than most takes several cups from the bucket. He splashes his neck and tells her the town is not conquered. It has been liberated by the People's Army.

Ulka laughs in his face. 'Which people?' She pulls the cup from his hand and turns up the path to fetch more water.

Lena takes Agata into her arms, planting kisses on her nose, looking at Romek's notebook crammed with tiny tally lines.

'Pages and pages of infantry. Thousands of them, Lena. My pencil's blunt.'

'But wherever are they all going to live?'

Ulka appears with the bucket. 'How are the stomachs going to be fed?'

*

The People's Army is to be billeted in homes in the town. When they're not at home sleeping or being fed by the town, the soldiers loll in the park with beer from the taverns. They play cards or throw stones in the lake, and piss their names up the trunks of the limes. When the weather turns cold the soldiers take their beers and piss inside, settling into the town hall and cafes, the library, cinema, hotels and bars. Without protest, the town takes them in. It waits for what will be done to it.

But rumour survives, staying alive in gusts blown along back alleys. Rumour scoffs when it can. These peasant soldiers keep carp in toilet bowls and can't fathom how their fish are flushed away. They consider toothpaste a delicacy and buy it by the crate. Rumour hears half these boys consider electricity the work of a sorcerer and worship forest sprites that eat babies at the full moon.

But rumour is a coy thing too, far too coy to mention all the roubles being spent in the town, and roubles buy so much more than zloty these days. Ulka sells her lacework to soldiers for their wives and sisters. Mama pulls out old recital dresses, and Ulka carts them off to the market square, laying skirts on the cobbles in a fan of extravagance amid scraps of paper and broken bottles. For a week, maybe more, roubles bounce on the kitchen table, sacks of grain tumble down the cellar steps.

Halfway through the winter, leaflets start to fall from the sky like a new kind of snow over town. The first time it happens people crowd the streets staring up, spitting paper from their mouths, shaking it from their hair. Grand proclamations flutter down, clogging the guttering and turn to mush beneath boots. Ink bleeds into the ground.

Ulrich comes by to take tea with Papa. He has twelve soldiers billeted in his hay barn. They are Ukrainians, like him, but unable to write one letter of their names. Not one letter! he exclaims, his finger stabbing the air. He tells Papa these cavalrymen without horses are little more than children. They have no idea

why they were taken from their homes and brought here. He
bangs his palm on the table. No idea!

He shakes his head. This is a bad business, all of it. But
what can you do? He takes a second slice of Ulka's poppy
seed loaf.

Two weeks after the blizzard of leaflets, Lena's family wake to
discover themselves citizens of a different country. Lena goes to
town. It is dressed as if for a party. Red posters paper the walls of
buildings, red drapes flap from the sills of first-storey windows.
Thousands of red chrysanthemums, hurled in celebration of the
new state, have turned to mush underfoot. Agata toddles on this
strange carpet, squatting to dabble her hands in pink puddles,
poking the petals that are staining her shoes. Agata grins. Pink is
her favourite colour.

From the bakery window Mrs Manowska sees Lena coming
and opens the door, a finger to her lips. She has four soldiers billeted to oversee flour distribution, but they're asleep. She brings
out a paper bag of milled rye. It's all she can manage. She whispers in Lena's ear, 'The rumour is we're to surrender our busi-
nesses to Ukrainians.'

A soldier staggers in from a back room, his tunic hanging loose
from his trousers. He stares at Lena, rubbing his jaw. 'Madam,
more beer.'

The door slams behind him.

'Don't believe the drunk show. They measure the flour to the
last gramme.'

'How's Adam?'

Mrs Manowska's mouth begins to tremble. Lena touches her
shoulder.

'They make him their pet. They have him run here and there
and give him foul words to shout for their amusement.'

'Madam! We perish of thirst in here!'

'I must go. Stay safe. Get your little girl home.'

Lena's route passes the telephone exchange, its walls covered in billowing red banners. Soldiers loaf on the stone steps

smoking cigarettes, now and then commenting to each other with smirks tucked into their fists.

Agata stops walking, rubbing her eyes. Lena squats down with a plum to bribe her into being carried. Behind her she can hear one of the soldiers laughing. The low winter sun is out, bleaching the steps, dazzling. And for a moment, when Lena next glances up, it isn't occupying soldiers she sees, but Anton, standing above her, his boots polished, the edges of his frame fizzing in the light.

'What?' she says, her voice loud in her ears. 'What is it you want from me?'

He stares back at her like a ghost. Which is what he must be, because this apparition is made from sunlight and her own anxiety, nothing more. But still Lena can't help herself. 'Are you angry?' she says, 'Have you come because I didn't go to Warsaw? But my family was here, Anton. Please understand. How could I go?'

She hears hissing. The soldiers elbow each other. She looks up and sees them laughing. She grabs Agata and runs.

It's only when Lena's halfway down the lane that she too sees the funny side. For just a moment she became a creature of superstition. In this new world she must take care not to leave her logical thinking behind.

A week later there's a businesslike knock at the front door. Pav runs up wagging his tail. Lena stands in the shadows near the kitchen watching Ulka investigate.

But it's only Ulrich and two of his soldiers.

'A sorry business all this, my sister,' Ulrich says, pulling a red-stamped document out of a satchel. A red armband is stitched to his coat sleeve.

'Will you look at that,' Ulka says. 'And with a red face to match.'

'I've had these boys bring six gallons.' He kicks the milk churn on the path beside him.

'Too generous a gift for these times.'

'You do what you can, sister.'

'Do you?'

Ulrich takes tea with Papa by the fire in the sitting room. Ulka beckons Lena to the crack at the door's hinge.

Ulrich is made a councillor under new laws. His Ukrainian blood is the cause of this demand on him, he says to Papa with a sigh. The position is unwanted, old friend, but what can you do?

Lena imagines Papa of old reaching out to pat Ulrich's knee. Sparks would have crackled in his tiny blue eyes. 'Really, old friend, how unwanted is it?' he would have replied.

'I could not turn this down,' Ulrich says. He sighs again. 'Am I right, old friend? I could not turn it down. Tell me, Jozef, I could not.'

Lena hears Papa's new hesitant voice. 'You could not.'

'There's no way I could.'

Silence. Perhaps Ulrich's now patting Papa's knee. 'How these times place a strain on our tired hearts.'

'Congratulations, comrade,' Lena says as he comes into the hall. 'That's a lovely red armband. You must be heading up in the world.'

He laughs without meeting her eye, his hand moving to finger the strip of material. 'Standard council issue. Nothing special about me, I'm afraid.'

'You're right there.' Ulka emerges with the tea tray. 'Well, councillor, let me show you to the door.'

Ulka steps outside with Ulrich.

The soldiers are smoking by the gate, tossing stubs into the flowerbeds. Ulrich seems about to summon them and leave, then he turns, rubbing his chin, his gaze shifting between Ulka and the open door. 'I almost forgot. There's to be a census of the state. I'm asked to record the names, ethnicities, professions and so forth, of each citizen in my district. Every person is to be accounted for.'

'But you know everything about us,' Ulka snorts. 'We've lived side by side for twenty years. I can smell a fart on the lane and know it for yours. Write that down if you like.'

The soldiers snigger. Ulrich bristles. He holds out the form. 'Lena, for instance, I must record whom she married and the exact nature of his employment. He's now of high rank, I believe. The Engineering Corps, wasn't it?'

Lena retreats further into the hall and creeps into the sitting room. She opens the window, watching Ulka take the document and glance down, her lips tightening.

Ulrich gives the churn a kick. 'I'll stop by tomorrow for the completed census. This milk has a good skin of cream. It shouldn't stand long on the step.'

Rumours swirl with the uncleared autumn leaves. They slip between winter's slicing rain. Under cover of night, rumours prowl around the outside of the house, saw-breathed beneath the windows.

Lena discovers Ala and Ulka at the kitchen table late one evening, sitting in darkness, speaking in whispers. She switches on the light. 'What's so terrible that it can only be voiced at night?'

'It's nothing, twig.'

'Really?'

'Only another little rumour from the hospital.'

'I'm surprised they don't pay you in little rumours, Ala.'

'Now, now.'

Lena looks at Ulka who is gnawing her thumb knuckle, and back at Ala who's staring at the table. 'So what does this little rumour concern?'

Ala glances at Ulka and then at Lena, and seems to lose her voice.

Ulka says it. 'They say bad things are happening to captured army officers.'

'Bad things?'

'In forests, twig. And off the side of ships.' Ala's face is a blaze of pink. 'They're being called traitors to the state.'

Lena walks to the sink and runs the tap. She fills a glass and drinks.

'I'm surprised at you, Ala, passing off stale gossip like it's fresh bread. I overheard all this rubbish at the grocer's yesterday. I'm actually expecting contact from Anton any day.'

She rinses the glass, and walks past the table, turning out the light as she leaves.

In bed she presses herself against Agata, sliding an arm under her back, tucking her legs around her, and turning herself into her daughter's shell. She stares into the darkness, feeling her daughter's soft belly rise and fall, and she tries to conjure the face of this child's father, an army officer out there somewhere in the world's noise and chaos – anywhere at all. But all she sees is a blur turning away, dissolving in a tunnel of light.

There's a tap at the kitchen window the next morning when everyone else is out. It's Ulrich, popping up from nowhere in his big coat, a pullet tucked inside a sleeve. A bird he says he doesn't need. She'll be a decent enough layer, he says, if on the puny side.

'But what a plumage she's got,' Lena says, taking the hen, stretching her chestnut wings.

Ulrich tugs his beard. There's something else he has to say.

'Get a job, Lena.' This is muttered as he looks about the back lawn even though there's only the two of them. His army boys are digging trenches over in the field. 'Find a way to be useful in town. Try to fit in, for God's sake. Become something other than an enemy officer's wife.'

'Is that what I am?'

'It's what they think you are. Get a job. It'll go better for you that way.'

'What will go better?'

But Ulrich is looking around and suddenly he is sprinting across the lawn as though fireworks are lit in his pants. He's leaping the fence back onto his own land, where one of the soldier boys is leaning on his shovel, watching.

Lena sits in her bedroom that afternoon.

She is at her desk, flicking through old notebooks. She has ten of them, crammed with diagrams, scribblings and diagnostic queries, the first page started when she was eleven and three months. Agata is behind her, on the floor. Lena has given her the amber and Agata is throwing it here and there and chasing after it. At some point Lena hears Agata start to scream.

Mama is at the door, watching Lena emerge from under the bed with Agata flailing with fury clutching the amber.

'She got herself stuck.'

'Let me take her. You get back to your reading.'

'You're sure?'

Mama laughs. 'Do you know one day when you and Ala were little I had to shut you both in a room.'

'You left us alone?'

'Only for an hour, maybe two. I went for a walk. After a few miles I decided to come back.' She laughs, lifting Agata and kissing her nose. 'Hush my cross little chicken, what do you say we give your mama a break?'

Lena reads her notebooks all afternoon. When she hears Ala return from work she goes downstairs. 'Might they need volunteers at the hospital, do you think?'

Because war rearranges the laws of possibility. This is what Lena thinks during the winter in her new country. And it might be possible to work at the hospital as if you've been there all your life, even though you have no skills and receive no pay. Ala agrees to ask around. A couple of days later she reports back that the chief paediatrician, Doctor Lasko, will see Lena in his office.

As it turns out it's not so much an office as a cramped cubbyhole off the corridor in the children's ward. Doctor Lasko, a wiry man with a halo of white hair, pulls the curtain, apologising for the smell. The office is next to the toilets. Lena looks around for where to sit and he apologises again, shifting a stack of files from a chair in front of a cluttered desk. His secretary was reassigned at the start of the occupation, which is how he describes the new state, casting Lena a wry glance. He gives up trying to find space on the floor and stacks the files on top of a book on the desk. By the way, has Lena heard there's a measles epidemic in town?

She hasn't.

'Funny what you do and don't get to hear about nowadays.'

'Thank you for seeing me,' Lena says, taking a seat on the cleared chair. She explains that she's required to no longer be the wife of a state traitor, but a useful and long-serving employee in the town. 'I'll understand if you can't help.'

'Nonsense, we need all the hands we can find.' He's peering closely at her. 'But I remember you.'

She shakes her head. 'I was put in the women's ward when I broke my leg.'

'You did just that, touched everything, you couldn't keep your hands off my blood-pressure cuff.'

Lena looks in her hands and lays a stethoscope back on the desk.

He laughs with delight, wagging a finger in the air. 'Good old Aristotle! The child and the woman are indeed the same! Please carry on, have a listen. It's an improved design with clearer acoustics – we can catch pneumonia far earlier these days. Your father brought you in ten or twelve years ago, you would have been eight, perhaps nine? He was helping us find a teacher for the ward, and you sat right there – it was a little more ordered – interrupting and insisting on knowing what everything did. My goodness, it's all coming back now. I was required to explain the principles of medical epistemology for half an hour. Your father kept apologising, but he was tittering behind his fist, the old rogue. How is he these days?'

'Up and down.'

'A fine man. One of the finest.'

'Yes. Yes he is.' A sudden thickness in her throat.

'But tell me about yourself. Have you been pursuing this passion of yours? It's possible for women these days, but you'll already know that, I'm sure. Before all this madness we had a trainee from Warsaw – a marvellous physician. I should hope the universities jumped at the chance of someone as smart and dedicated as you.'

Lena opens her mouth. There is much that could be said, but what's the point. 'Actually I've a young daughter, just turned one.'

'Well, that's a wonderful thing too. Keep her well away from the measles, won't you? House arrest until the worst is over.'

There's a rap on the wall. The curtain is pulled back by a nurse who raises her eyebrows and taps her watch. Doctor Lasko glances at his own watch and springs up. 'Good heavens, where does the time go? We'll walk and talk as we do the round.'

He sets off at a pace down the corridor. 'You'll see how stretched we are. All this upheaval and loss of personnel has consequences. We're a breath away from chaos, I can't pretend otherwise. Why don't you assist in the wards in the mornings?'

'You mean it?'

He laughs at her expression. 'We won't have you operating – not immediately. You have someone to take care of the child?'

'My mother.'

'Ah yes – what a voice that woman has.'

'It wasn't passed on.'

He laughs. 'Initially it won't be much more than donkey work, I'm afraid, bedpans and the like.'

'That's fine, I'll do anything at all.' Lena thinks perhaps she shouldn't be grinning, but she can't help it.

'We all muck in. And as I no longer have the power to officially employ you, I'm sorry to say that means I can't officially reimburse you . . .' He breaks off as a uniformed man passes with a rifle slung from his shoulder, then he bends to her ear, '. . . but should our new authorities make enquiries I'm sure we'll discover you've been nursing here for years.'

'I could start right now, organising those files if you want?'

'You'd do that?'

'Try and stop me.'

'This is going to work out marvellously, I can tell. But first you'd better come and meet some of our guests, a tremendous bunch we have with us at the moment. Let me introduce you to Jan. Jan's six. His particular passion – and you must always find it out – because passion is what tends to land people in here – well, his happens to be climbing, unfortunately he's a little too wild about it, which is why he's strung out in here with a smashed fibula and tibia, and not hanging from the top of a tree. Good morning, Jan. How was the gruel today, as atrocious as ever?'

And he strides off into the ward.

Winter deepens. Christmas is a quiet affair. At the vigil meal a place is set at the table for a passing stranger, but none turns up. Mama receives a note informing her that her services are no longer required for the advent concert. When Ulrich is approached for explanation, he rubs his beard and mutters that traditional peasant ballads were felt to be more appropriate. The family has handed in their passports as required. Ulrich is most relieved to hear this. His beard is shot with grey these days.

Through the new year and into the spring Lena kisses Agata on the nose after breakfast and flies out of the house with Ala to go to the hospital. The trams have stopped running so Ala and Lena walk. There are tannoys now in the town. Every morning along their route the tannoys talk to them. Recently they've been offering a year's supply of bread for information leading to the arrest of traitorous army officers.

Ala looks to Lena, and Lena shrugs. 'What? There's no bread around for a month, never mind a year, everyone knows that.'

Ala laughs out loud and squeezes Lena's arm. Ala whistles on her way to work these days and wears ribbons in her plaits. She doesn't say why.

At first, for four hours a day Lena washes floors, empties bedpans and reorders files. If time allows she also demonstrates conjuring tricks Romek has deigned to share, or reads fairy tales, or plaits bumpy cornrows into hair. She takes it on herself to fetch tea for shattered parents, and always adds a spoon more honey than they ask for. She makes beds and runs baths and smiles at everyone. At home in the evening she reads her encyclopaedia and starts a new notebook, this time featuring living patients. Whenever someone catches her smiling, Mama or Ulka mostly, Lena simply shrugs. 'People aren't allowed to be happy in wartime?' she says.

It's not just that she likes it. She's good at it, she sees that too. Over time Doctor Lasko starts to demonstrate procedures, and ask for her opinions about diagnosis or treatment. On occasions he tells her she's completely right. When he adds, as he often does, that she'll be as good as qualified when the war is done, and he'll fight any other hospital that wants to take her, she spends the whole day walking on a cushion of air.

Lena helps to set broken limbs and suture wounds, she monitors heart rates and learns to take blood. After a while she starts to think there's nothing she can't do. But one morning, when the matron asks her to change the sheets where a baby girl has been lost to the measles, she's blindsided. Lena touches her hand to the imprint of the small body. The sheet is still warm. She runs from the ward.

Doctor Lasko finds her in the corridor and takes her into his office.

'Sit down.' He pulls his own chair close.

'I was thinking of Agata.'

'Of course you were. Which makes me think of somebody who once told me we have to confront our fears. We get nowhere when we run from them.'

Lena fumbles in her bag for a handkerchief. 'A trite thing to say.'

'It was a girl with leukaemia who told me.'

She blows her nose. 'Thank you. Now I feel even worse.'

He laughs. 'Tereza was a remarkable child. They all are, each in their way. She was right, of course. You can stand in fear's shadow if you like. You can stand there an hour or a day. Some people stay there much of their lives. But wouldn't it be better to step out and face reality, whatever that may be?'

Lena thinks of the dead child's parents as they left the ward, the father holding up his stumbling wife. 'How do you cope? How can you go home and play with your own children, and sit enjoying your supper after seeing all this every day?'

He smiles softly. 'You have a point. To refuse to feel another's pain is also to deny it. But what would it serve if I neglected my family and sat in a corner drinking myself to death? Someone needs to do this job. Someone needs to turn up in the morning to help the next child who comes in.'

'So the dead ones don't matter.'

'I didn't say that. Every death is a failure I carry with me. If you lose that belief you lose what makes you a physician – the desire to ease suffering. After all, that's why we're here, you and I, isn't it? Personally I try to remember that for every death there's also a child who comes into this place and is cured. That's what helps me. You'll discover what works best for you.'

She scrunches the handkerchief into a ball and watches it unfurl in her hand. 'I've taken up too much of your time. I'll go and change that bed.'

'Wait a moment . . .' He turns to the row of books Lena's shelved along the windowsill. 'Perhaps for you knowledge is going to be the best defence against fear.'

He hands her a heavy hardback. 'It's a spare. Take it.'

Lena looks at the manual of paediatric medicine, fresh tears in her eyes. She draws back the curtain to leave. He's smiling at her.

'You'll make a superb doctor one day, Lena.'

'Because I can't change a bed?'

'Because you have the heart for it.'

Militia men loiter by the hospital gates in March. No one knows at first whether they're simply there to pass the time, smoking and telling jokes, the rifles on their backs rocking with laughter. Then a day comes when they're seen checking papers as people arrive for treatment. The rifles swing round and point at people's stomachs.

A man staggers up to the gates carrying a boy, long and lolling in his arms. The militia men continue to smoke and tell their jokes. Eventually one turns and asks a question. The man shakes his head. The guard shrugs and returns to his cigarette and his story. The man shifts the weight of the child in his arms. He reaches out and taps the guard's shoulder, but it mustn't be felt because he taps again. The guard turns, still grinning from his tale, but in a flash he's stabbing his rifle at the man's chest, then his forehead, forcing him back and back again. Eventually the man turns and stumbles away carrying his boy to the road. The guard slings his gun into a comfortable position and returns to his story. At its conclusion his friends laugh a long time and slap him on the shoulder. It looks like a good joke they're sharing.

Doctor Lasko turns from the window, his face tight. 'Come with me to the office please, Lena.'

She watches him take off his white jacket and pull on his overcoat, folding his stethoscope into a pocket.

He hands her his white jacket. 'Keep an eye on things here. Monitor the temperature and check the heart rate of the lad in bed three.'

'But where are you going? What do I say if someone asks?'

'I'm taking an early lunch. Back soon.' He walks quickly to the door to the stairs.

Lena does as he asks. She puts on the jacket and keeps an eye on things. She passes the mirror, sneaking glances at her reflection. She can't decide whether she's surprised or not to see a woman who looks like a medic. But she can't deny how good it feels.

Within the hour Doctor Lasko is back, but he doesn't remove his overcoat. She follows him into the storeroom watching him search through the pharmaceutical cupboards. The boy that was brought to the gates has malaria, he tells her. His name is Tomasz Wimieck. He's been in for this before.

'But I know the family,' Lena hears herself saying. 'His eldest sister was in my form at school. Give me the tablets, I'll deliver them on my way home.'

Lasko turns, raising a finger to his lips. He glances into the corridor.

'I'm sorry but I can't let you do that.'

'What do you mean? It'll be easy for me. It's on my way home.'

'You have a young child.'

'So?'

He scratches his head and looks at her intently. 'This isn't a game, Lena.'

'I know that.'

'Are you sure you do?'

But it's pounding in her, right now, the certainty. 'We're here to ease suffering. You yourself said that.'

'We are.'

'And you have all these children here to think of. Let me be useful.'

'Excuse me, doctor' – a nurse is at the door – 'you really need to take a look at the girl in bed seven.'

'I'll be along shortly.' He looks at Lena and the bottle of pills in his hand.

'I know where they live.'

'This once only.'

She takes the bottle.

'Wait there . . .' He runs to his office and fetches a thermometer case and a stethoscope. 'Check his heart rate and temperature. Remind them about the importance of fluids: a simple vegetable broth if he can manage it. Crush the quinine tablets in honey – two to be taken four times a day.'

There's a roaring in her ears as she walks past the militia. A waterfall of blood crashing inside her. She goes quickly in case they can hear it somehow, in case they can see she's not actually walking, but striding far above them – a giantess doctor in her white coat. Because they are no bigger than ants, these petty young boys, but she, she is on her way to her first house call. The Wimiecks' house is only three streets away. It won't take a moment for a giantess doctor to make it.

All afternoon at home she finds her thoughts returning to her visit to the Wimieck boy; sitting by his bed, lifting his nightshirt to listen with the stethoscope to the wheeze in his lungs, pressing it against his chest, finding the spot closest to the mitral valve. Most of all she remembers the way the mother gripped her hand at the door before she left. 'I don't know how to thank you, doctor,' she'd said. And there'd been no time, it seemed, to reply, 'You're mistaken, I'm no doctor. I'm just Lena Bem.'

'There's something different about you,' Ulka says, staring when Lena gets home. 'All this skipping about like someone's given you a key to a chest full of gold.'

Lena smiles. 'I have no idea what you mean.'

'There's apple strudel for supper. With cream. You'll tell me in the end.'

But Ulka's distracted from interrogation that evening because a far juicier subject lands on the dinner table when the strudel's finished and Ulka's gathering up scraped plates. It comes courtesy of an announcement from Ala. She has good news, she says, licking her spoon. She's to marry.

Lena splutters into her water glass. 'You dark horse!'

'Marry?' Mama shrieks, crossing herself three times. 'Mother of God, but this is from nowhere. I don't understand. Where's this come from?'

'It's very simple. I love him. He asked me. I said yes.' Ala pushes back her chair.

'Where do you think you're going?' Ulka says. 'You haven't even told us his name.'

'Molek.'

'Molek?'

'His name is Molek.'

'Is that some sort of family pet name?' Mama says in a weak voice.

'No, Mama.'

'Is it a village name?'

'I really must wash my hair now, thank you for supper.' And Ala is gone.

'Well,' Mama says to the silent table. 'Well, whatever sort of name is that?'

Lena finds Ala in the bathroom, kneeling with a jug over the bath.

'He's twenty-seven and a farrier.' She turns her head to grin at Lena. 'He's got marvellous hands. I mean he's totally wonderful all over, his hair's black like the devil and he's an ogre – he walks like one at least – and his forearms are something else, but his hands, my God, they're the most marvellous thing of all.' Ala lathers shampoo into a wobbling meringue on her head. 'He makes me laugh, twig. I can't tell you how he makes me laugh.'

Lena looks at her sister, grinning to split her cheeks. All this babbling is probably just a result of hanging her head upside down and blood rushing to the brain.

'How did you meet this marvellous-handed devilish ogre?'

Ala laughs. 'That's the incredible thing. He came in with an infected cut on his heel. Tuesday January seventeenth it was. It was ten thirty-one, I'd just come back from my break. Two minutes earlier and another girl would have booked him in. Just imagine.'

'I'm trying.'

'One second of looking at his pitiful, crumpled face and it was decided for me. Actually, it felt like it was decided without me. It was like some force whooshed me up and flung me round the ceiling, and when I was back down at my desk I was staring at him, and I knew I'd be looking at him for the rest of my life. Do I sound crazy?'

'Yes.'

'Pass me a towel. I think I'd stopped believing it could happen like that, but it really does.'

Lena sits on the edge of the bath, then she slides down to the floor.

Ala glances at her, twisting her wet hair into a turban. 'You all right?'

For some reason she's trying to remember Anton's face: the exact position of his features, the cut of his hair and how it parts, the precise shade of his irises. But all she sees is a narrow shape melting into the sun.

'So when you walk into the cafe what kind of cake is this ogre then?'

'He's the cake I want most at any moment – at every moment – whatever I want right then, it's always him.' Ala shakes her head and laughs. Lena could probably go from the room, all the way downstairs and out into the lane and she'd still hear Ala laughing. 'Did I tell you how good he is with his hands?'

At the end of supper the next evening Ala makes a second announcement. Molek has been good with more than his hands, so they're getting married the following week with only the priest and God watching. Mama sobs at thought of missing a second daughter's wedding. But given the thickening of Ala's waist, not to mention the fact church weddings are now illegal, it's a business best done on the quiet. A week later they make it official by filling in forms at the town hall.

Consequently there are accommodations to be made. Ulrich comes round at breakfast when Ala and Molek are taking a stroll by the San. He breaks the news that the council has requisitioned Molek's smithy. Fifteen men can be housed in the forge, and why would a horse need metal on its feet when working folk all over the world go shoeless? Ulrich consults his housing list. He's pleased. The Sadowski family will be seen to be helping. So, Mama says, this Molek of Ala's must be welcomed into the home and treated like a brother or son.

'Does that mean this Molek gets to share my poky room?' Romek looks up from the end of the table where he's shuffling sugar lumps under teacups. 'I can't have him watching rehearsals.' Romek is practising for a magic show he plans to put on in the market square. He claims the town is in need of entertainment.

'No, darling, this Molek will share with Ala now they're husband and wife.'

Agata drops her spoon on the table. 'This Molek.'

Everyone turns and looks at her.

'What did you say?' Romek sniggers. 'Say it again, squirt face, say it again.'

'This Molek.'

They all start to laugh. The titters go from one to the next like a current sent along the table. Even Papa smiles into his glass.

'This Molek,' Agata says. 'This Molek.'

'His name's Molek, little frog,' Lena says, shaking her head and wiping her eyes, 'There's no "this" about him.'

'This Molek is not This Molek.' Romek pulls a face, so Agata bangs her spoon and copies him. 'This Molek. Not This Molek.'

Everyone roars. And the damage is done.

As it turns out there are plenty of accommodations to be made. For one thing This Molek is fond of having a bottle of vodka at the supper table. It's Papa's vodka he likes, as This Molek's still has been requisitioned by the occupying army. And: 'Mother of God,' Mama whispers to Ulka in the kitchen, 'even for an ogre, have you seen how much he eats?' This Molek is also observed to be fond of an indelicate joke, the conclusion of which he enjoys most of all. Sometimes the sudden strike of his palm on the table makes both Papa and Agata jump at once. Sometimes when he shouts 'To the bottom!' a belch escapes from beneath his black moustache.

'Isn't he marvellous?' Ala sighs, sitting at the kitchen table, dipping her thumb in the pickle jar. 'Just look how he's sorting us all out.'

This Molek's plan, as he explains it, taking a break from carving up the back lawn to slurp sweet tea at the kitchen table, is to turn the entire garden – lawns, rosebushes and flowerbeds – into crop rows. 'Imagine it,' This Molek whirls an invisible pitchfork in the air, 'we shall create potato heaven.'

'He's thinking of his vodka,' Ulka mutters at the sink.

'So you're just going to plant potatoes?' Lena says.

'You don't like potatoes? Your daughter doesn't like potatoes?'

'I didn't say that.'

'Who in this world does not like potatoes?'

'I like potatoes,' Ala offers.

'Of course you do, princess. You are a sensible woman, which is why you married me. Potatoes we can trade. We might even exchange them for these roubles everyone loves. With roubles we buy a cow. From this cow comes milk. With this milk my princess will grow a strong baby when he arrives in the autumn.' This Molek beams at Lena, 'And there will be some milk for your little girl too.'

Ulka rolls her eyes at Lena.

'So,' This Molek says slurping, his black eyes glinting, 'please be so kind as to remind me what the problem is with chopping up all that pretty green grass?'

Ala titters over the pickle jar, as if her husband is the funniest as well as the most marvellous of men. It seems Lena can't stop bumping into them these days. They even go into the bathroom together, and when they emerge – after several knocks on the door – Ala is usually leaning against him, like she's somehow fallen into him and can't pull herself out. Only this morning when Lena was clearing the breakfast plates she glimpsed the glistening slug of This Molek's tongue disappearing into Ala's ear.

'It's wonderful that you've come up with all these plans, and the cow is an excellent idea.'

'It is, sister, it is that.'

'It's just I wonder whether you might leave a small corner of lawn for Agata to play on. It's not so easy to take her out these days, and summer's coming. Your child will also come to enjoy the grass in time. If you take up all the turf, who knows when we'll be able to replant it, you see?'

'I do, I do see. Molek will redraw his plans.'

Lena glances at Ulka with half a smile. 'You will?'

'With pleasure! You ask for a lawn? No problem! Would you also like a flowering border?'

'That sounds lovely, but it's not necessary, just a little grass would do.'

'Chrysanthemums perhaps? Chrysanthemums are no problem.'

'I really don't mind. Chrysanthemums sound nice.'

This Molek turns away from the table, his shoulders shaking. He slaps himself several times on the thigh. 'You nearly had me, you did! You did! Chrysanthemums sound nice.' He is waggling his finger at Lena, merriment popping in his eyes. 'But then Molek does some thinking for a moment, and what he thinks is, when your little girl is starving will she want to eat chrysanthemums? Will my son chew on a lawn? Why, Molek will do no such thing!'

Lena glances at Ulka who is scowling at the floor. Ala is giggling, her fingers paddling up This Molek's thigh.

'Excuse me,' Lena says pushing back her chair. Loud, manly laughter follows her to the end of the hall.

She finds Mama in the conservatory, humming Liszt on the daybed.

'We can't live with him, Mama, it's impossible. Today he almost accused me of wanting to starve Agata.'

'That's terrible, darling.'

'So tell him to leave.'

Mama doesn't open her eyes.

'Mama?'

'Darling, I really don't think I can. For one thing it would upset Ala terribly.'

'Have you seen them together?'

'They do seem wrapped up in each other.'

'Wrapped up? Ala's practically growing out of him.'

Mama raises an eyelid and smiles. 'Your sister is so full of joy these days, which is such a blessing in pregnancy. It will have a wonderful effect on the child.'

'Goddamn Ala.'

'Language, darling, please. Give it time. A new body will always rearrange the air around it.'

'Excuse me?'

'Ulka said it once.'

'I'm not sure she'd say it again.'

'That may be, but as we are without choice, hadn't we better make our peace with what it is we have?' Mama closes her eyes and Liszt resumes.

*

Lena finds herself thinking about bodies and the arrangement of air late into the night. She can't sleep; foxes are barking in the field, and Agata's woken for the third time flush-cheeked and unhappy from teething. Across the landing she can hear snickering and bedsprings, as if it's not three in the morning and there isn't work tomorrow and patients to be visited across town. She plumps the pillow and slaps it against the headboard. 'Come on, little frog, it's time to try to sleep.'

Agata shakes her head and sits up. 'No, no, no.'

Lena rubs her daughter's back, thinking about air and how her once solid husband has dissolved completely into it. She wonders if she were asked to describe him, what she'd say. Theirs was no world of wandering tongues or fingers paddling on thighs. Lena thinks of the last day she saw Anton. Most clearly she sees the file on the table among tomatoes sliced for a picnic.

'Should I have taken you to Warsaw, little frog? Is that what we should have done?' She thinks about her daily life – about the hospital, and she thinks how strange the world turns, because she is now doctoring after all. In a way her destiny has been delivered. She mulls this over with increasing satisfaction, yawning. Of course the only thing that really matters, logically speaking, is that she sleeps. Lena is going in early tomorrow.

Quickly, Lena.' Doctor Lasko beckons her into his office, his manner tense.

It's mid afternoon. She's just back from her rounds. The militia has been turning away increasing numbers of sick children from the hospital. These days she only returns to the ward to be seen eating lunch and receive fresh instruction from Doctor Lasko. She takes out her notebook with details of the children she's visited that morning.

'Put that away,' he says, glancing out into the corridor and pulling the curtain across.

'What's going on?'

He doesn't seem to hear. 'Your daughter's one, yes?'

'Heading towards eighteen months.'

She watches him bend to a drawer in his desk. His hand is trembling as he turns a key in the lock.

She says, 'Shall I tell you about the children I saw? I've written it all down. There's one, the little Janucek girl, who's worsening. I'm not sure the linctus is helping, her blood pressure's very low, so you might want to see her yourself.'

'I will, yes, thank you, Lena, that's excellent, really excellent.' He's nodding too hard for Lena to think he's listened. He pulls open the drawer and takes out a thin glass tube the size of a cigarette with tiny yellow pills inside, pressing the tube into her palm, 'Its name is Prontosil. There should be enough to treat one major bacterial infection in an adult. Two in a small child.'

Lena stares at the tube. 'I don't understand.'

'Put it in your bag. Do it now.'

She looks at him and pushes the tube into the lining of her handbag.

He passes a hand through his hair and smiles at her, but no light comes to his eyes. 'Soon there'll be no more antibacterial treatments available – not even in hospital. This isn't a town to fall sick in, Lena.'

'I don't understand.'

'Take the tablets home. Go now. Take the back stairs and the quiet streets, stay away from anywhere you've been today, and don't ever come back.'

'But I don't understand,' she says, panic rising in her. 'What's changed? Have I done something? You said I could stay here. That I would be a doctor here one day. When all this is over we'll fight to keep you on, that's what you said.'

He no longer seems to care. He pulls back the curtain. 'And now I'm telling you to stay at home. Look after your daughter. Go, Lena. Burn that notebook when you get back.'

She stares at him. All over she is trembling.

His lips move to speak then he simply shakes his head.

'The notebook,' she says quietly offering it to him.

He turns away. 'Lena, go.'

At the curtain she hesitates, thinking he's spoken. 'Doctor Lasko?'

'We did the right thing,' he says. 'We must remember that.' She looks at him, but he isn't talking to her. He's at the window staring out at the sky.

In the stairwell going down she's passed by four men coming up wearing red armbands and dark uniforms. They take the steps two at a time, rifle stocks snug in their fists, smells of motor oil and sweat in their wake. These men are nothing like the soft-faced boys who dispense mockery at the gates; they are muscular, intent. She turns to see them pause at the third floor. One of them pulls back the door to the children's ward.

Lena's legs buckle under her. She grabs for the banister, cowering, for a moment every part of her paralysed. The door slams behind the men and she's alone in the stairwell. Seconds pass. Breath comes with a spasm in her chest.

A minute passes in complete silence. Lena clings to the banister. Slowly she feels for the step below.

Head down, Lena passes the militia at the gates and turns onto the street in the direction of home. She can do it if she modulates her movements, if she imagines a metronome is clicking in her core. With this metronome she will automate herself, turn her body into a machine without sensation of any kind, without the capacity to replay images of armed men running up stairs, without a human heart that might rupture before it reaches a child at home. She must make herself a mechanism possessing only forward motion. Tick tick tick tick.

'Where's Agata?'

'Nice to see you too.'

Lena brushes past Ulka in the hall. She runs to the conservatory.

Ulka follows her, and puts her hand on the door. 'Your mother had a bad night with your father wandering again. Don't disturb her. Agata's fine.'

'If she's so goddamn fine, where is she?'

'Come with me into the kitchen.'

Ulka points out the window. 'The potato man has got himself a new employee.'

Lena runs out and seizes Agata so tightly that she yells and squirms to be free. Ulka opens the back door. On the kitchen table there's a bottle of plum vodka.

Ulka shoves a glass towards Lena. 'Drink.'

Lena shakes her head.

'It will help.'

'Nothing will help.'

Some hours later, when Agata's asleep, Ala knocks on Lena's bedroom door carrying a bowl. 'Are you sick?'

Lena sits up, squinting at Ala in the yellow light in the doorway, steam from the bowl curling around her like mist.

'Only Ulka said something was up. Why are you lying in the dark if you're wide awake? I brought you broth.'

Lena says nothing.

Ala doesn't leave. 'Doctor Lasko's been taken to the castle for questioning.'

Lena stares at her.

'Four policemen came and took him away. His wife tried to visit him but she was told he'd already gone. No one would tell her what that meant. They have three children, did you know, and she's expecting another the same month as me.'

As Ala talks Lena begins to feel herself tipping forwards off the bed. Although she knows her body doesn't in fact move anywhere, she has a vivid sensation of dropping through the floor, passing through the solid wood boards with ease, falling into the sitting room below. Ala talks and Lena continues to travel through floorboards and footings, then soil and rock down into the earth's liquid core. Untouched by fire she tumbles on, out of the other side into an emptiness beyond, falling without end because there's nothing solid enough in this universe to stop her.

Ala is staring at her. 'I said did Lasko say what he was up to, twig?'

'Promise me you'll look after Agata.'

Ala looks down at the bowl in her hands. 'I'm at work all day. You should probably ask Mama or Ulka.'

'Just make the goddamn promise, Ala. Is it too much to ask?'

'I promise,' she says quietly, putting the bowl on Lena's desk. 'It's pumpkin and caraway. Is there anything you want to tell me. If I can help—'

'You can't.'

Lena turns her face away and curls around Agata.

Ala slides down to the floor in the doorway. 'I'll just sit here a little while. My back's killing me.'

It was Adam Manowski, the baker's son. This is what Ala discovers the next day and reports back to Lena in the bedroom. Without enough of the correct medication his brain unravelled. 'Back again for a fucking chat, doctor? More fucking pills I don't want?' Rumour has it he went running onto the street in his bedshirt, hissing and hurling pills into the drain – pills that the new council had said (in typed, signed and stamped documentation no less) would be wasted on such a creature. And look, more than one diligent observer was rumoured to say, wasn't our council proved right? Rumour adds that Doctor Lasko has been taken from the castle, minus a handful of teeth, and marched into the birch forest.

'Are you all right?' Ala asks Lena. 'Really?'

'I guess they'll come knocking soon enough.'

Ala stares at her. 'Whatever do you mean?'

Lena looks at Agata, asleep on the bed, and she strokes her hair.

Ala sits down on the mattress next to Lena. She puts her arm around her. 'I never wanted a sister, you know. But when you came I got quite used to you.'

They sit together, their backs against the wall. After a few minutes Ala's head lolls against Lena's shoulder and Lena lowers her down beside Agata. She covers them both with the blanket, then draws up a chair and sits by the bed.

Lena reaches to Agata's tiny open hand, the fingers slackened in sleep. Anguish moves in her to touch it. The pain is slow and heavy. It is a cutting and a deadening; a plough being hauled through her chest.

She bends closer, touching her forehead to Agata's palm. She kisses the seams in the flesh. There is so much growing for this hand to do, changes that will happen imperceptibly, by day and night. Soon the fingers will learn to grip pens, to scribble and colour. In time they will shape letters and words. These hands might move over a piano keyboard as Mama hopes, or dice Ulka's onions. The infant nails will widen, they'll be trimmed ten thousand times, and painted in bold reds or perhaps shy pinks. And one day, when all its growing is done, when the muscles are strong and the fingers adept, this hand might come to wrap itself around another tiny fist.

The moon climbs and falls in the sky and Lena keeps her daughter's hand in her own, as an iron plough carves her heart to strips. She mustn't think of this hand's future – of that future happening without her. If she does, she cannot draw breath. But she cannot turn away. She watches Agata sleep, each mumble and hiccup and sigh. And she waits for a knock at the door.

But it does not come when Lena expects, and when day breaks she rises quietly from the bedroom floor, and goes to find This Molek. He's crouched outside Papa's shed, stirring eggshells into a pail of chicken shit, surveying lumpy earth that was once lawn.

'Good morning, sister. You too like the dawn?' he says beaming. 'Or was my wife's snoring driving you crazy?'

'Do you have tools?'

'I have.'

'Can you drill a hole in this?' Lena holds out the amber.

Wiping his hands, This Molek straightens up. He turns the amber in the sunshine, whistling in admiration. 'Where did you find this beauty?'

'Can you drill into it?'

'There's a spider in there, can you see? Poor little fellow.'

'It's actually a fly.'

'Thousands and thousands of years ago, you were crawling about on a tree, spinning your web, not looking where you were going.' He tuts and taps the amber, 'Always look where you're going, little spider.'

'It's a fly.'

'Fly or spider, it's an ancient marvel. What a beauty.'

Lena snatches the amber back. 'Can you drill into it?'

'Amber is soft, sister. If I drill, we'll break this beauty's heart.'

'It's dead. Its heart's already broken.'

He looks her over as plainly as he might a lame horse. 'Ala says you're troubled but you don't care to say why.'

'Can you do it? If not, I'll find another way, I don't have much time.'

'Sure, I can do it. A Polish man can fly to the moon if he chooses.'

She hands him the amber. 'It'll need some sort of cap fitting on the end.'

'For what purpose?'

She bites her lip and looks away.

'Lena,' he touches her arm, 'we are brother and sister now. It may be that Molek is not the brother you would choose, but please, you will put away suspicions. I cannot fit a cap without understanding its function.'

'Fine.' She feels in her pocket and takes out the tube of anti-bacterials. 'Don't ask me how I got them.'

He whistles, staring at her for a moment. 'All right, I don't ask.' He pours the tiny pills into the palm of his hand, peering as though he's panning gold. 'This is what Molek will do. I will make a tunnel up the centre of the amber and cap it with a short screw. It will not be pretty. It may hurt the little spider inside.'

'But will it keep them safe?'

This Molek pours the pills back into the glass tube and hands it back to Lena. 'Do you trust me?'

'Will you do it now? It needs to be ready as soon as you can.'

He touches her cheek with the side of his thumb. 'Ala loves you very much.'

'Will you do it?'

'Yes, sister. Molek will drop all his plans and do it. Now go away please. It will be ready soon.'

When Agata wakes up, Lena takes her into the bathroom to wash. She's running hot water when This Molek's hand appears round the door, holding out the amber.

'Try it.'

She uncaps the glass tube and carefully pours the Prontosil pills into the narrow tunnel he's carved into the centre of the resin.

He hands her a tiny brass screw. 'A perfect match for amber. Twist it.'

She feeds the screw into the thread. When she turns the amber upside down the pills rattle in the tunnel, making a thin yellow core.

This Molek beams. 'Perfect, yes? Now you say thank you, brother Molek.'

She stares at the amber in her hand.

'Thank you, brother,' he says. 'Not a problem, sister.'

Lena tucks the amber under her pillow that night, and though she tries to stay awake, she curls round Agata and is soon asleep. A third day has passed and it hasn't come for her, the militia's knock at the door.

It's early April when it happens. When she'd almost started believing she was safe. The hammering begins in the dead of night and is so forceful that Lena wakes thinking axes are bringing down walls. Ivan Pavlov jumps up, whining. Agata is also awake, her eyes wide and staring. Lena turns to her. 'It's all right, little frog.' And in a way, it is. The waiting is over, what she feared is here. It's almost a relief.

Doors are opening along the landing. Papa's voice is raised. 'What are you going on about, Zosia, what occupation? You're making things up to fool me. Get away, woman, you think I don't know how to put on a bloody foot?' Downstairs Lena can hear Ulka yelling – presumably to say she's on her way, they can stop their banging, spare the paint and the wood.

Lena pulls a sweater and skirt over her nightdress and sits quietly holding Agata on her lap. The surge of near relief has given way to nausea and a deep muscular heaviness, as though her body is inexorably being petrified.

'Lena?' Ala's face is at the door.

She looks up. 'It's me they want.'

'What are you talking about?'

She stands, lifting Agata to her shoulder and wrapping her with a shawl so she isn't cold. She takes the amber from her desk.

She only has to do what she's rehearsed in her head, that's all. She mustn't allow herself to think about her daughter's smell or smile, she won't look at her face or listen to her breath. 'Come on, little frog.'

Ala steps aside and Lena carries Agata onto the landing. Down in the hall, Ulka is tying her robe and patting down her hair. The noises have stopped.

Lena looks at her family in their nightclothes, their faces soft from sleep. Her voice comes from her like a slur. 'It's me they want. Don't worry.'

'You're making no sense,' Ala hisses, 'will you stop it.' This Molek has his arms clamped around her, like a great standing bear.

Lena watches Ulka at the door below, sliding the chain. In a moment, when the handle turns, everything will change.

She goes quickly to Ala. 'Take Agata for me.'

'Lena, what's got into you?'

'You promised.'

'I didn't think you meant this, not like this.'

'Take her, goddammit, while I can do it.'

'What's going on?' Mama says, her eyes glittering. 'I don't understand any of this. Lena darling? Ala? What's all this about?'

Ala looks away, her hand at her mouth.

'Just take her into your room and shut the door.' The words slur, iron weights her mouth. 'Don't come out until I'm gone, you hear me. I can't do it if I hear her crying.'

Ala's face is ashen. 'I'll keep her safe until you come back. Because you'll be coming back. I know you will.'

'Sure she will, princess,' Molek says, his hands rubbing Ala's shoulders, his soft smile for Lena. 'She'll be back by lunchtime, this one.'

'But where's Magdalena going?' Papa says.

Lena kisses the crown of her daughter's head where the hair swirls like a pinwheel since the day she was born. She hands Ala the amber and, prising Agata's fingers from her sweater, she kisses each hot palm. Ala takes the baby from her without a word and slips into the bedroom. The door closes.

'Lena?' Romek is touching her shoulder. But she can't feel him. Her arms are useless to her now, her chest cold as a sea wall. She starts down the stairs with no sensation of the boards beneath her feet. Behind her, Papa's voice goes on. 'Where's Magdalena going? Answer me, Zosia. It's not safe at this time of night.'

Ulka is drawing the bolts in the hall. She glances at Lena frowning, and she opens the door, pushing it wide. It takes several seconds for her to find her voice.

'You. Of all the people, you.' She turns back inside.

Ulrich; this is who steps into the house in his long coat, the one with the red band above the elbow, pausing at the mat to brush off his boots. Two soldiers barge past him, rifles raised, and a short, plump man in a grey suit and trilby enters, blinking beneath the hall light. He looks like a small-town bookkeeper, a briefcase clamped in his arms, his shoes slightly scuffed.

Lena walks towards the open door. There's nothing to keep her in this world now. 'I'm ready.'

The man glances at her and looks to Ulrich, speaking Russian. 'How many have we on the list, comrade, six I believe?'

Ulrich gives a small nod, his arms tight-folded across his chest.

'Six?' Lena says. 'No, it was just Doctor Lasko and me. No one else.'

'You piece of shit. You take her and I will kill you with these hands.' Ulka rushes at Ulrich, slamming him against the wall, then pushing him back towards the door. 'You have no place in this house, shit piece. Get out. Go shit in another family's home.' He makes no move to defend himself, taking her blows until one of the soldiers steps in and pulls her off.

'Ulrich, old friend!' Leaning over the banister, Papa waves with both arms. 'Wonderful to see you. Shall we get the board set up, what do you say?'

When Ulrich speaks, his eyes don't leave the floor, his voice is no longer that of a man who calls home his herd from a kilometre away. 'Every resident will make themselves known in the kitchen. No one is to attempt to leave. We have armed men placed at each exit with instructions to shoot if required.'

Lena goes after him. 'Just goddamn take me. I mean that's why you're here, isn't it? Let's get this done.'

'Lena,' he says hoarsely, 'I tried to prevent this. You need to know I tried.'

'What did you try to prevent? What are you talking about?'

He looks away. 'Tell your mother I tried.'

She stares at him and goes past him into the kitchen. Behind her, the sound of her family coming slow-footed down the stairs, and Agata, starting to cry.

'Please make yourselves comfortable.' The plump man removes his hat and lays it with his briefcase on the table. 'Go ahead, madam, and your husband also, sit, sit, please.' He indicates the chairs. Mama beckons Romek to her side and wraps her arm around him. Papa's fingers strum the oilcloth. At the sink, Ulka has her fists pressed to the draining board, her shoulders raised in a ridge. This Molek and Ala come in and Lena takes Agata back with a sob at feeling the weight of her child in her arms. She rocks and shushes her into quiet.

The man gazes round, his expression civil. Noticing Agata, he smiles like any parent on seeing a stranger's child and being reminded of their own. 'I'm sure you'll be wondering why we've asked you to assemble.' His voice is mild, as if he is commenting on the day's weather. He takes a pair of spectacles from his breast pocket and hooks them over his ears. He unbuckles the briefcase and pulls out a sheet of paper. Lena closes her eyes.

'I, Commissar Dravitch, hereby proclaim Central Committee Edict Forty-Seven concerning Enemies of the State.'

'What?' Mama whispers wide-eyed, 'whatever does he mean?'

'Magdalena Luiza Bem, wife of traitor Anton Janek Bem is henceforth classified an enemy of the state, second-class citizen, as is their progeny, Agata Magdalena Bem.'

'Agata? Whatever this is you can't mean Agata, she's a baby. No this is nonsense, this is ridiculous. Agata's not an enemy. She's not even two.'

The commissar glances up mildly and returns his attention to the document. Having served as a bourgeois suppressor of the education of the proletariat, Papa is also a second-class citizen and an enemy of the state. Mama is married to an enemy of the state. All progeny of this union are declared enemies of the state.

He stops and calls across to Ulka. 'A glass of water if you'd be so kind, sister, the night air is not so good for my throat.'

'But Blessed Virgin this is ridiculous,' Mama says, her voice wavering in the silence. She looks where Ulrich is trying to disappear into the wall. 'You tell him, Ulrich. Explain the wonderful things Jozef's done for the children in this district. Tell him how he's been an advocate for every one of them. He would have taken every needy child into our home if he could. Thirty years of his life, he's given to this work. You know the sacrifices he's made.'

Ulrich nods without looking up. 'It is true,' he mumbles.

'That's it?' Ulka spits, setting the glass of water on the table by the commissar. 'That's all you'll move your tongue for this good man, you pig?'

Papa smiles benignly at the commissar. 'Good water in this region.'

'Indeed, yes, very flavoursome.' Commissar Dravitch takes a sip and pulls back his sleeve to look at his watch. 'For the safety of the state, the enemies here listed are to be relocated.'

'Relocated?' Ala cries. 'I don't understand.'

'Mother of God,' Mama says crossing herself over and over, 'Mother of God they're sending us away.'

'Enemies of the state are allocated thirty minutes to pack necessities up to a maximum of two hundred pounds in weight per person. They may take only what can be carried on their person. Religious iconography, medicines and items of political propaganda are forbidden.' He stops and glances towards

Mama and Papa. 'It's not in the official documentation but I would suggest including articles of clothing for cold weather and food sufficient for a lengthy journey.' He looks again at his watch. 'Your transport to the station will depart in twenty-eight minutes.'

'We're to leave our home in twenty minutes?' Mama whispers.

'Twenty-eight minutes, madam.'

'Ulrich, is this true? Is there nothing to be done for us?'

Ulrich is rubbing his boot heel along the skirting.

The commissar slides the edict back into his briefcase.

'Wait.' This Molek steps forward. 'I'm not on this list. You made no mention of my name.'

The commissar glances from This Molek to Ulrich. 'The numbers appear to be out by one.' He takes a pen from his pocket. 'I apologise, comrade, local information is not always up to date. This can be rectified, we've space at the bottom.'

'No, wait.' This Molek puts his arm round Ala who is weeping into her hands. 'This woman is my wife. She's carrying my son.'

'Congratulations.'

'My father and mother came to this town from Kharkiv.'

'A fine city, I'm sure.'

'You will know of it. They were humble people who worked the soil. I shoe horses, as will my son one day. Cut us, and the Danube flows from our veins.'

'I understand.'

'So you will understand, comrade, that Ala is my wife, and you are right that you are out by one because she must stay here in the town with me where we will make a wonderful loyal family with our Ukrainian blood. You must strike her off the list. You are a reasonable man from the look of you.'

The commissar fiddles with his pen. 'You make some excellent points. However, I can see your wife's name on the list. Take a look for yourself.' He swivels the paper towards This Molek. 'I am required to transfer the list to my colleagues at the station with every name accounted for. Regrettably my hands in this are tied.'

'Untie them.'

'Regrettably that is not possible. You will understand I'm sure, it's nothing personal.' He looks up blinking and smiling at This Molek, the nib of his pen hovering over the paper. 'Your wife is leaving for the station in twenty-five minutes. But we have room for one more at the bottom.'

There is no sound in the room but Ala's weeping.

Mama pushes back her chair. 'Darling, sit down. Come, sit here.'

'But I have a baby coming in the autumn, Mama.'

'You do.'

This Molek looks at Ala and he smiles, stroking her wet cheek with his knuckles. 'You do, princess. You will have my boy and he will have his mother's sweet face.' Turning back to the table he slams his palm on the oilcloth. 'I am Molek Kravets, put me on your piece of shit list.'

No one speaks as This Molek's name is added and blotted with a slip of white card. Nodding to see it set in ink, he turns to Ala, lifting her chin, speaking to her for all the room to hear, telling her to hush because he loves her, she is his only life, if he stayed here without her he would have no life at all.

The commissar takes a circular stamp from his case and stamps the document in red ink at the top. 'So we have seven in total,' he says to Ulrich. 'In my experience the final number always changes, which is why you see I like to leave a little room at the bottom of the sheet.'

'Eight.' Ulka throws back her head and spits a gob of saliva on the oilcloth. 'Pick up your fancy pen and put my name down too.'

The man blinks, staring at the bubbling pool spreading towards his briefcase. Lena would like to think he looks a little afraid. 'Who is she?' he asks Ulrich, 'the maid? Well, sister, tonight is a happy night for you. May I be the first to offer congratulations; you are liberated from oppression. If I were you,

I'd take a walk down the lane under a very pretty half moon, or go and visit your boyfriend.'

'What's this rubbish you're talking? My name should be there. This is my family and Ulka Petrenko is the name you need to add. Do you need it spelling out?'

'Ulka, darling, please think about what you're saying.' Mama's voice is low. She's no longer crossing herself, but gripping Papa's hand and Romek's too.

'Uncap your pen and put it to that piece of paper, sir.'

'Regretfully, the list is now stamped and dated, and without additional space.' The commissar slides the paper into his brief-case and buckles it shut. 'I thank you all for your attention.' He turns to Ulrich. 'What time do you have?'

'Two thirty.'

Ulka storms over to Ulrich. 'You listen to me. You speak to your boss as one piece of shit to another. Tell him to take me or I won't answer for the consequences. You tell him that.'

She shakes him by the shoulders, her voice rising to a yell. 'For all that our families have shared these years. For all that's holy in you.'

Ulrich pushes her off. 'There's nothing holy in me.' He walks out the back door.

Lena can hear fussing in the hencoop as she runs to the bedroom, setting Agata on the rug and pulling the eiderdown from the bed. She rips a hole in the corner of the cover and pushes the amber through the tear, shaking the quilt until she's sure it has fallen all the way to the bottom.

Down in the hall Ulka's shouting, her voice rough and running on as though afraid of stopping and falling down for good. She's telling them all to pack their clothes, bring their thickest blanket and get downstairs. Each must take a portion of silverware. Mama is to bring her jewellery, This Molek, find your tools. Ala should take plates in her blanket, Romek the pans, Mama and Lena salted pork and potatoes, the pickled vegetables, sugar and eggs. 'Scissors, needles, hammer and nails!' Ulka shouts, 'soap and disinfectants too.'

Lena runs down to the hall with her bundle then hurries upstairs for Agata who's crawled beneath the bed. Crouching down Lena meets Ivan Pavlov's white eyes. Agata is lying on her belly beside him in the corner rubbing the fur up his back. He looks at Lena and his tail beats on the floor.

Lena can't trust her voice to say the words 'thank you' or 'I'm sorry', or even to tell him what she knows, that he'll be fine, Ulka will brush him and let him warm her feet at night, and spoil him with bones and pancakes as she always has. Lena reaches a hand to him and she pulls his ears, just as he's always liked best. Pavlov's tail thumps, he licks her fingers. 'Good boy,' Lena whispers, tears dropping into his fur, 'my dear dear good boy.'

Agata wriggles closer. Her fingers reach for the wetness on Lena's face. Lena turns away from the dog's gaze.

'We have to go now, little frog,' she whispers. 'Take my hand.' She pulls Agata out from under the bed and hurries from the room, closing the door without looking back.

Down in the hall Ulrich thrusts a squirming sack at her.

'I've knotted their feet and thrown in corn. Kill the black ones last, and only when you absolutely have to. They're the best layers.'

'Where are we being sent?'

'They don't tell me that.'

'But you knew they were coming for us.'

'They're coming for all of us, Lena. Some quicker than others.'

She looks into his eyes then, and she sees how it is. He is a man sick to death.

'If it wasn't you it would be someone else.'

She takes the sack from him and turns away.

'Maybe it's better it's you.'

And then, after all the frenzy of packing they stand in the hall, waiting in silence, bundled up in clothing too hot for the weather, as their blankets are unknotted and searched through by soldiers. Only Papa won't stop talking, asking where they're going and why they need to wear so many layers if it's almost summer. He's hot and he doesn't want to go on holiday, he says. There's too much work in the garden in summer, Ulka agrees with him, doesn't she?

Ulka is slumped on a kitchen chair, her head to the table, her face shut away behind clamped arms. Lena goes to embrace her but she doesn't respond. It's as if she's been sealed inside a chamber, as if she's the victim of a wicked spell.

Mama waddles in, fat as a bear in three winter coats, and sits beside her. Somehow she's made a smile come to her lips and she's leaning to Ulka's ear telling her the house is hers. Sell the piano, darling. Sell what you can. Promise me you'll sell the house if it will let you live well. Marry the butcher if he makes you smile every day. Build a life, darling. Have a child of your own. It will be a balm. Mama stops speaking to press a finger to her eyes. Whatever will we do without you, my daughter? Whatever will we do?

Mama tries to raise Ulka's head from the table but it won't lift. 'Mother of God, I promise you it's better this way. It's better your life isn't thrown away. That's the comfort I take with me.'

A soldier comes into the kitchen. 'Out. All out, make your way to the transport at the gate. Any luggage that can't be carried is to be left behind.'

In turn they go to Ulka, pressing kisses on her hair, hugging the hunch of her back. Lena leans her forehead to Ulka's shoulder. She says nothing since what is there to say? The only thing that matters is the truth they've learned this night: that there's something worse than being taken from your home; it is being the one who is left behind.

The soldier returns shouting and threatening with his gun. Lena settles Agata on her hip. She bends to lift her bundle and follows her family out of the house.

England

There's a girl tiptoeing in her bedroom, glancing back at the bed and opening the curtains a fraction, just enough to let in a slash of light, just enough to navigate by. Under her eyelids Lena has been silently observing this girl's explorations for a while. The girl throws back hair from her face and for a moment Lena sees Ala and her rippling yellow curls.

But of course it is not Ala who turns from the curtain and steps light-footed to the bedside table. Ala is long gone. Lena watches this cusp creature, half-girl half-woman, unaware of how her skin glows in the morning light. The girl takes the amber and turns it in her hand, peering at the bubbles of ancient air trapped in its skin. She spots the tiny brass screw head and she begins to twist.

'Nothing there,' Lena croaks. 'All gone.'

'Babby!' The girl starts. 'I'm so sorry, I thought you were sleeping.' She shoves the amber back in its place and wipes her hands on her jeans as though disassociating them from the crime.

Lena cracks a slow grin. The girl is flushed, embarrassed. Well, let her be. Let her find a way out of it. Escape is a good trick to learn.

'You have beautiful photos, Babby.'

Lena indicates she wants the white board and pen from the bedside table. The girl – Amy, that is her name – holds the board as she writes.

SHOW ME?

Amy picks up the photograph of the farmhouse. Long and low and white, a grey hill behind partitioned by stone walls. In the foreground a stocky black-haired toddler stands between the front legs of a huge draught horse. 'I like this one best.'

WALES. YOUR PAPA AND THE HORSE BLACKIE.

'I can't believe you and Dziadziu were farmers.'

Lena tries to laugh too. She shakes her head, the sound trapped by the growth in her throat. If she could only describe what terrible farmers they'd made, her and her husband and the little dark-haired boy, in that ramshackle rented farm in the first years after the war. The labour was easy enough. She'd gone up the ladder and whitewashed that building in three days. Her husband had dug out the well in a week. But the culling of young cockerels, or slitting the throat of the Easter pig? Even loading up the sheep for the business to be done elsewhere, as bemused neighbours suggested, well, it turned out neither of them had it in them.

WHY NOT FARMERS? she writes.

Because something must be done with a life. And what can be done when you cannot go back to your home country and you have no language or connection to the place you are in. And, sometimes, she would like to tell her granddaughter, a body needs a place to recover quietly, just as a dog finds its corner to hide with its wounds.

Amy is now fingering the one photograph that exists of Lena and Anton with Agata a bundle in her arms by an unlit advent hearth. She picks it up to examine. She sits cross-legged with the photo on Anton's side of the bed. Lena would like to tell Amy she's always been drawn to this. One of those girls who loved babies and cots and endless stories about other babies. Tell me about baby Agata, Babby, she would say, during those after-school teatimes in the house. Forever drawn to the one story Lena cannot tell. It was Anton who filled the silence. Who cleared his throat and told tales to satisfy the little girl over her pancakes. It is only natural, he said later in bed. Old people's war stories are fascinating; it is a suffering that can be sucked on like a sour sweet, the taste enjoyed and washed away. They had lain together in silence, one that had ceased to be uncomfortable, and he had held Lena's hand, as he had on the ship that sailed them and JoJo away from the steppe and everything it held in its soil, the first time he told her he could forgive her anything. The time she whispered, *But you know nothing*.

I know you, he had said.

The front door shuts.

'Oh Amy!' JoJo says, coming into the bedroom. 'What did I tell you? Babcia needs her sleep.'

Amy jumps up. Lena winks at her as she shoves the photo back on the table.

'Come on, out with you, my girl.' JoJo takes her shoulders and steers her to the door. 'Just putting the kettle on, Ma.'

Lena smiles, watching them go, father and daughter. Ala would approve of all that swinging hair.

People warn them they'll find it cold on the farm, too cold to stay. The neighbours also say this, but not to them.

She shrugs such warnings away. It's not so cold as places she has known.

Still, the neighbours worry about them. She knows this not by their words – because words mean nothing to her, and besides there is no common language between them. She knows this because a crate of eggs appear on the doorstep when they move in, followed by a mound of potatoes. And now and then a pair of boy's sandals, or a piglet, or a box of fluffy chicks might be discovered in the porch on a rainy afternoon. In December there's a fruitcake. In March a white hyacinth turns up on the mat. She cannot think why that makes her weep more than the other gifts.

It's quiet on the farm, down the end of a lane where no one comes. They drink the silence into themselves. Like the brown water from the well, it nourishes them. A year passes, then a second and third before they dare to ask the question, what do you do with a life when there's no war? When gods and men take no further interest in you. They settle into the farmhouse and they live quietly behind the walls with the harvest spiders. But just to be sure she takes up the back lawn and grows potatoes, storing them in mountains in the cellar alongside wobbling columns of waxed cheese. She pickles eggs and preserves apples and cures ham. Little Jozef is sent to the local school and in time he learns the language they need to get by. On market days JoJo walks with them five miles to town to trade the lambs and buy cornmeal and rennet. He takes his father to the opticians and them both to the dentist. He translates every letter and every report from school, some, Lena suspects, more accurately than others.

On the farm they rise early and work late. They eat cream and potatoes and autumn fruit. Some days she finds herself standing on the Welsh hillside, staring at the horizon. Some days her chest seizes like it's being grabbed by a giant's fist and squeezed, and she doubles over and thinks it's happening, what she wants is coming for her. Long ago she read it could happen this way, particularly to hearts made weak by labour or grief. But it doesn't happen. She stands on the hillside and thinks about the person who once told her that humans are cowards. They refuse to accept their lack of control, yet they don't act when they could, when it would be in their interests. Humans are irrational by design, he said to her. They cling.

What do you do with life when men put down their guns? When the god beneath the soil is resting his fingers or otherwise engaged? When you live in a country that isn't yours, that is neither here nor there, and your childhood dreams are broken into pieces too sharp to ever touch again? You eat cream and grow fat. You build reserves. In time you move a little around this country and meet other people who are neither here nor there. You don't talk about when you were alive somewhere else and what happened there. There's nothing for anyone to gain in this.

She and her husband acquire a reputation as breeders of sheep. She is invited to county shows, but her heart isn't in it. She watches lambs she's reared loaded onto trucks for the abattoir and one day the cheque turns red in her hands. When her old school friend hunts her down with news of work in a factory, she persuades her husband. An easy life, she suggests. Besides, the boy needs society. He needs more than two sad people on a hillside and a horse called Blackie.

So she writes back to Danushka, with whom relations are undergoing careful restoration. Why not? she writes. Are we not free as birds?

They sell their flock and the horse, and move to a town where they watch the television from comfortable chairs. JoJo grows old enough to leave them but does not go far, and in time he has a yellow-haired daughter who comes for childcare and strudel after school. At night Lena puts her hand to her husband's shoulder, or leans her head against his chest, and they might talk quietly about factory gossip or smile over their granddaughter's exploits. But rarely do they mention a time before – and never what they left behind on the steppe in a cardboard box.

One day, after sixty years of marriage, her husband turns cold in his sleep. It's an easy death and she is glad for him. She buries him in sunshine, his coffin wrapped in a red and white flag.

Margaret lifts Lena's wrist and takes her pulse. Gentle fingers probe her throat. JoJo hovers by the door. Amy is back in Anton's place on the mattress. And on the windowsill, the blackbird looks in, a worm surrendered in his beak.

Margaret is explaining what comes next. Lena will slip into unconsciousness for longer and longer periods. Margaret can help with the pain and ease her way. She has to ask again. Is this what she wants?

Lena turns from the blackbird and slowly nods.

'In which case, I'll fetch the rest of my equipment from the car.'

JoJo follows Margaret from the room. Lena closes her eyes. Beside her she hears a loud sob. It is time.

Breathing carefully to garner her strength Lena reaches to the bedside table and pulls down the amber. How heavy it now lies in her thin palm. She moves it towards Amy, tipping her hand so the amber falls on the mattress between them.

Amy turns, her eyes dripping.

Lena smiles. She must choose her words with precision. 'It's yours,' she says on a wisp of breath.

She tries to pour the rest of it into her look, all the other things she wants to say. 'It doesn't really mean anything, this gift, don't worry.' This is what she tries to tell Amy. 'Not if you're a rationalist like me. But you may be more like my old friend Danushka, the poor thing was a romantic, always believing in the power of her will right to the end. She used to laugh when I told her it was chance that made her think that way. But, listen, darling, it's not at all special, this piece of amber. At least I never thought so. Although I won't deny there were times it came in useful. My Agata loved playing with it, for one thing. And it was hard to lose. You can let go of everything you love, but somehow you won't lose this. You see, humans are sacks of bone and liquid. Bones crumble and liquid is easily spilled. But this resin won't rot.' She feels for Amy's arm. 'Think of it as something to hold on to in life. I hope with all my heart you won't need it, but you never know.' She tries her voice out loud one last time, 'Take it, please.'

Tears are rolling down Amy's face. She will be a sentimental sort in life, and what is so wrong with that? Sobbing, she looks at Lena, then at the amber on the bed.

'Take it,' Lena mouths, and she sees Amy's fingertips touch the amber and begin to curl in a slow caress of possession. Lena smiles. How light she feels.

She watches Amy turn the amber. A new noise is in the room, an irregular dragging sound. It's coming from her own body. Lena recognises it as a change in her respiration. Cheyne–Stokes, the name she remembers for such breathing. Her face slackens, too tired to smile any longer. Impossible now to keep her eyes open.

'Here you come.' That voice in her ear.

'You. Are you here with me? Will you stay?'

'Did you miss me, Magdalena?'

'All my life I did.'

The air is suddenly around the bed. Margaret is back, clinking and rustling, taking her arm, rolling back her sleeve, telling her she's going to insert a cannula for fluids, is that all right? JoJo is taking her hand. 'I'm here, Ma, I'm right here with you,' he's saying, his voice a little broken, but he'll recover.

Deep inside herself Lena is smiling. She'd like to tell Margaret to do as she likes, because she, Lena, is leaving now, going for good, untethered and rising from this body on the bed in this foreign country. She's too tired to open her eyes again, but the wind that was outside is now lifting, pushing, moving her heels. She has the energy for where she must go.

Siberia

They are to clear the taiga of its pine. Also the spruce and cedar. Moscow requires lumber to build houses, also sideboards and dining tables, bed frames and chairs. And this is not to mention all the railway sleepers that are needed, and not just in the capital, but to get to everywhere else you can think of in this magnificent country, so really it's best if the larch comes down too. The million square miles of taiga around them are to be felled trunk by trunk. This is what citizens of the second category do with their lives until the lives are over. There's no rush. There are plenty of citizens of this category to do it. There are plenty of lives.

The new arrivals, about fifty of them left over from the journey, sit with their bundles on the ground between two rows of wooden huts. It's midsummer, humid in this thin gap between the trees. Black flies hiss in the air. They've walked half a day, following guards down a track from the place, deep inside the taiga, where the railway sleepers came to an end and the door slid back a final time. Each has been offered a ladle of water pulled from a well in the centre of the camp. Now they sit or squat or lie in silence, gazing at the small wooden huts or the flies clouding above the well, the long barrack at the end of the camp, or the green canopy framing their view of the sky. And all the while a jaundiced man in grey clothes, standing on a tin bucket and speaking in Russian, is warmly welcoming them to their home for the rest of their lives. He unscrews a tin flask and takes a drink. A rifle dances on his shoulder and his trousers are held up by string.

'Will you look at them?' he says with a chuckle, addressing his remarks to a group of men also dressed in grey and tied with string, who lean against the wooden struts of the well scratching themselves or smoking. 'Don't our new friends look plump enough to eat?' He turns back to the arrivals, waggling a finger, 'Seems you've been sitting on your arses too long, comrades.' When he grins, as he does between gulps from his flask, his front teeth appear through his beard like tombstones jutting from long grass. 'I'm sorry to break it to you, friends, but now you've said goodbye to comfortable carriages with waiter service at your door. But don't fret because here we have something even better. Twice a day we fill your bellies to the brim; tasty soup at breakfast, and at supper, for those who present their quota ticket – bread.' He opens his arms wide. 'Work and there is bread. What could be fairer on this fair earth? Even for enemies of our state.'

Several people have given up looking at anything at all during this speech and are covering their faces with scarves or they're ducking their heads between their knees, or swatting at their ears. The commandant beams down from his bucket, 'Don't mind these flies, friends, they are our comrades too!' He swings his rifle and aims as if shooting ducks from the sky. 'I'll let you into a secret. The truth is we must all try get along because although your guards here are criminals by trade, since we've been living together with all you enemies, it seems our hearts are turning pure as the forest air. Your faces, my friends! Trust me, you have come among angels. Look around, do you see any wire fencing to trap you in? Any watchtowers? I give you my word no one who tries to leave will be shot. Have a go if you like.' He shades his eyes and looks down at them, grinning, 'Somebody surely would like to stretch their legs?'

Lena pulls Agata against her, whispering, 'Quiet, little frog, hush now.' Silence everywhere but for the humming of flies.

The man laughs. 'Come now, I'll throw down my rifle. There. None of my lads will bother you either. These angel boys prefer to save their bullets for the squirrels. There must be a volunteer, surely?' He shakes the last drops from his flask down his throat. 'Not today? That's very dull sport, friends. Very well, if anyone would like to run . . .' He turns and points into the spruce canopy behind the long barrack, 'Moscow is four thousand miles in that direction.'

As he enjoys his joke, there's the sound of shuffling and clanging, as if a group of lepers were materialising from the air to beg for alms. The new arrivals turn to see a procession emerging from the forest track. More extraordinary than mendicants, it is a carnival of rag people that shuffle out, dressed in torn skirts and pyjamas, all with a patina of filth and flashes of patched colour, their footwear flapping like drowning fish. Lena catches Ala's eye and looks away quickly. Some wear scarves or caps, but most are bare-skulled, their bony faces blistered by the sun. Behind the workers comes a tall bay draught horse and a blue-eyed piebald pony harnessed unevenly to a cartload of tools. A tall guard jumps from the cart and leads the animals behind the long barracks. The workers assemble into a thin queue in front of a hut that is shut up.

A murmur begins to spread through the huddle of new arrivals on the ground. How is it possible for these carnival creatures to be so thin-necked and yet for their skulls to hold their place in the air? What momentum keeps these bones moving forward and not falling down in a pile over their feet? They watch the workers, some fifty or sixty men and women and youths – Lena can see no small children in the throng – stand silent in the queue, paper slips gripped in bony claws. None of them shows any curiosity towards the newcomers. Their eyes are fixed on the hatch.

'Here it is, friends, coming up before your eyes!' the man on the bucket shouts, his yellow eyes twitching with excitement. 'This beautiful system, you will see a demonstration now. See the slips of paper, see the loaf and the scales, see the bread portioned fairly.' Laughing, he waves down those new arrivals who have stood up intending to join the queue. 'No, no, my naughty friends, the magic only happens with a slip of paper. Tomorrow

you might be in luck, let's see, let's all hope for you. In the meantime I'm sure you wish to settle in. Take a hut, you'll see there's
plenty of room for everyone. It's a tragedy that we never seem to
keep anyone with us long, no matter how we try.' He raises his
flask in the air – 'To your good health' – and he stumbles backwards off his bucket.

This Molek finds them a hut near the end of the row at the forest's edge. Its roof is covered in yellowing turf. To the side of the
door there's a glassless window frame and on each end wall, two
planked bunk beds. In the centre of the hut is a cylindrical stove
with a narrow metal pipe leading up and out through the roof.
Molek is on his knees at once striking a match and checking the
vent.

They drop their bundles on the beaten-earth floor. The whole
place is little longer than Papa's shed.

'We're all supposed to live in here?' Ala's voice is a whisper.
'All of us? I don't see how.'

Romek strides from one side of the hut to the other in four
long paces. He kicks the strut of the bunk. 'Are we sharing beds?'

'You're not, worm,' Lena says. 'I promise you that.'

Mama puts on a bright smile as if it's no worse than being
introduced to a dingy hall where she's required to perform. 'I'm
sure we can make it quite cosy with a curtain or two. Look,
there's even a row of nails where we can hang photographs.'
She opens her bundle and begins to rummage, wrapped over her
wrist are the rosary beads she's not removed since climbing into
the container on the train.

Lena kicks up paper scraps from the corner. She bends down
and lifts a passport-sized photo of a solemn-faced boy in a com-
munion suit. The boy has almond eyes and bent ears, and having
found him she doesn't know where to put him; he can't be left
on the floor, or added to the fire This Molek is trying to light in
the stove. In the end she leans him against the floor under a bunk
and moves away from his gaze.

'There we go,' Mama says, hanging her wedding photograph on the nail on the wall by the window. 'Better already. Now we just need to stitch up a couple of curtains, a sheet should do it.'

Lena stares as she goes rummaging in the bundles. 'Do you even know how to make curtains, Mama?'

'How hard can it be, darling?'

Ala sits on the edge of a bunk, slapping flies, a hand on her belly that has grown silently – miraculously – in the dark of the train. 'Do we have soap anywhere? I'd like to wash my hair.'

'We have treasure.' Romek waves a bent spoon he's found under a bunk. He reaches further and scrapes out spoonfuls of small black flies. 'And food.' He takes the surviving hen from the sack and sets her down by the flies. 'Dinner time, Blackie.'

Sucking her thumb, Agata toddles over to watch. Lena strips her of her clothes, running her hands over her ribs, pressing the hard wall of her belly.

'There's a few potatoes left and a little pork,' Mama says. 'Enough for a good soup tonight.'

'Do you even know how to make soup?'

'Now you're being ridiculous, darling. What do you think we girls had to do in the convent those three years?'

This Molek takes a bucket and goes for water, and Lena finds the scissors to hack Agata's hair while she's distracted by the hen. Later she'll shave her head and scrub her clothes in boiling water. Every day she'll check Agata's pulse at her wrist, and the temperature of her chest. She'll examine her eyelids for jaundice, her gums for decay. The state of Agata's legs and feet will need monitoring for ticks and burrowing insects, bites must not get infected. At night Lena will put her head to Agata's chest and learn the resting rhythm of her heart.

'We should all shave our heads to keep off the lice.'

'With respect I'm not an animal yet,' Ala says, curled on the bunk.

'I have to disagree. You might be carrying disease you could pass on.' Lena gathers up the mass of Agata's hair and dumps it in the stove. As casually as she can she says, 'I didn't see any other young children about, did anyone see any?'

'They're all at enemy-of-the-state school,' Romek says.

'Of course, worm, that must be it.'

'I'm sure there's a sensible reason,' Mama says. 'Agata's going to be fine.'

Lena is about to tell her how ridiculous she sounds, that nothing at all here is fine when she hears a man outside the hut.

'If you take water from the main well it doesn't need boiling,' he's saying to This Molek in Russian-accented Polish. 'But those who value their lives tend to avoid the water supply near the latrines.'

Lena looks up to see a tall figure in a long grey coat entering the hut. His hair is a dark copper flash, his face freckled and sharp-boned. He steps inside quietly, sawdust falling from his boots, and the stuffy air is suddenly cut through by a tang of pine and resin. The man looks round the hut and he smiles.

Lena stands, lifting Agata to her hip. She looks at this man. His wide white smile is the grin of a fox. 'Did you want something? Only where we come from, a stranger knocks before entering a family's home.'

'Lena, darling . . .' Mama murmurs.

The man looks at Lena. He's thin, but not so reduced as the workers they've seen. His gaze crackles with something like amusement. 'Is that so?'

She remembers him now – the guard who'd led in the horses.

'I was advising your husband to avoid the latrine well however desperate you become.'

'This Molek isn't my husband.'

'There are less painful exits from the world should you wish to make one.'

'How good of you to tell us, guard, we'll bear that in mind. It's always so nice to have a choice.'

'You think so?' He returns Lena's glare with that smile.

Yes, a fox, she thinks, come to charm the new hens.

'I'm not sure I'd agree,' he says. 'But that aside, if you wish
the luxury of a grave, you'd be advised to dig in the summer
when the ground is accommodating. Planning ahead also helps
prevent the spread of disease from unburied winter corpses. It
can be a problem in the spring. We like to recommend the preparation of at least one grave per hut.'

'You do?' Lena says, her fists tightening. 'At least one?'

'One or two.'

Lena sees his gaze flit round the hut, taking in Mama burrowing in the sack for the last of the potatoes, Romek hiding flies
in his right hand and offering his closed left hand to the hen.
She hitches Agata higher on her hip. 'A zoo would charge for
admission.'

He puts his hand in his pocket and brings out a black slab so
dense Lena at first takes it for peat. 'This is for your daughter.'

She stares at the slab.

'The taste improves when softened in water.'

She snatches the bread and shoves it in her pocket. Mama
thanks him.

'Does anyone have any questions?'

'Must everyone work?' Ala mumbles from the bunk.

'If you want bread in the evening I'd recommend it.'

'My sister's pregnant, can't you see?'

'My congratulations.'

'And my baby brother won't tell you, but he has a shrivelled
lung. Long ago my parents were told a physical lifestyle would
be out of the question for him.'

'My commiserations.'

'That's it? That's all you have to say?'

'The commandant was right. Life is lived simply here. If you
wish for bread you work.'

Lena scowls, wanting to tell him that she sees his contempt
though it's coated in civility. 'So you don't care? You let people
die and it doesn't bother you one bit that their blood stains your
skin. You'll carry that mark to heaven's gate.'

'Oh, I can't think I'll be ascending so high.'

'Lena darling, please—'

'He's come to mock us, Mama. And we have to smile and take it because he gives Agata a crust of bread.'

For a moment he's silent, unsmiling, and she is glad of it.

'Well?' she demands. 'Tell me that isn't so.'

'I quite understand,' he says, and she feels his words quiet as an ant on her skin, 'you're scared and angry. It's a big adjustment coming here.'

'You understand nothing.'

'As you wish.' He looks round, 'Does anyone have any other questions?'

'What parasites are in the water, guard?' she says.

'Comrade is our preferred term. Your question's one for a scientist or a physician. Regrettably we lost a capable surgeon a month ago. As I said the well water may kill you, but from what disease is anyone's guess. There are lice about obviously, I'm sure you're familiar with them now. The bigger worry is mosquitoes, particularly at this time of year. Pin fabric over those window frames within the hour and keep yourselves clothed.' He glances at Agata. 'They don't discriminate.'

Lena's heard enough. 'Come, little frog, we'll wait outside for This Molek to boil water, and you can have this great gift of bread.' Her hands shaking, she barges past him into the daylight to breathe fresh air and look over her child without talk of suicide or graves or disease.

Inside the hut he's still going on at Mama. 'Prioritise the care of your feet, hands and teeth. You're lucky, you've arrived in the best of the year. The shifts are long but you've time to prepare for winter. If you've brought seeds plant them. The soil's acidic, but some people have success. Soon there'll be berries about – blackcurrants, cowberries, cloudberries, and in a few months you can forage for fungi. Whatever you do don't let that hen out of your sight. The same goes for tools and boots. Everyone here is your comrade, but morality can be hard to find when . . .'

Lena storms off to be free of that voice, heading across the open ground with Agata, zigzagging around people hunched over buckets rubbing carefully at clothes, or their own thin limbs, with dripping grey cloths.

She hears her breath, too fast, it is much too fast. Around her the forest pulses green and black. Her focus blurs. Her chest tightens. Panic is everywhere inside her, it is a thousand rats in her brain. Because it is impossible for her to live in this place. This is not life, not here, this is not her life. She will not die here. Agata will not die here. Mama and Romek and Ala and This Molek will not. They will dig no summer graves, never will they do it. One death in this family has been enough.

She's over the far side of the camp when she sees the guard emerge from the doorway. He pauses for a moment glancing up at the crown of a tree before heading for the next hut along, his hands in his pockets, his stride loose and easy. He looks like a regular man entering a store on an errand, going about his business in a place of order and civilisation, rather than a criminal guard in a work camp at the end of the earth. He's whistling. It's as if he doesn't have a care in the world.

A metal pipe strikes a corrugated iron sheet, this the call to work at first light. The camp comes to life with wordless scratching and scuttling sounds; noises that seems to Lena to befit the movement of lice or beetles more than humans.

They join a queue at the hut beside the latrines, waiting for a ladle of soup. A hatch opens and a cloud of cabbage-smelling steam pours out. Lena holds out her cup and watches grey liquid splash in, the surface frothing and bubbling like dishwater scum. The guard titters at her expression. A goitre bulges his throat into a camel neck. 'What's wrong, flower? You think we chucked some soap in there to clean you up? We wouldn't put in soap, my angel, it's far too expensive to go in your soup.'

Lena drinks quickly then pushes the cup to Agata's lips. Mosquitoes dance on their breath. Agata does not want to drink and the soup spills down her front so she cries. The clanging metal sounds again and workers begin to move off. Lena straps Agata to her back and gives her the last chunk of the black bread to suck on. Romek stuffs the hen Blackie into his jacket pocket. He feeds her a beetle from his fist. She's not laid an egg in two weeks. This morning This Molek was spotted fingering his blade and muttering.

They fall in behind the workers shuffling up the track towards the trees. Lena keeps her gaze from the dozens of grass-covered mounds on either side. It's humid in the forest, the air thick with peat and resin scents. Here and there the brown needled floor turns to a sprawling carpet of acid-bright moss, sucking sound from their feet.

All day they labour in a clearing, in teams of two or four, expanding the space tree by tree, felling white pine and black spruce and elegant limbed larch; hacking down the vast winged branches, spreading sawhorses to reduce each amputated trunk into measured lengths, pushing these logs to the ground and rolling them into piles, shouting their quotas to a guard with a clipboard. Every five days the amassed timber is to be bundled in chains and dragged by the piebald pony and bay mare ten miles to the river's edge to be rolled onto barges for the south. It is just as the commandant said, they are clearing the taiga tree by tree. Halfway through the shift they break to receive a cup of water dispensed from a tall tin barrel. When the sun tips out of sight, a pipe strikes metal and logs are recounted, clipboards signed. A pencil scribbles on torn paper strips. In accordance with the percentage of quota fulfilled, each scribble specifies the gramme weight of bread to be received.

That first evening, after queuing at the canteen scales to receive her slice, Lena boils up the last of the salted pigskin in a pan of water on top of the stove. They each take a bowl and drop in lumps of bread to soak up the salt and juice. No one mentions the tremor in their hands as they lift their spoons, nor the welts that rise on their broken skin.

As they eat, faces appear round the door, offering introductions: their neighbours, an ancient count and countess, an apothecary with his wife and daughter, a girl a little older than Romek but with the hands of a fifty-year-old. Mama invites them in although they are far too tired for conversation and there's barely room for one family. But no matter, they are not large, these people; in fact crouching in the dusk of the doorway, they seem shaped more like ghouls than humans, their eyeballs murky and watchful, nostrils gaping cavities, and the slabs of their teeth too big for their gums. Under these jaundiced stares Lena drains the pan into a cup and holds out the dregs of the broth. The count takes a sip and hands the cup to his wife who wears an emerald silk scarf over her skull. A string of pearls sags at her desiccated throat. The count watches her drink and starts to talk of their arrival five months before.

'You will not imagine it,' he says, pressing a shaking thumb to his eye.

His wife lays a sinewy claw on his arm. 'They do not need to hear, sweetie. Not yet. They will not imagine it. Not yet they will not.'

'Everyone needs to hear. Everyone should imagine it. We arrived in January.' He blots his eyes and speaks of the dozens who died on the train, of chipping the frozen hair of corpses from the container walls, of babies thrown out into snowdrifts and the mothers who leapt after them.

'We lost someone on the journey,' Mama says.

'Just one?' the apothecary's wife grins, taking her turn with the cup, flicking her tongue along its rim and into its interior walls. 'You're lucky.'

'You think so?' Lena says, holding Agata close.

'Sure. Here you are lucky if you die standing up.'

There is nothing to be said to this, and no more food, so the guests nod their thanks and creep away into the night. The air around the lantern is a blizzard of tiny wings. A cockroach falls from the moss in the roof. Ala screams and Romek offers it to the hen. Mama takes to her bunk with her rosary beads.

'We need to make some sort of net for the beds,' This Molek says.

'We need lots of things.' Lena takes Agata to Mama. 'Watch her for me.'

'But where are you going, darling?'

'For a walk.'

'But you need to conserve your energy, darling. You look to be limping.'

'I'm not.'

'Show me your fingers, have you blisters? Should we pop them? Come, sit, let's look. What would Ulka suggest, do you think?'

'Mama, please, I just need some air. I can't breathe in here.'

*

It isn't clear to Lena where she's heading, just that she needs to go. In the dusk, groups of men are squatting outside huts, playing cards or draughts with fir cones and a board scored in the dust. A woman in a tattered floral dress kneels by the well staring at the hard ground as if waiting for it to open up in revelation. Lena watches her. She'd like to go over and tell her she understands, because she herself would like a sign. She wants it from the sky, and it wouldn't have to be much. *I see you*, Lena thinks. *I see you here and you are known to me. You are still known.* That's as much as the sky needs to say.

She keeps on walking to the edge of the compound, unsure whether to exchange the strip of dusky sky for the enclosing solitude of the forest. Behind her she hears the sound of whistling. It's one of the card players, causing his friends to look up from their hands and glance around. They grin. Other men purse their lips. The cacophony grows.

At the far end of the camp a figure is hurrying away from the guards' barracks, tucking something into the waistband of their trousers. From the smallness of the frame it might be a child, but in her movement it's clear she's a woman, barefoot and quick. Lena doesn't recognise her from the work party; she's pinched thin with a face as white as china. But all about her head is an extraordinary thing: hair, dark and wild, a bouncing tangle of energy. The men watch her and the whistling spreads from group to group. Female faces appear at half-open hut doors, spit flies down into the dust.

'What are you staring at?' the woman spits at Lena as she passes, entering a hut at the end of the row with a flowered sheet pinned to the windows. As the door opens, Lena thinks she hears a small child crying, 'Mama!' and words from the woman, no longer hissing but melodic and fluttering, 'I'm home, little bear. Look, my little bear, see what Mama's brought you.'

The door shuts. Abruptly the whistling stops, and fir cones hop again in the dust. Lena steps close to the covered window, listening to the women asking her little bear for a great big kiss.

And then she can't hear anything more inside, not clearly. Perhaps the woman is humming a lullaby. Or maybe she's taking the child's pulse or checking his gums, or hooking her limbs round him on the bed. She imagines the woman pressing her face to his hair and whispering a story as he gnaws at the bread. She's probably concentrating on the wall while he eats, so as not to watch his hunger nor allow herself to imagine all the horrors that may be visited on a child in this place.

Lena turns away and continues to walk towards the trees. She needs to get a grip on her thoughts, find a crevice in a rock or a rotten stump to shove them in. She mustn't think of Agata, her thin limbs and mute gaze, her face puffed from insect bites in the night. There's no good place where these thoughts lead.

Ahead is the main track towards the work clearing. To either side, between the trunks are narrow gaps, which may or may not be paths going nowhere at all. This forest is immense above and about her; a labyrinth without a heart, or a maze without an exit. You could live a thousand years and not find a way out of these trees, she thinks. You could live a million years in this place and never get home.

Panic is in her now, in her head, in her chest. Panic is a force heavier than these trees, it is falling down over her, felling every tall thing with it, it is crushing her bones to splinters, puncturing her lungs. A million years or one month? How much? How long is she to be here?

She cannot die here. She cannot live here. She cannot leave.

She bends over her knees to steady herself.

Move. If you move the sky won't fall down on you. The earth will not collapse under you. These things are proven, she tells herself. Move to stop panic screwing through the tissue of your heart. Move to stop thinking. Move to live.

To the left of the route to the worksite is a thin path blocked by a rotting larch trunk. She steps over and follows a gully of dead twigs and needles. High above her, the pines lean in and crack their joints. They creak and snigger. And why shouldn't they laugh, these trees that have everything they need? For thousands of years the sun and soil have been enough. When the last humans succumb to starvation, and saplings rise between the rotting huts, these trees will not even notice what has come and gone as fast as a needle's fall. They'll creep their roots through the soil and suck what's left from the human bones.

'We lost a man to a lynx a little further that way.'

The voice slices through her thoughts. It stops her dead.

'It's up to you, naturally, but I should warn you night falls quicker here than you'd think. To the wild animals' advantage.'

She doesn't turn round. She knows who's speaking. His voice is low, almost disinterested. She rubs her arms to dispel a sudden shivering.

'That's not to say some people don't choose this way to go. But you don't seem the type. There's your attachment to your daughter for one thing.'

'My attachment?'

'Is there another way I should describe it? I refer to the bond that keeps most women from running to the wolves.'

Lena lifts her chin. 'And what's the name for the thing that has a man creeping through the trees behind a woman?'

Were she to turn around and look at him, she knows what she'd see – that sly white fox's grin.

'I came here to find a moment's peace.'

Somewhere to her left she hears a cracking of branches.

'In which case I'll wish you good night.'

She listens for movement. Then she listens for silence beneath the creaking trees.

When she's sure she's entirely alone, she turns round, retracing her steps to the camp.

Mama is turning her hand into a paw, winding turquoise rags over her blistered fingers. 'I sang in Kraków Opera House three times wearing this dress. Such a lovely colour, a perfect match for the stage curtains. Your father always said I resembled a hummingbird in it.' She presses her clumped mittens to her lips. 'Naturally he considered it a compliment.'

They are on the march to work. Ala is staying behind in the camp. Yesterday This Molek knocked on the door of the guards' barrack and sold his pipe for a change in Ala's employment. She is to launder for the guards and clean communal areas in return for a quota of bread. When the apothecary's wife notes Ala's absence from the group, This Molek says, 'Everything's for sale in the world, you think here is any different?' Lena remembers the tiny woman hurrying across the camp last night to her child. The guards' barrack door closing as she went. She can't see the woman or the child in the work party.

They head deep into the trees. Mama points out specks of light vibrating on the forest floor. 'Join in with me, darling, I want to sing.' Mama weaves her paw through Lena's arm and starts humming the Ave Maria. This is the woman who went into a container on a train with hair gold as harp strings, and came out goose-white. Lena would have once considered such transformations anatomically impossible. Perhaps she took Papa's hair for herself, Lena thinks now, perhaps that's what happened so that one small part of him would not be left on a siding to be picked at by crows.

Mama sings and Lena shifts Agata on her back, wondering what she weighs. 'Keep your eye out for berries,' she tells Romek. 'Blackcurrants or cowberries. And if you find any don't feed them to the damn hen.' This Molek is joining in with Mama's hymn, others too, but Lena stays silent. She'll make her prayer to science and nutrition. You must choose carefully what to worship when your only wish is that your child survives.

All morning long under a burning sun, Mama sings hymns. She works at the cross saw with Lena, portioning a spruce into lengths, her turquoise paws darkening with fluid from her blisters. They were late to the tool queue and received a broken-toothed saw, the handles bound with fraying rope. Their quota requires two pine trunks dismembered by the day's end and they are barely halfway through the first. All this and Mama sings.

'Do you really think Papa can hear you?' Lena asks as they shift the saw to the third chalked line, bending to tease the first careful nicks through the bark.

Mama blows the dust from the cut to check the line. 'Does it matter, darling?'

'That you pretend a dead person can hear?'

'I think of it more as giving myself a little comfort. Would you choose to lie on a plank bed, or one with a blanket laid on top?'

'An imagined blanket, Mama.'

Mama wipes her brow with her sleeve. 'It is wonderful, isn't it?'

'What is?'

'Imagination. I've been thinking this all morning.' Mama bends back to the saw and begins to hum.

'Doesn't it make you thirsty all this singing?'

'A little.'

'So what will you do if the pony doesn't come with the water?'

'Why wouldn't it?'

'You've no idea whether it will.'

Mama stands up and stretches her back. 'Darling, you've no idea it won't.'

Lena looks to where Agata's asleep in the shade. 'She sleeps too much.'

'She's smiling,' Mama says, 'she must be dreaming of something good.'

When the sun's at its height, the cart does appear in the clearing, the blue-eyed pony in the traces. The workers lay down their tools and queue for a drink. Lena takes Mama's cup with her own. The red-haired guard is at the barrel, ladling water as easy as if he were serving drinks at a bar.

'You decided to come back from the forest then.'

She holds out the cups. 'I'll take my mother's portion too please, guard.'

'Nice porcelain, comrade.' He pours an extra half ladle in each cup. 'For your daughter.' He glances at Lena's trembling hands. 'You need to protect your skin in the day and expose it at night to allow calluses to form. You want it as tough as possible. The tremors will stop when the muscles toughen up. How's your little girl?'

'Hungry, what do you expect?'

'You could try cutting the inner bark from a trunk. Pine or elm are the most tolerable, I believe. Scrape out the green outer layers and take the bark where it's creamy and peels easily. It's rubbery and strong-tasting but edible I'm told.'

'You're told. How do you know it's not poisonous?'

'I've seen mothers do it for their children.'

She takes the water from him, blinking suddenly. 'And where are all those children now?' she hisses, turning away before he can say anything more.

Mama's on her back in the grass, resting her heels on the spruce trunk, her eyes closed and her pawed hands in the air. Lena tells her she looks like a stuffed bear and she smiles without opening her eyes. 'What were you talking to the guard about?'

'Why?'

'It looked like he was stroking your hands.'

'He wasn't stroking my hands.'

Mama nods dreamily. 'What do you think they're all here for?'

'Who?'

'Our guards. We know why we've been rounded up. But them? They must have done something terrible to be sent to end their days here.'

Lena says nothing. She kicks at a length of sawn pine. The bark is thick as elephant hide. Suddenly Mama laughs.

'What?'

'I'm thinking about your father. How that man loved to lie in the sun. Yet he burned a strip off his nose every time. How many summers did he have to learn this, and yet every year – off came another layer of skin. Do you think anyone ever learns anything in life?'

'I don't know, Mama.'

'Nor do I.'

The metal pipe clangs and Lena puts out her hand and helps Mama up. They drink their water and return to the saw.

There's commotion in the hut that evening. Ala, who can be heard but isn't to be seen, is its cause. A bedsheet hangs over the bunk where she and This Molek now reside. Ala is behind the sheet with the paring knife. Romek supplies this information grinning. She's been there a while. This Molek is also behind the sheet, Romek adds, begging Ala to hand over her blade.

The sheet flaps. There are sounds of slapping and Ala shrieking, 'Get your hands off me, I'm going, I swear it. Let me go or I'll take your eye out, I'll take them both. Better to be eaten by wolves than to die with this shit in my bones.'

Lena holds Agata on her lap, encouraging her to take the spoon and feed herself. She stirs the bowl of bread and boiled water with her finger, picking grit and husks from the dark bog. 'Don't worry, darling, Aunty Ala's just a little upset.'

'I'm more than a little goddamn upset!'

'I'll speak to them, princess, I promise you,' This Molek is saying in a steady voice. 'If you give me back my knife I'll go over there right now.'

'And I should trust an oaf like you? Take your hands off me. Just a spot of laundry, princess, a bit of general cleaning, princess. The shit has soaked into my hair, I can smell it. What kind of husband sends his pregnant wife to mop up turds all day? No husband I know. Only an animal would do that.'

'Animals don't have latrines,' Romek says.

'And you can goddamn shut up, worm.'

A yellow plait comes flying out from behind the sheet. Agata climbs off Lena's lap and toddles to get it.

A second plait follows.

'There,' Ala shrieks. 'How does your princess look now?'

Silence. Followed by mumblings. The sheet ripples with renewed commotion.

Romek walks the hen close to the bunk to eat the day's dead flies from the floor. 'Don't worry,' he says to Agata in a loud voice, 'Aunty Ala and This Molek are no longer fighting.'

'Is there no privacy left in this world?' Ala screeches. 'And everyone keep your goddamn hands off my goddamn plaits.'

Lena lies with Agata on the quilt on the bottom bunk. She's lowered a sheet, knotting it round the frame to keep out what mosquitoes she can. Above them Mama is snoring, the rosary dangling from her hand. On the other top bunk Romek is juggling pine cones. Now and then one thuds into the roof and a scattering of bugs falls down and starts him coughing.

It's stifling under the sheet. Lena has bathed Agata twice but her skin is sticky with heat. 'Say Mama,' Lena whispers, stroking her fingers through Agata's stubbled hair. 'Just once. Say Mama, little frog, and I'll know we're going to be fine.'

Agata's belly protrudes in a hot hard dome. Lena rubs it gently. 'Little frog, you need to drink more. Tomorrow we'll take a good drink of water in the morning to fill us up.' Lena's own stomach growls and turns on itself. She's saving half her bread for Agata's breakfast. Another pine cone thuds into the roof and beetles smash down on the floor. The hen goes scrabbling after the insects.

Lena sits up. 'Can't you stop goddamn juggling and go and dig up some worms for that goddamn bird, Romuś, so she lays some goddamn eggs? The forest must be crawling with goddamn worms. Feed her properly. Otherwise it won't be This Molek but me throttling her in the morning, with my own two hands, I swear I will.'

Agata is wide-eyed, watching.

'Mama didn't mean to shout. I'm sorry. I'm sending my little frog a message. Are you ready?' She kisses Agata's cheek three times, watching for a smile. 'I love you. Did you get the message? Mama's sending it again – I love you.'

She reaches into the hole she ripped in the quilt, stretching down to the bottom corner. She pulls out the amber, checking the screw is tight and she hands it to Agata. 'What can you see? If we look really carefully we might just spot Ulka. See that strand of hair jumping about her ears like a rusty spring? Looks like she's making pierogi. Yes, can you see, it's pierogi for Ivan Pavlov. He loves the onion and potato ones best. Strange animal. Can you see Ulka stretching the dough with the heel of her hand. Ugh, look at Pav, sitting there drooling all over the floor.'

Agata's lips move slowly.

'What is it, little frog?'

'*Dziadziu*,' she whispers.

'Dziadziu?' Lena's throat constricts. 'He's probably having pierogi too. Dziadziu doesn't miss a meal if he can help it. Do you know Dziadziu likes paprika in his pierogi with lots of garlic? He always asks Ulka to fry them on both sides till they're hard as nuts. Ulka grumbles, but she'll do it. She'll do anything for Dziadziu.' Lena turns the amber round. 'Look, can you see Pav's tail wagging? Now he's full of pierogi he's chasing squirrels in the lane. See how he leaps at the trunks, all four legs off the ground at once? Do you see? Nine years old and he still believes he's got springs in his feet. Ridiculous. When he was a baby like you he wanted to jump into everybody's arms and be carried. Ridiculous bouncing dog.'

Agata's eyes are closed. Mama has turned to her side and is no longer snoring. Behind their sheet Ala and This Molek are snickering. It's still light. Lena watches Agata's ribcage rising and falling. She pulls back the sheet and goes to the shelf where This Molek keeps his knives.

Outside the men at their games glance up from the dust. Lena ignores them. She walks close to the end hut with the flowered fabric at the window frame. It's quiet inside. There's a gash in the curtain, and Lena would like to look through it to see how life is lived here with a child. But the men's eyes are on her. She turns away and heads into the forest, taking the same turning at the rotten larch that she took the evening before, thinking only about her immediate purpose and her steps; simple things that can be controlled.

Ahead of her a broad pine stands in the space it has made for itself, moss carpeting its roots in acid green. Lena goes to the tree and rams the knife into the bark, stabbing to break through the crust. There's green beneath. Lena scrapes at this until she sees a spongy white layer soft enough to gouge. She pulls out a thin strip. The bark is pulpy and smells of sawdust, and she has less than will cover the palm of her hand. But still if she leaves it to dry in the sun tomorrow, she may be able to grind up a flour in time for supper. It could be baked on the stove or boiled for breakfast. Even better she could give it to Agata to suck during the long day, or at night when Agata lies awake listening to a gobbling hen.

'Beautiful evening.'

She stops scraping. She had not heard him come.

'You again.'

'Me again.'

She does not need to turn, she knows where he is, a few feet behind her. A stripe of light will be catching the copper stubble on his jaw.

'You're following me. You've no right to.'

'Is that what you think?'

'Have the decency to admit it.'

'I came to enjoy the forest. Perhaps it was you who followed me.'

Now she turns, her knife clenched in her fist.

'That's quite a look,' he says, grinning. 'Are you taking lessons?'

'I'm trying to work out whether you're mad or just plain offensive.'

'Is it madness to want to appreciate the colours of the forest on a midsummer evening?' A red tail dangles from his coat pocket. He has a catapult in his hand.

'You mean in the prison we're going to die in? My family, at least. I've no idea about you.'

He tips back his face to look at the pine. 'Taller than a church steeple,' he says. 'For thousands of years these trees have existed without human interference.'

'As they will once we're gone.'

'No doubt. How are your hands?'

She turns back to the trunk to start on a new patch of bark.

'The first weeks are the worst.'

She strikes at the tree with her blade.

'Would you like me to take a go? It can't be easy after a day with the saw.'

'No, thank you.'

For a moment he's silent.

'They say there are two possibilities for how life goes here. Would you like to hear them?'

'No.'

'The first is that it gets worse.' He steps closer. 'And the second is that it will get even worse than that.'

Her hands tremble with the effort of working the knife.

'There's a third possibility,' he says.

'I don't want to hear it.'

'The third possibility is that life improves.'

She can't help herself. She laughs out loud.

'What's so funny?'

'Only that my mother and I were trying to decide what manner of criminal was wicked enough to be assigned to this life.' She faces him. 'But now I understand you don't have to be a thief or a thug to end up in this place. Insanity, that's what brought you here. You're a madman, that's why they threw you out of the civilised world.'

He's gazing at her with such intensity the knife slips in her hand.

'Some people say life improves if you've something to believe in.'

'Some people suggest eating trees.'

'Would you care to hear a story?'

'I don't believe in stories.'

'There was once a species of animals that grew greedy, that's how it starts.'

'I don't need to hear how it continues.'

'Don't listen then. Shut your ears from me, but stop for a moment and enjoy this sliver of daylight before it vanishes. It'll never be here again.'

'Please,' she whispers, 'please, please will you leave me be.'

'You must be tired.'

'You underestimate me.'

'I'm sure I do. But come and rest for a moment.'

It pushes back and forth between them, this current, like a repelling magnet.

'No.'

'As you wish.' She watches him go to sit by the pine, leaning back against the trunk, folding his arms, stretching his legs out in front. She watches him stroke his knuckles over the moss like he could not be in a place of greater comfort. 'To continue the story, this species was formed by a god underground.'

'It might have been a goddess.'

'Who's telling this story and who's listening?'

'I'm doing neither,' she says picking up her knife and walking around the pine out of sight.

'No one's quite sure why the god decided on fashioning this particular species, after all he'd done pretty well in shaping trees and birds and some wonderful wolves. Possibly he was feeling experimental, but it's not for us to question a god's motives.'

'Utter nonsense.'

'You have something to say?' He is leaning round the trunk.

'You should question everything.'

'Is that what you think?'

She says nothing.

'Do you ever wonder where it gets you?'

He's wrong, but she's not listening, and in a moment she's going to walk straight past him back to the camp.

'As it happens it was an imprecise recipe the god followed; two parts soil to one part spit, but he must have known what he was doing because he moulded the clay into lumps. These he set down in warm pools.'

Silence.

He's looking up at her. 'Come, sit.'

'No.'

'This moss is very comfortable, but as you like. The following morning when he checked in his pools there was no sign of the creatures, not one blob. It seems they'd grown wriggly in the night, and each and every one of them had crawled out of the water onto solid ground. Whether this was by accident or intent it's hard to say, and we shouldn't speculate, but the god let them be for a while.'

'I do understand evolutionary theory if that's what you trying, very crudely, to describe here.'

'It's not. To reiterate, the god let them be.'

'Ridiculous.'

'Why is that?'

'He makes them and abandons them.'

'He was probably curious to see what would happen. I'm speculating now.'

'So this is some parable about free will?'

'Again, no.'

'Because if it is, it's a funny story to choose.'

'Do you know how to listen?'

She steps back to the far side of the pine and slides down. She shuts her eyes. His voice goes on, as it probably would even if she weren't there.

'Before long the animals looked around and noticed trees nearby. They decided they wanted these more than the ground they were crawling on, so they grew tails and climbed into the canopy.'

'Just like that.'

'Yes.'

'Ridiculous.'

'Once up high they watched the birds flying in the air—'

'And seeing birds the creatures decided they too wanted a piece of sky.'

'Precisely. But unlike the birds they'd nothing on their bodies that would enable flight. They waited in case their bodies grew wings like the tails that had grown so simply, and in this time of waiting they became impatient for sky and rather forgetful of where they'd come from.'

'Spit and mud.'

'Glad you're paying attention. But unlike the tails – which had dropped off by this point – no wings grew. It's not for us to speculate why. So instead they built machines.'

'Again ridiculous. This is all completely ridiculous.'

'Flying machines that would take them into the sky. From the sky the creatures looked down and saw the ground in all its murk and beauty which reawakened their desire for it. Each of them craved to lay claim to their own piece, because beauty isn't often a thing people want to share.'

'People have been fighting long before planes were invented.'

'I'm ignoring you now. Which is when the god ran out of patience.'

'You're saying we're the creatures and we've been dumped here because an entirely imaginary underground god wants to teach us a lesson. This is a fairy story.'

'We make good fertiliser, I'll say that much for us.'

He's standing over her. The darkening trunks are bars around them. 'Here.'

She looks up at him. A squirrel lies limp and glassy-eyed on his palm.

'Don't be proud.'

She nods and stands up and takes the squirrel, shoving it into her pocket. 'You're not buying me. Just so you know. Not for listening to your stories or for anything else you have in mind.'

'That's funny.'

Even the way he stands has too much ease to it.

'You really don't care about anything do you?' she says, watching him stretch his catapult, aiming at the canopy above. 'No, hold it, I don't want to know.'

He steps past her, his tread silent on the forest floor. 'You'd best get back. It'll be night before you know it.' Pushing aside thick greenery, he disappears from sight.

Lena hurries into the camp, fingering the silky fur in her pocket, her heart racing. Tomorrow evening she'll skin the squirrel and stew it so the meat infuses the water and the bread. She'll cook it until the flesh disintegrates and flavours the broth. The bones can be boiled a second time. The stew will fill Agata up and her eyes will shine. Lena will tickle her daughter's full belly and Agata will squirm, kicking her legs. She'll giggle and Lena will keep on tickling until Agata shouts: 'Mama, stop!'

The apothecary's wife is squatting outside her hut in the darkness, her shoulders hunched high like a vulture, scouring a pot with an ashy cloth. She lifts her head as Lena approaches.

'You have a lot of energy for evening expeditions, I'll say that much for you.'

Lena clutches the squirrel and pushes open the hut door, smiling. 'Goodnight.'

Mama brings it up when they're resting from the saw. It was the goitred guard who dished out the water this time. Viktor, he's called; Romanian, petty thief, watch your silver. The apothecary's wife, Hania, has already filled them in while they were dragging branches to the pyre. Viktor had been the mastermind behind the theft of a bagel cart, mule and all, Hania whispered, except that when he carried out his heist the cart was on its way back to the bakery entirely empty. Hania found this eye-wipingly funny. Now look at him, she said, Viktor has all the bread he needs.

Lena gives Mama her water and sits on the spruce they're limbing. Sap leaks where the last branch was removed. She holds her cup to Agata's mouth. The worksite is quieter than usual. A team of men, This Molek and Romek included, have gone with the red-haired guard and the horses to the river to load the barges with timber. They will camp overnight. This Molek has taken a bedsheet he hopes to fashion into a net for trout and salmon.

'I have a squirrel, Mama,' Lena says, taking Agata on her lap to cuddle.

Mama looks across, squinting from the sun. 'A squirrel?'

'I came across it in the forest last night. We can make broth for supper. We'll boil it in the big pot and steep the bones so it will last a couple of days.'

Mama nods slowly. She looks to where the guard – Viktor – is pouring a second ladle of water into a woman's cup. They're both laughing as water overflows and splashes on the ground. 'You know, darling, women here have to be careful.'

'I'm not sure what you mean.'

Mama leans towards her. 'You've seen them surely, the extra-ration women.'

Lena laughs. 'Is that what they're called?'

'It might not be something to laugh about, darling.'

'I'd like to laugh about something.'

'Only Hania, the apothecary's wife—'

'Can mind her own business.'

The women eat the squirrel in the hut that night. Ala washes the hide and pins it on a hook. Something soft for the baby, she says. They sleep well with a taste of squirrel on their tongues. Even better, the next afternoon the men return with fishtails sprouting from their trouser waistbands so Ala shrieks, and Romek and Mama jig round the hut singing silliness about salmon suppers. Before they feast Mama says grace. Afterwards Lena settles Agata and slips out of the hut.

He watches her come. He's lounging against the base of the pine, peeling a thin larch stick with a small blade. It's as if he's been waiting for her.

'I don't know why I'm back,' she says.

'You could have chosen a different direction.' He is whittling the stick into a thin white cane. 'I've another story, if you'd like to hear it.'

She steps around him towards the pine.

'Leave the poor tree alone for a moment.' He looks up grinning, his teeth white in the grey evening. 'Come on, take a seat. Many things might be said about living out your days in a forest, but no one could deny that moss is very accommodating. This colour reminds me of chartreuse.'

'I don't think I will, thank you.'

'As you wish. In any case it's a short story tonight.'

'I don't want to hear it.'

'It's called the tale of a girl with strange powers. Will that entice you?'

Lena looks at a train of black ants crawling across the gash she'd made in the trunk. She had pounded the dried bark into a paste and left it on the stove hoping to create a biscuit, but it had crumbled and smelled so bitter Agata clenched her teeth and turned away. If she could only find some sweetness that would help. 'Is there honey anywhere in the forest?'

'There was.'

'So there still might be some?'

'There was before the camp came and everything else ran away or was eaten. My story begins with a little girl growing up in a small village in the middle of nowhere.'

'I said I didn't want a story.'

'I'm talking to myself.'

'You think you have an answer for everything,' she says quietly.

He stops whittling and looks at her. 'Is that what you think?'

'Do you?' she says.

'I have my own ideas for how best to live.'

She snorts. 'Everyone has ideas about that.'

She watches him whittle. 'Were you a pianist once?'

He laughs this time. 'I don't believe so. Anyway this girl in the village was different from everyone else. Her mother knew it first, of course, her child's difference, because one day her daughter approached her in the kitchen with tears in her eyes; she wasn't more than six years old at the time. When asked why she was crying, the girl replied, "But, Mama, I don't want you to die so soon."

'The mother smiled and knelt down and replied, as mothers are wont to do, that she wouldn't be dying for a very long time, and certainly not until her daughter was grown with children of her own.

'But the girl wasn't placated. She took to clinging to her mama day and night, and refused to leave her sight. Within a week the mother had slipped on a dirty flagstone and an infection had developed in the heel of her foot. The girl was standing by the bed when the woman breathed her last a few days later.

'After the funeral the father took his daughter to one side, for his wife had told him about the strange scene in the kitchen. Adopting his sternest tone, he told her she must never speak of death to anyone again.

'Why? the girl wanted to know. But the father simply held her shoulders. He told her she was too young to understand. She was to promise him. Could she do that?

'The girl loved her father so she agreed. However her presentiments didn't leave her. On the contrary, as she grew in maturity she only had to look at someone for a matter of seconds to know how many years or months, or weeks even, that person had left to them. But true to her word she said nothing, and each time her premonition became reality. You'll know where I'm going with this.'

'I saw a gypsy once.'

'Yes. And how did that work out?'

'Her premonitions were complete nonsense.'

He looks at her a moment. 'I'll continue. When the girl was ten she repeated her question to her father who worked as a train conductor, asking why she shouldn't speak to people about their deaths. It might be helpful for them to plan ahead.

'It was a summer evening when she brought this up, and fortunately her father was in a good mood, sitting under the apple tree with a glass of plum brandy in his fist, so the time seemed ripe for conversation.

'Her father replied that people preferred to think about life and living. He raised his glass. "Ask me something else," he said.

'She thought about this. She was a smart child and what she said next was, "What would you do if you had a year to live, Papa?"

'He shook his head and laughed heartily. He'd not been the one to give her brains. "I would fish in the river and we would picnic, your brother, you and I."

'"And would you get less angry with the rude passengers on your trains?"

'He laughed. "Perhaps I would."

'She was nodding at him, nodding and nodding, his strange little daughter, and she was doing it in such a way that the father suddenly felt a great urge to swallow down his plum spirit and pour another glass.

'He stared at her as he drank, but she said nothing more.

'"Do we have any of that cheese around?" he asked when they went inside for the night. "If the weather holds, I was thinking we might have a picnic tomorrow."'

The guard stops whittling and lays down the stick. He takes up a second twig and begins again.

'Are you making a baton?'

'No.'

'Is that the end of the story?'

'No.'

'What do you want me to say? I've told you I don't believe in fairy tales.'

'What do you believe in?'

'I'm a rationalist. You should talk to me about things that can be proved.'

'Such as?'

'Science. It tells me when a pulse is too low or a temperature too high. A fairy story won't cure malaria or set a broken leg. A story about a picnic doesn't feed me.'

He digs in his pocket and finds a slice of bread.

She looks at it.

'This is what you're here for, isn't it? Take it. Feed your daughter.'

She doesn't meet his eye. 'I'm not one of those. You should know that.'

'One of whom?'

'Those women, the extra-ration ones.'

He begins to laugh then; it surprises her how deeply it comes from him, she hasn't heard him laughing like this before. He

throws back his throat and the sound is a cannon turned boom-
ing at the crowns of the trees. She waits for him to see she isn't
smiling and stop. But he goes on like a madman taking his fill of
a lone pleasure. He wipes his eyes. 'Seems to me those women
are making fairly rational decisions.'

Lena hates him then. How easily he finds his amusement in
this miserable place. 'I'll have you know I'm married.'

'Was that a rational decision?'

She snatches the bread and tucks it into her waistband. 'I
won't be coming back.' She stands and sets off walking back as
fast as she can.

'That wouldn't be a very rational decision,' he calls after her.
'Besides, I haven't finished the story. The end's the best part.'

She rages back to the camp, thumping her thighs with her
fists. As she passes the end hut she hears a low crying sound. She
pauses then pushes the door and goes in. Lying in the corner of
a bunk beside a red toy car is the small boy; he's perhaps three or
four years old, grey trickles on his puffy face.

'Don't be afraid,' Lena says quickly. 'I'm sure Mama will be
back soon.'

He stares at her, his dark hair sticking up, his eyes on her
bread.

She breaks off a chunk and she goes to him, putting a hand
around his thin shoulders. 'Sit up. Slowly now. Suck before you
chew. How's that? Better?'

Outside whistling begins.

She strokes the boy's hair and smiles. 'I think I hear your
mama coming.'

She kisses him and slips out. It's very dark, and the last shadows of card-playing men are watching a tiny figure with black
hair hurrying away from the guards' barracks. The men turn
their heads the other way to take a look at Lena. She waits for
the whistling but they simply return to their games in the dust.

Agata is giggling. It's a sound so forgotten to Lena that it jolts like a blow to the chest. She looks round from the pyre and sees her squatting over something on the ground, hands clamped to her mouth in delight. Kneeling beside her is the red-haired guard, just as engrossed.

'We can get another three branches on top,' the apothecary's wife says, scarlet in the face from the pyre's heat. She spits out a wad of the bark pulp that they all keep in their cheeks these days. 'Watch the grass on your side, Mrs Bem, those embers need beating down.'

'Just give me a moment,' Lena murmurs, flicking ash from her forearms and walking away. 'What is it, little frog, what's making you laugh so much?'

Agata points to a curved tin pot. It has a quick grey mouse inside, its paws scrabbling to get purchase on the metal sides.

Behind her the apothecary's wife is raising her voice, calling Lena back. But she can't take her eyes off Agata's delight.

The guard tips the pot into his hands. The mouse's pink nose appears twitching through the gap between his thumbs. Agata giggles.

'Would you like to stroke her?' He parts his thumbs slightly to allow Agata's finger in. 'Feel that galloping heart?'

'Be gentle,' Lena says.

'Yes, we have to be careful, mice are delicate creatures, we don't want her to die of shock.' He turns to Lena, his eyes bright as Agata's. 'Have a look, she's a beauty.'

Lena peers into his cupped palms. 'She looks like she wants to be free of you.'

'I thought your daughter might enjoy a pet.'

The apothecary's wife is calling again, shrill and sounding close to tears, shouting that all the branches must be incinerated before the pony brings water, that Lena is not being fair, she isn't thinking of the needs of others, there are so many branches, comrade.

Lena watches Agata wriggling a finger after the mouse again.

She bends to him, unable to shed the smile from her face in time. 'Don't let it die.'

'That's quite a command.' He slips the mouse back into the pot and covers it with a cloth. 'So, Agata, what shall we call her? We need a name that befits such a determined creature. Then we must build her a home.'

Lena kisses Agata's hair and returns smiling to the pyre.

'The girl says to her father, "What would you do with a month?"

'The father stares at his child. It's early summer again, almost time to taste the first glass of plum spirit under the apple blossom. He's eating his breakfast when she comes to him and says this. The bread is transformed to concrete in his mouth, too solid to swallow.

'On this occasion her timing is not so good. His fist crashes down on the table. "Haven't I warned you about talking like this?" He thumps the table a second time, the head of a rusted nail jamming in his flesh.

'She watches him. Despite his determination to be furious, he finds his thoughts turning to the age of the offending nail, wondering when it was hammered in and by whom. His fingers spread and move over the knots that gleam in the planks; it seems to him they are as beautiful as eyes in peacock feathers. His thumbs feel the difference in gradient and texture. He moves his hands further.

'"Would you stop going to work on the trains, Papa?"

'"What?"

'"Would you stop going to work on the trains?"

'He blinks and takes his knife to the loaf, intending to lop off a second corner and do it quickly so as not to think any more of his daughter's witchcraft, which after all is only what is whispered of her. He saws through the loaf, hoping to lose his fury in action. The knife's bone handle is a sleek, cool weight in his closed palm. Was it always such a good fit, this is what he's suddenly thinking, or have years of usage by him and his father, and grandfather before him, shaped it this way? He wonders what sort of animal gave its bone for this utensil. His hand rises to his brow to blot a trickle of sweat and he stares at his daughter sitting before him. He remembers a story about a king, Midas – everything this king touched was transformed.

'His daughter smiles at him, clear-eyed. He sees hazel flecks in her irises he hasn't noticed before.

'He clears his throat. He needs to bring his thoughts back to an unshifting place, a familiar place where he can keep them under control. He lifts the bread and smells its yeasty odour. Somehow he is reminded of caramel, the sort his wife made on feast days. He bites.

'His daughter is still smiling. Does he only imagine her expression is a little sad under the skin? "Would you stop work, Papa, with a month to live?"

'A drink is needed to get this bread down his throat. The dough turns to glue in the cavities of his teeth. The water is soft against the sides of his mouth, against his gums. He's never noticed water's skin before. It passes over his tongue and down his throat in an easy stream. Tears come to his eyes. How has he never noticed the softness of water's skin?'

'But you're crying,' Lena says to the guard.

'The story makes me happy.'

She looks at him, his narrow stubbled face, the beads of tears rolling over the pale bone curve of his cheeks. 'Who are you?'

'Does it matter?'

The air is cold on Lena's skin. Dusk is turning the space between them to a deep blue. 'Everything matters or nothing matters,' she says.

It's her hand that reaches to his face, wanting to interrupt the rolling tears, unable to hold back the need to press each of her fingers against his cheek. It is as if his face is an object of intimate familiarity, something that has worn down over centuries to reach this easy fit against her hand. 'What would you do with a month?'

He lifts his hand and covers her fingers with his own. 'This. I would do this.'

They stand in the quiet forest and night drops around them.

The nerves in her hand tingle.

She had stood in the trees cupping his cheek until the blood ran from her fingers and left the length of her arm. He had looked at her face as she touched his skin. Nothing was said between them and she could hear nothing from the forest around them. If life was continuing it was happening else-where. She stood before him, her palm to the hollow beneath his cheekbone, the pad of her forefinger at his eye's corner, feeling the beat of his dark lashes. It was a form of death to stand in the forest and touch him in this way. She didn't know why it felt like this, but she knew it also for a death a person might come to desire.

'You smell of the forest,' she had said to him. 'You'll smell of the forest as long as you live.'

He had covered her fingers with his own, pressing his callused skin over her swollen knuckles. She knew, like this, he was mak-ing a mould of her. When he removed his hand the imprint of her would peel with him.

'Are you cold?' he said.

'I'm not.'

But life had to be happening somewhere because night was falling down.

Now he weaves her fingers in his, crossing bone over bone, and he leads her through the trees, twisting beneath branches in the dark until they step out onto the track to the camp where a ris-ing moon is blanketed by clouds, the night's silence edged by the sound of bodies breathing behind planked walls. Darker than the sky are the two lines of huts, drawing the blackest of the night inside themselves.

'Wait,' he whispers. He stops, pointing to the left of the track where the oldest burial mounds are grown over with silvery grass. A dim shape is crouching there, barely visible in a dip between the mounds. 'I wondered when she would come back.'

'She?'

'The snow hare. See her?'

Lena studies the shadowy form for movement. She can just make out flattened ears and the pulse of breath shifting dark flanks. Lena is taken with a desire to creep forward and put a hand towards this crouching life, to reach out to it very slowly so the hare might also reach to sniff her fingers or accept a blade of grass. She would like to feel the thump of its heart inside the pelted ribs.

'She comes here?'

'Why not? I saw her here last winter. This may be her home.'

'Here? The camp?'

He's grinning at her. 'Get a good look. In winter it'll be almost impossible to spot her. She becomes a snow queen in winter.'

'Will she survive?'

'She's made for winter.'

'Will she have young that also survive?'

He lets go of Lena's hand and creeps towards the mounds. Without warning he claps. The grass ripples in a line into the forest undergrowth.

He turns to her, laughing at the expression on her face. His white teeth glint in the dark. 'Would you have her make her form here and become someone's dinner?'

And there is silence, ripping a gap between them, and the night air is pushing this gap wide open, pushing them apart. Lena looks at him and she thinks there will always be this pushing between us.

'They'll be waiting for you,' he says.

She watches him move away from her, stepping across the beaten earth steady and quiet as a fox. Within ten paces he has been swallowed by the night.

Lena blunders against the hut door coming in. There's a scratching sound, which may be the mouse in its pot, or the hen turning to resettle its feathers on Romek's bed. Some other sound is missing but she can't think what it is. She steps carefully towards the bunk, groping so as to avoid the stove.

'Is that you, Lena darling?' Mama's voice cuts through her thoughts.

It's the sound of sleeping bodies that's absent; the lip-smacking, swallowing and grunting noises of animal bodies unconscious of themselves. She looks towards the low bunk and sees eyes, tiny white buttons, then the dark forms of three people sitting in a row along the bottom bunk.

'We need to talk to you, darling.'

'You waited up, Mama?'

'We did.'

'Where's Agata?'

'She's here asleep, waiting for her mother.'

Lena steps towards the bunk. 'I'm tired, Mama, can we discuss it tomorrow, whatever's on your mind.'

'Better not, I think, Mrs Bem.'

Lena peers in surprise. 'Hania? Is that you?'

She makes out a shifting in the dark, a movement on the planks where she should be lying down with Agata.

'Your mother invited me,' the apothecary's wife says.

'Mama, whatever is all this?'

The third person – This Molek – of course it is – stands in front of her, his bulk in her way. In the hut's closeness she smells salmon on his breath. 'You're to stop seeing this man.'

'Excuse me?'

'You bring shame on this family, sister.'

'I bring bread for my daughter,' Lena hisses. 'I bring bread to stop my child starving in this hell on earth.'

'So it's true,' Mama says, her voice catching. 'Hania, you warned me of this and I prayed to heaven you wouldn't be right. My daughter has become one of them.'

'One of them, Mama?'

Mama is silent, sniffing.

'An extra-ration woman? Is that what you mean?' Lena looks along the shadowy faces, grateful for the dark, grateful that none of the dim white eyes seem to meet her gaze. 'And if I had?'

No one speaks.

'If I had become one?'

'If you had?' Mama's body is rigid. 'Tell her, Hania. Tell my daughter what you told me.'

The apothecary's wife straightens like a pronouncing judge. 'What do you know about this man?'

'What business is it of yours, Hania, what I know?'

'Mother of God, Lena, please—'

'I know as much as I need to know, Mama. He gives me crusts for Agata and asks nothing in return. He found a mouse, it made her giggle all day. He made a home for the mouse. Agata spoke today. She said "mouse" over and over. I feed her bread in the morning. It's in my pocket now and it makes my heart burst because I know she won't feel so hungry during the day. This bread keeps Agata alive and you sit here with your tuts and frowns and tell me to stop seeing him. No one is going to forbid me from keeping my child alive. I thought you of all people, Mama, would understand that. If you could get off the bunk, Hania, and return to your hut, I'd like to go to bed so I have strength for tomorrow's work.'

The apothecary's wife is clucking her tongue as Lena speaks. She levers herself up and shuffles past to the door. 'I can see my information isn't wanted.'

'Tell her, Hania,' Mama calls out. 'Tell her what you know.'

The woman stops at the open door, thin as a meat hook in the moonlight. 'This man you visit in the trees at night is a murderer. The bread you take from him is soaked in blood.'

All the next day she looks for him, but he's not in the canteen serving soup nor is he supervising the working party. He doesn't bring the water in the middle of the day. When they return from logging and she's received her bread portion, she breaks a piece for Agata and heads to the guards' barracks.

The one with the terrible goitre – Viktor – beams to see her coming. He's sitting on the step, coughing and rolling a cigarette using a scrap of newspaper. 'Missing lover boy already?' His voice is hoarse; she hears the catch in his breath between his words.

'I don't know what you mean.'

He hawks on the ground and strikes a match on the sole of his boot. 'How much does he pay?'

'I beg your pardon?'

He leans towards her and sniffs sharply, as though deciding on fish in the market. 'Three hundred grammes? Four hundred? I'm happy to match that.'

Lena's cheeks flame. 'How dare you.'

'You're tempted though, flower, I can see.'

She grips Agata's hand and turns away. 'Let's go, little frog.'

'Such a shame really.'

Lena freezes. She glances back despite herself. 'What is?'

'Didn't he mention it to you? Been sent to town to deliver the log sheets and collect the wheat for your delicious bread before the winter comes in. He didn't mention it? Funny, because there's a place for a woman on every cart.'

Lena stares at the smirk sliding across his face.

'After all, it's a long journey and it's nice for us to have someone to warm those places the sun can't reach. Seems he looked elsewhere for company this time, but don't take it to heart. Natalia's got quite an action on her, the commandant says. There wouldn't be many women who could match that. But come, I don't like to see ladies disappointed. I'll give you a try-out. Two rides and a cock suck for six hundred grammes, and maybe if we get something regular going you can share my cart next spring. What do you say, blue eyes, do we have a deal?'

'Go to hell.'

Agata's shivering with cold now the sun's dropped, but Lena doesn't go straight to the hut, instead she walks down the row and without knocking she pushes open the door of the hut at the end. There's a wooden spoon and a couple of bent forks on the stove, a heap of rags in the corner of a bunk. On the floor, upside down in the dirt, a child's red toy car.

The first snow falls on the camp six weeks later in September and there's still no sign of the guard or the woman and child he left with. The snow comes in the night, a heavy blanket, erasing one world, restoring a memory of others. Lena dreams of a forest in the mountains and blizzards there. She dreams of a man melting into white, a man who rarely enters her waking mind, but now and then creeps round the corner of a dream to pinch at the marks his spectacles make.

The snow continues to come down as they queue with cups for soup. Lena and Mama take turns with Papa's old ushanka. They wear layers of sable and mink and mitts stitched from a ripped stole. The cold burns like a poker in Lena's thigh. These days Agata stays behind in the hut with Ala and the mouse and hen, and the stove that must never go out. Mama begged Romek to keep inside as well, but the family need every piece of bread now that Ala's waiting not working. Besides, Romek says, stamping footprints in the ice, just imagine what December's going to look like. This Molek cuffs Romek's ear because no one wants to imagine that, and This Molek is twitchy about leaving his wife in her condition. Anything could happen without him, he says, any day it could happen. But a day's bread is a day's bread. Salmon is a distant memory. Lena walks quietly in the forest thinking of other things that have become nothing more than memories.

All day they work while snow falls like a shedding of infinite pale grey scales. The snow settles into white towers on tools and hats and red raw skin. They're all carnival people now, their bony frames layered in gaudy rags as if for a pantomime show, but one that is whitening into oblivion; a show that no audience will ever come to see.

Concessions are made to the quota because of the weather. The blue-eyed pony delivers lukewarm soup with weevils, which the guards joke are added for flavour, and the smudge of sun starts to slide away in the middle of the afternoon, shortening the working day. These are blessings to count when fingers don't bend and the icy air peels the lungs. Once the siren sounds for the return to camp, Lena shuffles to walk beside the count, watching how he moves, barely lifting his knees, choosing his track in the middle of the main crowd where there's body heat and the snow is beaten down. The count's wife is never seen at the worksite. The rumour goes that the commandant is paid off in jewels from a chest under the countess's bunk, which is why she can't leave the hut, and also why she hasn't yet starved. Lena would like to ask the count if there's truth in this rumour. She would like to ask if other rumours passed around about people in the camp are founded on truth. Most of all she wants to know if the snow makes it difficult for a horse and cart to return from the town. If a person should want to return.

'You're not taking care of your feet,' the count tells Lena, shaking his head at the splits opening in the toes of her boots. 'Listen, girl, you'll never survive winter at this rate. You need footwear like mine,' he waggles an iced clump above the snow and lets it fall. 'Every morning wrap your boots in rags. Use as many as possible. Four or five layers if you have them. Drench the rags with water. When it freezes the ice will provide extra insulation against the snow.'

Lena waits for more. The count can usually be relied upon to offer an array of survival tips, but it seems his piece is said. They shuffle on quietly, now under the shelter of the trees where the air is a little warmer and the earth still brown.

'Will it be very bad?' Mama asks, breaking the silence as they approach camp. 'In the winter?'

The count puffs out a rapid sequence of breaths. Shorter exhalations waste less energy he maintains. He smiles, green eyes sparking in his shrunken face. 'That depends. What temperature do you require of your purgatory?'

'But how are we to . . .?' Mama says.

The count lays a grubby paw on Mama's arm. 'Save your strength, dear lady, and enjoy the autumn. The mosquitoes have left us, that's a blessing.' He shuffles to take his place in the queue for the bread scales. 'Don't forget to chew fifty times to aid digestion.' He nods and falls silent like the rest of the workers, clutching his quota slip, preparing for the most important moment in the day.

The canteen hatch opens and the first in line passes over his slip holding his breath and staring as the knife starts to make its way through the dense black loaf. Weights are slid onto the scales, the cut slice is dumped in the pan and the scales tip. The queue remains silent, all eyes are on the guard's hands while a corner is shaved off the man's slice and it is returned to the scales. Behind everyone's eyes rapid calculations take place, assessing the density of the day's batch, the guard's mood and sobriety, the precision of the cut, the benefits or otherwise of a crust – harder and heavier, it is argued by some, but more filling because of this. Comparisons matter. Each portion is contrasted against the one before. Is it better to be earlier in the queue when the guard is less bored, or later when a more relaxed attitude might have taken hold? To smile or try a joke, or not? Because every variable matters. And when all these possibilities become too much to think about, the first moment of biting can be imagined, the act of swallowing solid matter rehearsed. It is quite the most important part of the day.

'Lena!' A shout behind her. This Molek is loping through the snow towards the bread queue, a bucket in his hand, a stunned look on his face. 'Lena, sister!' – causing several workers to turn tutting and muttering, as if Mass is being disturbed. He thrusts his slip at her. 'Tell them you're collecting my bread for me.'

'They won't let me.'

'They have to today.'

'What is it, what's happened?'

'You want to know what's happened?' This Molek takes her shoulders. 'You want to know?'

'Whatever is it?'

He lifts her in a bear hug, yelling into the air, 'He's happened, that's what's happened.'

Lena's chest tightens. 'He's back from the town?'

'Who's back?' This Molek roars at her expression. 'My son! My son came today! Congratulations, aunty!' He turns to Mama, arms outstretched. 'Zosia, your grandson is the most beautiful baby in this shithole world, excuse me.'

'And Ala?' Lena says, smiling quickly. 'How's she? Does she need me?'

This Molek pulls her close. His arms grip her as if he would crush her. 'Incredible. She is incredible. But she must wash. My princess demands to be clean.' This Molek lets Lena go and holds up his bucket. 'So here I am. An obedient servant always. Get my bread, sister.'

He sets off in a running shuffle for the well to check if the water is frozen.

When Mama and Lena enter the hut, the stove is raging and Ala lies beneath two quilts, a tiny dark-haired companion peeping out at her side. She looks up and, as Mama bears down, Ala smiles the creamiest smile Lena may ever have seen. 'He got himself out easily enough. As you can see he took his father's hair.'

Lena laughs and glances at This Molek. He is on his knees throttling the hen. 'Let's hope he doesn't take his father's hands.'

'I shan't let him have those, they're all mine.'

'Your Molek is going to boil broth tonight, princess.' This Molek holds up the bird in his fist, its claws still clutching at air. 'You need strength. My son is a prince, he must grow strong for all the great things he will do in his life. I have seen into his eyes and I know this.'

Ala beams at Mama. 'We're calling him Jozef, after Papa.'

'You should,' Mama says fiercely. 'You should call him this to honour that man. And we should give thanks because this is a good thing that's happened today. This is life starting again, a new healthy life. We have been blessed.' She lowers herself onto her knees by the bed, pulling the rosary from her pocket.

Lena hugs Agata and whispers, 'Now we have little Jozef, you'll have to be my big two-year-old frog. Mama's sending you a message. Are you ready?' She kisses her nose three times. 'I love you. Did you hear it?'

'Again,' Agata says and giggles.

Lena's heart leaps. 'Did you say again, little frog? All right, here we go.'

'Again.'

'Come see your cousin, Agata,' Mama says.

'He's asleep,' Ala protests.

'Never mind, he must know his family.' Mama turns back the quilt and plucks out the naked baby. 'Jozef, listen now, I am your babcia and I will sing to you because every child should hear music before they open their eyes. Listen now, this is the tune of your dziadziu's favourite nocturne. He had me hum it for days on end when we met. Such a ridiculous man, your dziadziu. Days and days, that crazy man.'

Mama starts to hum, little Jozef hunched in her arms, her shadow a giantess slipping along the walls. This Molek sits beside Ala kissing her hand, and Agata plonks down in Lena's lap for more kisses. Mama hums and Jozef sleeps, and a trance falls over the hut. It's easy to imagine the whole camp soothed by her voice drifting into the night.

Once Lena had asked Papa what it was that he'd fallen in love with: Mama's crystalline soprano voice presumably, or the charisma of her performances. No, he'd said, not at all. It was Mama's character he'd noticed, something in her determination for happiness that set her apart from the rest. There was no one alive with her zest. Lena had watched him closely when he'd said this, wondering if there might be a veneer of mockery to all this effusion. Now she looks at Mama waltzing round the stove and water runs from her eyes.

'Papa would have loved to meet Jozef.'

Mama sways closer. 'Perhaps he's watching right now. He's the world's nosiest man, your father. You think he'd miss his grandson's birthday?'

'I wish I could believe like you, Mama.'

'You can, darling,' she says, 'any time you choose.'

Lena shakes her head. 'I'm sorry I'm not like you, Mama.'

Mama spins on, smiling.

'Why are you smiling?'

'Imagine how dreadful that would be, darling, if you were.'

This Molek takes the hen between his legs to pluck, throwing the feathers at Agata so she shrieks and jumps to catch them.

The hut door bangs back revealing Romek, snow-covered and triumphant in the doorway, a whole black loaf balanced on his head. He's been teaching the commandant card tricks in return for stale bread. 'He definitely likes me. He's asked to learn juggling tomorrow and . . .' he spots a feathered bottom between This Molek's thighs.

'Ala had her baby,' Lena says.

Romek turns and climbs up his bunk. He slams the bread against the wall. 'Murderers, all of you.'

Mama goes after him. Romek cries, his sobs high and childish, and Lena is sorry for him. He hurls Blackie's harness at This Molek's head. He swears never to come down. And he stays in the bunk hurling the loaf at the roof until the smell of the broth is too good.

It's really quite unnecessary to walk to the guard's sleigh during the break and ask for a portion of soup because now there's snow everywhere it won't be thirst they die of. Snow is cleaner than cold soup. If she were giving out medical advice she would call it a safer bet than a bout of diarrhoea. Lena tells herself this watching the pony stumble through drifts into the clearing, a fox-haired driver in a long grey coat at the reins. Stubble has grown to a coppery thicket on his cheeks. Lena watches him come and reminds herself the soup will be nothing more than dishwater with weevils. She doesn't need it. She watches workers queue and the guard lift down the barrel and turn the lid, dipping the ladle and pouring languidly. She watches his eyes for a glance cast over the clearing.

'Well?' Mama says thrusting the cups at her, because recently their policy has been to join the queue early, when the soup is thin, rather than wait until the end when the dregs may be thicker but frozen solid.

Lena trudges towards the sled. She lifts her chin. She has nothing to be ashamed of.

'How are your hands getting on with the winter?' he says to her, stirring the barrel, his voice so low it's like a rumble inside her own head.

'I'll take my mother's portion too, guard.' She won't look at him while he ladles the soup. The pony is snorting and pawing at the snow, probably hungry and cold like the rest of them. She watches its hoof strike the ground, sending up a blue powder spray.

He's filling Mama's cup first.

Lena watches the pony but she knows his eyes are on her, boring into her as if he thinks he can drill in a bolt and haul up her gaze by will alone, as if he believes himself to have this power. As if he thinks she has no will of her own.

'You should remember I'm not a free man,' he says. 'I'm given orders and I fulfil them. I'm a prisoner here as much as you. Perhaps more so in a way.'

She looks into the cups. The liquid is repugnant: grey with floating weevils and gelatinous lumps. She hears herself blurt, 'And I know why that is.'

'You do? That's good you know.'

She turns away, her face hot with fury. She doesn't want to walk off and let him see how her leg moves so stiffly in this cold.

'I've something for Agata,' he calls after. 'I'll give it to you at the camp.'

'You're a free man. Freer than the rest of us. Do what you want.'

Raisins. Wrapped in newspaper, perhaps one hundred grammes, perhaps there are as many as two hundred of them. He hands the wrap to Lena with her quota of bread. She says nothing, walking away from the hatch and the eyes of the queue before she unfolds the paper and her heart lurches. Taking Agata out of the hut and keeping a finger to her lips she puts a raisin in her daughter's mouth.

'Suck it slowly.'

It's dusk but she can see the spark in Agata's eyes. She feeds her four, one at a time and no more. She takes a raisin for herself, moving it around her gums in a trail of sweetness, keeping it in her cheek until it disintegrates. In the bunk Lena lies awake, Agata slumped against her sucking on her thumb. She listens to Mama chewing and swallowing in her sleep. They all eat plenty in their sleep. The stove is roaring – the one thing in the hut that's never hungry – but Lena's back is stiff with cold. Soon they'll need to hump every piece of clothing on the bunks and crawl into a bone heap together. Behind the sheet by the other wall Ala is whispering to little Jozef as she feeds him. Romek's coughing. All day he's been coughing. His quota wasn't completed and the commandant was too drunk to bother with any magic lessons.

Lena thinks of the three sheet-covered mounds they'd passed on the way back from labouring, mounds which hadn't existed that morning when they'd left.

The count had shook his head at the sight. 'Didn't make it beneath the earth, poor devils.'

'What will happen to them?'

He'd glanced at her. 'You really want to know? There'll be no thaw until April. The wolves, at least, might get a decent meal out of it.'

'Not just the wolves,' the apothecary's wife had sniggered in Lena's ear, making a dumb show of eating with knife and fork.

'I refuse to believe that happens,' Lena said.

The wife sucked her cheeks so the hinge of her jaw was visible. Her cheeks were sprouting the soft down of starvation. 'What tricks will you try next to keep your daughter alive?' She turned her head into her coat and began to croon like a wolf.

The count put a hand on Lena's arm. It was good he did because her fists were shaking. She looked ahead where smoke was rising from roofs in the camp – an illusion of domesticity and community. At the end hut where flowered fabric hung in iced stalactites, no chimney smoked, drifts of snow still blocked the entrance. She looked away. What business was it of hers?

Lena counts out the raisins at night on the bunk, dropping them one at a time through her fingers into the wrap of newspaper. Where does a man find raisins anyway? She counts them three times over. Two hundred and twelve. Five a day for forty days. She rolls the wrap and tucks it down her quilt, shunting herself around Agata, moving her arm beneath her child's head, feeling for a pulse at a tiny wrist. Nothing can happen for forty days. Not while there's such sweetness in life. In the morning she'll give Agata two raisins before she leaves for work. Three more, one at a time in the evening. This will be the way to do it. Forty bright-eyed days.

Lena tries to sleep. She finds herself thinking of the weight of the paper wrap falling from his hand into hers, wondering about this man walking through an unknown town seeking out raisins for a child at the end of the world.

'I need to speak with you,' he says as he fills her soup cup.

It's the bay mare, not the pony, in the clearing, harnessed to the traces of a high-backed black sleigh, a nosebag hooked to her bridle. The soup has come far earlier than the workers are used to. Men have stared with envy at the mare's heavy nosebag – possibly it contains something as nutritious as oats – they have squinted at the sun and turned muttering to their comrades. It's too early for soup, everyone understands this; there will be too many cold hours of the day to fill when the soup is gone. Women begin to move in small groups towards the sleigh, sniffing and wiping noses on sleeves, straightening skirts, sliding quick glances at the guard. One or two are taking their portion of soup but hanging around. He does not seem to see them.

'Give your mother her soup and come straight back,' he says to Lena almost under his breath.

'Is that an order?' she asks.

He doesn't answer. He stirs the liquid in the barrel and pulls out a ladle, taking the cup of the man next in line.

'Are you not drinking?' Mama says when Lena hands her both portions.

Lena glances back. The guard is screwing the lid on the barrel.

'Look after Agata for me, Mama. Make sure she drinks it all.'

'Where are you going?'

'I don't know.'

'Darling, where are you going?' Mama repeats, her voice climbing. Lena shakes her head and makes her way back to the sleigh.

This Molek rises from the stump he's been splintering, rewinding rags across his palms like a prizefighter. The apothecary's wife straightens, a hand to her spine. Behind her, Mama is calling out Lena's name.

She walks up to him at the sleigh, lifting her boots out of the snow. He's buckling the horse's yoke, checking the shafts.

'I'm sent south again,' he says without looking up. 'I'm heading back to the camp, then I'll be travelling on, overnighting in a village and then spending a night in the town. The trip will take three days, four at most. Come with me.'

'You're not choosing another woman this time?'

He leads the mare in a wide circle so she faces the track into the trees. 'They like us to take women who have children. They think you're more likely to return.'

'The last one didn't.'

She watches his eyes for a flicker of something – irritation or anger perhaps, or even grief. She isn't sure what's there or what she wants to see.

'There's a market in the town where you'll be able to trade possessions. Don't make a fuss, just follow me into the forest. You'll have a few minutes at the camp to gather items you want to sell from the hut. We need to leave now if we're to make the settlement by nightfall.'

She stares at him. Steam is rising like a thousand serpents from his sheepskin coat. He tightens the mare's traces.

'Come,' he says to her. 'I'll lend you my coat.'

'No.'

'You want me to order you?'

'Nobody orders me.'

'Is that so?' He laughs in her face. Easy as a lunatic, this is how he laughs.

'They say you're a murderer.'

'Is that so?'

'Are you?'

He slaps the mare's rump. The sleigh begins to move off towards the trees.

'Darling!' Mama is breathless, fluttering beside her.

Lena turns and hugs her.

'Lena? I don't understand. Where is it he wants to take you?'

'Look after Agata, Mama, I'll be back soon enough.' And she's off, she's running, her boots flapping as she stumbles to catch him, stepping in the treads he's left behind.

'The woman's son was ill,' he says. 'We stayed in the hospital a month. The snow came. My return was delayed a further two weeks waiting to exchange the cart for a sleigh.' He glances at her. 'This is how it goes here.'

Huddled into her coat, only her eyes exposed, Lena is staring at the snow-swept tundra. Her eyes ache from trying to absorb the vastness of the plain that stretches to the horizon. Behind her, the taiga is reduced to a thin black band between white earth and grey sky. She'd not thought the trees could end so soon. Perhaps she'd stopped thinking the forest had any sort of end, or that her body would ever move through open space again. Her lungs don't know what to do with all this air.

'You've no response to make?'

The sky is empty of life but the tundra is not entirely featureless, not if you stare hard enough. Here and there yellow grass stalks poke from the snow, thin as hairs on a feather. When the wind blows the land ripples far into the distance. It's like they've become mites riding on the hide of a mighty beast. The bay mare jogs methodically south. The snow hare may be out there somewhere, belly to the snow, lying low in her winter disguise.

'It's not my business how other women live.'

He looks at her, beside him but separated on the bench by an inch of air. A deerskin hide is draped over his lap which Lena has refused to share. A rifle lies on his knee. 'It's not,' he agrees. 'Regrettably it didn't end well for either of them.'

The sun is already descending, a grey stain in the western sky. Lena balls her hands in her mittens and presses her chin into her coat. She thinks about the jewellery she's wrapped in a scarf and tucked into a tear in the lining. She thinks about the bundle behind her on the sleigh, all the things she raced to gather up to sell in the town. This the third time she has been required to pack as if life depends on it. Has she chosen well?

There's no sign of a village on the horizon. She leans forward and watches the horse's knees moving like pistons through the snow. Their lives are completely dependent on the limbs of this animal.

'We're lucky it's not blizzarding. Sit close to me if you won't take the hide. The most effective way to stay warm is to share body heat.'

Lena laughs, sudden and hard.

He turns and looks at her.

'You're not the first man to tell me that.'

But she doesn't have to say any more. She won't be unpeeled by him, picked over for his entertainment. She inches away, bending over the core of herself, bracing her arms against the wind. The horse jogs on, loose-reined, clumps of ice clinging to its fetlocks. She stares out across the tundra searching for a sign of habitation.

'Did the little boy live?'

'No.'

'How old was he?'

'Four.'

'Why was he taken to the hospital?'

'Dysentery.'

'I mean, why wasn't he left here to die like the rest of us?'

'His mother had a good friend in the camp.'

'What happened to her?'

'She didn't choose to return.'

'You let her stay in the town?'

His eyes are narrow, watching the horizon.

'You didn't force her to come back?'

'She made her own decision about what to do. In the circumstances there was no way I could prevent it.'

She looks across at him, hunched over the reins. Lines fan from the corner of his eye, ice is a sugar crust on his red beard.

'Perhaps it was for the best,' he says. 'She did what she wanted. How many of us can say that? How much of our lives do we waste clinging to things, often things we don't want? I admire that woman. She saw clearly. She didn't hold on to what she didn't want any more. She had the courage to act.'

'Am I your good friend? Is that your expectation for this journey?'

He throws back his throat and laughter booms across the tundra. She wonders how far it might travel looking for a place to stop.

'How easily you find your amusement,' she says.

'Is that what you think?'

'You don't deny it?'

He shifts his rifle to the side and lifts the hide, digging into a sack at his feet. He hands her a chunk of frozen bread. 'Eat some of this if you can, then try to sleep. If we're lucky we'll make the village before nightfall.'

'And if we're not?'

'Eat.'

She's woken by the crack of gunshots, two, fired in succession. She lurches upright. He puts out an arm to stop her tipping off the front board.

'Elk,' he says, laying down the rifle and picking up the reins to slap the mare into a canter. 'See them?'

A cloud of snow is churning in the distance like a tornado scudding across the plain. He grins at her. 'We'll eat well tonight.'

'We'll never catch them.'

'We don't have to catch them. Just keep your eyes on the snow.'

After a few hundred yards they see dots of red in the white. He grins at her and slaps the horse on. The dots become a trail and this turns wider and more meandering, like the course of a river seen from above.

'We're heading east,' she says. 'Don't we want to travel south to make the village before night?'

'Are you hungry? So we head east.'

'And gamble our lives away for meat?'

He grins and doesn't answer.

'How long will it take?'

'How strong is an animal's will to live?' He urges the horse again, grinning. 'It's very tasty, elk stew.'

Lena looks up from the blood trail to the sun spreading its stain on the distant horizon. The elk herd has disappeared from sight.

'Please,' she says. 'There's nothing out there.'

He shakes his head, pointing. She can just make it out; a dark form lying prone in the snow.

The fallen elk must be the size of a pony, its head propped by jutting antlers. Bullets have ripped dark holes in the skin on its throat and shoulder and the exposed muscle shines purple. The elk's gaze slowly follows the sleigh as it comes to a halt. Blood trickles in a half-frozen estuary down its stiffened forelegs.

'Look in the back and throw me the rope.' He jumps down with his rifle, shifting it against his shoulder as he approaches the elk. She watches the rifle's barrel end push into a whorl of hair between the animal's eyes.

His gloved finger moves to the trigger.

She looks away and hears the cracking of bone.

The sun is no more than a hump on the western horizon by the time the elk is trussed behind the sleigh. When he climbs up beside her, his gloves are dark and wet.

'It's going to be pitch-black soon.'

He turns the horse in a wide arc and slaps it into a trot. 'Let's find you some hay, Marysia.'

'There's no sign of any village.'

'There isn't.'

'You have blood on your gloves.'

He moves himself next to her so their sides touch, telling her to lean against him. 'You need to stay close and stay awake. No arguments.' He pulls the stiff hide around her. 'Now's the most dangerous time of day.'

'For wolves?'

'Hypothermia. Keep your eyes out for the village lights.'

'If they exist.'

He grins. 'They exist.'

Lena's jaw is clattering. Cold throbs in her core, slowing her heart. He leans across her, tucking the hide under her knees. 'Can you feel your feet?'

She nods.

'And the leg?'

'Yes, fine.'

'Talk to me. Start now and don't stop, understand.'

'I've nothing to say to you.'

'I doubt that.' He glances at the horizon and slaps the mare into a canter towards the south. 'What happened to your leg? And why do I hear your family call you "twig"? Let's begin somewhere there.'

A handful of lights pulse in the distance, yellow and impossibly faint. The luminescence is shy like glow-worms, or fairy lanterns in children's stories. Lena stares. It is somehow impossible to think the lights won't be suddenly snuffed out. Impossible to believe they can exist at all beneath such endless black sky.

'Here's our accommodation for the night,' he says. 'Thank me if you like.'

She's pressed against him but she can't see his face in the dark. No doubt he's grinning.

'We'll use a little fat to fry the meat, add some smoked garlic and dried mushrooms and a splash of local vodka to enrich the flavour. You like potatoes? They'll be available now we have meat to trade. It will taste even better than St Petersburg venison stew.'

He talks on and on about types of stews, until she thinks she'll go mad with it, and the lights grow stronger, twenty or thirty of them set in a ring. All else is dark. Dogs are setting each other off in peals of excitement.

'But who'd choose to live in this place?' she says.

'Choose?' He laughs at her. 'People live here who have always done so.'

'But it's desolate.'

'Life is without adornment, that's true. But they have their families and everything they need. You won't believe the heat inside those huts. It's like walking into a sauna. It melts you. In a few minutes we'll be there. We'll trade a hind quarter for milk, bread and potatoes, and we'll feast and sleep in the warmth.'

She looks at the dark edge of him, the shine of his teeth in the black. 'Why are you always grinning? Only a lunatic would grin like you.'

'What more is there to want than a full belly and a warm place to rest?'

'And in the morning when we're cold again?'

'We'll have full bellies in the day and meat for supper.'

'And when we return to the camp in winter?'

He laughs.

'There's nothing goddamn funny in that.'

'Can I ask you why you always look so far ahead of yourself when right now we have everything that our bodies need.'

'And that's supposed to console me? I should forget about Agata, and my sister's baby, and my family who are going to sleep tonight hungry and cold?' She tries to keep the tremor from her voice. 'One dead elk is no answer to that.'

He slows the mare to a walk. 'Perhaps thinking so much is no useful answer either.'

'No,' she says. 'You're wrong. If you stop thinking you might as well stop bothering with everything.'

'Oh, Magdalena,' he says turning. 'You don't see it, do you?'

'You know my name.'

'I know your name.'

She shakes her head over and over to rid herself of what – him? – her own thoughts? 'It's you that can't see it. If you embrace all the suffering that life hands out it's too much to bear. If you refuse to embrace it, what kind of person does it make you?' She looks away from the lights, turning her head where there's nothing in the world to see. 'I don't know if it can be borne, all the suffering there is in life. All the suffering that the people I love must endure. I don't know if I can bear it.'

'This,' he says, reaching to touch the ridge of her jaw with his thumb. 'Can this be borne?'

What is the name for it, the line of fire that runs down her throat? She used to know the name for all sorts of things. What is this gunpowder trail rushing her nerves?

She lifts her chin from his touch. They're close enough now to see the pale clump of settlement huts, to smell the bitter smoke rising from holes in turf roofs. Dogs run up, a swirling pack of yelping excitement. Lanterns dance through the dark.

He raises his arm in a sweeping wave, calling out in a dialect she doesn't understand.

Lena pushes back a thick wooden door and enters the hut they've been given. Heat pours over her. It submerses her, stunning her senses and buckling her knees. The floor is covered in animal skins and leather cushions. A small cauldron hangs from a tripod over a dung fire in the hut's centre, the smoke rising to a hole in the roof. Lena crawls towards this fire and curls on her side, closing her eyes.

Some minutes later in a blast of cold air, he comes in. He lays a slab of dark skinned meat on a ledge built into the mud wall. She watches him lift the cauldron's lid, releasing aromas of herbs and hot starch into the air.

He turns, grinning. 'Potato and wild garlic broth to start?'

'It's not ours, it belongs to the family who had to leave the hut for us.'

He takes two clay cups from the ledge and dips them into the cauldron. 'Sit up. Drink. That family will be feasting on elk tonight.'

Lena sips the broth. Her stomach fills. Tears come to her eyes.

He smiles. 'They smoke the garlic in the ground for a year.' He's dicing a slab of muscle on a wooden board, throwing cubes of meat into a shallow pan. She watches him move along a row of clay pots by the wall, sniffing and pinching dried herbs, crumbling tiny showers of dust into the pan. He shifts the cauldron off the tripod and holds the pan to the flames, shaking it as the meat begins to sizzle.

'You look like a chef. How you move, that's what it's like.'

'The body doesn't let you forget these things.'

Now he balances the pan on the tripod above the fire and kneels close, pushing cubes with his finger, flipping them over into their own bubbling fat. He uncorks a bottle from the shelf, splashing liquid into the pan. The hut fills with a rich gravy scent. 'Give me your cup. Eat, but slowly and not too much, your stomach won't handle the richness. Take this spoon. Wait, it's hot, don't let it burn your mouth. Wait a little longer. Now, try it now. Tell me, is it good? Can you taste the chocolate flavour in the flesh? The sorrel leaves? Wasn't that a wonderful generous elk?'

She has to smile at his talk. 'I'd forgotten eating could be like this.'

'Pleasurable?'

'Yes, I suppose so.' But that word, or any word is not enough to describe the fever in her brain and the tranquillity in her blood, her muscles' slow easing and the wash of gratitude across her skin.

'This is why being a chef is the best job in the world. Knowing when a person sits down to a meal that, whatever they're carrying in their hearts, when they eat the body won't be obstructed from its pleasure. There's nothing that can be confused or misconstrued in a mouthful of food.'

'Unlike when you're talking to someone, you mean?'

He grins at her. He's pinching cubes from the pan, one at a time, throwing them into his mouth and nodding his head from side to side as he chews, as if every mouthful requires individual assessment and is not exactly the same. If she was closer, her knuckles might reach out to rub against the beard on his moving jaw.

'What?' he says.

'I don't know your name.'

'Grigori Aslanov.'

'Grigori Aslanov,' she says, tasting the sound of it.

The look he throws back is a blade moving through her.

It is a cold unzipping of her skin.

She looks away.

'Ask me what it is you think you have to,' he says.

She puts down her cup. For a while she keeps her eyes on the orange shift and glow of the fire and nothing is said between them. He moves to stoke the flames and sits back on his heels facing her.

'Ask me.'

'All right,' she says, and she looks at him. 'Did you kill someone?'

'Yes.'

'Did you mean to?'

'At the time, yes, I did.'

She looks away, nodding.

'Go on.'

'All right,' she says. 'But now you feel remorse for it?'

'If you want to hear that I go about dragging a chain of guilt at my ankles, no, as it happens I don't.'

He stands and goes to the ledge. She watches him begin to dice more meat. 'You feel no guilt for killing someone?'

'It was a drunken brawl in a restaurant. Was it planned? No. Were the consequences regrettable? Certainly. Do I live with the consequences? What do you think?'

She watches him slide cubes into the cauldron and return it to the tripod over the fire. 'You have no remorse,' she says under her breath. 'You're a killer without remorse.'

'You want honesty from me? Very well you must take the answer. I had a temper in those days and I was proud. The circumstances were banal. A diner with a gut full of vodka complained about a perfect steak. It was the end of a long week. I'd also been drinking too much.'

'You killed someone over a meal?'

'He refused to pay the bill and disrespected my sister in front of the staff. I swung at him with a bottle. He fell back against the corner of a table. An unfortunate landing, you might say. The man was a party apparatchik so I was tried in the morning and sent north on the next train. Like I say, an unfortunate evening all round.'

She's quiet for a moment. She doesn't know what to do with her hands that wanted to reach for his beard.

'How matter-of-fact you are.'

'Listen,' he says leaning towards her, the knife's point in the air between them. 'Would crying a sea of regret bring the man floating back? You think an ocean might do it? Would going down on my knees in prayer to his ghost rematerialise him?'

'So you forget about it. How convenient for you.'

'I live as best I can. I enjoy meat when it comes my way, a warm fire, a cup of spirit in my hand. Perhaps you're scornful because you know a better way to live?'

'I've nothing to feel guilty for.'

'Unlikely to be true but convenient for you.'

'Not as convenient as pretending nothing matters. A useful attitude for a murderer to take.'

'This,' he says, his voice as fierce as she has heard him, 'this is what matters. It's the only thing that matters. Here. You and I on the edge of the world, teetering on the precipice of our lives. One gust and we're gone. We're nothing, you and I, Magdalena, pieces of bone wrapped in skin. We don't control the wind. But what we do today – now – in this moment, with all we have in this moment – that we may never have had before or have again' – he demands her gaze – 'don't you see? Tell me you see it. This matters. Now matters. That's all there is.'

Lena looks back at him, at the unyielding black in his eyes. 'You're wrong,' she says. 'The future matters. Without a belief in something better there's no point carrying on. If I can't believe in that for Agata, what sort of mother am I? Why drag her through this hell day after day?'

'There is no why.' He leans towards her, the knife trembling in his hand. 'There's no why to living, Magdalena. We freeze and starve, and we have nothing certain ahead of us but more freezing and starving, and yet we go on fighting to draw breath at any cost. You tell me why?'

'Because we have the strength and imagination to hope for better.'

'No, Magdalena. Because we're no different from animals staggering on in the snow until our hearts give way.'

Suddenly he's standing, pulling a heap of skins from the side of the hut. He drops three in front of her. 'Roll yourself inside to stay warm, it will get cold once the fire dies. Colder still if fresh snow comes down through the vent.'

'Where are you going?'

He throws another three skins by his rifle near the door. 'Get some sleep, we leave at dawn.'

They reach the town, such as it is, by mid-afternoon the following day. Here the snow lies in patches on beaten ground. The settlement buildings are crude timber shacks and corrugated sheds, between them Lena sees bent trees dropping the last leaves of the year, but few signs of life. No motor vehicles travel the streets, there is only the odd mule cart hauled by a thin animal slipping over frozen ruts.

They follow the main road to the side of a railway line, passing a wooden building with a peeling sign in a script Lena can't read. She watches a tall blond man in a peaked cap sweep the gutter with a bundle of twigs, his gaze briefly meeting hers then sliding into the distance. A heavy-skirted woman squats by the road, sprouting onions and potatoes spread in a heap on a coat. Behind her, a crow hops back and forth eyeing the vegetables.

'This is the station. Tomorrow morning you can barter here,' Grigori says to her. The first words he's uttered since they left the village. 'The market starts early.'

'But who on earth comes?' Lena asks, looking down the empty street.

'Plenty of folk. Three types in particular. Peasants from the villages turn up seeking practical items – ironware, utensils and the like. The nomads who pass through will be looking for items they can trade further on, and lastly there'll be settlers who may be interested in any jewellery or trinkets you have. They tend to shop for souvenirs.'

'Souvenirs?'

His eyes don't move from the road. 'Reminders of what they had in the southern cities in a life before exile. These people generally choose to settle near the railway but there's no way back for most of them. This town will be their home until the end.'

Lena glances over her shoulder at the blond-haired man. 'But still they stay near the station?'

'I'd call it a kind of self-inflicted torture, but I guess you'd say it's hope.'

She looks at the closed, dust-covered door of the station building. 'Do trains really run through this town? This far north?'

'Once or twice a month in summer. That's according to a schedule inside drawn up by Moscow fantasists.'

'Why don't you try to leave then? Take a train south or west or anywhere rather than returning to the camp. The commandant would hardly care.'

'And what would they do to my parents and sister if I did such a thing?'

'Some would do it anyway.'

He looks ahead down the line of sleepers, where they stretch to a distant blur. 'So that's what you think of me,' he says.

The mare knows her route. She turns off the main street, dragging the sleigh down an uneven track towards a long corrugated building at the edge of a dark ploughed expanse. A thin red flag hangs from a pole to the side of the building's door.

He tells Lena to stay in the sleigh while he delivers the quota information.

She wraps the deerskin around her, staring at the drooping flag, trying to think how long it's been since she saw red banners in her hometown, if it still can be called that. A year? Longer? The woman who watched her child paddle in chrysanthemum puddles may as well be a stranger to the one in this sleigh, this is what she thinks.

A sack lands on the ground next to the sleigh. She looks up.

'I have to get the flour loaded.' He unbuckles the mare from the traces. 'Take Marysia to the trough, then go and find her some grazing. There's a patch of common ground beyond the field. If anyone asks what you're doing, call me.'

'What if I run off? I might mount her and ride away.'

He hands Lena an empty sack, and he smiles, just for a moment, for the first time that day. 'Do as you wish. But if you return bring firewood, twigs for kindling if you find any.'

When she comes back he's crouching by the sleigh runners, building a pyramid of twigs with handfuls of hay tucked in the centre. He takes the kindling sack from her and tells her to tether the horse to a bolt at the water trough. There's a bucket with allocated oats. The sun has gone, pulling colour from the sky, and she shivers.

'Where do we sleep?'

'Usually beneath the sleigh.'

'Usually?'

'I've traded some meat for a night in the depot for you.'

'And you?'

'I have to keep watch over the flour.'

She looks at the stack of sacks. 'Why don't we leave it all inside for the night and load up in the morning? You'll freeze out here.'

'I'll build a wall from the sacks and sleep under the sleigh.'

'But it doesn't make sense.'

'You might think that, but Moscow has a different understanding of what's logical. Papers have been signed today.'

'They could be signed tomorrow.'

He strikes a match to the hay and kneels over it blowing, shielding the blaze with his hands. 'The building isn't open tomorrow.'

'But I'm sleeping in there tonight so it will be open.'

'Not officially.'

'We could take the sacks back in when the workers have left and bring them out in the morning. No one would see us.'

'We could. But that would be an unlawful appropriation of our nation's assets.'

'Not unlawful, you signed for them.'

'On a different day. An investigation would be opened into my actions. The delivery would be impounded for the investigation's duration, and no flour would get back to the camp in time for winter.' He sits back on his heels, still as a priest, watching the curling filaments of burning hay.

'But it's ridiculous,' she says.

'We could take the risk if you want, and you're absolutely right of course, it's both ridiculous and unlikely we'd be seen.'

Lena is silent.

'So what do you think?' he says. 'Do we take the risk?'

'Why do you always push me like this?'

'Is that what I'm doing?' He turns to her. Amusement crackles in his gaze.

'Sleep under the cart,' she says.

When the fire's strong they roast meat skewered on twigs. He warms a pot of broth brought from the settlement. Steam dances in the gloaming, and they eat in silence until their stomachs are full.

She watches him wipe the pot with a crust of bread.

'What do you miss most?' she asks.

'Salt.'

She laughs at him.

'Sure. Perhaps more than anything. I dream of White Sea salt. Hummocks of it on the shore. Cities built of it. Saint Basil's cathedral shaped from it.' He throws back his face and he too laughs. 'Every night at some point in my sleep I dream of salt.'

The shadow shapes of two men leave the building. One of them padlocks the door, glancing towards their fire, stooping to slide something beneath the trough. He runs to catch up with his colleague. When the men have disappeared into the darkness on the lane, Grigori goes to the trough and retrieves the key and fetches two glasses of hot tea and a white loaf from the depot. They dip hunks of this soft bread in the tea. 'Pomorka salt most of all,' he says. 'Even five grammes would do.'

Lena pulls the deerskin tight and stares into the fire. Cats are fighting somewhere nearby. She thinks how much she'd like to see a cat again. Even a wild scrapping one. 'I never wanted to be anyone else in life. Whatever's happened to me I've still always wanted to be me.'

'That's how we're supposed to feel, don't you think? It's built into our design. A useful survival attitude.'

She shakes her head. 'Right now I think I'd quite like to be that cat out there.'

'The one that's winning?'

'Even the loser.'

He smiles and says nothing. The night is cloudless and the land so flat that the sky is a dome of indigo, pricked by stars. 'There's your salt,' she says. 'Up there above us. Millions of flakes of it.'

He empties the dregs of his tea glass on the ground. 'Tell me, what is it you dream of?'

She shakes her head. 'I don't want to talk. You tell me something else.'

'Sure.' His voice, quiet as an ant on her skin. 'Anything you like.'

'Your sister. Tell me about her.'

'Tasha? The light of my life.'

'You're close?'

'Not in age. She came fifteen years behind me. My mother had her very late in life, when they'd given up hope of another child.'

'Is she married now?'

He smiles, 'Tasha will never marry.'

'How can you be so sure?'

'My sister was born a little different from others.'

'Different how?'

He adds a branch to the fire. 'Perhaps because she has more joy in her heart than anyone I know.'

'She doesn't think too much?'

'She doesn't.'

'Unlike me.'

'Unlike you.' He takes her glass and shakes the leaves out. Then he reaches behind him into his bag and brings out a bottle of spirit. She watches his pale hands twist the cork, the slide of the carpal bones in his wrist pouring the liquid into the glass. 'But even better than all that, my sister makes superb custard. Silkier than the drapes in any palace in the world.'

Lena snorts. 'Custard is custard.'

His fingertips brush against hers as she takes the glass. 'I disagree. Custard is consequence. When someone is patient with it, custard returns the respect. Tasha has patience.'

'Which is why she puts up with you.'

'And why her custard is sublime.'

'I have no patience.'

'You don't.' He raises his glass and knocks it back, all the while staring at the branches popping and spitting and collapsing into the fire. Shadows stroke the bone curve of his face. Zygomatic. The name for the bone of his cheek.

'You should check the stove's still lit inside the depot,' he says.

'How long before you get to see her again?'

He nudges a branch further into the heat with his boot toe. 'Twenty-two years and three months.' He doesn't look up at Lena. 'I will see her again.'

'And if you don't?'

'She's here.'

'Where?'

He taps his head. 'Everything I need is in here.'

'Except salt.'

'Except Pomorka salt. It's cold. Get inside. Take the skins. Stoke the stove.'

'And you?'

'Go ahead. I have my flour sacks to comfort me.'

He points out a good spot on the beaten ground beside the railway building. Dozens of people are already there, opening sacks, arranging their wares. It's just past daybreak. The vendors, mainly women, are setting out pans of yaks' milk, potatoes and turnips, baskets of dried berries, jars of boiled eggs. There's no obvious organisation to the marketplace: an old man offers strings of minnows and a stack of empty sacks alongside a girl laying down a neat grid of paper icons. A boy unwraps a stone to sharpen knives next to his mother's cage of sparrows and four brocade slippers.

'Listen carefully to me,' he says, taking her arm as she pulls her bundle from the sleigh. 'These people are not soft.'

'I know that.'

'They will look at you and see your hunger. Don't fool yourself that such a thing can be hidden. They will read your desperation. Remember that. The nomads who pass through will sell on what you trade for ten times the price. Remember that and pause to think before you make any deal. You brought jewellery?'

'Yes.'

'Show me.'

She unfastens her sable and takes a knotted green scarf from a rip in the lining. 'Diamond earrings, three of Mama's gold necklaces, a string of pearls. Papa's watch.'

'That's everything you have? Are the stones genuine?'

'Of course.'

'And the gold?'

She looks at him.

'I have to ask. All right, give them to me.'

He unknots the scarf, glances inside, knots it and then tucks it in his coat. 'I'm going out of town to find spirit and tobacco for my colleagues. I'll try to bring back something useful for you. What is it you wish for most?'

'A hen that lays. That will keep on laying through the winter and never die.'

'A magic hen. Very well, I'll be back with one when I can. Wait for me here.' He slaps the horse's rump with the reins. 'Don't smile,' he shouts back to her. 'They'll see you're even more nervous than you already look.'

For a while it seems everyone is walking past Lena's spread blanket without even a glance, then she realises some people are passing and returning and passing again. She sits up straighter. By the time a pair of boots stops and a hand reaches down to poke at Ala's silver-backed hairbrush, she's ready. With a face of stone and a finger pointing to her mouth she says, 'Food. I want food.'

When the market eventually disperses, taking with it This Molek's wrench and file, a pack of cards she pulled from Romek's bunk, scissors, crockery, silver picture frames and Mama's Bible, Lena has amassed such treasure she could weep over: two bags of rye flour, a honeycomb, a kilo of cloudberries, another of cowberries, twelve pickled eggs, several seed potatoes, two strings of dried minnows, a swede, and a bucket of lard. Best of all are the raisins, two hundred grammes worth. She takes one to taste, imagining a shower of them splattering into hot water, sinking, softening, expanding. She imagines Agata growing fatter before her eyes.

'Well?' he calls from half a street away. 'How did you do?'

She jumps up, grinning, running down the road to meet him with her bundle in her arms, laughing as she runs because she knows she's turned back to a child again, wanting to show Papa the sugar mice left by the Christmas angel beneath the tree.

'Taste them,' she says, holding out the wrap of raisins. 'Try the honey too.'

'It's good,' he says running a finger over the comb. 'Nearly as good as salt would be.'

'I can't wait to see Agata's face when she has some.'

He's grinning too. Like kids, this is how they're grinning, a shine in the eyes, an ache starting in the jaw. And she knows the thump in her blood and the rush in her ears is simply because she has food for winter, that's all it is, but still the air between them, the push and pull in the air between them . . .

'We need to get going,' he says, turning.

He climbs on the back of the sleigh. 'Give me the bundle, I'll strap it with the flour. I'm afraid I couldn't find your magic hen anywhere. The last one was sold yesterday.'

Lena tries not to let her disappointment show. She tries not to notice it creep under her skin, not today, not with all the honeycomb and berries and lard she now owns. 'Somehow I didn't think you would.'

'Come, hand me the bundle.'

Lena lifts it up and as she does she gives a small cry.

'They call her Creamy,' he says.

She's staring into the face of a small white nanny goat, kneeling on the flour sacks, tethered to the side of the sleigh.

'Creamy for the taste of her milk. I'm afraid there's not a family jewel left. But I do have two sacks of hay.'

Lena's legs are liquid, she might just fall down.

His hand is stretched for Lena to take. 'Come and meet her.'

He helps Lena up into the back of the sleigh, and she crawls towards the goat who eyes her but doesn't pull away. She leans her forehead against the animal's neck, breathing in its acrid living heat. 'Give us milk,' she whispers, 'and I'll protect you with my life.'

When they arrive back at the village, the hut is prepared. Broth simmers in the cauldron over the fire, the elk carcass, split down the backbone, lies in two halves on the ground. Lena tethers the goat to a hook on the wall with a pile of hay. She crouches, her hand on the animal's warm flank, watching it chewing steadily. Grigori tells Lena the village chief will provide five large sacks of dry grass in return for the remaining elk meat.

'Will it be enough?'

'To see her through the winter? Who's to say.'

'She has to live.'

He uncorks a bottle of spirit, pouring it into two tin cups. 'Stew for supper?'

She knocks her cup to his. 'Milk for breakfast.'

'You're smiling.'

'That's hope for you.'

They eat their fill of meat and broth. She hears herself talking to him about her morning at the market, she talks like she can't stop, like he must hear each of the bargains she made and how they came about. He listens, loading the fire and they lie on cushions either side, and she is smiling.

'Tell me about your husband,' he says to her.

'There's nothing to say.'

'You have a child together.'

'I don't know whether he's alive or dead. Usually I try not to think about what's happened to him.'

'And how is that?'

She takes a drink. 'It wasn't a marriage I wanted. People told me it was for the best.'

'Why?'

She swills her cup. 'Various reasons. At the time I thought the arrangement a catastrophe. I had other ideas about my future.'

'You had plans?'

She gives a short laugh. 'Yes, I had plans. You could even say I got myself caught up in notions of destiny, believing I'd do important things. I presumed I'd have a choice. I thought choice existed.'

'Life's not so bad without it,' he says quietly. 'Once you come to accept it.'

'No,' she replies, looking straight at him, 'you're still wrong about that.'

'I suppose it depends how much truth you want to live with.'

The vodka is hot in her stomach. She throws back the last of it, feeling a scorch in her throat. 'My husband isn't a bad man, that's true too. There are lots of truths around.'

He takes her cup to refill. She closes her eyes, listening to the liquid's splash. The goat is rubbing a shoulder against the wall. Dung hisses and spits on the fire, and outside a gust nudges a clod of turf on the roof. And beneath all this is the silence between them.

'Here in this hut right now it's almost like being in a place outside of time.'

He hands her the cup.

'What I mean is perhaps when we return to the camp we'll look back and discover today never happened. That's how it feels.'

'There's a goat by the wall, how will you explain her?'

'Maybe she'll be gone in the morning. Maybe she's out of time too.'

Lena closes her eyes again. She doesn't need to look to know he's moving around the hut. She doesn't need to hear it. She can feel it in the push of air, because there's always this force with him, and there's always this smell of him. With her eyes closed and her hearing dulled, she could track him from a mile away, the scent he carries of soil after rain. She smiles, she could tell him this, how she'll always be able to track him down from his smell.

But she doesn't, and she won't look at him, however much her eyes want to see what he's doing. She'll never tell him how he seems to move through this life, which is no sort of life, easy as water flows, how he laughs at nothing at all, and makes a sound to crack open the earth when he does. She won't give in to the desire to go to him and raise a hand to the curve of his cheek. Because she's more than a body, isn't she? She has to be more than a sack of bones and longing.

She hears him come to sit by the fire. She wonders how far away he is. If she's very still she might catch the edge of his breath, or the sound in his throat as he swallows.

'There were once two people made of skin and bone,' he says. 'A woman and man drawn together by something they couldn't articulate or understand.'

When she doesn't interject, he goes on. 'Let's call this compulsion, with a degree of imprecision, a natural force. At first it seemed easy for them to try to deny it because, like the most powerful things in life, like kindness, say, this force can't be seen. But still the force that drew these two bone people together didn't go away.

'They were unsure what to do about this feeling, which if I'm honest I'm dressing up a little, and is simply a name for animal desire. They were unsure because the feeling was complicated by time and place. Above all, it was tangled in human worries, which have a reproductive energy, even though worries are often bred from nothing but air.'

She begins to laugh. She opens her eyes. He's kneeling on his heels to the side of the fire. She could touch him right now if she chose, she might reach a hand to his shoulder and dig her fingers into the hollow beneath. 'You're sly, bone man.'

'Please don't interrupt. You see there was little time available to these people and no certainty about the future, and being creatures made from bone but possessing human minds they worried about this. But still the feeling between them did not disappear.

'It happened that they were offered a tremendous gift – a single evening out of place and time and consequence. A night without hunger, cold or exhaustion. To their human way of thinking it was all they could be sure of.'

'You've really no shame, have you?'

'You think shame would be useful?'

'It would be normal.'

'But would it be useful?'

'Go on.'

He shakes his head and looks at her. 'You've stopped my train of thought.'

'So go back a bit and carry on.'

'No,' he says.

'No?'

'I think that's my story about done.'

'You do?'

'I do. Do you like it?'

'Well . . .' she says and she stops because he's kneeling like a monk before a votive candle, as grave as she's seen him, and she gives in to the silence between them.

He turns his head to look at her.

It's as if she's being drawn on a line towards him, as if there's a hook in her belly and she's being reeled out of the water and pulled to a place she has to go but knows she'll be unable to breathe. She stands and she walks to him and she slides down against him. She puts her lips to his cheek, she runs her mouth down the ridge of his nose to his cracked pale lips.

'I would like to see your ribs, bone man.'

Unbuttoning his heavy grey shirt she peels it from his shoulders. Her palm goes to lie against that place where his heart beats, her fingers slip into the gullies between the bones.

His hand moves to her throat, gripping her neck between thumb and forefinger. He pulls her mouth down to his, vodka and meat on their tongues.

She strips off her woollen jacket and tattered sweaters and two blouses, rimed in dirt, and he touches the nipples that stand from her shrivelled breasts. The air is thick with the smell of their unwashed bodies.

He lays her on her back.

'Tell me if I hurt you.'

'You won't hurt me.'

His gaze takes in her thin grey frame. 'Magdalena, my heart's breath.'

He wipes a tear from her cheek. He doesn't ask why she's crying, and she doesn't say. Perhaps he already knows what she's coming to discover: that there is nothing greater or less in life than this – the slide of skin on skin, the knock and rub of bones. If there's just an evening left to them in the world, this is how it must pass, if there's just an hour, or the minute ahead of them.

When he sleeps she covers him with a rug. She lays her ear to his chest listening to the thump of his heart. A dread thought comes to her. How improbable that this muscle should beat on as it does, alone in its dark cage and without rest.

'Sleep,' he tells her.

She imagines it a mail horse endlessly galloping in the night. How much hope it requires to believe a horse will keep on running without a stumble or pause, second after second for decades of time. Impossible to believe this heart can keep going on so long.

He turns to his side so he might wrap her body in the length of his. 'Sleep.'

She wakes in the night to blackness and his touch on her forearm.

'Sleep,' he says to her.

She tells him she's been dreaming of him moving through the span of her life. Just now they were in a hut in the forest, white-haired and arthritic with a goat at the door. 'The peculiar thing is how unremarkable it was; you were in the house I grew up in, and you were old in the hut in the forest. I dreamed you were my past and future.'

He takes her hand in his. 'I'm your present, Magdalena, that's all.'

She lies her ear against his chest, willing the horse to slow its stride and conserve its movement, willing the road to continue for hundreds and thousands of miles. 'You're more than that. You have to be.'

His fingertips weave between hers. 'Don't think, sleep.'

This Molek grabs her with both arms and plants kisses on her forehead and mouth. He encloses her in a rib-crushing hug, so she pleads for mercy. 'All this for one small goat.'

She'd led the animal into the hut at suppertime, and Ala had turned and screamed, then started to cry. Mama's rosary fell into the water boiling on the stove.

But no one cares to salvage it. They all crowd round where This Molek is running his hands over the goat's legs, inspecting each hoof. He peels back her lips and taps her teeth. 'Young enough. Strong enough. What shall we call you, girl?'

'She has a name. Creamy.'

'Creamy the goat,' This Molek says, peering in her fluffy ears, running his hand over her sharp spine. 'Come to give my son milk, have you, girl?'

'Terrible name,' Romek says, emerging from his bunk, legs first, landing on the floor with a coughing thump.

'You look dreadful, worm.'

'You don't,' Ala says beaming at her. Ala's black-haired son is snuffling like a mole for her breast. 'You look like you're about to start dancing.'

Lena kisses Agata on the nose and scoops her up. 'Do I?'

This Molek has the goat by her cheeks and is blowing into her nostrils.

'Do you think she likes that?'

'She does.'

Ala is still beaming. 'What sort of cake is he then?'

'Cake?' This Molek says. 'Don't talk about cake, princess, you are cruel.'

Lena laughs, 'I don't know what you mean.' She swings Agata round and round and sashays six steps in each direction, the length of the hut. Only four days away and she's forgotten the filth and stink of this wretched place and how thin everyone is. 'Did you miss Mama? Did you miss me?'

She's light, Agata's far too light. She can't have weighed this little when Lena left. But there will be milk to strengthen her bones. And lard and honeycomb, and raisins to suck. 'But look at you,' she says, licking Agata's nose so she squeals. 'Look at this grubby hair. Do I have to lick you clean like a baby goat?'

'It's only been a couple of days,' Romek says. 'I doubt it's grown.'

Lena laughs. 'Everything grows, Romek, haven't you learned that yet? If something's not dying it's growing, that's how it goes in life.' And she begins to twirl round the stove.

This Molek pokes his head up from the goat's udders. 'Have you been drinking, sister?'

Lena laughs but she can feel them all staring. Well, let them stare while they can. She whirls Agata like a plane in the air. 'We've got a goat, we'll have milk for breakfast. Mama, have you seen her properly?'

Mama is at the stove, pulling out her rosary on a fork. She doesn't answer.

'And the market,' Ala says. 'How was that?'

Lena laughs, 'Yes, that, I forgot.' She goes outside and brings in her bundle, dumping it by the stove. 'You unwrap it, Mama. Goodness, we got so much.'

'We?' Ala says.

'Grigori warned me to be tough. You should have seen the way a woman ended up begging me to take her pickled eggs.'

'There's eggs?'

'Eggs and so much else. Mama, do you want a spoon of lard in that water? Some minnows perhaps?'

Mama is drying her rosary so Lena unwraps her bundle and holds up her treasure a piece at a time. Minnows are thrown into the pot on the stove. 'Just a handful,' Mama says quietly, 'and one spoon of lard because there are several mouths to feed and for who knows how long.'

'There's hay for the goat, Mama.'

'So I see.'

'Grigori bought her.' Lena laughs. 'I asked for a hen, but a goat is incredible, isn't it? He did well, didn't he, Mama?'

Mama is ladling out the broth. She takes a moment to nod.

For a moment the only sound is scraping and swallowing. Romek is the one who brings it up – what everyone really wants to ask – when they're each dipping bread into their second cup of broth. He's holding his spoon towards the stove to watch the tiny beads of fat bobbing in the liquid.

'So are you officially one of them, twig? Not that I'm not grateful for the goat and everything.'

'One of what?'

'You know, those women – what do they call them here? Viktor's even got one now.'

'Romuś,' Mama says in a low voice, 'eat your soup before it cools.'

'It's fine, Mama.' Lena is helping Agata feed herself with a spoon. If she helps too much Agata pushes her hand away.

'Extra-ration women? Is that what you mean, worm? Yes, I suppose I am. Actually I've some news about that.' Lena turns to Ala when she speaks. Alone of everyone in the hut her sister is smiling, and what Lena would like to say to her is: 'You're right, Ala. I never thought it could be like this, but this man is what I want most at any time of any day, I understand it now. What I want most – it's him.'

'News?' Mama says, turning her cup in her hands. 'What sort of news do we need to hear, darling? Do we need to hear it right now?'

But she doesn't get to answer because the door is pulled open to the cold, and it's him, Grigori, his shoulders wet with snow, stamping his boots on the floor. 'Good evening,' he says looking round, and to Lena, 'I've lit the stove.'

Mama's cup falls to the floor.

Lena goes to her. 'There's a small hut vacant until the next transport arrives in the spring. I'm sorry, Mama, that's what I needed to tell you.'

Mama stares at her, her lips trembling.

No one speaks.

This Molek clears his throat and steps up. 'It's not that we're not grateful to you, comrade. A goat, I mean, a nanny and in such productive health. But—'

'Has she told you she's married?' Mama's voice is suddenly strong and clear enough to reach the back of an auditorium. 'And her husband, we must presume he's alive, we've heard nothing to the contrary, she's told you of him? Anton is his name. Lena made vows of marriage to him in a chapel before God.'

'Grigori knows all this, Mama.'

'And still you proceed without thought of your sin?'

'How is sin useful to any of us right now, Mama? We have a goat.'

Mama turns away. 'A goat has no power to absolve.' She goes to her bunk, turning to lie on her side, facing the wall.

'It saves us, Mama. The goat's milk will save Agata and little Jozef. Can't you at least see that?'

'I'm tired, Lena, it was a long shift, please let me rest.'

'And I'm happy, Mama, isn't that what matters? And yes, Grigori was responsible for a man's death, that much is true. I presume that's what you want to hear? Pray for me if you like, Mama, if it helps you. But will you be happy for me too? Will you try, Mama, because I'm happy with him. I wasn't sure it was possible to feel this way, the way you felt with Papa, but now I see it is.'

Ala puts her hand on Lena's shoulder. 'I'll talk to her.'

'Come,' Grigori says. 'Give it time.'

Lena wipes her eyes. She lifts Agata to her hip and looks at Ala. 'Keep the food here and the goat, it'll be safest with you and the baby in the day. I'll come back in the morning for milk and my clothes.'

Mama speaks out from the bunk. 'And, Agata, is she to live with you in this place?'

'She is, Mama.'

Lena wraps a quilt over her daughter, kissing her brow. 'I missed you, little frog, how I've missed you. Snuggle in close, it's cold out there.'

She follows Grigori to the door.

'Extra ration,' Romek says as they leave, 'that's the name for the goat.'

No one whistles that night as Lena follows him in the dark to the empty hut. It's too cold to stand outside for more than a second and no one with a wish to live would be there willingly.

Winter deepens and no one whistles as each day Lena walks between her family's hut for milk and food and the place where she passes the night with Grigori. December comes and a work team is assigned each morning to clear a path between the canteen, the latrine and the track into the forest. Sometimes when the work siren sounds curtain scraps are raised at the huts' windowless frames and legs appear dangling. Boots land in waist-high snow and shovels must be taken to the drifts blocking the hut doors. In the worst of the weather some doors do not open at all.

No one whistles as Lena walks up to Grigori to receive her ration of soup at the midday break. Eyeballs shoot out and quiver on stalks, but observe in silence. They follow the ladle's journey from its dip in the barrel through the air into her cup. Lena isn't surprised. Rumour is the one thing that thrives on the world's edge. Rumour says extra-ration women receive a different sort of soup in their cups. This soup consists of cream and dill and morsels of chicken breast.

No one whistles, but now and then at the shift's end if a quota is declared incomplete, Lena's elbow will be taken and words breathed in her ear – acid-stomached, cabbage-stinking words begging for intercession.

'But I have no special power over anyone,' she will reply, looking away. 'Please believe me, I work for my quota just like you.'

And the worker will stare at her, on occasion venturing a foul word or comment, usually quickly snatched back and tucked under the breath. If the person has the energy for it, they might spit at her rag-covered boots as they walk away.

One afternoon when there's neither snow nor sun in the sky, the count stumbles over a length of larch he's dragging to the depot. Too weak to rise, he's carried back to camp between This Molek, the apothecary and Romek. This Molek shakes his head as he goes. The man weighs less than Agata, he says. Lena hurries ahead to warn the countess. The old woman raises herself on an elbow on her bunk. 'Welcome, young lady,' she rasps, 'what an unexpected pleasure.' She is wearing a pink taffeta gown and an ermine coat. Beneath the bed is the trunk that's rumoured to contain all the gemstones the count uses to buy his wife's daily bread. It is also overflowing with fine fabrics. The countess listens to Lena and beckons her close. 'It is beginning,' she smiles, her teeth shining in the dark of her mouth. 'The god in the earth is fingering my husband's bones before he cracks them for the marrow.'

'Nonsense,' Lena replies. 'He'll be up and about in hours, you'll see. He wasn't injured, just a little cold.'

The countess pinches Lena's wrist with her thumb and forefinger, her grip surprisingly strong. 'Is it true, what I hear? You're an extra-ration woman to the murderer?'

Lena looks away. 'I don't think that's your business.'

The countess laughs a long time, her breath damp with decay. 'Good on you, I say. When I'm dragged under, come and help yourself to my gowns. Don't let them go to waste on window curtains or God knows what else. They're Parisian silks, they should be admired by a man.'

That evening Lena's sitting on the bunk checking through Agata's clothes for lice, when Grigori comes in carrying a bundle of offcuts for the stove. At once she asks him for bread for the count and his wife. The countess is raving, she's got the hunger madness in her brain, she tells him.

'Insanity is not such a bad thing when the end approaches,' he says, opening the stove door to refuel the fire.

'But you can get them extra bread?'

He stops, a log loose in his hand. 'Magdalena, my heart's breath, where am I to find this bread? Every ounce of flour is accounted for.'

'You could ask the commandant.'

'I've no more sway with him than I do the wind.'

'You could at least say you'll try.'

'And if I try today for this man who's dying anyway?'

'He might not die.'

He throws the log into the flames. 'That's not what you just said.'

'He's a good man. He gave Agata some marbles.'

'And tomorrow do I do it for another good man, and the day after for the next? I live in a world where there's a limited amount of bread and a crowd of starving people. Where do you live? Please don't tell me it's a place with a magic baker's shop full of loaves for whoever wants them?'

She stares at him.

'I don't know you,' she hisses, standing and walking slowly towards him. 'I thought I did, but I don't.'

'That's not true. But what you seem to have forgotten are the circumstances of our existence.'

'I'm curious. You'd have me starve also, if I didn't make my quota?'

He steps towards her. When he faces her, his breath is cold. 'You're missing the point. You want to imagine, as all the rest do, that I've some control over life and death here. You'd like to believe some control is possible in this world. You still don't understand, do you, Magdalena? When are you going to understand?'

'That's right, silly me. Please tell me the story again, teacher. We're creatures of skin and bone put here to learn we've no control over anything. We should wish for nothing, expect nothing; live like animals while we treasure our hunger and cold and exhaustion because it's all we have? Well I don't want it.' She shoves him with her hands, slamming his chest. 'I won't have it. Not like this.' She spits on the floor. 'The wolves out there have more morality than you.'

'Mama?' Agata is tugging the hem of her coat. 'Mama?'

'Come here, little frog . . .' She turns and bends down to take Agata into her arms. 'Mama's just a bit sad. Let me kiss you. Here and here, also here. And Mama is happy now. You see how happy you make your Mama? And now it's time for bed,' and she heads to the bunk.

Behind her she hears the hut door close. She rummages down the hole in the quilt and finds the amber. For a moment she holds it towards the glow from the stove, rattling the tiny yellow pills in their tunnel. She pulls the elk skin high and gives Agata the amber to turn as she pleases. 'Where shall we go tonight, little frog? Shall we see what Ulka's cooking in her kitchen? Can you see Ivan Pavlov crouching under the table where he believes he can't be seen.'

The next morning as they assemble for the work party, packed close as herded cattle to stay warm, the count shuffles up and takes her hands, squeezing her fingers between purple thumbs. His eyes are big as moons.

'So you found some bread from the magic bakers.' This is what she says to Grigori in the evening. He and Agata are grooming the goat with Lena's hairbrush, Ala having requested the productive but pungent Extra Ration, as the nanny is now known, stay in their hut at night. Lena adds a handful of minnows to the pot and glances at the pair of them, intent on an examination of the goat's callused knees. Agata is wearing three sweaters, but even so Lena can see the jut of her shoulder bones.

'If you ask me to hand over my ration again, Lena, I'll do it.' He doesn't turn to look at her. 'If you want to tell yourself there's a choice here, that we have the power of life over death, I won't try to dissuade you.'

'You saved a couple's lives yesterday, aren't you content with that?'

'I wasted my bread.'

'Nonsense,' she says, watching the minnows spinning in the bubbling pot. 'Nonsense,' she repeats to herself.

Two days later the count fails to appear for the working party. That evening his body is taken to lie among the mounds by the gate. In the morning his wife follows him.

Lena cries quietly in the night when Agata is sleeping. 'We could have done more. We should have done more for them.'

'You'd give them the milk you feed your child?' he whispers. He is hooked around her back like a question mark. 'There are choices you can make in this place. Choose who to save, Magdalena, because it cannot be everyone.'

'Tell me a story,' she says to him when she still can't sleep. 'A happy one.'

So he tells her about a white bird who saw too much. A bird who was awake early in the morning and watched the god in the ground pulling frozen and starving bone people below the soil to feed the earth. A bird whose feathers turned black from what it saw.

'That is not a happy story.'

'The orange beak,' he says.

'What about it?'

'Hope. I left in the hope for you. I would have thought you'd like it.'

They make it to the other side of winter. Mama calls it a miracle and no one disagrees. During the coldest months a third of the workers in the camp have stopped moving and lain themselves down. Like shipwrecks exposed by a shore tide, the retreating snow reveals scraps of cloth and leathered bone, earlobes and wisps of hair. If Lena were to choose to step close she knows she would see mouths stretched wide to eat up the forest, crooked, beckoning fingers, or the curling yellow nail on a toe demanding a trim. But she is still living and the living do not choose to step close to the dead, and as the weeks pass it becomes possible for her to think of these body parts as nothing that ever resembled humanity. The mounds are a scrapyard of defunct, obsolescent objects. One morning a man from each hut is assigned to drag the corpses into the forest and bury them in more compliant ground. Romek goes and receives, for this service, an extra ration of bread.

But still, spring is coming and the bone heaps are a reminder not only of death, but of survival. *We are not there.* This is the phrase muttered by workers passing the burial pit in the trees, crossing themselves and kissing their thumbs, lifting eyes to thank gods or fortune, the superiority of their constitution or boot leather, or the milk from a small nanny goat.

We are not there, Lena thinks, undressing Agata each evening to crack the lice in her clothes, to press her gums and record her pulse, and measure her height against the door. *We are not there.*

In the dusk a patchy white-brown hare is sometimes sighted taking a cautious path along the edge of the camp, or a blackbird might appear above the workers in the clearing, singing boldly from the safety of the highest branches. The sun regains its colour, and, of an evening, hut doors are left ajar for a moment or two. Singing is heard, argument and laughter. Draught pieces slam down on the ground and talk turns to future plans: potato seeds to be sown, locations suitable for grazing, the grass that might be harvested for hay. This Molek has heard that the river is thawing, log shipments are to resume. Remember that salmon, he says. He is knotting a net from the countess's underdresses. When he is done it will be vast enough to stretch across the river, and in a single night he and Romek will trap every fish that flicks its tail downstream. They will need four horses to haul their catch home, he says.

Hope is a virus spreading between the survivors; a delirium hot in the veins. If one winter can be endured, the next must be easier. This Molek pronounces it a certainty, dandling the baby to strengthen his legs. 'My son will grow taller than this forest,' he says. 'He will be a free man one day.' No one disagrees with such fever dreams, especially not little JoJo who does not cry so much these days. Like Agata and the rest of them, he has learned not to expect. But he is a handsome thing; all black eyes and blacker hair. Even the commandant stops in his tracks one evening to hold out a crust for him.

Then a day comes in spring when the siren is late to sound. The workers assemble but the canteen doors remain closed and spoons rattle in empty cups. A whisper of anxiety begins to move among them, only stopping when the door of the guards' barracks swings back and the commandant appears. He hitches his trousers, yawning, his arm around a young woman with short dark hair.

'This,' he shouts to the camp, 'is a sign of comradeship between worker and guard.' He turns to the woman, bending her back as if in a passionate dance, kissing her at such length that one or two of the guards start to applaud.

The commandant rights the woman and wipes his mouth. 'What are you lot looking so worried about? You want to get to work, is that it?'

No one answers his ringing laughter.

'But it's May Day, friends.' He pauses, then shouts his punchline. 'I am very sorry but you cannot work! Mother Moscow forbids it!'

'But we want to work,' a voice shouts from somewhere. 'We want our bread.'

The commandant opens his arms wider than a conquering emperor. 'On the grave of my mother, I promise you shall have your bread. Today we holiday, criminals and state enemies alike, celebrating our solidarity as workers in our great nation. Free rations will be served for all! Yes, my hungry friends, today no one is second class. Every one of you is a valued comrade. And so, I wish a happy holiday to you all!' He blows kisses in the air and swivels the woman towards the barrack building. The door slams, the workers stand silent.

A day without work. A day with bread. What should be done with this unusual day?

Of course it might be passed in sleep, but then the sun is up and the air warm. The desire to be out of the huts beneath this sky for a few hours is strong. And look, the canteen hatch is opening, and the short guard named Olav is slicing up bread.

They take their rations, the family, and head to the logging site where they can lie under the sun. Mama packs a little of what they have left over to eat. Romek brings a kite he's fashioned from a shirt and sticks. The goat comes too, towed by Agata on a lead of knotted stockings.

This Molek lights a campfire and they sing songs, passing a pan of milk and a cup to dip, and bread smeared in the last of the lard. The apothecary creeps to join them, offering a bottle of ethanol in exchange for a cup of milk. Conversation moves backwards to a world before. Mama is persuaded to reminisce about Papa. She sips from the ethanol bottle and splutters. My goodness,' she says laughing, 'Papa wouldn't have lasted a minute at the saw without a fudge lodged in each cheek.'

Lena and Romek get up to try to fly the kite while Grigori whittles a toy for Agata from a length of spruce. She asks for a mouse like the one that died in the winter. His blade slips and cuts his index finger beneath the second knuckle. He binds it in a cloth. When Lena sees the blood she takes his hand to examine. 'Really you should have this closed with a stitch, but at the very least it needs washing properly, you should go back and clean it, get it out of this dirty rag.'

'I have a mouse to finish,' he says, wrapping the cloth back over. And the sun is high and warm. Lena lies back against him and closes her eyes.

Mama sings arias from Mozart's *The Magic Flute*. The earth turns, nudging the yellow sun from view and they pack up their cups in the trees' spreading shadows. Stepping quietly through the forest they return to camp, listening to birdsong, marvelling as if it hasn't been heard before.

That night when Agata's asleep clutching her toy mouse, Lena boils water and washes herself. She spreads a sheet on the hut's dirt floor and lies down naked, watching Grigori strip to the skin to take his turn with the water.

She watches him dip his rag in the pot and rub his face. He takes a cup and douses his red hair to black and she talks to him. 'Slowly, bone man,' she says, or, 'Wash that arm again. Let me see how the water makes its river down your elbow.' Or she says, 'Turn now, and make a cascade on your back for me. Slowly, bone man, show me that again.'

He kneels dripping in front of her. How beautiful he is to her, this man of bone.

She touches his pelvis and tells him this. 'How beautiful you are to me.'

In her head words come like music: *clavicle, acromion, scapula, ilium, sacrum, femur, tibia, talus, calcaneus.*

He lowers his face to her neck and puts his nose to her skin to smell her here and there. Each of her ribs is traced by a finger and the cave of her navel circled with his thumb. He lowers his mouth and takes her nipple between his teeth.

She grips his hips and pulls him onto her. 'Look at me, bone man, look at me.'

He pushes himself inside her. His gaze locks to hers. And when they come they share each other's breath.

'Is it possible to be on the edge of life and feel as happy as you have ever been?'

'It's possible, my heart's breath, it's possible.'

Side by side they lie holding hands. Some minutes pass and Lena raises herself above him. She begins to bite at his jaw and throat and shoulders; small bruising lozenges, sucking the blood to see it rise to the surface of his skin. Because she needs to see this blood, to know it runs in him. She needs to brand him, to claim the flesh as her own. She tells him this. 'If I could, I would score your bones. I would scar your heart's chamber with my teeth.'

'What is this thing?' she says to him. 'What is this need in me for you? Would we share it if we met in another time or place? If we encountered each other at a party, say, one where you wanted to dance and I did not, would it be the same? Tell me,' she insists.

'We're here. Does anything else matter?'

'If I could climb inside your skin, bone man, I would. I'd curl up so small you wouldn't notice me, or perhaps I'd ride your breath down into the insides of you. From there I would travel everywhere that is you. There wouldn't be a part of you that hadn't been visited by me.'

He takes her fingers and traces the coast of them, each promontory and inlet. He turns her hand as if it isn't callused flesh, scarred and swollen, but a sculpture from antiquity.

Suddenly she lurches up, staring ahead at the dark walls, her heart pounding in her chest. 'What happens when this ends? What then?'

He has her hand and he rubs his lips along the knuckles of her fingers. 'We are grateful.'

'YOU'RE BURNING UP.'

Lena has her hand on Grigori's chest. It's coated in a sheen of sweat. 'Look at me,' she says. His gaze is glittering, shifting, it slides away into the dark. Beneath him the quilt is soaked. She takes his wrist, pressing to the artery. Too fast. This pulse is far too fast. 'What's happened to you?' she whispers. 'Bone man, what did you do?'

If he hears her he doesn't answer. His hands are clenched, the tips of his fingers pressing into his palms. Unfurling his index finger she removes the rag he bandaged over a cut. The skin is swollen, leaking pus.

Lena takes a blanket and scoops Agata from the far side of the bunk. She carries her into the night to Mama's hut. When she returns, Grigori opens his eyes and says, 'What should we do with an hour? We must do something because I have to go.'

'Hush,' she answers him, 'hush now, you're going nowhere.'

Lena dips a cloth in the water pail and lays it across his forehead. He's tipping back his jaw, mumbling through his teeth. She takes a second cloth and wipes his face, his bulging rigid neck, his limbs. She would like to examine his finger properly only it's too dark to see. She sits beside him monitoring his pulse, thinking back to her time in the hospital, wishing for a stethoscope to check his heart and lungs. Too fast, it's far too fast, this pulse. Her own blood roars with dread.

'What are you doing in my life, bone man? Why did you come and disturb me like this?'

The night thickens. Beetles hiss in the roof. They drop to the floor and scuttle into corners. At her ears, mosquitoes scream. Grigori's hand grips her arm. He tells her he must go.

'You can't,' she says to him. 'You say there's no choice in things, but you're wrong. You came to me and I won't let you leave me.' She raises his head and tries to give him water in a cup to drink but he can't unclench his teeth to swallow.

The night begins to thin. He opens his eyes and looks hard at her.

'Go to work, Magdalena. Get bread.' His breath is a quick, shallow sawing. 'You need to work if you want bread.'

'Hush,' she tells him, 'close your eyes, rest.' She lies by his side, wanting this hot sick breath on her face. She hums nursery songs, as she did once in a children's ward in a hospital in another life. She wills the day to come, and in the meantime she watches each draw of his lungs. And if his heart stops, she'll pound on his ribs and break open the cage of him. She'll bully his heart back to life.

When light begins to leak through the fabric at the window Lena gets up. The work siren sounds and the camp begins to stir. She looks over Grigori's thin body, his tensed muscles, the yellow tinge to his skin. Fear is a stone dropping in her belly.

The hut door bangs back against the wall; the guard Viktor enters, coughing, taking his time to swagger around, eyeing the clothes draped over nails, the stack of porcelain plates, the jar with sprigs of fireweed and sundew that Lena has set under the window. He kicks a rug and saunters over to the goat, bending to poke the udders.

Lena says, 'We milk her in the evening.'

'That so, flower? How much do you get out of her? A pint? Two?'

'Not so much at the moment.'

'Warm though, when it's fresh.' His goitre bulges from his shirt.

'Yes.'

'Creamy.'

'Yes.'

'Aren't you the lucky ones.'

'Grigori's sick, we need help,' she says. 'Will you help us?'

He doesn't seem to hear. 'Cosy little nest you've got going here. Might try a similar arrangement with the furnishings myself. My girl's quite a fan of a rub down on skins. It's the friction, she says. Drives her *wild*.' He turns from the goat, and kicks the frame of the bunk where Grigori's lying. 'Up you get, comrade, you're needed.'

'I told you he's sick,' Lena says quietly.

'And there's a consignment to drive to the depot.'

'He can't go anywhere, look at him, he can't even stand.'

Viktor coughs and spits on the rug. 'Sorry to spoil the party, nursey, but the chief's pissed with lover boy here. Pleasuring himself is all well and good, but to do it in work hours, what does he take this place for, a brothel? Pardon my language, flower, those are only our leader's words. Between you and me, I'd be careful, or lover boy will be banged up for good. Worse maybe. Our chief's a reasonable man, but he's a temper to match the best of them.'

'Perhaps the commandant wants to come here and get him up himself.'

'Now, now, sweetie.' Viktor kicks the bunk harder.

Grigori doesn't open his eyes.

'Do you have medicines?' she asks. 'There must be supplies reserved for guards? I'd keep my mouth shut if you found some, I swear it. If you don't, we'll need to get him to a hospital straight away.'

'You think so, nursey?'

'I think he has tetanus. We can't wait.'

Viktor sighs, his eyes bulbous, glittering with a show of pity. 'That's too bad.'

'He's really sick. Look at him. If it was you lying there, you'd want help.'

Viktor begins to giggle, covering his mouth like a schoolboy, his breath high and whining. 'You're really not the smartest, are you? How do I make it plain? It's not just you lot that are disposable round here.'

Lena stares at him. 'I'm sorry for that,' she says. She takes his hands. 'You're a decent man. I know you'll help me if you can.' If that goitre were treated, he wouldn't be so old at all. Not much older than Romek. 'Please, Viktor, you have to help. We need to get him to the hospital. We could ask about medicine for you too, when we go, they may have iodine there. That would make you feel so much better, I promise. It would take away the tightness when you breathe.'

'You think?'

'It's the only thing that will help the goitre. The cough will clear up too.'

'What a clever little nurse you are.'

She makes herself smile. 'Could you drive the cart to the town? Would you ask the commandant for me? Would you ask him?'

He looks down at her hands holding his. He sniffs. 'What's in it for me?'

'Milk. A cup of goat's milk. You'll see how creamy it is. You'll love it.'

'A cup?'

'Yes. The moment we get back I'll bring you one, full to the brim, still warm.'

'Every morning.'

'Every morning?'

'A nice warming drink will be just the thing to get my bones moving.' He grins at her. 'Such pretty eyes you have. I wondered what our favourite murderer saw in you at first, with all that scowling, but I can see you're a sweetie underneath.'

Lena steps back from him. 'But you know I can't do that.'

He glances at Grigori. 'You hear that, friend, she can't do it.'

'I can't give you a cup every day. I just can't.'

He tuts and shakes his head. 'You hear that, Grigori, she says she just can't.'

'My whole family relies on the milk,' she hears herself whisper. 'My child and the baby need it. We already give a cup to the commandant each morning. We don't have any more to share. It's not mine to hand out.'

'You sure about this, sweetie?'

'I can't,' she whispers. 'I just can't do it.'

'Well, isn't that a pity.'

'So will you ask?'

'Sorry, sweetheart, but I just can't do it.' He shrugs and swaggers out.

She bangs her fist on the door of the guards' barracks until it opens. The commandant is bleary-eyed, yawning, his breath foul in her face. One of his front teeth has turned entirely black in his smile. 'Good morning, blue eyes.'

He leans against the door frame, retying his trousers, looking her over as she speaks. He is like a livestock breeder wondering whether to expand his herd.

'Lie with me,' he says. 'That's my price.'

He laughs at her expression. 'It's not such a bad offer, blue eyes. I have certain talents, so I've been told. And let's be frank, it's the only offer you're going to get round here.'

'I don't know,' she says quickly looking down. 'I need to think.'

'Think away. I'll wait right here.'

He reaches to her hair and coils a strand around his finger, letting it unwind slowly. 'Nice,' he says. 'Very nice.' He scratches his beard, his gaze travelling over her once more, then he turns and opens the barrack door. 'Mull it over. No rush. Come back tomorrow. You know where I am.'

The door starts to close.

'Wait.'

She looks up and gives a slight nod.

He grins and kicks the door wide. 'Come on in then. Nikki's here of course, but she's up for anything that one. She has beautiful hair too, we're growing it out. We'll make a lovely threesome, you won't be disappointed. Are you a top or tailer?'

'Wait,' she says, stepping back. 'Not now.'

'Not now, you say?'

'Afterwards. I'll do anything you want afterwards. When he's back from the hospital. I have to go with him to look after him, and we have to go now.'

'You do?'

'Straight away.'

'Well, what are you standing here for? Run along, precious one, go pack up your nighties.'

Lena is already halfway across the camp when she hears a whistle. The commandant is bent over his knees, hissing with laughter, a hand waving her down.

'Sorry, darling!' he shouts, straightening, wiping his mouth of an excess of mirth.

She looks back at him. 'But we agreed—'

She turns around and walks towards him, a roaring increasing in her head. 'But I don't understand—'

'The horse was needed to get the logs down to the barge. It left with Viktor half an hour ago. Poor Viktor, that one's always stepping into the breach. The man deserves a medal.'

'But you said—'

'Cheer up, blue eyes, it's not all bad news, at least we've worked out your availability.'

The world turns silent as Lena returns to the hut, only there's a whining in her ears. She doesn't feel the sun on her skin. The hut smells of syrupy sickness. The goat pulls on her tether, bleating for food.

Lena props back the door to the daylight and goes to Grigori. She peels back his lip as you might a horse, and tries to prise apart his clenched teeth. She sits beside him stroking his drenched hair, watching the quick rise and fall of his jaundiced chest. 'There's no more time left,' she says to him. She knows what she has to do.

Gently she turns him onto his side and pulls the quilt from under his body. She makes her voice loud and confident for them both. 'You've got tetanus from the cut on your finger so I'm going to treat you and you're going to get better.'

A flicker of something across his eyes. A hiss between his teeth.

'That's what we're going to do,' she says more firmly. She gropes inside the quilt for the amber. His eyes are open, following her movements. He jerks his arm as though he would grab her if his fingers weren't clamped into fists.

She moves from his reach, and she finds a knife and dips its point into the screw head at the base of the amber, twisting until the tiny brass stopper comes out. Yellow pills fall into her palm.

Behind her, he's hissing through his teeth. He's trying to raise himself on his elbows.

She wipes water from her eyes, taking a cup from the shelf and a spoon to mash the pills. 'I'm going to treat you with anti-bacterials' She is talking louder and louder as she grinds the pills to drown out his hissing. 'The name is Prontosil. It will fight the infection. You don't need to worry, you're going to be fine very soon. You're going to live.'

She wipes her eyes again and pours the crushed tablets onto the spoon. With a cup of water from the pan she goes to him. She takes his coat from the wall and pads it into a thick pillow, then grabbing him under the arms, she hoists him against it. 'You will need to open your mouth for me.'

The spoon is trembling in her hand.

'Come on,' she says. 'Help me.'

He is slowly, very slightly, moving his head from side to side.

She can't wipe her eyes because she's holding the spoon and the cup. Her vision blurs. 'I don't think you understand. You need to do this. You need these tablets, Grigori. You need them now otherwise you'll die.'

She can't get his teeth to part.

'Please, Grigori, please.'

He is trying to turn away.

'No,' she says standing up. 'No, you don't understand, we have to do this.' She fetches a butter knife. Prising the flat blade between his upper and lower teeth, she works it, twisting until she has wedged his mouth open. 'Don't fight me,' she says, her tears dripping on his face as she holds back his head. 'Don't you love me, bone man? Don't you want to live?'

He closes his eyes.

She pours the crumbled tablets into his mouth and then the water. Tilting his chin she pulls out the knife. Her hands are shaking. She rubs his throat until his oesophagus moves.

The sun is a white square on the back wall of the hut. She goes to the window and lowers the fabric to let in the light. Her hands are shaking.

'You were just like my old dog,' she says, trying to smile. 'He hated taking medicine.' Grigori stares into nothing while she bends to kiss him. Water seeps out from his eyes. She sits watching him cry. It is like looking at a spring in a rock face that will not run dry.

In the end she goes out of the hut and she lies down on the ground and looks at the sky.

When she returns he seems more peaceful. His eyes are closed and his pulse is a little slower and perhaps steadier. Does she imagine his brow is not so hot? She lies beside him on the bunk, turning the emptied amber in her hand. 'Agata and I travel anywhere we like when we're looking in here. Where would you like us to go?'

She takes his balled fist in her hand.

'I'll tell you a story. Once there were three creatures who were nothing special; beings made of bone sewn into bags of skin – a mother and her daughter and a man. They lived inside the earth's great forest, in a hut they'd built of timber planks. Its roof was moss piled upon moss, there were rag curtains at the window and a small white goat tethered in the corner. The trees provided wood for their stove so they were never cold. Outside the hut the woman grew potatoes and cultivated wheat from seeds gathered on the tundra. In the summer they foraged for herbs and garlic, and for cloudberries and blueberries, and mushrooms in the autumn. The man went fishing in the river for trout and salmon, and once a year he brought down an elk and skinned it, curing the meat so they had more than they ever needed to eat. Although it should be said they lacked for salt. And this is as much as these three people did for work. On dark evenings they sat inside and played games: chess or draughts with pieces he'd whittled from wood. From time to time they told the child stories about the world they'd left behind: a place of plenty, but also a world of complications and expectations, and with so many unimportant worries buzzing in the air. Here the only things in the air were birds. These three creatures lived in their hut and did no harm to the animals or the forest around them. And down in the quiet earth, the god decided to leave them to play out their lives. Every night they held each other as they fell asleep, smiling because they knew they were as happy as people could ever wish to be . . .'

He's sleeping, his head heavy as a boulder against her, his breathing steady. She turns and kisses his lips and then she lies back closing her eyes and she dreams of a hut in a forest and Agata, grown taller, playing with two small children in the mud.

By the evening his temperature has dropped. His jaw softens and she feeds him a few spoonfuls of milk. He takes this from her and his eyes are dry.

The next morning she leaves him and goes to work taking down a larch. When she returns, he's sitting up. She comes in with Agata, undressing her, taking a cloth to wash her, combing her hair, breaking a crust for her to suck.

She feels his eyes on her and she goes to him. 'What is it?'

He moves his lips carefully to speak. 'Whatever price you paid for my recovery I hope it wasn't too high.'

That night she lies against him and it comes to her again, this need to talk.

'We could do it. It isn't impossible. We could live in the forest. When all this is over, we could stay here. It wouldn't take much to get by. I've been thinking we need a billy goat, just one. Then we could breed, sell goats to the commandant, buy our freedom and live in this place like the settlers do. Perhaps one day we might even have brothers or sisters for Agata. It could happen and we'd be happy, wouldn't we?'

'Settle here?' he says slowly.

'Why not? What else is there to want?'

He lifts her hand, rubbing the split and broken nails of her fingers against his lips.

'Say something,' she says. 'Just say whatever you're thinking.'

'I'm thinking it's dangerous to dream.'

But Lena dreams and life goes on. The summer sun warms them and they're grateful, while the god in the earth sends mosquitoes to keep their feet on the ground. Lena thinks back to their arrival a year before: the despair and hunger, and the panic that shadowed each day. But now, with the sun browning her bones, and the goat grazing in the clearing, she watches her daughter play with a stick doll in the grass outside the hut and she thinks why shouldn't Agata grow well enough in this place? Maybe Lena can get back to the market before winter and trade what she has left for a hen. With eggs and milk her daughter will grow strong. Or she could take everything the family has left and find that billy goat to breed and provide meat, fresh meat. Grigori will know how this goat might be found. Yes, Agata will grow as well as any child in the world. Ala has announced she's pregnant again, a second cousin is coming. Life is happening here. Lena dreams bigger – of a settlement with children running around and goats. Why not? she thinks. People can regain their freedom and all can be well. Different but well. And Grigori will finally understand what it is to hope, which is only what every parent does; if not for themselves, then for what will come after.

For a moment there's only warmth.

No sight or sound, no knowledge of colour or black, just a sensation of spreading heat.

Then she sees her. The pieces come together in Lena's vision like a mosaic assembling, and she sees the brown steppe in bright light, and the running girl.

'Wait,' Lena cries out. 'Please, I've something to say to you.'

The little girl stops. Lena hears her say, 'What is it, Mama?'

Lena hesitates. 'I will know. Soon enough, little frog, I'll know what it is.'

The girl disappears over the horizon. Lena is left in heat and light. And then movement, she is setting off again, being carried forward. But she can't see in the light and everything is speeding up. Time is on the run from her.

Wait.

Wait, slow down, please.

'Lena . . .'

There's a man standing by her side at the railing of a ship. It's not the bone man, not Grigori. The man is straight-backed and narrow. He holds a black-haired baby she doesn't want to touch. The man is looking out across a vast blank sea. He is telling her that forgiveness is possible, always.

Wait.

What is she saying to him? Yes, she hears herself speak.

'You're wrong,' she's saying. 'I made a choice.' The words are dead weights on her tongue, she can barely shift them. 'I made

*my choice and it was the wrong one, Anton, I can't ever be for-
given.'*

'Wait!' – but it's Romuś screaming this, she can see him standing on the planks of the pony cart, screaming at the work party
who are about to swap stations – Romuś who was sent to the
river depot with Grigori and a consignment of larch, and here
he is, two days later, back in the clearing, fish heads peeping
from his trousers. It's a beautiful summer day – you might
actually call it the height of summer, one of those days when
even the sawdust smells good. Hymns have been rising from the
work stations, some dirty jokes were also thrown in the air, an
eagle has hovered over the taiga to much general admiration –
and now Romek is shouting, 'Wait! Stop, everyone! Lay down
your tools!'

Saws and axes lose their rhythm. Faces lift and eyes narrow.
Lena sees it happen around the clearing, glances turn towards the
grinning youth on the cart. Then heads shake and lower, and the
sounds of work resume. Because when there's no interruption to
your labour, it's possible to get lost in life's smallest pleasures;
an old school song or the carryings-on of ants at your feet, or
perhaps the saved crust dissolving into sourness in the pouch of
your cheek. You focus on these pleasures and make a chain from
them, and you follow this chain one link at a time until the siren
at the end of the day.

But Romek is crazy. Just look at him, he's pulling whole loaves
from a sack and hurling these loaves at people's heads, and the
guard – it's Grigori, actually – is standing beside him doing
nothing at all to prevent this. Romuś is yelling, 'Didn't you hear
me, you bumpkins, stop working now!'

This Molek scowls more than most, because if the guard won't
do his job, then he'll have to be the one to tell his young brother
to quit fooling around, disrupting everyone's daydreams, not
to mention wasting precious bread. But Romek jumps from the
cart, fish slipping out of his trousers at his ankles, and he runs to

This Molek, shoving a loaf at him. 'Take this to Ala, there's as much as we want until we leave.'

Lena looks across the saw at Mama.

'We leave?' Mama says.

'It's all written down! It's official!' Romek shouts, his arms windmilling in a madman's dance, 'Grigori, show them the edict!'

And now people drop their tools. They wander towards the cart to see this raving boy, because lunacy is always interesting, and who can resist bread. But as they approach, the workers suddenly eye each other, nervous because perhaps the boy isn't completely raving after all – the guard is holding up a sheet of cream-coloured paper – look, there is thick cream paper, stamped red in his hands.

'Grigori, translate it for them!' Romek is unstoppable, jigging on the cart. 'It's insane, wait till you hear, you won't believe it.'

Lena looks over at Grigori and the funny thing is he isn't meeting her eyes.

'It's all true,' he says, holding the sheet like a king's proclamation, turned outwards in front of the workers so everyone can see the words printed on the document, so they can all bear witness to the circular stamp in red ink in the top corner, the signature in black at the bottom. 'A new pact's been made. You're no longer second-class citizens of the state.'

'We never were!' someone shouts. But people are far too nervous to laugh, too confused at suddenly finding themselves in a scene they've never imagined, even in their most glorious daydreams.

'You are hereby re-designated citizens of your homeland, free to join a new army – your own country's army – and unite forces with our glorious motherland against the great evil in the world.'

'You see!' Romek screams. 'I told you! We're free!'

'But this is impossible, a new army?' This Molek says it with his axe loose in his hand. 'This is crazy. We're free – just like that?'

'Crazy, just like that,' Grigori agrees. 'Release passes will be provided and transport arranged to the local town. There's no information as to what happens after. I guess that part is up to you.'

Mama turns to Lena, her eyes are streaming, her rosary pressed to her lips.

Grigori continues, 'There are letters at the camp from loved ones in your country. Regrettably their delivery has been delayed a year or so by war.'

Across the clearing people are clutching each other open-mouthed, they are falling to their knees. Mama is down on her knees. Lena looks at her with her beads turning in her hand. But this is no work of a god, she thinks, at least not one in heaven with ordered plans. No, the world has simply spun on at random. Here, at the end of the earth, it's by chance alone they are reprieved.

Crazy! Just like that! – these are the words flying through the air, batted back and forth in cries and trembling. Lena runs towards the cart, calling to Grigori, but he's already driving the pony out of the clearing, leaving Romek and the paper edict surrounded by dancing men.

Back at the camp, Viktor stands outside the canteen, hoarsely shouting names and handing out thin envelopes with red crosses in the corner. He's all smiles like it's Christmas morning. Telling people to rest up now, read the news from their loved ones, transport is coming, a train is on its way. He calls Lena's name.

She finds him near the pine where she first encountered him a year before. He's lying on his back in the bright moss, staring up at the pine's dark canopy.

And she, where is she? It's getting harder to tell where she is.

The mosaic shatters into pieces. It reforms for a moment. Nothing sustains.

She's pacing in and out of spots of light in the clearing, a sheet of paper, pale as dried skin, in her hand.

'It changes nothing,' she says.

He bats a fly from his forehead.

'Didn't you hear me, this news changes nothing. I'm staying here.'

He smiles but doesn't speak.

She steps closer to him. Panic beats in her, it is a wild animal trapped in the cage of her chest. 'Don't lie here making out you don't care. I said I'm staying with you.'

He lifts his head, shielding his eyes from a shaft of light. 'It's a nice sentiment.'

'How dare you.'

'You received a letter from your husband.'

'It changes nothing. It was written two years ago. I'm staying.'

'So you keep telling me.'

The animal turns in her. It hisses, beating the bars, knocking at her ribs. She can't keep still. She can't bear it. How her heart needs to hate him.

'You would have died if I hadn't treated you.'

'I would.'

She can't bear how he lies here as unconcerned as the trees. It is like his hand is reaching into the cage of her and squashing that life within. His hand is squeezing her heart to a pulp.

'You don't want me to stay. That's the truth.'

Silence. Bending and flexing between them.

He doesn't take his eyes from her as he gets up.

Cutting through the sunlight he comes to her. 'No, Magdalena, I don't want you to stay.' The breath of each word hits her face. 'I don't want you or Agata to ever see another winter in this place. And nor do you. Despite this performance, you know you have to get Agata away from here. You'd never choose for her to face death again – which is what winter brings with it year after year.'

'You presume to know so much.'

He reaches for her hands. 'That night. The snow hare. Remember her?'

'The one you terrified into running away? Is that the one you mean?'

'If that's how you see it.'

Silence. Always this pushing, this pulling in the air between them.

'What of it,' she says, not meeting his gaze.

'I know you're really no different to that hare, Lena. It's in your nature to protect your young.'

'Well?' he says. 'Tell me you're not a mother. Tell me I'm wrong.'

Lena blocks his words with her hand. Lena is thinking of Mama. She is thinking how Mama had stood in the camp watching her walk back from the canteen turning a thin envelope in her hands – a letter from Anton, captured in the first campaign.

'Shall I take Agata while you pack for the train?' Mama had said as Lena approached. Then she had said, her eyes brimming as she looked across, 'At last we can let ourselves think it.'

'What, Mama?'

'That Agata will grow up. That there's going to be a future for her.'

Lena had stared at her mother. A warm sensation ran from her mouth to her chin as she did. She touched her skin and found she had bitten her lip until the blood came. Lena had turned from Mama and walked into the trees.

Now she steps towards him.

'Come,' she whispers. 'Come and be with us all.'

'Join up? A soldier in your husband's army?'

'If you wanted. Or we could go elsewhere. We could go anywhere we liked, you, me and Agata. Come with me. Anywhere in the world, it wouldn't matter.'

'You know what they'd do to my parents and sister if I did?'

'You don't know that for sure.'

'Magdalena—'

'You really don't know that.'

'Magdalena, listen . . .' He takes her hands, rubbing his thumb over her knuckles, frowning, as if searching for something infinitesimally small buried in the skin.

'I mean this thing we have, this thing, you said it matters' – she says shaking her head – 'living fully right where we are, you told me this was the one thing that matters, and what I can't understand is—'

'Please, Magdalena—'

'– does it matter? Do I matter?'

He has her hands in his. He is pressing her fingers to the bone as if he would crush them.

'Or was I simply something to fill the time?'

He stares at her and she sees how sadness has swallowed the light from his eyes. 'Magdalena, my heart's breath, you must listen to me . . .'

And she shakes her head over and over at him because she wants him never to stop saying her name but she doesn't want to hear it, what he's going to say. She doesn't want to feel it, the way his voice moves on her skin, the way she has presumed she will hear it for years and years of her life. She shakes her head to prevent him starting what she cannot bear to hear end.

'This is simply how things have turned out for us.' He raises her knuckles to his lips. 'You will get on that train with Agata, and I will stay here and serve out my time. It's our responsibility to accept how it is.'

'No,' she says, 'don't you dare dress it up like that. It's simply that you're weak.' Hatred is surging in her because she cannot bear it, the truth he makes her see. 'You do nothing. You fight for nothing. You let everything just happen to you.' She jerks her hands from his grip. 'And you let everything that matters be cast away. I can't accept it. I'll never accept it. I won't be weak like you.'

For a moment he stares at her and doesn't speak. From the camp comes the sound of voices, a jumble of tone and pitch. There is unfettered laughter and song.

He steps close. 'Do you remember the first night in the village? We talked and I said to you that we're simply like any other animals, trying to survive in the snow, our lives driven only by chance? But you see I was wrong to say that. You've taught me we humans have something special, we have an awareness of our luck. Meeting you, Magdalena, that's been mine. You have been the fortune of my life.'

She shakes her head. She is sobbing, her hands cupped to hold up her face. 'So come with me, bone man. Come with me.'

He opens his arms and draws her body to his. His fingers move up and down her spine, ordering and accounting for each vertebrae. 'Whenever you think of me I'll be right beside you. You'll never get rid of me.' The smell of him is resin and soil after rain.

He holds her until she quietens. His thumb takes the tears from her skin. 'You need to go now and prepare for your train.'

She looks away. She knows that when she leaves what beats in her will die. A hollowness will be left. This emptiness will be as vast as the tundra.

'I can't.'

His thumb moves slowly over the contours of her face. He touches her nose, the slight cleft in her chin. 'Go.'

She cannot look at him but she can't look anywhere else.

'I can't.'

'Then I'll make it easier.' He takes her hands, turning her palms, and he strokes her callused fingers, each in turn. 'I love you, Magdalena. This time we've shared was my life's great joy. Whenever you choose to think of me, know my thoughts will be of you.' He kisses her quietly on her lips, and he turns and walks towards the thickest of the forest, pushing his shoulder at the heavy greenery, forcing his way without breaking stride.

'Wait,' she whispers.

'Wait!' she screams, blundering after him, stumbling and falling on her knees.

She is howling into the moss.

But he'll return, she thinks. Any moment now he'll turn and come back. He'll touch my shoulder and take my hand.

She presses her howling mouth into the moss and she waits. Because this can't be how it ends.

No hand reaches down to raise her up.

She sits up and stares about in each direction. There are only trees, their trunks solid like bars and black. Across the forest floor there's a single flicker of movement, such as a hare might leave in its wake. She can hear nothing but her own rasping breath.

'*Are you here? Are you here now with me, Grigori?*'

'*I never did leave you, Magdalena, I never left.*'

'*I want it over. It's too much for me.*'

'*It's happening, Magdalena. You are getting to where you need to go.*'

'*Where is that, bone man?*'

'*You will see.*'

'*Will you stay with me? Will you stay when it happens?*'

'*I won't leave you, my heart's breath, not until it is time.*'

Uzbekistan

Warmth everywhere and a falling, a white tumbling.

Is she rolling into a lake? No, it's not that, she's moving, sitting crammed on a bench in a train. It's so hot and crowded and she has Agata lolling against her, her daughter's hair dark with sweat. On the bench opposite there's Mama with the goat wobbling on her knee. Mama who is looking at her with eyes brimming with love. Lena turns her head. Outside the window, the green of the taiga has given way to a white and black blur of birch.

This Molek is laughing. Standing above her, his shirt drenched and stinking, he's throwing little Jozef in the air, entertaining the carriage with jokes about camp guards and mules. How broad he's grown these last days. Squatting in the aisle, Romek is doing cup tricks with crusts of bread.

How long have they been travelling? Getting on and off this train. Sleeping on station platforms, rising and boarding at the engine's whistle. Not retracing their journey home, but heading south, across brown earth, always south.

This Molek is talking too loud. At the next village stop he's going to steal a pig. A boar will be roasted and his son is going to cut his first tooth on its sweet crackling skin. There are bound to be vegetables coming up in all those fields out there. Turnips and potatoes. A woman shouts, 'Turnips to roast with the pig!' Everyone is talking too loudly, talking because their mouths have found possibility exists again in the world.

'Look, princess!' This Molek is laughing to Ala, 'A field of beetroot! A pen of geese!' He shouts at the top of his voice,

'Driver, slow the engine, you hear me! Let us eat roast goose tonight with beetroot cream!'

The carriage roars its approval. Ala smiles quietly at her husband, her hand on her belly where a second child is just beginning.

And she, where is she?

Staring out of the window as the fields give way to flat steppe. Lena's eyes are pooling and dropping tears on her daughter's head. It's like a nausea caused by the draw of a powerful magnet, caused by the wrong sort of gravity in the world. She shuts her eyes but it pulls her, this antigravity, wrenching her molecules, separating willing from unwilling surely as oil parts water, as her body travels south with her daughter.

Now nothing. There is nothing.
  No colour.
  No noise.
  No girl running on the steppe.
  Where's the girl? Where is she?
  'Step right up, ladies and gentlemen, come see the most amazing show on earth. The world's strongest man, sword-swallowing ladies; sights to befuddle and astonish your eyes!'
  Suddenly she's swinging through the air on a trapeze, there's too much air. She's spinning out of control.
  But this is not her show. This tent is not where she needs to be. She's not a creature of air, not yet.

A different tent is coming together in its mosaic pieces. Yes, this is it. The pale-brown one, its pitched roof and sloping walls large enough for a single family, not a circus. Sufficient for her family to lie in an ill-tempered pile, listening to the complaints of families in other tents nearby. Hundreds of tents, thousands, brown as the soil of the steppe. But not as many tents as flies.

Romek is the first to laugh when the train pulls in and there is no more track ahead of them, just tents and dust. 'This is it? This is where our country's great army is being reformed? This is where we're to live?'

This Molek rubs an elbow at the grime on the window. 'Someone is making a joke, that is for sure. A bad Russian joke.'

Dust and thin yellow dogs come to greet them. And flies, fat and screaming, although who's to say they haven't travelled with them from the forest to this flat brown land? The black flies scream in clouds around the large pale tents where men from other trains queue to be assigned a place in war.

For more than a week they have been living in the tent. Waiting for this army that is to reform, taking its shape from all these dusty bone people. Every day a hundred or a thousand more arrive at the station and tents go up, like a pox spreading across the steppe. And why not bring more? – this land is vast. There are makeshift ovens baking unleavened bread, and wells full of water, and there is nothing to do but wait.

Lena is inside the tent, out of the sun, stripping Agata to run her thumb down clothing seams and crush what she finds, when Ala's face appears at the flaps. 'Come quickly,' she hisses.

A man in military uniform is moving from tent to tent along the row. A slight, stiff man, dirty and limping, methodically making enquiries. He's not the first of his kind to do this. Many soldiers come hobbling through the camp, bending to tent flaps, asking for information. Some even clutch photographs of what they seek. To Lena, watching him approach, the man seems to be emerging from the dust, rematerialising from remnant parts. It could be a ghost she sees, filthy and grey, only that Ala called her out, which means Ala recognises him too.

'Are you all right?' Ala asks, putting her arm around Lena's shoulders.

She watches him come nearer, her stomach twisting, her mouth dry, keeping Agata in front of her, gripping her child's shoulders like she is some kind of shield.

He is two tents away, limping slowly, the edges of him shimmering in the heat. How slight he is. And pale. Has he always been so slim?

'Stop!' she shouts across to him. 'Don't come any nearer.'

'Lena?' he stares. 'Lena?' his voice hoarse and splintering.

'Don't come any closer. Go wash yourself. Please go and do it now.'

He stands on the beaten path between the tents, ten or twelve dusty paces between them. A tremor in his left leg. She stands, gripping Agata. His clothes are filthy as a beggar's, but he still has his spectacles. All this and he has his spectacles. How can a pair of lenses reconcile this trembling man with a husband she once shared a life with in the mountains?

People move past them with water buckets or bread, or bundles of clothing. Ala has gone inside the tent. They are both stuck in place on the track. Lena opens her mouth as if words might come and these words might give her feeling.

In the end he speaks first. 'I had to see if I might find you. I hoped so much, and now my God . . .' his voice runs out.

And Lena's heart moves for him and words begin to come, 'We're glad to see you, Anton, very glad. We have all been worried for so long. But lice are everywhere as well as rumours about what they carry. You can see for yourself there are far too many people in this place and too few latrines. Return to the tent when you're clean and we can talk. That will be how to do it.'

Agata is staring at Anton.

He is trying to smile, lifting his spectacles to wipe his eyes. 'She's grown so much.'

'Of course. She's a little girl now; full of her own opinions.'

'Agata,' he calls, leaning forward, a hand on his trembling thigh. 'Papa's here.'

Agata turns, diving into Lena's skirt, burying her face in fabric.

'Agata, my little Agata—'

'She's shy, that's all,' Lena says, adding softly, 'she hasn't forgotten you.' She sees the anguish in his gaze. Again her heart moves for him. 'It is good to see you, Anton. Give her a little time. Go and wash and come back clean.'

He nods and turns away, limping into the heat. In her head, an echoing tread of boots on polished floors.

Anton returns when the sun's low, bringing a bucket. He's shaved and wearing a khaki uniform. His leather boots look new, but the shirt hanging from his shoulders is soaked in sweat, and his face is pallid grey.

'What's the matter with your left leg?' she asks.

'It's nothing. I've brought water for you from the base, I'm assured it's clean. Also an apple.' He bends towards Agata, holding out the fruit.

Agata ducks behind Lena.

'Give it to me,' Lena says softly. She takes the apple and bites off a chunk. 'Try a piece, frog.'

'She's not had an apple?'

'Not for a while. We do have a goat though, don't we, Agata?'

'Extra Ration,' Agata says looking up at him.

'Extra ration?' He smiles at her, and looks at Lena.

'Romek named her,' she says. 'That's the goat's name.'

'I see.'

Lena opens her mouth to speak, then looks away. The air dances with heat. It's as if the past two years, hers and his, have risen up on the track between them, and these years are implacable and unscalable as mountains. And in her ear she hears a whispering of a man in a faraway forest.

Anton clears his throat. 'So you all—'

'Survived the winter, yes. Ala had a baby and is expecting another. Which is something of a miracle.'

Agata appears from behind Lena's legs. 'Apple.'

'Apple what, frog?'

'Apple please.'

In silence together they watch her eat.

'She always loved apple. You used to stew it and mash it with cream for her,' Anton says. 'It was the first thing she ever ate.'

'You remember?'

'I remember.'

She smiles at him. 'Can you get more?'

'Soon I hope I can.'

'We need good food and clean water too, and to be away from all these flies and lice. We need soap and new clothing and something to do.' Lena gazes over the camp where the latest arrivals queue in hope of tents. 'Why were we brought here, Anton? There's nothing here for us.'

He pushes up his spectacles. His nose is too thin to hold them in place. 'I'm assured food and medical supplies are arriving imminently. Uniforms are coming for the men. Barracks are under construction.'

'And for all these women and children, and the grandmothers and the men too old to be soldiers?' Lena beats flies from her face. 'They told us we were going to be free but the truth is I curse the day we got on that train.' She bites her tongue to avoid saying any more, to avoid telling him – pointlessly – that freedom means nothing when you're trapped on the boiling steppe without decent food or medicines or any sort of occupation. It is only a different kind of prison.

'It's not your fault, of course,' she says. 'I'm sorry.'

'I'm sorry too. This isn't how I would have you live.' His eyes don't leave Agata, he's watching her swallow the last of the apple and lick her palms of juice.

Lena notices a pale line down his cheek, silver welts on his wrists. 'Was it very terrible for you?'

His eyes blink several times before he answers. 'The thought of seeing you both again kept me going.'

'Well,' she says softly, 'here we are.'

She looks at him, blinking and nodding, a twitch of things unsaid on his lips, and she reaches to touch the sleeve of his tunic. 'Here we all are.'

He pulls a watch from his pocket, one she's not seen before. It trembles in his hand. 'I must get back to headquarters. There's much to be done and too few officers left to do it.'

'Are you well, Anton? Only your thigh?'

'A minor infection.'

'Can you not rest a day or two?'

'I'm assigned to the command of a new regiment.'

'Another promotion?'

He tries to smile. 'There's not so many of us about now, so . . .' He presses his lips together. It's not just his leg, or the watch in his hand, every part of him seems to be quaking.

She puts her hands on his arms and holds him until he steadies.

'I'm sorry, thank you, I'm fine.'

'I'm sorry too, Anton.'

They stand facing each other, husband and wife.

'I'd like to kiss you, Lena, if I may.'

She nods and he leans towards her, his lips brushing briefly on hers. He puts a hand to Agata's hair, then he turns and hobbles away.

The next morning, Romek and This Molek stand in the queue of men hopeful of joining the new army of displaced and dis-possessed people. Ala and Lena take the children to find shade beside the trains that have ground to a halt at the terminal.

'It must be strange for you,' Ala says, wafting a black fly from Jozef's mouth. He's flung out asleep across her lap, his belly moving with quick infant breaths.

'Strange how?'

'Seeing Anton again after everything. This Molek said you wanted to stay behind in the forest.'

Lena watches Agata shunting the amber in a line in the dust. *Choo choo*, she says crawling after it, *choo choo*.

'I think I've stopped believing I can do whatever I want in life.'

Ala laughs at her, shaking her head. 'You took your time about it.'

So Lena has to smile. 'Why was everything always easier for you?'

'Do you ever think about it?' Ala asks as Agata reverses her amber train.

'About?'

'The gypsy. What she said to you.'

'Should I?'

Ala points to This Molek, who blows her a kiss. 'There's my man getting his uniform.'

Lena looks over at him, pretending to march on the spot and she laughs so hard Jozef is startled from his nap. 'No chateau though.'

'Who needs a chateau.'

Agata looks over and frowns trying the word.

'It's like a castle, frog. Your Aunty Ala was going to live in one, but then she fell in love, poor thing.'

Ala snorts. 'You can't deny it. She got it right. The fortunes she gave us.'

Lena says nothing. She watches Agata pushing the amber back along its imaginary track, grinding a rut into the dust. She'll never get used to the sudden plunging sensation in her stomach whenever she looks at her daughter. Every day it is like falling from the sky.

'Is it better to love or be loved, do you think?'

'It's easier to be loved,' Ala says, 'but better to try to have both.'

Lena puts her arm round her sister and kisses her cheek. 'Papa was right. You're smarter than you look.'

Ala laughs and for a while they watch Agata play. Little JoJo wakes and Ala puts him to her breast.

'I wonder what Agata's going to remember of this time.'

Agata lifts her head at the mention of her name. 'I remember everything.'

They laugh.

'Come on the train, Mama.'

So Lena goes to crouch in the dirt and shout *Choo choo.*

Ala calls to her. 'Will you look at Romek!' They watch their younger brother step up to the recruitment desk and swing his arm in a salute, not a hint of mischief on his face. Lena wonders aloud when he did all his growing up.

Ala shakes her head. 'How many lungs does that boy think he has?'

'I'll have a word with Anton. Surely they won't accept him. Do you really want This Molek to go?'

Ala frowns and begins to say something. Lena is listening and nodding.

And she could linger in this moment. She could stay sitting with her sister in the shrinking patch of shade, swatting at flies and riding Agata's amber train. She could close her eyes from a burning sun, dawdling with her daughter while her sister explains something about her husband. But Lena feels herself separating from this place, lifting away from the ground.

She doesn't want to go.

Lena tries to resist but she is sucked into the air, as if she is being drawn inside a great wind, a tornado perhaps, carrying her away from the steppe. She is powerless against this force, pulling her into the future, to a place she doesn't want to go.

One, two, three, four.

Moments come to her with the flickering speed of a camera shutter:

Anton falling down on the track.

Anton being carried to a jeep to be taken to a military hospital.

Groaning in the tents around them as neighbours sicken.

A chorus of groaning, constant as the sun or flies.

One, two, three, four, Romuś counting corpses taken off in sheets.

Lena screaming, 'Stop that, stop it at once. Bring Agata inside.'

The goat bleating. Agata crying. It's too hot in the tent.

Romek leaves to join the army, This Molek too, promising to return soon as Ala claws at his face and weeps.

More people come. More and more, shimmering in the distance. Fifty thousand, a hundred thousand. Who's counting?

'It's like the exodus from Israel,' Mama says, sitting outside the tent to watch. She is shivering despite the heat.

'But where's everybody going to live?' Ala asks. 'Whose water are they going to drink?'

Mama moves her hands up and down her legs.

'What is it, Mama?' Lena asks.

She smiles. 'A little aching, darling. My bones are old, that's all.'

There is no word of Anton's condition from the military hospital. Rumour takes the place of information here of course, coming in shouts of anger and songs of lament. Rumour sings of contagion carried by lice, the work of a god above them or below, it really doesn't matter any more; a god who has little love left for what he made. Rumour says this is why they've been assembled in their thousands; it makes for a more convenient death. If you are nothing more than a bone creature you don't have to be long in a hot and crowded place before you grow sick and die. Foolish to have thought there might have been another purpose to you, or place for you to end.

Lena is shouting at the woman handing out bread in the canteen tent. Where are the medicines? This is what she demands. This isn't liberation, it's mass murder.

The woman tries to quieten her, taking her arm, leading her aside. 'Aid is coming. There's a hospital and more will be built.'

'For the soldiers who matter to them.' Lena shrugs off the woman and spits on the ground. This morning Mama was feverish and unable to stand.

'He was right,' she says to the woman.

'Who?'

She shakes her head. 'Why did we ever imagine anyone in the world cares for us? We're here because the soil is poor. Our bones will fertilise the dust.'

Mama lies on the mat, her teeth chattering.

Lena holds her head up and gives her water to sip from a spoon. She doesn't know whether it's better to have the tent flaps open for the air with the flies coming too, or the heat that will boil them alive.

Mama turns and vomits on the ground. She apologises. She asks to be taken outside to make no more mess. Lena wipes her face with a rag, then raises her head and asks her to drink. Mama whispers that her head is sore.

Lena unbuttons her mother's blouse.

Mama is watching her, smiling.

Lena opens Mama's blouse. All across her chest is mottled. Lena stares at the rash; a spread of inflammation from Mama's belly to her throat.

'Darling?' The air moves beside her. Mama's hand is reaching for Lena's cheek. 'You mustn't be afraid, darling,' she whispers, smiling. 'Someone needs to take care of Papa. You know how hopeless he is on his own. Quite hopeless.'

Lena takes the rosary that has slipped from Mama's grip, and weaves it back between her mother's fingers. She lies beside her, holding Mama's hand. She thinks what she needs to say and she tells her this. 'You always did your best for me.'

That night Lena and Ala sit either side of their mother and they whisper Hail Marys until her eyes close for good.

*

The next morning, Ala complains of a headache behind her eyes. Lena comes into the tent with bread and water and stares at her when she says this. The air is hot and sour. Ala is lying on Mama's mat, now that Mama has been taken away to lie in the ground.

'It's just a headache,' Ala says, shivering on the mat.

Lena knows she should go to her, check her sister's temperature and pulse, look for signs of a rash on her chest. But she doesn't do any of this. Because what would it serve? she thinks. What's the point of a diagnosis if there's no remedy to give?

Ala is watching her. She asks Lena how she is.

'Useless.' Lena hears her voice come from far away. 'Everything I know is useless.'

'Take JoJo out for me, will you? I need to sleep this off.'

Mechanically, Lena goes to Ala's little boy, taking up his unfamiliar weight and settling him in a sling against her back. Lena takes Agata's hand. 'Let's go, frog,' she hears herself say, 'we need to get this hungry goat to some grass.'

'Lena?' Ala calls as they leave. 'Take my boy a good way off. You understand? A good long way.'

Agata drags the goat, thin and unwilling, and they make a wavering procession through a camp full of sickness and sorrow. Lena's mind is a blur of chasing thoughts. If they keep walking for fifteen minutes, maybe twenty, they'll reach open ground. In thirty minutes they might see a ridge. If they climb it, Lena might see wherever the military hospital is in the distance. In a day they might make it across the steppe and fetch help for Ala. No one will be able to turn away two small children and a lieutenant colonel's wife.

She hums as she walks to drown out the babble of the camp.

Agata begins to complain. She's tired. It's too hot. Her mouth is very thirsty, she says. Lena bends to her. 'Mama's sending a message to her little frog. Are you ready?' She kisses her cheek three times. 'I love you. Did you hear it?'

'Again,' Agata whispers, blinking solemnly. 'Again.'

In the distance tents are being hammered into the ground to accommodate more people and the things that breed on them. A long line at the latrines. Elsewhere, the excavation of a great square pit.

'Feed me,' says the god in the ground.

'Never,' Lena hisses, gripping the children and scanning the horizon.

She can see no ridge, no hospital, only tents and dust.

Jozef is wriggling and starting to cry for Ala. Agata clings to Lena's skirt, her expression blank. Flies crawl undisturbed on her lips.

Lena turns around.

'Typhus.'

'Excuse me?' Lena says.

A woman waiting her turn at the well is saying the word to an old man. Lena interrupts, asks how she's so sure about that. The woman laughs. She was a biologist once, she says, believe it or not.

'Can anything cure it?' the man says.

The woman shrugs. She's a broad-framed woman with skin flaps where flesh has shrivelled away. 'Antibacterials would do it of course.'

Lena stares at the woman.

'Antibacterials would wipe this out.' The woman is turning to Lena, 'Steady now,' she's saying, 'careful with your baby.'

Lena's legs have gone from her. 'You can't be sure of that,' she says.

The woman is grabbing her, calling for help.

Lena is being lowered to the ground against the well, Jozef in her lap. Agata crouches beside her, holding tight to the goat. 'You can't be sure,' Lena says.

'Take some water.' The woman holds out a cup and watches her drink. She puts a hand to Lena's forehead. 'You don't have a fever.' The woman sits beside her, dipping a cup for Agata and Jozef. 'I have to get back to my father,' she says then, standing with her bucket. 'Will you manage getting up when you're ready?'

Lena opens her mouth and says nothing. She watches the biologist disappear.

That night as fever takes hold of Ala, Lena steps outside where the air is black and cold. The sky dazzles with its stars. They are bright as salt crystals.

Lena kneels, pressing her forehead to the ground. It is the only thing left to do.

'Take me,' she whispers to the earth, the words catching in her throat. 'Take me, but leave my daughter. Let her grow.' Lena whispers this until she doesn't know whether the words are sounding in the world or will forever live inside her. 'Leave my daughter. My daughter needs to grow.'

Inside the tent, there's the sound of quick, shallow breathing, a sweet smell. She sees the shapes of sleeping bodies and creeps to Agata who lies on her side on a mat nearest the opening, the amber tight in her small fist. Agata's hair is sticky, her skin hot, but then all the air in the tent is hot. Lena draws back the tent flaps to the cold night and curls herself around her child, tucking a hand under Agata's belly. 'Mama's secret message,' she says, kissing her cheek three times. 'Did you feel it? I'm doing it again. Again?' *Let her grow*.

When Lena wakes the tent is stifling. There's a stink of shit and vomit. Ala is lying very still on her front in the corner, her yellow hair spread about her. Little JoJo is sitting up between her legs watching a gecko on the tent wall.

Lena looks at the gecko for a long time, summoning her courage.

'Agata, darling, it's time to wake up,' she whispers.

She feels for her daughter's shoulder, her face. She feels a puff of hot breath on the back of her hand. 'Time to wake up, little frog.'

Lena turns and sees the rash across Agata's chest. She hauls her into her arms.

Outside the heat is a white wall. Lena staggers into it, Agata slipping in her grip. 'I am a lieutenant colonel's wife!' she screams as her legs give way. 'I demand medical assistance.'

Blackness now, a liquid, shifting murk that folds time in on itself. It folds time into smaller and smaller pieces until no such thing is left.

A voice summons her. She shakes her head, resisting.

The voice goes away. It calls again. In the end she rises, emerging as if from stagnant well water.

There's a heaviness on her face, like a layer of extra skin she doesn't want. She wants her skin flayed from her. The voice calls her, insisting. She doesn't want her eyes to open. She wants to stay in the liquid dark. But the voice calls her.

'Anton.'

He removes a cloth from her forehead and dips it in a bucket. He wipes her cheeks and throat. 'I came as soon as I was able.'

She watches him replace the cloth in the bucket and she doesn't want to ask.

But she cannot not ask.

'Where is she?'

He hesitates. 'You need to rest. You're through the worst.'

'Where's Agata, Anton?'

His gaze slides to the ground. Lena is afraid to look in his eyes. She is afraid to turn her head towards the ripening sweetness in the air. She creeps her hand to the edge of her mat and feels the piece of amber lying on the floor. She feels the tiny screw hole for a shaft in its core. She reaches further and touches Agata's arm. There's no warmth in what she feels.

'You see,' she says to him. 'You see what I have done.'

Lena lifts her daughter's body and lies beneath it. She presses her chin to Agata's skull and wraps her arms round the stiffened limbs, already mottled where blood has stopped circulating. It is like clutching a rubber doll.

Lena starts to rock her daughter's body, rolling from side to side as if such movement might cause Agata's heart and brain and blood to start once more. Back and forth Lena rocks her dead child.

Anton goes from the tent and falls down crying in the dust.

Lena watches her husband cry.

She watches her hand reach to him. But she cannot help him up.

Because Lena is flying now.

She realises she can fly anywhere and watch anything she chooses. She could go to the farm where little Jozef is riding on Blackie's wide back. Dear little JoJo who held her tattered life together, who gave her and her husband some purpose in their grief. JoJo who grew and became a man now weeping into his hands by an old woman's bed. She could go to comfort him.

And she might go elsewhere after that, return to a hearth with a dog called Pavlov and a rabbit boiling in a pot. Papa sucking peppermints in his fireside chair.

Or she might fly far away, fly to the edge of the world and a forest, and live a life in a one-bunk hut with a bone-thin man who wears a sheepskin coat and a fox's grin, live a life she has yearned for, with a murderer, no less, who has years left to serve. What do you think, bone man, shall I come?

Bone man?

But there's no sound around her, nothing at all.

Only the world is getting brighter.

The air is lifting and everything around her is still and washed in white. And she realises she's done with travelling.

Lena watches the girl who comes running into this brilliant light. Soft-footed, this girl, running unevenly because it's new to her. A slip of a thing, never even been to school.

Lena starts to laugh. She has to laugh out loud because she knows at last what it is she has to say to this girl. There's no more sorrow. It's gone from her. So too the need to grieve and beg forgiveness for a decision taken long ago. It's all gone, lifted away.

And the light that is all around Lena is inside her too. She is made of light.

'Wait,' she says to the girl running into the shimmering light. 'Take me with you. Little frog, I want to come with you.'

Agata stops. She turns and smiles.

She holds out her hand.

ACKNOWLEDGEMENTS

This story was a long time coming. I'm grateful to friends old and new for their support along the way. Special thanks to Den Harman, Gabrielle Murphy, Anna Sadowy and Rosalind Beardshaw, who held out a light when I found myself in dark places. Thank you too, Fiona Shaw, for your writerly generosity in a new town.

The book owes a huge amount to the wonderful Jocasta Hamilton and Helen O'Hare. Your passion, commitment, and editorial brilliance strengthened and elevated this manuscript. I'm deeply grateful to you both. Thanks also to Abigail Scruby, Martin Bryant, Judy Spours, Sara Marafini and the team at John Murray for excellence in midwifery. And of course there would be no *Snow Hare* at all without Clare Alexander, whose insight, experience and support I continue to cherish, and who gave this story its name.

I'm grateful to my family and that mighty network of British Poles for a childhood rich in the traditions of Poland. If I close my eyes I can still hear Babcia telling me, reluctant but resolute, about the war and everything she lost. Her courage, resilience and humour I do not forget. I'm also proud of the next generation; my nephews Mieszko and Wojciech, who tell me they are neither Polish nor British but citizens of the world.

Lastly, most importantly, Bea, this story's for you. You are the sun around which I turn.

NOTE ON SOURCE FOR *THE SNOW HARE*

The inspiration for this story came from conversations with my grandmother near the end of her life. She had been one of over a million Poles deemed to be 'Enemies of the State' during the Soviet occupation of Eastern Poland in the Second World War. Along with her family, my grandmother was deported to a labour camp in Siberia. Other Poles were relocated to forced settlements in the farthest corners of the USSR. Conditions were brutal; it's believed as many as half the deportees died within the first two years.

In 1941 when Stalin broke with Hitler, Poles were released from the labour camps. But without food or money, and with local overseers keen on keeping a cheap workforce, the majority of exiles struggled to get out and were forced to take Soviet citizenship in 1943. Those that did escape, my grandmother's family among them, made their way to Uzbekistan where a new Polish Army was being formed. Here, in unsanitary conditions, with promised food and medical equipment slow to arrive, typhus raged. My grandmother lost her father and four-year-old daughter at this time. Subsequently, she and my grandfather travelled with the Polish Army and an exodus of civilian refugees across the Caspian Sea to Iran, Palestine, and finally Britain, where they settled.

READING GROUP GUIDE

Dear reader,

Several years ago I sat at the kitchen table and faced my grandmother. Between us, a plate piled high with biscuits and a Dictaphone. "Baba," I said, "it's time to talk."

During my childhood, my grandmother had been the stereotypical Polish babcia; a pope-loving, fur-wearing, cake-baking matriarch; the life and the soul of our family. Yet this seemingly uncomplicated and much-loved woman held in her heart a terrible grief, one that had never left her. She never spoke about it. And we grandchildren knew better than to ask.

But as she neared the end of her life, I realized I had to find out what had happened in her past. Records mattered. We needed a family one before it was too late.

So we sat together for two days, and, reluctantly, she talked. First she spoke about her youth: a time of dreams and dances, and the thrill of life as an officer's wife. Then came the war, and her country's partition between Germany and the Soviet Union. She remembered deportation to a freezing Siberian logging camp and a daily struggle to find food for her young daughter. Dates and places were lost to her, but not the details: jewelry bartered for an onion, her wedding dress used as a mosquito net. Anything and everything done to stay alive. Finally she came to speak of a typhus epidemic that swept over the steppe.

You can't imagine it, she kept saying, as if she too couldn't believe what had happened on her journey from southeastern Poland to refuge in Britain by way of Siberia, Uzbekistan, and Palestine. *Really, Paula, you cannot imagine this.*

I didn't want to imagine. The tapes went into a box.

Years passed. My grandmother died. A decade later, pregnant with my daughter, I took out the box. It felt like I met my grandmother again, but this time as the young wife and mother she'd been. I was stunned—not just by everything she'd gone through, but by the contrast to my own easy life, one where I presumed freedom and choice absolute rights. I decided I needed to try to tell my grandmother's story. But how? Biography was restrictive, so I turned to fiction.

I found accounts of other Poles who'd also been deported from the Soviet-controlled east. Several were written from a child's perspective, and I remember reading through winter evenings while my daughter slept upstairs, warm and well-fed. The sheer variance in the ways people suffered came to haunt me. I was also surprised that this history seemed to have received little wider attention. No one knows for sure how many Poles were exiled, but over a million is a fair estimate. It started to feel important that I try to make *The Snow Hare* some sort of testament to them too.

I came up with the character of Lena: a girl with grand ideas about her future, determined to live the life she wants. But, deported with her family to the Siberian taiga, she loses all hope. This, I came to realize, had to be the crux of *The Snow Hare*. How does a human find meaning when made powerless by global forces? How can Lena survive and find a way out of despair? And so a story began to grow in this frozen forest at the edge of the world. A story about what it is to be human, how important it is, in the darkest times, to dream and hope, and, above all, to love and be loved.

(And Baba, I'm grateful that you talked.)

I hope you enjoy the book.

My best,
Paula

QUESTIONS AND TOPICS FOR DISCUSSION

1) *The Snow Hare* explores how memories can haunt us throughout our lives. Why does Lena see the little girl and the "bone man" in her final days? Were you surprised by who these characters turned out to be?

2) How do you feel about Lena's character? Did you like her? Does that matter? Is she a different person at the end than she was as a child in Poland?

3) One of the novel's central questions is how much control we wield over our own lives. To what extent does Lena have agency? What happens when an external force — such as war — deprives us of our choices? What do you think motivates Lena to keep going?

4) On page 279, Lena tells Grigori, "Everything matters or nothing matters." What does she mean? Do you agree?

5) How does the novel explore romantic love? Do you think Lena loves Anton? How does meeting Grigori change her? Do you think she makes the right choice in the end?

6) Discuss the novel's title and the scene on page 281. What does the snow hare mean to Lena?

7) On page 261, Lena's mother says, "I'm thinking about your father. How that man loved to lie in the sun. Yet he burned a strip off his nose every time...Do you think anyone ever learns anything in life?" What does she mean? Why do you think she says this now? Do the characters in *The Snow Hare* learn something?

8) Discuss the portrayal of motherhood in the novel. Are some mothers better than others? Is that a fair question? Do you think motherhood changes Lena?

9) *The Snow Hare* is inspired, in part, by the author's grand-mother's life. Do these real roots change how you feel about the novel? And is there a story in your own family that has shaped how you understand history?

10) In 2023, after the Russian invasion of Ukraine, Eastern Europe is again at war. How do today's circumstances compare to those of World War II? Did reading *The Snow Hare* change your perception of these circumstances?

11) As a child, Lena dreams of becoming a doctor, but her life takes a very different course. What did you dream of being as a child? How has that played out for you?

12) Were you surprised by how the novel ended? What did you hope would happen?

ABOUT THE AUTHOR

Paula Lichtarowicz is the author of the novels *The First Book of Calamity Leek* and *Creative Truths in Provincial Policing*. She studied English literature at Durham University and has a master's in psychology from the University of East London. When not trying to write, she works as a documentary maker in Yorkshire. On a good day she sees a kingfisher on the river. In fact, a day doesn't really get better than that.